A Handbook of the Theatre

for little theatre groups, teachers, youth organizations,

and students –

outlining the preparation and activities of those involved

in the production of a play

A Handbook of the Theatre

by

Esmé Crampton

HEINEMANN EDUCATIONAL BOOKS
LONDON

Heinemann Educational Books Ltd

LONDON EDINBURGH MELBOURNE AUCKLAND TORONTO
HONG KONG SINGAPORE KUALA LUMPAR NEW DELHI
NAIROBI JOHANNESBURG LUSAKA IBADAN
KINGSTON

PN
3155
C7

ISBN 0 435 18186 6

First published in Canada by © Gage Educational Publishing
Limited 1964
Second Edition 1972
First published by Heinemann Educational Books 1973
Reprinted 1978

Cover and text drawings by

Brian Jackson

Published by
Heinemann Educational Books Ltd
48 Charles Street, London W1X 8AH
Printed by photolithography and made in Great Britain
at The Pitman Press, Bath

Illustrations and Tables

Average Production Schedule: Six Weeks' Rehearsal two weeks preparation, three rehearsals per week

WEEK	DIRECTION	DESIGN	PRODUCTION	STAGE MANAGEMENT	PUBLICITY, BOX OFFICE, HOUSE MANAGEMENT	ACTING
8th Oct.	Read Discuss Discuss Read Research	Read Discuss Read Discuss Research	Read Discuss Enquire re theatre rental, etc. Announce times & dates of casting	Read play		
15th Oct.	Discuss Decide Casting sessions	Discuss Decide	Apply for rights and enquire re royalty, etc. Start to select staff Discuss budget PRODUCTION MEETING	Attend casting Start prompt copy	Read play	Casting Read play
22nd. Oct. 1.	1st Reading 2nd Reading Block/run half Act I	Complete model set Complete costume design Measurements for wardrobe Order materials	Check design and orders – eye on budget Order materials PRODUCTION MEETING	Attend rehearsals Start props Tape outline of set on floor Continue prompt copy Take blocking	PUBLICITY Consider publicity Attend Readings 1st Release	1st Reading 2nd Reading Block half Act I Learn lines
29th Oct. 2.	Block/run Act I Block/run Act II Run Act I – no books	Assemble materials Start on set and costumes	Start carpenter, wardrobe, and begin co-ordination of all depts. PRODUCTION MEETING	Prompter available Props coming Take blocking	PUBLICITY Prepare handbills Mailing list Posters BOX OFFICE Ticket material to printers	Block Act I Block Act II Run Act I – no books Learn lines
5th Nov. 3.	Block Act III Run Act III Run Act II – no books	Set and costumes on way	Co-ordinate all depts. Check insurance, licences, etc.	"Dummy" props & furniture complete Real props & furniture coming Sound effects ordered Prompter busy Take blocking	PUBLICITY Sell advertising and start program Posters ready Continue releases BOX OFFICE Tickets back	Block Act III Run Act III Run Act II – no books Learn lines

Date						
12th Nov. 4.	Run Act I Run Act II Photos	Set half completed Fittings begin	Co-ordinate all depts.	Finalize effects, cues Prompter busy Effects becoming available	PUBLICITY Posters out Photo call Releases out Mailing list out BOX OFFICE Advance sales open	Run Act I Run Act II Photos Check lines
			COMPLETE RUN-THROUGH PRODUCTION MEETING			
19th Nov. 5.	Crowd work Polish of exits, entrances, etc. Final run in rehearsal room Music chosen Lighting discussed	Set three-quarters completed Further fittings	Co-ordinate order, rental of extra lights, etc. Effects Select staff re parking, coffee and checkroom, ushers, etc.	Crowd blocking Final assembly of props and furniture Prompter less busy	PUBLICITY Program to printers Cast release photos BOX OFFICE Advance sales HOUSE Check with producer re staff	General rehearsals and polishing Final run in rehearsal room Fittings
			PRODUCTION MEETING			
26th Nov. 6.	First run in theatre Technical rehearsal Photo call First dress rehearsal Second dress rehearsal	Period of bustle Special artwork Completion of set & costumes 'Setting-up' Photos Technical rehearsal First dress rehearsal Second dress rehearsal	Co-ordinate needs for 'setting up' – eye on ticket sales and publicity Technical rehearsal First dress rehearsal Second dress rehearsal	Assemble all furniture, props, and effects at theatre Help with 'setting-up' Technical rehearsal First dress rehearsal Second dress rehearsal	PUBLICITY Program back Interviews Photo call Releases BOX OFFICE Advance sales HOUSE Special reception arrangements, etc.	Final fittings Line rehearsal Check lines Interviews and photos First dress rehearsal Second dress rehearsal
			PRODUCTION MEETING PERFORMANCES			
3rd Dec.	Assess production	CARPENTER Help strike set WARDROBE Clear costumes	Check budget Pay bills Close books	Supervise striking of set, etc. Close production	PUBLICITY Keep publicity clippings – reviews BOX OFFICE Financial report HOUSE Check cleaning, etc.	
			GENERAL MEETING			

Contents

Acknowledgments

The author would like to acknowledge with thanks the help of the following, who read and commented on the chapters and sections indicated:

Chapter I. Introduction to Theatre

Dr. Murray Edwards, who received his doctorate in Comparative Literature from Columbia University. He has been a producer with the CBC and Assistant Director for Continuing Education at York University. He is currently an Assistant Superintendent for the Ontario Educational Communications Authority.

Chapter 2. The Director

Mr. Douglas Campbell, who has acted and directed at the Stratford Shakespearean Festival and at the Old Vic in London, England. He has been Artistic Director of the Tyrone Guthrie Theatre, Minneapolis and is currently at the Crucible Theatre in Sheffield, England.

Chapter 3. Stage Management

Mr. Jack Hutt, who has been with the Stratford Shakespearean Festival since 1954, first as a stage manager and currently as Production Manager.

Chapter 4. Design

Setting and Costume: Miss Tanya Moiseiwitsch, who has designed for the Stratford Shakespearean Festival, the Old Vic, the Royal Opera House (Covent Garden), and the Tyrone Guthrie Theatre, Minneapolis. She is currently at the Crucible Theatre in Sheffield, England.

Lighting: Mr. Philip Rose, President of Century Strand, Inc., Hawthorne, California, who has been responsible for equipment and lighting designs for theatres in Britain and North America, including the Old Vic Theatre in London, the Grand Theatre in Quebec City, and several other projects in Canada.

Make-up: Mr. Mervyn Blake, who studied at the Royal Academy of Dramatic Art and acted in England with the Young Vic and the Shakespeare Memorial Theatre. He has acted with the Canadian Players and the Manitoba Theatre Centre and on television. He is currently in his sixteenth season with the Stratford Shapespearean Festival.

Chapter 5. Production

The Producer: Mrs. Florence James, Drama Consultant to the
Saskatchewan Arts Board, who has been director at the Playhouse
Theatre in Seattle and is a member of the Board of Governors of the
Canadian Players.

Publicity: Miss Mary Joliffe, who has been Publicity Director for the
Stratford Shakespearean Festival, the Metropolitan Opera National
Company, Expo '67, and the National Arts Centre in Ottawa, and is now
with the Toronto Arts Foundation.

Chapter 6. The Actor

Miss Frances Hyland, who began acting with the Regina Little Theatre
and then trained at the Royal Academy of Dramatic Art in England.
She has acted in London's West End and has starred on Broadway,
at the Shaw Festival (Niagara-on-the-Lake, Ontario), and at the
Stratford Shakespearean Festival. She appears frequently on CBC
television and has appeared extensively in Canada's regional theatres.
She is a holder of the Service Medal of the Order of Canada.

The author would also like to thank: the front-of-house staff and
electricians at the O'Keefe Centre and Hart House Theatre in Toronto;
members of the Stables Theatre and of the Rosedale-Moore Park
Association; the University Alumnae Dramatic Club in Toronto for
discussions concerning costume and equipment; and Miss Heather
McCallum and staff of the Theatre Section of the Metropolitan Toronto
Central Library.

In addition, acknowledgements are due to: Harper and Row,
Publishers, Incorporated, for permission to quote from *Our Town*, by
Thornton Wilder; Samuel French, Inc., for permission to quote from
A Marriage Proposal, by Anton Chekhov, English version by Hilmar
Baukhage and Barret H. Clark; and New Directions for permission to
quote from *The Glass Menagerie*, by Tennessee Williams; to Miss Isobel
Wilder for supplying the photograph of her brother; and to others
who have offered or permitted the use of photographs and drawings,
especially to the Red Barn Theatre, the Virginia Museum Theatre, and
the Stratford Festival Theatre, Ontario.

Special thanks are due to the encouragement and interest of Mr. and
Mrs. Ken Watts of the Simpson's Collegiate Drama Festival, to
Miss Helen Dunlop, Education Officer in the Curriculum Development
Branch of the Ontario Ministry of Education, and to Mr. Patrick
Drysdale of Gage Educational Publishing Limited.

Author

Esmé Crampton holds the Teacher's Certificate of the Central School of
Speech and Drama, the University of London Diploma in Dramatic
Art — Stage and Teaching, and the International Phonetics Certificate.
Following three years in professional theatre, she taught and directed
in England, Australia, and the United States.

She has worked in Canada since 1954, and has had wide experience in
teaching speech and drama, in directing and adjudicating, and in
lecturing on theatre and theatre arts. She was for two seasons voice
coach at the Stratford Shakespearean Festival, and she was the first
director of the Manitoba Theatre School. In 1961-62 she studied in
England and, before returning to Canada, visited Russia to see theatre
and observe drama classes in Moscow, Leningrad, and Kiev. She was
for four years Lecturer in Theatre Arts at the College of Education,
University of Toronto. In 1968 she was awarded a Canada Council
grant to study Creative Drama at the London Theatre Centre in
England.

Miss Crampton is currently Speech Consultant at the Faculty of
Education, University of Toronto. She is a past-President of the
Canadian Speech Association and was a member of the executive
committee of the York '71 International Conference on Teaching and
Learning English, serving as Co-chairman of the Drama Commission.
She has published a number of articles on speech and theatre arts,
including contributions to the *Dalhousie Review*, the *Canadian Speech
Communication Journal*, and *Teacher Education*. In addition, she has
compiled *Drama Canada* (published by the Guidance Centre, Faculty of
Education, University of Toronto), showing trends in drama in Canadian
education during the past twenty-five years.

Illustrator

Brian Jackson studied Stage Design at the Old Vic Theatre School in
London, England, and he then spent three years in the Property
Department of the Old Vic Theatre. He came to Canada in 1955 as
Head of the Property Department for the Stratford Shakespearean
Festival. He soon became a full-time designer, and he has designed
settings and costumes for many productions at Stratford, where he has
worked for sixteen successive seasons, and for the Canadian Opera
Company. From 1964 to 1965 he was designer for the Manitoba Theatre
Centre, and he has worked for four seasons at the Vancouver Playhouse.
In 1971 he designed *The Marriage of Figaro* and in 1972 *Cosi Fan Tutte*,
both for the National Arts Centre in Ottawa.

In 1963 Mr. Jackson was awarded a Canada Council grant for advanced
studies, which allowed him to spend a year studying design in Europe,
and in 1967 he was awarded the Canada Medal.

1. Introduction to Theatre

"Beginners, please!"
"Quiet, everyone."
"Houselights."
"Curtain – going up!"

A routine such as this is used at the beginning of every performance of every play that is ever produced, and is preceded by weeks, or even months, of preparation. Whether the play is being prepared by one of the Stratford companies (Eng., Ont., or Conn.), by a little theatre or high school group, or by an alumni association, the pattern is similar and the principles are the same.

There is one special attribute of the production of a play which is part of the magic – and the mystery – of the theatre; because of the particular approach of the director and designer, the interpretation of the cast, and the personalities of all who are involved, it becomes, necessarily, a *version* of the play. So in a good production an audience is vitally alert, literally holding-the-breath, knowing that each moment can only be retained in the memory; there is no going back, holding the page, or reversing the camera, for the action will never be repeated in quite the same way – ever, in the whole of time.

A Play

A play starts life in the mind and heart of a playwright, who expresses his ideas, characters, and situations in words that are written to be spoken in the form of dialogue. They are the outcome of the thoughts and feelings of his characters, based on his central idea, or theme. He so chooses them that they indicate all that is going on in the sense of action, and re-action. The action may be of two kinds: outer, as indicated by Henry V's "Once more unto the breach, dear friends, once more"; and inner, as in Hamlet's "To be, or not to be – that is the question."

At the same time, these words and their resultant actions carry the story, or happenings, of the characters forward – towards an inevitable end. They are active, not narrative, as in the descriptive prose of a novel, or in the long stage directions of certain playwrights. A play is essentially a showing of a story by action, rather than the telling of a story through narration; the dialogue is written to be spoken aloud, in public, rather than read to the self, in private. No matter in what form it is written, from the rhythms of verse and good prose to the meaningful nonsense of the Theatre of the Absurd, it is the sole expression of the author's intent. It may come hot from his hands into immediate rehearsal; it may be spoken two hundred, or two thousand, years after his death; but there it lies, eternal, the one lasting and material object in the ephemeral world of the theatre.

The playwright is subject to certain requirements not common to other authors. He orchestrates his writing so that it is pleasing to the tongue and to the ear; he catches the speech rhythms of his characters, just as the composer has a sense of each instrument in his orchestra; he conceives these people in terms that are larger, in varying degree, than the average we know in ordinary life; for if they are to be effective they must "show," or be projected, to some hundreds or thousands of people at the same time. He is communicating, not at first hand to an individual public, but at second hand, to a collective known as an audience – doing so through the medium of actors, aided by designers and staff, all of whom are guided by a director.

There are further conditions to the making of a play. The events are not, even though they may appear to be, slap-hazard slices of life, taken and repeated exactly as they would happen; or stage time would run as real time instead of "turning the accomplishment of many years into an hour-glass." So they are of necessity an arrangement, or contrivance; a selection, giving an impression; by nature, artificial; but by appearing to be natural within their context, art. A mere copy of life would be dull because, if it is to be successfully communicated, any event requires editing to be of interest. So a good journalist arranges facts, and so a lawyer plans his brief. If the playwright were merely to record events, the result would be repetitive; an actual tape recording of men planning a bank robbery could last some hours, but would be unlikely to sustain the interest of others after the first minutes of curiosity. If such planning were to show the gradual turning of one member of the gang against the rest, the entire action could be concerned with this one meeting. Selection is likely to be made on the following counts: of the importance of the event in relation to the total idea;

the most effective moment at which the action should begin; what it should contain, or reveal to an audience, and when it should end.

As the action of a play is therefore condensed and selected to the writer's purpose, so is the dialogue – the words conveying a total impression by means of a certain economy. It is a convention in theatre that a performance rarely lasts longer than the two or three hours traffic – with intervals – of the stage. There is no time to waste, and this urgency in itself helps to forward and condense the action.

Because the playwright is going to share his story, not with individuals but with people coming together, as it were, in communion, this very communion becomes a vital element which goes beyond the material aspects of comfortable seating, well-equipped stages, and other paraphernalia which help in the presentation of his work. When people are so gathered, it becomes much easier to touch their emotions, and to affect not only their minds, but their hearts. For emotion is catching, and when a laugh is caught, or a moment of grief shared, then the audience is participating in the performance, and the playwright's work becomes a vital and living experience.

Thus the theatre becomes a wonderful place of discovery – of finding out almost what it is like to be other than the self, to see another's viewpoint, to wonder how we might react in similar situations, to try out in our own small way the experience of being emperor or slave, princess or drudge. We explore, we enjoy, we learn from seeing other human beings in action. Laughing with those more foolish and more clever than ourselves, we sense with relief that our own worries are nothing in comparison to what can happen to others. So we are refreshed, and a sense of balance is restored. We may also find a new appreciation of theatre, of the skills of staging, of the costumes, and the music; and we may, if we are fortunate, hear good speech well spoken.

ELEMENTS OF DRAMA

Now we should consider other factors which influence the playwright, and so affect all concerned in a production (or bringing-to-life) of his play.

The action of a play is designed to show people in conflict; conflict is the essence of drama, and drama is a showing – by doing. The showing is to be seen, and the place in which the drama is shown is a theatre, which originally meant a viewing or seeing-place. It is interesting to note that we have three main associations with this word: one is the theatre as a building in which we see ourselves in many kinds of action; the other two provide settings for the basic conflicts of life and death – the operating theatre, and the theatre of war, the purpose of one being the reverse of the other.

Conflict may have extreme results: it can end happily – in life, or sadly – in death; but naturally between these two extremes are many variations, and plays will contain elements of both. While most comedies should leave us in good spirits, a great tragedy will not depress; man may be beaten in conflict, but when his spirit transcends even the most terrible results, we leave the theatre elevated, sharing the memory of his triumph.

Every story requires a turning-point, or climax. Will the hero kill the villain? boy get girl? or the little man win a fortune? The climax will decide the result, bringing about the reversal, or change of fortune, in the lives of those with whom we are becoming involved. When, in tragedy, this reversal is accompanied by a self-recognition of what is happening, and when this realization is caught and shared by the audience, then we are witnessing a play that may be called great.

These important points of reversal and recognition were among those noted by the Greek philosopher Aristotle (384–322 B.C.). Because Plato and Socrates doubted that a practising poet could set down an approach to his art, Aristotle wrote an outline of the conditions of drama, known as the *Poetics*. Some of his points, such as those relating to the unity of action (that there should be one plot, and no sub-plot) and to time (that the action represented should last not longer than twenty-four hours) are still applicable to some plays, but have not been universally accepted for some centuries. In fact, as we shall see later, too great a regard for such laws, for the form rather than the content, curtailed the development of drama in Italy during the Renaissance. Aristotle found that language, or diction, is the chief vehicle of the poet's expression, that speech is the proof of feeling, and that the spectacle, or visual atmosphere of a play, should have an emotional attraction of its own, so that the force of the drama would be felt apart from the performance of the actors.

He pronounced certain developments in character as poor drama (or conflict); a virtuous man, for example, going from prosperity to adversity, or conversely a bad man from adversity to prosperity; and he also suggested there is little interest in the downfall of an utter villain. All of this may be found in the simplified form of drama known as melodrama, or the current, less violent form known as soap opera, where situation is more important than character, and where there may be reversals galore, but comparatively little recognition. Aristotle claimed that drama proceeds from man's own frailty, known as the tragic flaw, and that tragedy arises from the terrible and pitiable actions of people near and dear to each other. He stated a theory that has since caused much controversy and should be regarded as applicable to the drama as he knew it over two thousand years ago, but which does contain a definition which many still regard as the aim of a great play: "Tragedy is an imitation of an action that is serious, complete, and of a certain magnitude; in language embellished with each kind of artistic ornament, the several kinds being found in separate parts of the play in the form of action – not narration; through pity and fear affecting the proper purgation of these emotions." This is known as Aristotle's theory of catharsis, and perhaps, very occasionally in a playgoer's life, the experience still occurs when there is a complete sense of identity with the action, and when the emotions of pity and fear cleanse and refresh the spirit.

TRAGEDY AND COMEDY

Drama, conflict, and reversal are not all a matter of tragedy; they also occur in comedy; and the difference between them depends – literally – on the way we look at things. Horace Walpole said, "The world is a comedy to those that think, a tragedy to those who feel"; and so it becomes a question of the balance between the two, and the proportion with which we experience events. When the world grows off-color, we may indulge in a first-class suffer, and experience everything in terms of our feelings; but when we can see and think about the same situation from a distance, we gain a new perspective – and may even be able to laugh at the events. In this way laughter restores balance, provides a way of getting our own back, and helps maintain our morale. It is worth remembering that almost every situation can be either tragedy or comedy, depending on the way we experience it; it is customary to think of death as being tragic – but how many times do we laugh when certain characters die? Pyramus has a wonderful time at the end of *The Midsummer Night's Dream*; so does Lomov, whom we shall discuss later, in Chekhov's *The Marriage Proposal*. By their very performance the actors will not let us "feel" their death, but will let us perceive the event more through our eyes than through our hearts. Then another element of comedy occurs: the unexpected; both characters, to our delight, revive, and so the enemy is cheated. The unexpected is useful in comedy for, like a necessary sense of pace, it keeps our eyes and ears hopping, so that feelings do not have time to catch up with events – nor reason and logic snort too often at situations we might otherwise consider ridiculous. This can happen when a comedy is acted without a sense of pace, or in such a way that we cannot believe in the events.

Conversely, the proverbial slipping on a banana skin can be serious (Who wants to break a leg?), especially with hospitalization, mounting bills, and work hours lost. Again, everything depends on how it is performed, and on our association with the character. If it happens to the little man, the tramp, with whom we sympathize, and is so controlled by the actor that he attracts not so much our eyes but our hearts, we may feel for him; if it represents the literal reversal of the person in authority, who in this case is not popular – the admiral, the general, the policeman, or the judge – their balance is in all ways upset, and we have a satisfying sense of "How are the mighty fallen . . . ."

Audiences sometimes laugh, disconcertingly, at what the actor considers to be the wrong thing. The reasons can include not only the way in which the incident was performed – even with the best of intentions the result may not seem as hoped – but also the fact that both tears and laughter are ultimately a physical release of tension. In the theatre this will mount as the conflict rises, and is often called intensity because it exists to a heightened or larger-than-life degree. If, however, too much intensity is allowed to rise too soon – or in the wrong place – the audience will find a release in mistaken laughter. It is worth remembering that while the result may lie with the audience, the cause lies in the performance.

But when an audience shares a release at the right moments, it becomes corporate, rekindling the result through very proximity, and spreading it like a bush fire. A small audience that is widely scattered is difficult to play to, particularly in comedy; so is an audience containing few who can "see" the funny side of things; but a good laugh – or a cry – becomes wonderfully infectious when everybody on either side of us is doing the same thing. Then we enjoy the play even more with this refuelling of our common understanding.

Byron wrote, "All tragedies are finished by a death, All comedies ended by a marriage"; and both start more or less in the opposite direction to their end – comedy taking the hero from the bottom of his world, up; and tragedy from the top of his world, down. While these statements are necessarily sweeping, for there are countless variations within, they can provide us with a picture of the general trend. If we regard comedy and tragedy as the opposite ends of a see-saw, we shall find the more extreme elements in both as we progress further from the central point of balance.

On the one side, in great tragedy we find insight into character, developing in strong drama into events that lead to a reversal, but less recognition. Then we find comparatively little inner life in soap-operas and most Westerns, and move to the all-good heroes and all-bad villains of melodrama – with Sweeney Todd and his devilish barber's chair, and poor Maria Marten with trouble in the Red Barn. And so to Grand Guignol, with stock characters and a glorious wallow in the horrors of Dracula, and of Dr. Jekyll and Mr. Hyde.

On the other end of the see-saw we shall find comedy, with (near the centre) the wit of the comedies of manners such as *The School for Scandal* and *The Importance of Being Earnest*, sometimes labelled "high comedy." These catch and reflect the spirit of an age, commenting on the morals, the conventions, and the fashions of speech – which help to "date" comedy more than tragedy, but which in these great plays catch a lasting humor, so that they are still regularly performed. Then comes "low" or broader comedy, providing less that is verbal and more that is visual, and needing a strong sense of characterization. Next we come to farce and, finally, the custard pies of slapstick – as far removed from the probable in comedy as is Grand Guignol in tragedy. But all that is good in comedy has a quality of fun, and the shared exuberance of laughing with – not at – other human beings. We recognize in them qualities that exist in ourselves – joyous quirks that are the reverse side of the tragic flaw, and that contain the widest variety of amusement.

At the opposite ends of our see-saw, situation takes over entirely; but near the centre, high comedy and great tragedy require a most subtle understanding of people, and often the two elements intermingle. Chaplin can make us laugh and cry; Olivier can make us cry and laugh. Either ends of the see-saw may veer farther from the likely happenings of our ordinary world, but if at the time we believe that Bottom is transformed into an ass – even though one moment of reason would tell us this could not possibly happen – or that the Witches in Macbeth really exist, then we contribute our own spirit of belief to the magic of the theatre. For as Mr. Puff, the author in

Sheridan's comedy *The Critic, Or A Tragedy Rehearsed*, says at the beginning of his so-called tragedy *The Spanish Armada*, "A play is not to show occurrences that happen every day, but things just so strange, that though they never did, they might happen." Perhaps this "might" is one of the major drawing-cards of the theatre.

The Nature of Drama

Man holds a primitive belief, derived from his instinct for survival, that the acting in advance of an event can turn the outcome to his advantage – wishful thinking put into practice. Where he is faced with a coming conflict, he may, at one level, stick pins into an image of his adversary; at another level he acts out the coming hunt, in which he must kill if he and his family are to eat, thus safeguarding his present survival and, through perpetuation, his physical form of immortality. Then, instead of using a lifeless image as his rival, one of his fellow men agrees to dress up as the beast by wearing a mask; so the hunter enacts life, and the beast, death. Together they perform the ritual of the hunt: sighting, stalking, chasing, fighting, and the kill.

Already we have a plot; and already we have what are termed the twin levels of consciousness, both men pretending these actions at one level but retaining control at another. Without this second level the fight could become real and, instead of the continuance of their lives, the result could mean their own immediate death. At the moment, both will be performing for the sake of trial movements on the part of the hunter, and the possible evasion and counter-attacks of the hunted – what is now sometimes called a "dry run" of an actual event. But if they are also using these movements to show what might happen for the benefit of younger, less experienced, members of the tribe, they will probably enlarge the action somewhat, so projecting to a first audience – with a likely increase of ferocious growls and grunts – and interpreting, or making clear their actions, in order to share them with others.

Such dramas are often the means by which man foresees, safeguards, and builds all his designs; and this enactment can help us to bring our coming conflicts and problems into focus. So we try to foresee the events of an interview, the needs of an exam, or the rigors of a dental appointment. Used positively, this power may enable us to accept and construct from the coming experience; used negatively, it degenerates into worry; like all power, we have to learn to put it to good use. Another form of bringing conflict to light is used in what is currently called "role-playing" for those receiving mental-health treatment. Here it becomes a form of showing, or self-realization leading to acceptance, working the mental and emotional ills out of the system by acting – which is doing.

All of this stems from a further power, latent or otherwise, in all of us: the power of the imagination, which is defined by Webster as, "The act or power of creating mental images of what has never been actually experienced, or of creating new images or ideas by continuing previous experiences; creative power. Imagination is often regarded as the more serious and deeply creative faculty, which perceives the basic resemblance between things, as distinguished from fancy, the lighter and more decorative faculty, which perceives superficial resemblances .... The ability to understand and appreciate imaginative creations of others, especially works of art or literature."[1]

Thus the imagination is a most useful tool in projecting ahead, whether it be at the root of all good organization, the solving of a mathematical problem, the design of a bridge, or in all artistic creation – or even in solving the best route to the parking lot when on our way to the local store, with due reference to one-way streets and "No Left Turns." Memory plays a part; but the putting-together of memory for constructive purposes lies with the imagination. Even when we reach the store, we shall still use this power; we may not now hunt and kill our own food, but we plan, see, and taste in advance, arranging our meals, pre-testing for popularity and price. So, in the process of selecting and serving our food, we still use the power of imagination.

While imagination leads to a further understanding of events concerning ourselves and our society, it also, as the dictionary suggests, enables us to envisage another's point of view. This is invaluable when we wish not merely to express and try out ideas for our own sake, but to express so as to share, or communicate, with others – when it is essential that, in some form or other, the communication has a meaning and is significant. Here lies the root and purpose of all art. When we use drama to further our own purpose, it remains a useful form of sympathetic magic; when we use it as a means of communication with others, and we re-create an experience so that it may be shared by many, then drama becomes an art.

It is largely through the arts, via an awareness of the senses, that we receive impressions and can in turn express our own points of

Webster's New Twentieth Century Dictionary of the English Language (Second Edition, New York: Publishers Guild, 1957).

Development of the Stage: 1. The Greek Theatre

This and the seven following pictures were specially drawn by Brian Jackson to illustrate the author's explanation of the development of the stage through the ages. The other pictures in this series are on pages 16, 19, 22, 24, 25, 29, and 31.

view. Through observation, we take in; and then comes the need to express out; so we read, listen, and look; and we write, compose, and paint. By these means we also establish a sense of life in times and places other than our own; while language, for example, divides, art speaks a common grammar. As with people, nation may speak to nation through the arts with a more common understanding than has ever been supplied by the barriers of politics. Likewise, century speaks to century – the art of each catching and retaining forever the flavor of the sound, the color, the speech, the music, and the line of costume and furniture; of the stories that become legends; of the discoveries of medicine and science; of worlds of thought and the new world of space. We, in turn, continue the process, distilling our own age, providing the material of our arts through which those who live centuries ahead will view our twentieth century. So we communicate to others, and so we are linked with those that have been and those that are to come. This applies particularly in the theatre, which is a reflection of all the arts; plays written over two thousand years ago are still produced; those written by Shakespeare nearly four hundred years ago are performed everywhere; some now being written will express this age in the centuries to come.

The Story of the Theatre

The origin of formal drama – in the sense that it is performed in a certain place at specified times, using a definite play, or script, and for the benefit and participation of the entire community – lies in religion. In ancient Greece the important figure of worship was Dionysus, god of nature and more particularly of wine (his Latin name was Bacchus), whose rites of birth were celebrated each spring, and of death each fall. The audience participated through their own representatives, a chorus of approximately fifty, who spoke in question and answer form to a leader. He was, therefore, the first actor, and the very first was called Thespis. He stood on the *thymele*, or altar, in the centre of the orchestra, or dancing place, playing the role of a god or a priest. The entire celebration was possibly linked with some form of sacrifice, for the Greek meaning of the word tragedy is – goat-song.

Because great festivals of drama were planned for the entire community, the theatres were vast, seating over sixteen thousand people on the curve of a hillside, half surrounding the orchestra below. A second actor was soon introduced so that conflict could develop, and eventually a third, with some playing many roles. The chorus was later stabilized at fifteen. Women, incidentally, never performed in the Greek theatre.

Since the theatres were so large, the actors were padded so that they could be seen, wearing tall masks and special clogs (*kothurnii,* sometimes nine inches high) to give added height. They soon became separated from the chorus, performing on a long, low platform at the back of the orchestra, named the *logeion,* or stage. Movement was used very little since it would have been clumsy; and so it was left to the chorus who, with smaller masks and only slightly padded, commented on the action. They were still representatives of the audience – rather, as we shall find later, like the single chorus, or Stage Manager, in *Our Town.* The productions were a combination of singing, chanting, and dancing, resembling more a strange, ritualistic opera than performances with which we are familiar today.

GREEK TRAGEDY

The fifth century B.C. was the great age of Greek tragedy, established by the writer Aeschylus (525–450 B.C.), who was a majestic poet and laid the foundations of plot. He is said to have written ninety plays; seven are extant, of which the trilogy or three-part drama of *The Oresteia* is the most famous, containing the *Agamemnon, The Choephori,* and *The Eumenides.* Sophocles (496–406 B.C.) was an idealist, concerned with the interplay of character and situation, who brought a serene dignity to his plays. He was eighteen times winner of major festivals, wrote the last of his hundred or so plays when he was over ninety, and is best-known for his trilogy of *Oedipus Rex,* consisting of *Oedipus Tyrannus, Oedipus Coloneus,* and *Antigone.* The first part of this trilogy has been produced by the Old Vic and Stratford, Ont., companies during the last two decades, the latter production also being televised and filmed. *Antigone* has been adapted by the French playwright, Anouilh, and this version was first presented in Paris in 1944, under the nose of the Nazis, who failed to see that it represented a woman's stand against tyranny. Euripedes (480–406 B.C.) was a humanist, showing life not as it should be, but as it is. He introduced a slightly humorous element, and the innovation of a prologue. Versions of his *Medea* are known today through the performances of Judith Anderson and Eileen Herlie, and in 1962, at one of the ancient theatres at Epidaurus, near Athens, Katina Paxinou, the Greek actress, played Agave in his play about the female worshippers of Dionysus, *The Bacchae*. So our generation is familiar with characters who grew somewhere out of myth and legend, and who have been acted over a life span of nearly two thousand five hundred years.

GREEK COMEDY

Tragedy, to the Greeks, concerned human duty as told in legend. The original meaning of the word comedy is "revel," and the form began with a large proportion of disrespect for the very ideals which were the aim of tragedy. Taking the shape of lampoon, or satire, it deliberately upset the balance of values – de-bagging statesmen, poets, and dramatists; providing, as always, a safety valve against authority, and being topical rather than universal. (Comedies are rarely produced except in period; they are dependent on the modes, morals, and speech of the time; few survive beyond their age: tragedy can be transposed, and modern-dress and eighteenth-century Hamlets are not now uncommon.) In the Greek comedies the chorus was often disguised as animals to give a thin covering to what we should consider libellously topical allusions. The fourth century B.C. was the great age of comedy, by which time tragedy was already suffering a decline. Aristophanes (448–380 B.C.) established the golden age of Athenian Old Comedy, writing forty-four plays, eleven of which remain. One of his best-known is *The Frogs*, which still retains a certain humor; it begins with a slave who is forced to cart his master's belongings down to Hades, since he wants to find a poet – and good poets, he has discovered, are all dead. One century later Menander (342–291 B.C.) began a form later known as the comedy of manners, writing one hundred and five plays in thirty years, and evolving such traditional characters as the Rich Old Man, the Youth, and the Devoted Servant.

THE ROMAN THEATRE

The Roman theatre brings us to a perpetual cycle of development in all theatre: there is a rise to a zenith, lasting comparatively few years, when considerable activity is capped by the work of one, or a very few, great dramatists. This peak becomes a meeting place not only of writers, but of good actors, and of an audience that is both large and drawn from all ranks of society; it often coincides with a new approach in the design of the theatre building. When all these elements meet, as in the times of Ancient Greece and Elizabethan

England, the result is great theatre; when there is a meeting of two, we may find good theatre; otherwise the result is likely to be less than mediocre.

After such a rise comes the beginning of the fall; there is an attempt to repeat successful patterns; in lieu of better material, imitation leads to conscious effort and embellishment; decline falls into decay. Then a new beginning starts in obscurity and, perhaps nurtured by the rise of those other elements of audience and actor, shines forth as a light upon the way, in turn to be copied for its own sake, until the whirligig of time brings the inevitable revenge.

So it was with the Romans, who were mostly plagiarists, turning the theatre and their drama into elaborate copies of the Greeks. Religious feeling disappeared, and so did the policy of non-violence on stage (hence all those Greek messengers); gods became fierce and furious rather than bodiless spirits of fate, and theatres were built on flat ground rather than in the natural hollow of a hillside. Architects could now raise the *cavea*, or auditorium – first on scaffolding, and then as a permanent structure facing a larger, higher stage, taking precedence over the orchestra, which soon disappeared from use. Theatres were considered useful in keeping the people entertained, and were built at all the major cities in the Empire, including Sabratha in Africa, Aspendus in Asia Minor, Orange in France, and Verulamium (St. Albans) in England.

The Roman playwrights took the more sensational of the Greek dramas as a basis for melodrama. Because of popular taste, Seneca (4 B.C.–65 A.D.), a lawyer and philosopher, wrote to be read rather than performed. The comedies of Terence (195–159 B.C.), born a slave, and Plautus (254–184 B.C.), predecessor of Ben Jonson, are important because they establish a link between their basis of Greek comedy and the Renaissance – and so to Shakespeare and beyond.

Performances now degenerated from the religious ceremony of the Greeks to a debased form of popular entertainment, competing with gladiatorial combat, the flooding of the Colosseum for a sea fight, and the feeding of Christians to the lions. Blood and spectacle were in demand, and the demand was supplied in full. Actors, understandably, lacked repute; their profession was barred, again understandably, to Christians, who were also forbidden to attend performances. Finally the rift between religion and drama (to be repeated in our continuing cycle) was largely responsible for the closing of theatres in Europe by the sixth century, while in the East they died under the Saracens in the seventh and eight centuries.

Meanwhile St. Augustine of Canterbury (who died in 604 A.D.) wrote that drama could be a suitable means of education, and in this he was not prophesying to the wind . . . .

THE DARK AGES

Theatre, meanwhile, died; but somehow actors, tumblers, jugglers stayed alive, touring Europe in small, straggling groups, reverting largely to what had become a debased form of mime (acting without words) because it presented no language problem. These groups were forerunners of the individual troubadour, and they travelled with carts, probably used as portable stages. Their chief descendant is thought to be the Commedia Dell' Arte, a particular kind of drama we shall later find in Italy between the sixteenth and eighteenth centuries, in which the actors improvised upon chosen situations with the use of stock characters, and which was to have some influence on the theatre of France and England.

Drama, however, has always been a good way of telling a story, especially in times when few people can read or write. The instinct to impersonate, to celebrate and re-create legends through the simplest forms of song, dance, and action, remains. Even when the pattern is repeated and we find, in other ages, theatre suppressed, plays burnt, and companies turned vagabond, the structure may fall, but actors and audience persist.

THE MEDIEVAL PERIOD

In view of the previous cycle of events, the next official recognition of what was to grow into theatre came from a surprising direction. Drama, as we have seen, was first a tool of religion, an aid to communicating to the people facts about the gods; within a thousand years it was so out of hand as to be banished by another form of religion, which happened to use singularly dramatic rites in the celebration of the Mass. These, since Latin was the official language of the church, were spoken in a tongue foreign to those who worshipped and were largely incomprehensible to the simple congregations. To share, or communicate, the message of religion, a few additional lines of dialogue were inserted and spoken, or sung, as question and response among the priests. The first of these was a four-line interpolation at Easter about the continuance of life, or the Resurrection, known as the *Quem Quaeritis* (Whom Seek Ye?).

Soon more of these small dramas were added to the services in celebration of the Christmas and Easter festivals, but were still enacted by priests. Then more elaborate productions were created, with members of the congregation taking some roles; and soon the performances, colored by a sense of humor, were spoken in the vernacular and given outside in the churchyard. Again the wheel turns full circle for, by a papal edict of 1210, the clergy were forbidden to appear on a public stage, and the drama was no longer controlled by the church.

Development of the Stage: 2. A Medieval Pageant

Just over a hundred years later, in 1311, the feast of Corpus Christi was proclaimed, and from sunrise to sunset on one of the longest days of the year a series of mystery, or Bible, plays was publicly performed. Each incident was acted on a cart, or pageant, sometimes two-storied and always much grander than those once used by the travelling groups of acrobats of a few centuries before. The actors progressed through the town during the holiday while the people stood at the street corners and in the market place; after each incident was performed, its particular pageant moved to the next location. The total series was now organized by the local guilds of craftsmen; the actors were members of these guilds and were paid for their work, and these productions were the chief form of public entertainment in the fourteenth and fifteenth centuries.

The mysteries were composed of a series of single incidents. The next development was to a longer, still anonymous, type of drama known as the morality play, which told of the struggle and final triumph of virtue over vice. The most famous of these was *Everyman,* an English adaptation of a Dutch original; and between 1450 and 1600 the personifications of Good and Evil remained popular.

Parallel with this advance from mere story into the new delving into man's inner character and conflict, came the Interludes, which were more entertaining, of a less religious nature, and of known authorship. They are mentioned in the records of the early professional companies who performed under patronage and were known as the Lord Chamberlain's Men, the King's Men, and others. Without such protection, or form of licence, actors were classed as rogues and vagabonds, and could be imprisoned for giving a performance. By the early sixteenth century they were producing their plays on simple platforms for their lord's entertainment, sometimes as part of a banquet, already serving an age-old function of adding prestige to a household and impressing important and sometimes foreign visitors.

THE RENAISSANCE

Meanwhile in Italy there was the discovery, known as the Renaissance, of the classics of Greece and Rome, which aroused a fresh interest in the arts, the sciences, and in man. This was reflected in the great surge in the development of English-speaking drama within the fifty years from the Interludes of Thomas Heywood to the *Hamlet* of Shakespeare, culminating in the greatest meeting of playwright, actors, and audience yet known in the story of the theatre.

It is interesting, however, that in Italy, where there was such enthusiasm for the classics and such total acceptance of the theories of Aristotle, the Commedia Erudita of the court circles attempted only to copy, rather than explore, their form. The result was lifeless, more dependent on music than on drama, which probably drove the players of the Commedia dell'Arte to travel as they did among the people, developing the characters known to us as Punch, Harlequin, and Columbine. One positive outcome of the period, however, was based on the discovery that the Greek plays contained a form of recitation to music, and it was in imitation of this that the new dramatic form of opera was evolved by a group of the Florentine court known as the Camerata. The first major work in which music became the equal of, and not subordinate to, the libretto was Monteverdi's *Orfeo*, produced in 1607.

SIXTEENTH CENTURY

In England plays were now written and performed in three main centres of learning: the Schools, the Inns of Court, and the Universities. In the schools they were considered a useful means of learning Latin. Nicholas Udall, headmaster of Eton, was adept at placing native characters within a classical construction of acts and scenes, as in his first English comedy (based on Plautus and Terence), *Ralph Roister Doister* (1553). Young lawyers regarded drama as a form of recreation as well as of education, and *Gorboduc* (1562), by Sackville and Norton – the first English tragedy to be written in blank verse – was modelled on Seneca. University students were familiar with the Roman comedies, and Lyly, of the Choir School of St. Paul's Cathedral, wrote several plays in which the style was heightened out of proportion to reality. Accepted by a Court audience, Lyly did much to fashion the previous rough verse so that it was the more ready to be used by Shakespeare.

One office with which we are all familiar was already established by this time: that of the Lord of Misrule, known in schools as the Boy Bishop and in Scotland as the Abbot of Unreason, who was appointed to arrange the plays at Christmas and other festivals. There was also a permanent official known as the Master of the Revels, who by the end of the sixteenth century became official censor of plays. When the Licensing Act was passed in 1737, by which any person performing in an unlicensed building could still be classed a rogue and vagabond, the censor's work became the responsibility of the Lord Chamberlain's office; and in England censorship and licensing still come under his jurisdiction.

Meanwhile more companies of actors under patronage were formed, producing plays by writers such as Kyd and Marlowe, who provided thundering, magnificent verse within Senecan tragedies of revenge. In 1587 Edward Alleyn, an actor so respected

that a school was named after him, scaled the heights of Marlowe's
Tamburlaine the Great – which in 1955 was presented by the Stratford,
Ont., company in Toronto and New York.

Design of the first theatres. There was now a need for a place in
which actors would reach their growing audience, for their plays
were becoming more popular, and were essentially public – in the
widest sense – in their appeal. They were full of the tremendous

Development of the Stage: 3. The Elizabethan Stage

sense of discovery of the time, supplying verse for those who wished
to listen, and plenty of blood and action for those who wished to
look. The natural choice fell upon the general meeting place of
the inn yard, centre of food and drink, used by all travellers, and
frequented by all society. These yards were open to the air and
provided a circular, galleried surround to a pit, in which the
groundlings could stand; a temporary platform was built on
scaffolding so that it jutted into the audience on three sides, the
back galleries being used for dressing-rooms and often as part of
the play for alcoves or balconies. Not only was there a sense of

direct contact – with the actors performing raised up amidst the audience – but certain members of the audience and friends of the patrons almost mingled with the play, being allowed to sit on the edge of the stage. This custom was accepted for nearly two hundred years, until it was discontinued by Garrick in the eighteenth century.

The basic design for the construction of the first building raised for the performance of stage plays was a simple adaptation of the familiar inn yard. The Lord Mayor of London made it plain that continued performance within the city would be unpopular, for actors were considered carriers of the plague (which put an end to all activity for over a year in 1593), corrupters of morals, and a nuisance to merchants through distraction of apprentices. In 1576 the actor-manager, James Burbage, of the Earl of Leicester's Company, opened the Theatre outside the city limits on the south bank of the Thames. More theatres of this type were built nearby, including those named the Globe, the Curtain, and the Swan, and the staging of performances remained the same in such public theatres for nearly seventy years. Until, like the moth to candle flame, it seemed that the charges against actors and their like were resoundingly declared proven when, in 1642, the Puritans closed all theatres for the nineteen years of Commonwealth rule.

SHAKESPEARE TO THE COMMONWEALTH

Meanwhile the greatest meeting of audience and actor was joined by the writer William Shakespeare (1564–1616), who, between approximately 1590 and 1610, wrote thirty-six plays, of which sixteen were published in his lifetime for performance in this type of theatre. Like most playwrights, he was a plagiarist, re-adapting the Chronicle Histories, basing the *Comedy of Errors* on Plautus and *Hamlet* on Kyd's *Spanish Tragedy*. He created characters that were large, and therefore ideal for the theatre; but he wrote them in depth. He used poetry with delight, and more than compensated for any lack of scenery on his stages with an enormous variety of verse and of prose. He was a man of the theatre who knew his trade and his public – from the favorites of the groundlings to the preferences of the Queen.

When Shakespeare died, in 1616, at the age of fifty-two, the theatre, the plays, and the mood of the times were already changing – a useful example of Ben Jonson's dictum that "the drama's laws the drama's patrons give." The cycle that we have met before continued to turn drama into a copy of the past; the political scene was less stable, and there was a growing division between court and people. (James I, who came to the throne in 1603, believed in the Divine Right of Kings; Elizabeth had known there could also be a Divine Right of People.) The appetite for plot at the expense of character crept in and an elaboration of the spectacular appeared. Tragedies of horror and revenge were set in Italy, probably influenced by Seneca and the Borgias combined. A new form of entertainment, called the masque, was evolved and first imported into England from Italy and France during Elizabeth's reign. First cousin to opera and ballet, it was essentially a court entertainment, housed in private theatres that were roofed in – protecting patrons and scenery, and providing an elaborate setting for the spectacle. The playwright Ben Jonson (1572–1637) – once imprisoned as an actor, the author of *Volpone* (1606) and *The Alchemist* (1610), satiric comedies still often performed – collaborated with the architect and designer Inigo Jones (1573–1652) to produce the most elaborate results.

The Puritans soon regarded the theatre with deep misgiving, and the theatre retaliated in full measure by lampooning their behavior. Once again a split between theatre and religion became open conflict, and religion, temporarily, won. In 1642 all theatres were closed by Act of Parliament. But people continued to want drama, and somehow actors continued to act; performances of a sort were given in fairgrounds, and *A Midsummer Night's Dream*, for example, was adapted and condensed into *Bottom, the Weaver*. Plays that lay dormant were taken off their shelves and printed, as often as not producing a muddle of versions since the original prompters had cheerfully sold different copies to rival acting companies.

Meanwhile a monarch was beheaded; a people warred at home; and a court went to France.

THE NEW WORLD

Now another migration of a different kind was occurring. Rising prosperity created a desire for the ownership of land, which was a popular investment as there were no banks; but much of the land in the Old World was already sold. To better themselves, and to find religious freedom, people began to explore and settle in the New World. Craftsmen and builders took axe and plough to make civilization in the wilderness – in Virginia, New England, Pennsylvania, and the West Indies. Many of these took to the new Quaker form of religion, making the Christian qualities a way of life rather than a way of dogma as practised by the Puritans. By the end of the seventeenth century, when the struggle with the land had begun to earn the settlers some leisure and a little money, there were reports of stage-plays being performed in New England; one actor, Tom Aston, made a name in Charles-Town in the south before continuing on to New York, which then had a population of four thousand people.

Development of the Stage: 4. The Restoration

FRENCH INFLUENCE

In Europe, the influence of the French court was now to determine the trend of English-speaking drama. The theatre existed for one section of the community, and members of the court took part in the entertainments, with special enthusiasm for a new form of action in dance known as ballet. In 1653 Louis XIV played Le Roi Soleil in *Le Ballet de la Nuit*. One of the greatest French dramatists was Corneille, who wrote his most famous tragi-comedy, *Le Cid*, in 1636. Racine's *Phèdre* (1677) adapted the legend used two thousand years previously by Euripedes in *Hippolytus*. Comedy, however, had been lagging, and was regarded as more suitable for fairground plays than for providing wit for the entertainment of the court. Then Moliere, who began his career unsuccessfully in Paris, toured the provinces for over a decade, and returned a brilliant actor and writer. His *Tartuffe* (1644) is a marvellous satire on religious hypocrisy, and, though seen privately, was publicly suppressed for many years; his best short play, *L'Impromptu de Versailles* (1664), was commissioned by the King as a deliberate answer to attacks made on his private life; *The Miser* (1668), nearly three hundred years later, was one of the first plays to open the new Tyrone Guthrie Theatre in Minneapolis.

THE RESTORATION

In 1660 the monarchy was restored in England; Puritan narrowness was replaced by Restoration licence. It has taken the theatre almost three hundred years to recover from the resultant prejudice. Actresses appeared for the first time, and men of fashion paid more to see them in their dressing-rooms than for the seats that could still be bought on stage. Theatres existed in London only, playing to the court, and the king granted patents to only two companies, led by Davenant and Killigrew. Values changed, marriage was ridiculed, intrigue became popular, and vice was considered virtue. The comedy of manners was continued by Congreve (1670–1729), who achieved great subtlety in *The Way Of The World* (1700) (in which Edith Evans gained recognition when she played Millamant in 1924). In the oblong, narrow theatres, the fore-stage, relic of the Elizabethan apron, could now be entered by two doors on either side and in front of the proscenium arch. This frame to the stage, which had been imported from Italy for the earlier masques, now set off the picture in the recessed area of the stage. The inner stage was regarded as a means of suggesting location and changing background – which was accomplished by the use of movable shutters in a series of grooves – with the occasional aid of a table or chair. It was never considered that actors would mingle with the furniture.

EIGHTEENTH CENTURY

The eighteenth century marked a first return of ordinary, untitled people as the characters of stage plays. Goldsmith (1730–1774), with *She Stoops to Conquer* (1773), and Sheridan (1751–1816), with *The School for Scandal* (1777), retained all the wit, but none of the licentiousness, of the Restoration Theatre. Both Sheridan and David Garrick (1717–1779), a great actor in what was primarily an age of actors, were so respected as to be buried in Westminster Abbey. It was Garrick who finally banished the audience from the stage, and concealed bare lighting from the auditorium. With the Licensing Act in 1737 drama could only legally be given at Drury Lane and Covent Garden; but with the rise in population

Development of the Stage: 5. The Eighteenth Century

and the new prosperity of the trading classes, there was a growing demand for popular entertainment. Put in six songs, and any straight drama could be termed a musical, or burletta. Larger theatres were built; action became more important than dialogue; and, for lack of good lighting, subtlety was lost. To make way for more seats, the fore-stage, or apron, disappeared and the actors retreated behind the proscenium arch into what has become known as the "picture-frame" stage, from which they have only recently re-emerged.

NINETEENTH CENTURY

The nineteenth century saw a continuance of the spectacular; Vesuvius erupted nightly; ghosts arose from Gothic ruins; characters became types; and a hopelessly unnatural poetic justice formed the basis of melodrama. (This form first implied the use of music to convey a character's inner feelings, a device which later proved useful in the days of silent movies.)

Development of the Stage: 6. The Nineteenth Century

The stage became a machine; better lighting, elaborate scenery, and more funiture were added, until someone was needed to control these extra facilities, and the stage manager was born. The mechanics of production assumed a vast importance; actors were lost among the set. Scenery could be changed by sliding screens in grooves, or placing them in slots, by flying (raising) it out of sight above the proscenium arch, by using traps and, eventually, revolves. Although in 1843 an Act for Regulating Theatres had revoked the Licensing Act, breaking the monopoly of the two major theatres, "show" for the sake of show was now fully established in the minds of managers and public alike.

More people could now afford leisure and culture, and a new class of society arose. In the theatre the pit, originally a standing-place and later occupied by benches, was changed; the front rows became seats known as stalls; the back rows were pushed back under the first row of boxes, which was now raised to become the dress circle, or balcony. So the theatre began to cater to all society, and in 1865, to attract new money, a carpet was laid in the stalls; women were soon encouraged to attend by the addition of matinées to the regular performances. The theatre began to achieve a respectability and acceptance unknown for years. Historical accuracy became fashionable, and education took over what religion had rejected. Shakespeare re-emerged, accurate in text but submerged in pageantry; scholarship and classical research were combined, like medicine, for the common good; lecturers on ancient music and Fellows of The Royal Society became the high priests of the learned approach.

Wealth was emulated, and values were materialistic. People went to the theatre to see "real" life, and romantic ruins gave way to box-sets, real doorknobs, and cups and saucers; interior scenes changed from the bedroom of the Restoration to the parlor of the eighteenth and the drawing-room of the nineteenth century. Society was in; modes and manners were laced into convention; the sentiments of "When-did-you-last-see-your-father" melodrama and of "Tennis-anyone?" comedy were perfectly acceptable; politeness was all, and inner feeling and satirical criticism were out. With a growing audience, longer runs were established; *Henry VIII* played for a hundred performances in 1855, *A Midsummer Night's Dream* a hundred and fifty in 1856. Type-casting was created, and a new type of performer was needed who could speak, talk, and walk like society, off-stage and on. The theatre, like a photograph, was a replica of life; plays were constructed to a formula, so that the audience had the comfort of knowing what to expect; and, as their earnings increased, playwrights gained greater recognition. The times were secure and so was the theatre, housing trains with real steam, live horses, and rabbits.

THEATRE IN NORTH AMERICA

Meanwhile, there was expansion in the New World, developing within one hundred and fifty years from the garrison theatricals of the military and their wives at Halifax, Montreal, and Fort Pitt (now Pittsburgh) to theatres that within the first decade of the twentieth century were equal to any in the world.

The early military operations over, theatre followed the frontier, opening in New Orleans; two theatres were supported – precariously – in St. Louis by 1820. After the Civil War, Chicago became the theatrical centre of the West, and in 1862 Brigham Young built a large theatre in Salt Lake City, capital of the Mormon State of Utah. By the 'fifties there were theatres in Texas and in California, and soon the railroad linked a continent; companies could travel and began to tour via what is still referred to as "the road."

Philadelphia supported the famous Chestnut Street Theatre in 1794; but this was soon overshadowed by the Park Street Theatre in New York. One of the actors completed a first trans-Atlantic appearance, playing at Drury Lane in 1813; his name was John Howard Payne, composer of *Home, Sweet Home.* Elsewhere in the North, theatre was disguised (under the cloak of education) to be acceptable to religion; so Boston had a playhouse as early as 1792, but it was called The New Exhibition Room, and the famous Boston Museum opened in 1843; early productions of *Othello* were given under the name of *A Moral Dialogue Against The Sin Of Jealousy.* Theatres on both sides of the Atlantic shared the same plays and players; London's actor-managers Macready, Kean, and Kemble toured in the early years, as did Irving and Ellen Terry in the latter part of the century; Augustin Daly (1839–1899) built his own theatres in New York and in London. Plays varied from Richard Tyler's *The Contrast* (1787), a New World version of *The School For Scandal*, to melodramas by Belasco, with blood dripping from the ceiling as a wanted man lies hidden, wounded, in an attic. By 1879 the new Madison Square Theatre was one of the wonders of the theatrical world, equipped with an elevator-stage, air-conditioning, folding chairs, and an orchestra "pit" above and behind the proscenium arch. Within thirty years many smaller but well-equipped theatres were built in Canada, including Her Majesty's in Montreal (1899), the Grand in London, Ont. (1904), the Walker Theatre in Winnipeg (1906), and the Royal Alexandra in Toronto (1907).

NEW TRENDS

Theatre everywhere was becoming socially acceptable and even a potential money-maker, when rumblings directed against the then Establishment, the trite, the ham, and the sentimental created a further turn of progress. All the arts were beginning a counter-revolution against the long-term effects of the industrial revolution – the over-elaborate, factory-made, cheap-labor products of the time.

Henrik Ibsen (1828–1906) created a new approach to drama by making characters of equal importance to a strong situation, and by showing women who acted on opinions of their own. Shaw (1856–1950) brought social conscience into the theatre, and Chekhov (1860–1904) presented an inner life through reaction of character to circumstance, while Stanislavsky (1865–1938) counter-acted an outmoded approach to acting which was then particularly prevalent in Russia, always isolated from the rest of the artistic world.

William Poël, once a manager of the Old Vic when it was still a Music Hall, presented Shakespeare for the Elizabethan Stage Society on a bare platform, clear of all trappings. This was the first echo of the now re-accepted custom of performing a play amidst, rather than separate from, an audience, a custom brought about by many needs, not the least of which is the comparative expense involved in mounting a conventional, picture-frame pro-duction.

'TWENTIES AND 'THIRTIES

The audiences during World War One clamored for escape from a killing reality in a world that was changing faster than they knew, and they were supplied in the main with spectacular record-breaking musicals. In the post-war world in the States and in Russia, experiment answered the need to explore new means; and, as in the newer theories of the age-old art of acting, the approach appeared to eclipse *what* was being done by attracting to the *how*. All the "isms" became fashionable, and constructivism, futurism, formalism, and surrealism were rampant in the theatre as they were elsewhere. O'Neill became the star of the American drama, and on both sides of the Atlantic – perhaps in an unconscious effort to keep theatre alive during the days of economic crisis and to re-live past glory – there was a return to the chronicle play, now linking theatre both with history and with education. A generation of playgoers grew up on a diet of episodic pageants with large casts, including *Victoria Regina* and *Abraham Lincoln* (by a British playwright), *Elizabeth the Queen* (by an American), and *Richard of Bordeaux* (the best). Lesser ranks such as St. Joan, Elizabeth Browning, and Florence Nightingale took history seriously; *1066 And All That* did not. Realism was explored by American playwrights; exuberance and vitality were reserved for musicals.

Development of the Stage: 7. Early Twentieth Century

Meanwhile the Little Theatre movement was keeping theatre alive in communities and colleges; and the British Drama League (formed in 1919) and the Dominion Drama Festival in Canada (formed in 1933) did much to aid theatre in the days of the depression – and to build an audience, and often provide actors, for the great resurgence of drama during World War Two.

'FORTIES, 'FIFTIES, AND AFTER

Then – revivals of classic plays simply staged and greatly acted; a small return to verse led by Eliot and Fry; the bitter epics of

Brecht made known outside Germany; the clean sweep by Osborne of drawing-room comedy; muddy plays among cellars, attics, and sinks; the deliberate use of the absurd in making sense out of nonsense, and nonsense out of sense. The poetry of the pathetic in Tennessee Williams; the struggle for communication in Albee's world of non-communicants. The theatre treading carefully through the age of the atom, of technology, of astronauts and space – surrounded by marvels, but still surrounded by man.

And now – a further trend in the making? Another turn in the cycle, this time, perhaps, with hopeful signs. All sections of the community attend the theatre; the last decades have provided good, if not great, playwrights: Miller, Williams, Rattigan, Dylan Thomas (a might-have-been-greater), Pinter, and Wesker. We have witnessed a rise of international stars: Gielgud, Olivier, Plummer, Evans, Thorndike, and Ashcroft, with a new generation on the horizon. The actor-manager has almost ceased to exist; his private financial backing has been taken over in part by government grant, and in some cases by municipal and public funds; he has given way to a new leader in the theatre: the artistic director, who needs diplomacy with boards and committees as he needs technical knowledge with actor and designer. Finally, new theatre centres are developing away from the larger cities.

Theatres are casting off cumbersome, expensive machinery, and contact is being re-established with an audience. Location – where the playwright names it; time – where he places it; the need – for a language to give expression to this return to a wooden scaffold. The newly designed, Elizabethan-inspired theatres at Stratford, Ontario, Chichester, Sussex, and Minneapolis, Minnesota, may be the first of many. New buildings are appearing; the theatres are there, the actors are ready, an audience is being created. Now the need is for the playwright.

Mounting a Production

The purpose of this book is to discover the work – and responsibility – of everyone concerned in the fascinating process of bringing each production, or version of a play to life; and we will follow an outline of the preparation required, from producer to prompter, and from director to assistant stage manager. Each chapter should be regarded as part of a whole; it is never enough for an actor to know

Development of the Stage: 8. Mid-Twentieth Century

only about acting, or a director only about directing; a production is created by a team, and the more each person understands what is done by others, the better his contribution to the whole.

AREAS OF RESPONSIBILITY

The following diagram will show the tree, or main division, of work in the theatre. In later chapters, part of it will be subdivided to show the work of certain departments in more detail.

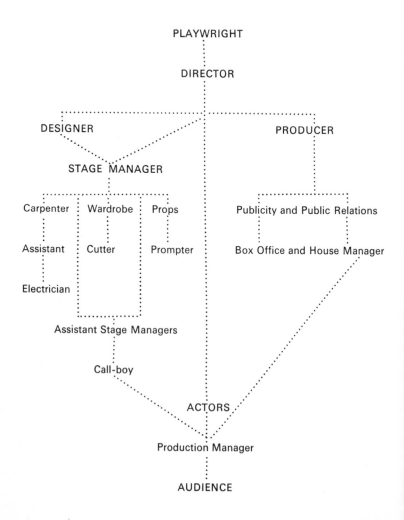

It takes three points to make a straight line, and the work of the director, for example, is to line the playwright, through the actor, to the audience. While the writer is the mainspring, the director is the pivot of production, and his authority should be regarded as complete. A particular version of any play will be largely the result of his main approach, colored by the work of the designer and the cast.

Ideally the director works in close collaboration with the producer, who is responsible for all business matters and, literally, for producing all physical requirements of the play. He is the coordinator who plans the budget, supervises all rentals – from theatre to costumes – checks that everything will be ready on time, and is an expert at the tieing-in-of-the-last-minute-ends.

The designer completes the triumvirate which gives form and shape to a production even before rehearsals begin. He is responsible for the entire visual aspect, or spectacle, of a production, often designing the set as well as the costumes, and having considerable influence in the lighting of the result; but, like everyone else, he accepts the fact that final decisions lie in the hands of the director.

The stage manager is the personal assistant to the director, and supervises, as his title implies, the management of everything connected with the actual staging of the play. We shall find that, when it has been set by the director, he eventually takes over the production and is responsible for the running of each performance. He prepares for this during the rehearsal period by marking in and practising the signals for all cues, allocating them to his assistants, checking the position and details of the set, and supervising the listing of furniture and properties. In this way, all the people in his department become invisible partners to the actors, aiding and abetting the performance; in this way sets will be changed smoothly, and lighting and sound cues given so that they are integrated within the total production.

The actor is responsible for an interpretation of his role that, again, is ideally the result of collaboration between himself, the writer, and the director. He is also responsible to many others, and should attend rehearsals on time, learn his lines as needed, and be available for costume fittings, publicity interviews, and other calls as required.

These people, then, are the main branches of our "family tree"; their work, and that of their assistants, will be discussed in the following pages. For those who will want to read more, there is a reading list at the end of each chapter. Some of the lists are longer than others, for while everyone has views about acting (and haven't we all?) and many theorize on directing, we tend to forget that the more technical subjects of stage management and lighting are just as interesting; to some, they are more satisfying, because they are dealing with tangible equipment, and with tangible results.

CHOICE OF PLAY

The choice of a play is rarely a matter of easy decision, except on those few occasions when a director, actor, designer, or producer has something he is burning to do, and everyone else is prepared to burn along with him. It usually means careful selection with the following points in mind.

Which of your actors, directors, or designers are likely to be available? though often no one really knows until the very last moment. Is the choice to be part of a season's program, so offering variety and contrast to previous comedies or tragedies? How many in the cast? it is often easier to do a heavy production earlier than later in the season. Exams, for example, and other commitments can make inroads into a potential cast after Easter more than at any other time during the season. Then, an audience is rarely a ready-made commodity: it has to be built, and led, and kept loyal to a group; as far as anyone can tell, will the choice appeal? A diet of far-out Theatre of the Absurd, such as Ionesco's *The Chairs* and *The Bald Soprano*, is unlikely to meet an immediate response from a community new to theatre; but occasional productions of this nature could create considerable interest among an experienced audience.

Conditions can also influence choice: a small stage with little wing-space may limit all plays to those with one set, though it is surprising what imagination and ingenuity can do; it may even lead to discarding the conventional platform, framed by the proscenium arch, and building a stage out into the audience. Budget, too, will determine the scale of the production: a few hundred dollars in hand could mean the affirmative for a costume play; no dollars in hand could mean trying a classic, which would be good or else it would not still be performed, and would be less expensive because it would not be liable to royalty fees.

Remember that if the choice is for a play which belongs to a period other than our own, it should be regarded in the light of its times to help make it acceptable to our own. So a Restoration comedy, or some of Shakespeare, could give offence if played as we would regard the same situations today; but if performed in the spirit originally intended, it will retain what is truly amusing, for while convention and fashions may change, human nature does not. Similarly, it would be best to discover the type of theatre for which the play was written, and to consider the audience for which it was originally performed; both are likely to have some influence on a current production. A Greek tragedy could never be played in intimate style because it was neither written for nor performed in intimate theatres; so even if played in a small theatre, it should seem, within reason, big. Be sure to delve into all conditions of the age, known to romantics as "the perfume of the centuries" and to realists as "the stink of the period": the clothes people wore, the houses they lived in, the food they ate and drank, the music they listened to, the pictures they painted, and the furniture they sat on.

Then remember that whenever the selection is finally announced, it will rarely meet with unanimous approval. So be as sure as possible that the play will be worth doing and that the characters and situations are believable; and then stick with it. Try a couple of questions: Is this a play we can continue to rehearse, and will we continue to find more in it? Is this a play which could be seen at least three times and would each time continue to enrich our experience?

ORGANIZATION OF A THEATRE GROUP

The size and management of theatre groups vary enormously. Some are vast, with hundreds of acting and otherwise active members, becoming more specialized each season, playing to a membership and to the general public, often selling tickets in terms of hundreds of thousands of dollars each year. Others are small, with just enough members to produce plays on a limited budget, providing lively and varied experience with everyone pitching in to do everything. Size is not always an expression of quality; in 1939, for example, the winning group in Canada's Dominion Drama Festival produced an original play about the depression called *Relief*, and came from a small community in Alberta with a total population of under one hundred.

Most organizations take color from their leader, depending on his particular interest in theatre, whether it be design, production, carpentry, direction, or acting. Few people, or productions, start completely from scratch: an actor usually wants to try a role he has already seen performed – with a hunch that he has something to "say" about it, and that he can do it a lot better (who, among performers, doesn't?); a director begins with a play he has seen, or acted in; and somewhere within every group there will be people who are prepared to pool their experience of one kind or another. Similarly, many start with one-act plays, using them for try-outs and interesting studio productions (simply produced) for new actors, directors – and sometimes for new writers.

There can be no one rigid way of creating theatre. What seems to work for the people and conditions in one group will not necessarily apply to another; but there are common pitfalls which can be avoided. There is a general pattern and certain principles which will in time lead to results; it is these which we will now set out to explore.

Reading List

Masters of the Drama, by John Gassner (Dover).
The Theatre in our Times, by John Gassner (Crown).
The Development of the Theatre, by Allardyce Nicoll (Harrap).
The Theatre and Dramatic Theory, by Allardyce Nicoll (Harrap).
British Drama, by Allardyce Nicholl (Harrap).
The Live Theatre, by Hugh Hunt (Oxford).
Playwrights on Playwrighting, edited by Toby Cole (Hill and Wang).
The Craft of Comedy, by Athene Seyler and Stephen Haggard (Muller).
The Seven Ages of the Theatre, by Richard Southern (Hill and Wang).
The Living Stage, by MacCowan and Melnitz (Prentice-Hall).
Drama on Stage, edited by Ralph Goodman (Holt, Rinehart, and Winston).

2. The Director

Actors are as old as the earth, playwrights as old as the Greeks; but the director is a comparative newcomer to the theatre. His job is fashioned out of that of the stage manager, who, until the end of the last century, helped position the minor actors while the major ones fended for themselves – usually down-stage of the star, who never took direction from anyone. The coming of the *problem play* of Ibsen and Shaw and the *play of indirect action* of Chekhov, however, meant that actors had not only to stand, deliver, and emote, but to think in terms of the play being as important as the performance. This new trend took its being more from the stage management than from the acting side of the theatre. Belasco, for example, was a stage manager in San Francisco before becoming the first well-known American director.

The director has the most interesting and challenging work of all the people concerned in the production of a play. He is finally responsible for the entire presentation and so for the joint effort of everyone involved. He needs a knowledge of the technical departments of design, lighting, and stage management in order to co-ordinate their work; he must also have a proper regard for playwright and actor, a sense of artistry to create magic, and an understanding of what is practical and significant in terms of the medium of theatre. This dreamer of dreams who needs both feet planted on the ground of possibility (and of human nature) is ideally a jack-of-all-theatrical-trades – and a master of two: directing attention via the imagination of actor and audience, and sustaining the thread of a play.

It is essential that he is able to communicate, since his function is to join the play to the public. He must first understand the the material, then communicate his understanding in terms useful to everyone from the actor to the prop-girl. Through them he passes on the total effect (more or less as he intended) to the audience, to whom, if his work is good, it will often pass unnoticed.

Some actors are good directors, but although the experience is a help, this is not a necessary combination. An actor may see a play as revolving around a certain character almost by habit, whereas the director requires an extra analytical sense to see all parts in relation to the whole.

The director can exercise the greatest living influence in the theatre, particularly in a situation where theatre is growing. He is the leader, the decider, the suggester-extraordinary, the perpetual guide, often having both the first and last word during the weeks of preparation and rehearsal.

Directors, like actors, become legends and leave a lasting influence through new approaches and different trends. Among the first was the Duke of Saxe-Meiningen who in the 1880's amazed the public with his fantastic discipline and his meticulous use of crowds. He was followed in the next decade by William Poël who, reflecting the first contemporary desire for simplicity, presented Shakespeare on a bare stage with the minimum of set after three hundred years of comparative rant and rave; and by Stanislavsky, who, by the turn of the century, was creating another form of artistic revolt, substituting realism and inner meaning for blatant artificiality. Every generation has its crop of innovators, revolutionaries, and international giants, such as Reinhardt and Guthrie. But while they lend much, they can only interpret or embellish the material they present. Not even the greats can make a silk purse out of a poor play; ultimately the playwright exercises the lasting influence in theatre.

The function of the director of a play is often compared to that of the conductor of an orchestra, for they both lift symbols from a printed page and, via a company of players, blend them into the harmony of performance. But the function differs in complexity. The conductor is concerned only with music: with content, form, the blend and tone of instruments, with rhythm and phrasing marked by the composer, leaving some allowance for tempo, pace, and touch. After comparatively few rehearsals the players (who need some proficiency to have attained orchestral level) read the score as the conductor, in person, leads the performance. Whereas the director of a play is concerned with all the arts: with choreography of movement and sculpture of grouping, with painting in the color, line, and form of the set, and even with the music of language (which, as spoken by the actors, should not be noticeable, but should be present to complement the sense of the words). He then rehearses the sometimes inexperienced players for many weeks until they have memorized the "notes" of their score so that they are used as the natural and inevitable expression of their "instrument" or role. Next he co-ordinates the total effect with appropriate sound, light, and music cues; and he finally exits – gracefully – from the stage, leaving the actors to conduct and re-create each performance from their memory of the arrangement he has provided.

There are few rules about directing a play, for it is largely a personal affair that each director sets about in his own way. By virtue of the theme, characters, and situations inherent within it, and his own reaction to the author's treatment, every director will have a somewhat different approach to every play – and even to a different cast in a familiar play. While maintaining that all-important thread of meaning and story, he is continually adapting to needs and conditions, as, in turn, a good actor adapts to every director and every author. The approaches are legion, but the sequence which he now sets in motion is similar, and for practical purposes we will discuss it with reference to a play that is already a young classic, and with which many of you will be familiar: *Our Town*, by Thornton Wilder.

Let us clarify one point about our discussion. However clear the author's intent, each interpretation and set of conditions of perform-ance will always result in a slightly different production of his play. So this chapter does not set out to show how *Our Town* should be directed, since all readers will gradually come to their own con-clusions about that. Were this the purpose, it would be better shown as a highly detailed acting edition of one version. There is no magic way or formula, any more than there is one way of conduct-ing Beethoven's Fifth Symphony. But there is your way, and to help you express it we will try to discover *what* a director does, *why* he does it, and *when*, so that you may relate this to the many levels of production of different types of plays.

Preparation

Time and care spent on preparation will enable a director to come to rehearsals knowing what he wants of a play and what he hopes of the performances. Fifty per cent of his work should be complete prior to the first reading after the play has been cast. A proportion of this time will be spent in discussion with the producer and in experiment with the designer. Then the director will already know *what* is to be done, *when*, *why*, and *by whom* within the total production unit before beginning detailed work with the cast. It is often thought that all a director does is to tell the actors what to do and where to go (and that this is not always very complimentary). He needs, however, a grasp of the total creative and artistic side of a production, just as the producer must understand the business side. Therefore the director is also a planner who is able to administer his plans into action. Grand ideas, great concepts, and a marvellous sense of the author's intent are not enough without the ability to transmit them to others in practical terms, and so carry them into effect. There are bound to be bumps, potholes, and crises along the way; but careful preparation will at least ensure that everyone travels the same road. As the dramatist Oscar Wilde commented, "There may be division of labor, but there must be no division of mind."

An important part of the preparation before you lies not only in a thorough knowledge of the play itself, but in the advance collection of certain facts which, from both the artistic and practical standpoints, will have considerable bearing on the weeks ahead, and on the final results of the production.

We will discuss the artistic preparation first, since the play ignites the spark and kindles the fire which awakens the creative ideas and sets tumbling the imagination of everyone involved: director, designer, actor – and eventually of the audience. Rarely do you hear people say, "Let's act" or "Let's direct"; but the phrase you often hear is, "Let's do a play."

THE PLAY

You will find that the process of becoming familiar with a script falls into three main divisions: basic knowledge, from theme to background, linked with conditions of performance; the composition of scenes – or changes of action – within the acts, which it would be helpful to consider while the design is still under discussion; and the blocking of moves for each actor. The sequence of this preparation will vary, but you may find it best to allow a few days between working on each division, since the intervals will give you a sense of perspective. Your decisions are soon to affect the work and time of others; it is important to discover what you sense about the play, for, while details change, the main approach then remains constant.

Read the play. Read it many times. Let it soak and seep through you. Then do everything that is advised in the admonition, "Read, mark, learn, and inwardly digest." Come to know the play as a craftsman knows his material: a sculptor his stone, a carpenter his wood, or a conductor his score. You may not understand all of it at once (especially if you are attempting one of the classics), any more than you can comprehend a great book or symphony at first acquaintance. There is unlikely to be one flashing moment of inspiration to guide your total concept of the production; the better answer may appear gradually, and it is as well not to rush the process.

Theme Discover what you consider to be the theme or main core of the play and how this is presented, and whether, for example, it is comedy or tragedy. Opinions can vary and change, but it is your own that counts. Sometimes the greater the play, the more varied the conclusions to be drawn from it. Until the nineteenth century *The Merchant of Venice*, for example, was approached in a very different way from that accepted now. Shylock was portrayed as a comic butt, until Edmund Kean turned him into a fiendish butcher. This interpretation has again been tempered to a different meaning, sometimes to reveal a misunderstood, tragic figure, aware of racial difference, who loves his daughter only slightly less than his ducats.

Beware of pigeon-holing the great plays and, equally, of looking for deep, inner meanings in what could become all atmosphere and pretension (*Dark Of The Moon*) or symbolic treatment of a well-constructed Who-Dun-It (*The Gazebo*). Often "Boy gets Girl" is at the heart of the matter, sometimes woven into the "Ugly Duckling" theme, which is the basis of Cinderella, linked perhaps with the legend of a famous sculptor and his statue, Galatea, and so down through the ages to Shaw's *Pygmalion* and to Lerner and Loewe's *My Fair Lady*.

The theme of *Our Town* could be said to lie in the author's awareness of the wonder of life balanced in the value of the everyday event, to be crystallized in Emily's words, "Do any human beings ever realize life while they live it? – every, every minute?" This awareness may not be the same as your own; if the author's treatment is one with which you do not agree or cannot accept, it is probably as well for you not to do this particular play. Theatre, remember, is "organized make-believe," and there should be belief in the material if there is to be faith in the play.

Plot If the theme of a play is likened to a clothes-line, then we can see how the plot, or thread of story, is pegged to it and illustrates the dominant idea. Thornton Wilder has clothed his theme with the story of two families living in a small New England community between the years 1901 and 1913, showing them as somewhere typical of us all "in our growing up and in our marrying, and in our living and in our dying." By setting the action in the past, he has used a perspective of human beings against a background of the cycle of Time, ranging from the 1890's to Ancient Egypt to the 1930's. Consider the contents of a cornerstone for the new bank: after the *New York Times* and the local *Sentinel* comes a Bible, a copy of the Constitution, Shakespeare's plays – and so to Babylon which "... once had two million people in it, and all we know about 'm is the names of the kings and some copies of wheat contracts and ... contracts for the sale of slaves. Yet every night all those families sat down to supper, and the father came home from his work, and the smoke went up the chimney, – same as here. And even in Greece and Rome, all we know about the *real* life of the people is what we can piece together out of the joking poems and the comedies they wrote for the theatre back then." We also move ahead of the action with mention that "Doc Gibbs died in 1930" (a reminder that he was almost contemporary with the original audience, since the play was first performed in 1938), and we see Joe Crowell, the paper-boy we meet in Act 1, who is pointed out as "Going to be a great engineer Joe was, but the war broke out and he died in France." The plot, then, concerns the story of the Gibbs and the Webb families (highlighting the characters of Emily and George), set in a New England foreground against a background of Time.

The sub-plot, or subsidiary story, would be the next consideration in many plays. A sub-plot can be muddling, but it can also complement and give focus to the main plot by providing a contrast to it; an example is to be found in Malvolio's hopes for Olivia's hand in *Twelfth Night*. In *Our Town* the sub-plot consists more in the introduction of a gallery of characters than in the intrusion of a subsidiary story. These characters are gradually seen to evolve round the central lives of Emily and George, so making the fabric of the community. We have the Baseball Players, George's contemporaries, providing an age-old commentary on weddings, and the Stage Manager remarks, "There used to be an awful lot of that kind of thing ... in the old days, – Rome" (the past again), and then, "We're more civilized now, – so they say."

Climax Find the climax of the play. This is the point towards which the action leads, inevitably in tragedy, sometimes obscurely

but none-the-less inevitably in comedy. As we have already discussed in Chapter 1, it marks the moment at which the conflict
reaches a peak, and may be recognized by the protagonist and
reflected by a change in attitude. In *Our Town* we do not have an
ordinary illustration of conflict – as between husband and wife in
the near-melodrama *Angel Street*, or between man and social environment in *Death of a Salesman*. Nor do we have the literal resolve
and recognition we find with the twins, Viola and Sebastian, in
Twelfth Night. But we do have a change between Emily's line,
"Oh, earth, you're too wonderful for anybody to realize you!"
and her question to the Stage Manager, "Do human beings ever
realize life while they live it? – every, every minute?" There, at
some moment, comes a development or change of attitude which
prompts that second line; and it is then we catch her first acceptance of death. Returning to the graves on the hill, she shows
Mrs. Gibbs that she realizes how blind humans are, and from her
and Stimson and the other Dead we have what is in essence a
musical coda, as we digest and learn of their more mature attitude
until the final resolve, "They don't – understand – do they?" "No,
dear. They don't understand." In a sense the Stage Manager
brings down the non-existent curtain of the play, finishing on a
note of the continuity of life with the mundane phrases: "Tomorrow's going to be another day. You get a good rest too. Good-
night."

Thus Emily's question to the Stage Manager is to provide the
focus of the production, and it is a help if this moment is in your
mind when you discuss the set, lighting, and costume with the
designer. Later you will be thinking of it in another section of
your preparatory work, when you come to blocking the actors'
moves; for the grouping of the chief characters and proportionate
setting of the minor ones make for visual clarity. Clarity of intent
is an essential part of communication.

Spectacle Now is a good time to consider an integral part of the
presentation of the play: the visual aspect, or spectacle, on which
you and the designer will collaborate literally to help "show" the
author's intention to the audience. In a play requiring a formal set
you will probably be taking careful note of the best position for
entrances, fireplaces, windows, different levels, and stairways, so
that you will meet the designer with a general approach in mind
and with ideas in the making to help transmit the dialogue into
spectacle, or show. (*Show* is a word we also use in connection with

movies and television and the whole entertainment business of which theatre is a part.) While the visual aspect of theatre is part of the "show," it should never be mistaken for the whole of the show. The matter lies in the language.

Language The choice and arrangement of words and phrases used to express the thoughts and feelings of the characters, upon which the theme and plot depend, are the key to the play. Even in moments of silence, which can become the most telling part of a production, the hint still lies within the words. They provide the first flavor, are the medium of the writer's intent, and should be respected by you and by the cast. Notice the form of the language and whether it is in verse or prose, which, if good, will in either case have its own underlying rhythm – look at the precision and balance of Shaw, or the trotting elegance of Wilde. If necessary, consider the fashion current at the time of writing; when the poet T. S. Eliot, for example, was trying to inaugurate a revival of verse-plays in the 'twenties and 'thirties the form was unfashionable, and he so disguised his free verse that it almost passes as prose.

Thornton Wilder uses a prose that is simple and colloquial; the style is never high-flown, and the most color is given to the Greek-and-Chinese-Chorus-philosopher-representative-of-the-audience-common-man-and-god Stage Manager. His function is to move Time back and forth and to introduce the scenes and characters. He mentions birth or death with simple everyday phrases and clichés, which perhaps touch us the more nearly for their or'nari-ness, yet weave a spell through the gentle irony of the accepted, almost inarticulate, expressions. In the last act the Stage Manager describes the Dead as, "waitin' .... Some of the things they're going to say maybe'll hurt your feelings – but that's the way it is .... And at the end of the play he says, "There are a few lights on: Shorty Hawkins, down at the depot, has just watched the Albany train go by ..." and then, "Tomorrow's going to be another day. You get a good rest, too. Good-night."

It is from the style and treatment of the language that the style and treatment of a production should be conceived – the one, which will differ with each director, being the natural outcome of the other. Beware, however, of that directorial feast known as a *stylised production*, which is often a fair example of that old dig about bringing coals to Newcastle. This is forgivable only when the play is not good and needs disguise (so is it worth doing?), or if the director honestly believes that it is only by extra means (*King*

Lear gone Japanese or Eskimo, *Troilus and Cressida* dressed Edwardian, or *The Alchemist* done modern) that it will have meaning for the current audience. Then it is only in safe hands when the director knows exactly what he is doing (you can break the rules when you know them) and can disguise, if momentarily, implied anachronisms and sore points. This awareness must be balanced by an equal grasp of the intended style by the entire cast. One role – lead or extra – out of flavor, and the taste is spoiled.

It is a help if you can become "in tune" with the playwright just as a pianist develops an ear for a composer – for his nationality, his period, and his temperament. For there is an inherent style, or manner of expression, in every good work, whether of poet, painter, sculptor, or architect. If you can become sensitive to this, you have an awareness to share with the cast, with the total production unit, and with the audience. Use of this awareness makes for a clear production.

Characters Become familiar with the characters who are to perform the spectacle and speak the language. Watch their growth, which is presented in the episodes of *Our Town* more as a fact of time than as a process of inner development. Look for their influence on one another – for example, Emily's on George after he is elected Captain – and see how their lives become interwoven. Look at their hopes for the future, such as Mrs. Gibbs' ambition to see Paris, France. Although in this play the characters are clearly defined and require little invention, keep a reasonably open mind as to interpretation, for an actor may come to casting with a different approach which can be incorporated usefully into the production.

Background Study the background of *Our Town* as suggested under "Choice of Play" in Chapter 1. Have a clear picture of those elements you are likely to need most, which in this play would mean costumes, hair styles, and furniture. See if you can trace any small-town newspapers of sixty years ago; listen to the music of the period – from the hymn tunes to the popular songs the characters would know; take a look at those "Whistler's Mother" pictures which would grace the front parlors. Remembrance of this material will help provide atmosphere for the play and, if necessary, an extra source of imagery for the actors. Find photographs of the times; read about those New England communities in their open valleys among the mountains; and imagine those graveyards with the sweeping views and the iron flags of their Civil War Veterans.

Consideration of these facts will help you decide on your interpretation and creative approach to the play. Now you need to know the conditions under which it is to be performed, since they may influence, if not the flavor of the production, at least the scale on which it is to be achieved.

CONDITIONS

Ideally a director will stand by his original concept no matter what the practical considerations, though he must always be prepared to adapt to conditions. These are more often dictated by budget and size of the theatre than by any other facts.

Budget The budget will be discussed in detail in the chapter on the producer, but for the present it indicates the opportunities for the type of production you have in mind. Since it is usually limited, it presents an immediate challenge to director and designer. But providing whatever allowance there is – whether forty dollars or four hundred – is handled with care, any lack need not be detrimental to a production which is built on a good play. When directing and acting are based on imaginative belief and a firm knowledge of theatre, *anything* can be achieved with almost *nothing*. Results are sometimes the more exciting because attention is directed entirely towards performance, the audience supplying the background within its own imagination – so becoming involved and, by giving, participating in the play, the game, the illusion. When the audience is involved in the *here* and *now* of this particular performance, the play becomes a living and memorable experience.

You may not be involved personally in the spending of the budget, for this is likely to be done by the heads of the technical departments; but, after discussion with the producer, you should know that the allowance for each is geared towards the needs of the production. Because in *Our Town* there is a minimum of set, the costumes, though simple, will be especially important. The action could be the more effective as a spectacle if there were enough money to buy or rent a sky-cloth; but to use it well and provide that extra sense of distance might require extra lighting equipment. The hard facts of the budget will soon determine a decision for or against such ideas.

Size of Theatre   If at all possible, go and see the theatre for yourself; if not, enquire about the following: the dimensions of the stage, including wing-space and any cross-over (or way behind the set – or sky – so that the cast may enter and exit from different sides of the stage) and the width and depth of the acting area. Know the seating capacity and arrangement of the audience, for the sight-lines (discussed in Chapter 4) will influence your work with the designer and your blocking of the play. In later rehearsals you will need to help the actor judge the size of his performance in proportion to the theatre. Take a preliminary look at sound and lighting equipment, for these could well tip the balance of the budget. Note whether there is an orchestra pit and any steps up to the stage, which could be useful in *Our Town*.

Audience   The audience has already been mentioned in the section relating to choice of play in Chapter 1. Although performances undergo a subtle change each night, because a play is not only inter-play between characters but also between actors and audience, a production should not need any touching up or playing down, especially to an audience of children. Sometimes it may be necessary to adapt the approach for special occasions – if, for example, there is a request from schools that the running-time last not longer than two hours to fit within a schedule. This would mean cutting the play, and here factors would include such points as time suggested, total suitability to cast or audience, and the necessity to clarify or tighten the action – often required in the sometimes sprawling classics.

Schedule   It is helpful to work back from the production date on two counts: deadlines, as outlined in the Average Production Schedule, probably discussed with the producer; and rehearsal schedule relating to the work of the cast.

Rehearsals, like packing, always take longer than you can have, and within every production that is ever mounted there is somewhere a race against time. There is no set limit for the entire preparation; six to eight weeks' rehearsal is usual for a three-act play, and, depending on experience, a one-act should need three to six weeks – with often not more than two weeks in either case for advance discussions, selection of staff, and casting.

Take the time available for each rehearsal into account when planning the number of rehearsals to hold each week. Something can be accomplished in two hours; more, of course, in three. Two rehearsals a week should be the minimum, with special calls for those in lead roles, or for others in minor scenes that can be rehearsed separately. Remember the duration of the run can have some bearing on the length of final rehearsals. If it is to be of only one or two nights, the cast may be able to continue into the small hours to gain a final spurt. A week's run, however, depending on the play and the experience of those involved, will make demands on any who hold a full-time job by day, and they will need energy not only for the first performance but also for the last.

DISCUSSIONS WITH THE DESIGNER

Now that you have discovered something about the play and the conditions under which it is to be performed, you will have ideas and some fuel to bring to early meetings with the designer. You should work in close collaboration with him so that, while you have suggestions about the main approach to the play and practical requirements of the setting, he provides the flavor and fills in the details, which you in turn use in relation to the acting and pointing of the play. Although occasionally the entire concept will be clear to you both from the moment you pick up the script, once again it is as well not to expect results too soon. Meet well ahead of rehearsals since he, too, will need to digest ideas before turning them into decisions; but ask him to supply a scale model and ground plan by the time of the first reading. Then the cast can see the set and its proportions; you will have material with which to work on the blocking; and he will have so many clear weeks to supervise the construction and organize the painting.

The same process should apply to the costumes. As mentioned in Chapter 1, these often come under a separate department, but results can be best when one designer is responsible for both set and costumes. In the same way decisions are made, color schemes and sketches are made ready, measurements can be taken, and the whole process of ordering, cutting, and fitting is set in motion as the cast goes to rehearsal.

CHOICE OF STAGE MANAGER

This, before casting begins, is a good time to choose the most important person on the production staff: the stage manager (not to be confused with the character of the same name in *Our Town*, whom we will continue to label with capitals). It is possible to mount a play without a designer, a wardrobe mistress, or even a producer, and sometimes a director is faced with all these tasks in addition to his work with the actors; but a good stage manager is essential to the actual running of a production. You may have an experienced person in mind or, if new to a group, you may find there is an almost resident stage manager who will know the local ropes. However, it may be a case of finding a volunteer at the end of one of the casting sessions. When you meet him, explain what you hope for the production as far as your ideas go at the moment and, if he is new to the work, what you wish him to do. Show how he can help by preparing the prompt copy in advance, and help him to adapt the sequences of his work to this particular play, as suggested in Chapter 3.

Casting

Good casting is an essential part of a good production. It means selection of those who will eventually bring most to the roles and to the play. The process of selection is bound to depend on comparison and contrast, on relationships and total impression, and, as a result, it is not always a matter of immediate use of apparent talent.

APPROACH

There are two main approaches, known as *type-casting* and *casting against type*, and most directors employ a smattering of each. Their use often depends as much on the director's courage to give someone a role that might not obviously be theirs as it does on choice of play.

Type-casting is the more usual approach in the well-made play of the past eighty years, with more-or-less set characters requiring little variety of interpretation and asking for certain types of performance. Such characters are often based on appearance and physical attributes, so that naturally the director looks for Middle-aged Parents, Beautiful Daughter, and Good-looking Son; he may think himself lucky if those who *look right* actually *sound right*, so that he can fit people into roles as coins into a slot machine.

In the long run *type-casting* can be a trap since, while it apparently saves time, it also hinders the development of an actor who needs to explore and meet the challenge of a wide variety of roles. If he is always cast near his own age and personality, how is he to stretch his imagination and technique and grow? In time his work will become dull – a repetition of past performances, providing directors and audience with variations on the round and sound of his own personality. (A similar fate could also befall the director who only worked on one type of play.)

Casting against type is the less obvious and more interesting approach, needing perhaps encouragement and faith in an actor who has yet to prove himself versatile. Often it is first explored in classical plays because the roles and their language are much wider in scope and far less confined in expression.

So be hopeful of surprises and beware of making snap judgments on appearances. Imagination, personality, and vitality are important; but, as Tyrone Guthrie once put it, "Theatrical talent can often be hidden under the most forbidding bushels."

Final choice in casting may be the result of a blend of the following methods:

1. A certain play is chosen because certain people are available and able to play a certain lead or leads, which means key roles are cast before many even hear about the play. While this method makes for clear decisions, if used too regularly it could cause dissent within a group.

2. A large organization may hold informal auditions once or twice a season, at which all interested in joining are invited to read or perform two or three speeches from different plays, to give some idea of their range and ability. These can provide useful reference for casting sessions and, linked with the first method, could help suggest future choice of plays.

3. Public casting sessions are announced – whether "public" to the public or "public" to the group – at which anyone interested is invited to come and read any number of roles of the newly-chosen play.

4. Private casting sessions are held when certain people may be invited to read certain roles on an individual basis. This may save time in a large organization but, because of vocal and physical contrast, should be backed by a joint reading before final decisions are made.

We will discuss our casting with reference to the third method, since it is that most commonly used. Much of the session will be routine, and part of it probably dull owing to poor reading, which may, however, cover a potentially good performance. Sometimes something interesting happens when, after your present study and preparation, you hear a character take life, realize there is another approach to a scene, find unexpected talent, or see development in an actor you have watched in previous seasons.

BEFORE CASTING

Casting, like all meetings which have in a sense to be "chaired," requires its own preparation.

Try to see that it is well publicized "to whom it may concern." Two sessions are usually best, since not everyone is likely to be free at the same time, and you will want to make sure of finding the most suitable people and of offering equal opportunity.

Ask for someone, preferably the stage manager, or an assistant stage manager if already selected, to have a form ready for any new names, addresses, phone numbers (home and business) and experience. If he can take these notes, and any extra particulars you might need, your attention can be directed towards the play and the selection of the right talent.

Check that there are enough clear copies. The layout of dialogue and close use of brackets and italics in acting editions are often confusing to newcomers; previously used copies may be marked, cut, lined, and dog-eared, and they will make the task more difficult. Should some actors arrive with different editions, ask them to use those provided, for cues, cuts, and page numbers are not always the same, and variations in these matters can waste time.

Have a firm idea of the particular speeches and situations which will give a good test of the characters and of the needs of the play. Relate these to voice and contrast of personality as an aid to balance and conflict. You will have to adapt many of your ideas, but clear thinking will help final decisions.

DURING CASTING

Be punctual. Give a brief synopsis of the play. Announce the dates of performance, dress rehearsals, and possible rehearsal times. Some people may not be available; others might feel they can make changes if needed.

When there are going to be two sessions, it is a good idea to say that casting will be complete by a certain date, and that those required will be notified. A mention that there will also be a need for various assistants could be useful, and, if possible, give the names of the heads of the technical departments so that those interested will know who to contact. This is one way of building a good production unit and of remembering those who may be helpful in the future.

There is much to be done in a short time, so ask for reasonable quiet since all need a fair chance to concentrate and to listen to the lines of other characters. Decisions soon to be made will affect the work of the next few weeks, with final proof resting in performance.

Explain how the session is likely to run – trying to give everyone present a chance, hearing odd speeches, taking a run at a few scenes, and looking at some mimed action to give the less good readers an opportunity and to test everyone's ability for the particular play in hand.

Events now vary with each director, depending on the number of people present, the play, and the variety of roles to be cast. The usual sequence is to hear everyone in the room read once. Sometimes you will know from the first sentence whether there is a "natural" for a role – for the Stage Manager or Emily, or Doc Gibbs — and this is especially encouraging when found early among the leads, for you then have people round whom you can build the whole production. More often it seems you have three suitable Mr. Webbs and no Georges, until you are doing mental permutations deciding on one as Mr. Webb, fitting another into Joe Stoddard, the undertaker, and selecting the third as Emily's cousin, Sam Graig.

Look for acting ability – an obvious point, but one ounce of this outweighs many previous hopes which may have been visually ideal, and can change the balance of the casting. Watch as well as listen to the readings; some people "give" at once and will help others and so influence the whole production. Others, unwittingly, may give solo performances, and occasionally you will hear an expressionless voice with a face that is working earnestly – usually a sign of tension and trying too hard, through lack of control and awareness.

Some people will give a clear and instinctive interpretation of a role they have only just met; others will mumble and stumble because they find reading at sight difficult and, with little grasp of character, have little to project. Even where there is not too much talent apparent on the surface, look for people who are reasonably mature in outlook, who have a real wish to accomplish something and are unmannered in themselves. With encouragement, and by the assumption that they can tackle a role, both you and they may be surprised at results in a few weeks' time.

Note who is adaptable by chopping and changing the roles occasionally. Ask for a different approach if you think this would bring a potential Mrs. Webb in line with your concept of the author's intention. The attitude towards direction is almost as important as the ability to act, for theatre is a co-operative affair and it would be difficult to achieve a balanced standard if any of the cast were wooden in this respect.

Suggest a sequence of imaginary, or mimed, action – opening windows, chopping wood, pulling blinds, cooking, feeding chickens, and pushing the lawn-mower; to avoid self-consciousness or much copying of others, have everyone do it at once. It won't take long for you to see those who can do this naturally and well and those who might do so with time.

When you know a second casting is ahead, try to sound non-committal even though you are pleased with general results. Enthusiasm helps any production, but it is a pity to raise individual hopes before an announcement is made. Before the end of the session, invite everyone present to do a quick reading of any particular role they would like to try. Occasionally this produces some surprises, and it does mean that all have a fair chance.

If, after a second casting, you are fortunate enough still to have a choice in some roles, it is wise to call an extra, or final, session, asking all those on a short list to attend.

AFTER CASTING

When you are new to a group, the producer or stage manager may help with advice on casting, as they know something of everyone's previous experience and dependability. All judgment in the arts is only a matter of opinion (and one man's meat . . .), but often agreement of opinion is a deciding factor. Since the production is finally your responsibility, rely on your own assessment of the potential that lies within an individual. Try to think ahead in terms not of what someone can or cannot do now, but of what he could do in six or eight weeks' time. With experience, you may be able to hunt out a performance as a customs officer finds contraband – somewhere, by instinct.

Try to be impartial if anyone contacts you about a certain role he wants to play. There should be no pressure from either in or outside the group.

Remember to take note of possible alternative casting and the need for understudies. People sometimes have to drop out of productions, and a quick scribble now may be a useful reference when casting for the future. You are unlikely ever to have time for special understudy rehearsals, and they would not start until after Opening Night in the case of a long run. Often, in an emergency, someone who has been constantly at rehearsals (such as an assistant stage manager or the prompter) and who knows the course of the production, steps in – and in such a crisis theatre provides a marvellous example of what *can* be done.

When casting is complete, try to see that everyone is notified at the same time by the same method. Sometimes the final decisions are made and announced at the end of one of the sessions, but with large organizations it may be done by phone or by a note in the mail. People like to hear such news firsthand, and direct contact saves rumor. Whatever the method, it is a good idea to add a reminder as to date, time, and place of the first rehearsal or reading, and to indicate future rehearsal times.

Production Meetings

When there is a producer in a theatre group, he should call and chair production meetings (see Average Production Schedule), so we will consider them in more detail in Chapter 5. They deal with routine matters which need constant checking, and it is best to discuss these at special times rather than interrupt rehearsals, as this would affect the work of the actors. Production meetings are important for the smooth running of performance and so for final rehearsals – Technical and Dress – and for the total co-ordination and assembly of set, costumes, furniture and props, music, sound effects, and lighting. They will cover advertising, ticket sales, and the program, and should be attended by the heads of all departments as required.

At the first and probably general production meeting, with everyone concerned present, it would be helpful for you to give a brief synopsis of your approach to the play, and for the designer to show preliminary sketches for the set and costumes. Circulate a cast list, with phone numbers, as this will soon be needed by the wardrobe department, who are likely to ask for measurements at the first reading, and by the publicity department. The latter will want the correct spelling of actors' names for first press releases, and will soon be wanting information on the previous experience and background of some of the cast.

As these facts are made known, they help create a sense of participation among the technical departments, and also ensure selection of staff well in advance. Someone appointed to the box office now, for example, will do a better job for knowing the play and appreciating the plans for it than if he were appointed ten days before opening night.

The question of budget and various allowances will arise, and here your preparation is important, for you should begin to know what you want with regard to lighting and costumes before these factors are discussed.

Present your schedule as it affects the routine of the department heads, bearing in mind that they will not be able to handle everything at the first meeting:

1. Deadline for any costume parade that you might require prior to the time of the dress rehearsal.

2. Any special equipment needed – for example, an extra dimmer board to be bought, rented, or borrowed by the electrician in time for the technical rehearsal.

3. Music which might be required for the final week of ordinary rehearsals, such as more voices singing the hymns in Acts One and Three, which will be taped because of a small stage which allows room for only a small crowd.

Check that all technical staff know the dates and place of final rehearsals and performance. Later meetings are bound to include questions on complimentary tickets, publicity interviews, costume fittings, and cast parking at the theatre. Always think ahead and, as far as possible, encourage others to do the same. Every production presents snags, but emergencies can be met if the schedule is reasonably under control.

Preparation of Scenes

Now is a good time to return to further preparation of the play and to look at the content and division of acts into scenes, and of scenes into phrases, which we may define as sections of the action (inner or outer) making a sense of their own in relation to the whole. Just as each act will have a shape – the sequence of daily life from early morning to night in Act One – so within this pattern are various scenes, each having its own sub-sections or phrases. Your clear understanding of these divisions and your working communication of them to the cast are part of the shaping of the play for the audience.

Thornton Wilder, as the Stage Manager in *Our Town*

In all good plays, most experienced directors would probably agree
as to the main division of these scenes, or changes and developments
in the course of the action – not merely the divisions as marked by
a blackout or lowering of the curtain (at the end of Act 1, Scene 2,
for example), for they are indicated by the writer. In music such
development would be indicated by phrase marks; but in a play,
if in any doubt, look more carefully into the script. This is an
instance of collaboration with the playwright, and the signposts
are there to be used.

MAIN DIVISIONS

With Act One as our reference, let us look into these divisions as
provided by Thornton Wilder. If we call the Stage Manager's
long opening speech Scene Nought, we will find there is a sub-
division which is part of this introductory section, starting as the
visual action commences and he says, "There's Doc Gibbs comin'
down Main Street . . . ," which surely begins the second, or (b)
phrase of this scene. You could if you wished, divide it again into
(c), (d), and (e) phrases with the mention and appearance of
Mrs. Gibbs, Mrs. Webb, and Joe Crowell. (The question as to
how much to analyse the script in great detail when you come to
rehearsal depends on the time and the cast available.) Be aware
of these differences – each point so far, for example, indicates a
slight variation of attack in the Stage Manager's voice – but
remember that you will need to find the balance between over-
burdening an inexperienced actor with finesse of detail, which he
cannot assimilate and will not have time to reassemble within the
total study of his performance, and allowing him to ride roughshod
through the nuances of light and shade, main theme and subsidiary
action which are provided by the author – and which the audience
is paying to see.

The next main division comes when the characters begin to
speak for themselves after Joe Crowell's introduction and with his
"Mornin', Doc.," which brings us to Scene One. Here we have a
sequence, backed by Mrs. Webb and Mrs. Gibbs preparing breakfast in the background and leading to the introduction of Howie
the Milkman, with the purpose of setting the atmosphere of
Grover's Corners, from the weather to the arrival of twins, to the
engagement of the teacher, to the fate of Joe Crowell in World
War I.

Then with Mrs. Gibbs' line, "Good morning, Howie!" we could

consider that the second scene starts, for the following sequence begins with the dialogue of the two women who have not yet spoken. But we already know *who* and *where* they are, *what* they are doing, and *why* they are doing it; you will find Thornton Wilder has the great faculty of any good playwright for setting the circumstances and following them with a scene which is logical and, to some extent, expected. Of course they are going to call the children to breakfast, for that is what they have been busy preparing. We are first introduced to the Gibbs' household, and then the next, or (b), phrase begins when Mrs. Webb speaks for the first time with her "Emily! Time to get up! Wally! Seven o'clock!" – and the scene alternates between the (a) phrases of the Gibbs' and the (b) of the Webb's, apparently oblivious of each other yet so orchestrated that they take turns carrying the "tune" of the play. The purpose of Scene Two is to get the children off to school.

There is a change of tempo, the noise ceases, and one kind of bustle is superseded by another as Mrs. Gibbs sees Rebecca off, collects corn, makes suitable clucking sounds (so that the audience is all prepared for the chickens) and comes outside to a different location to begin Scene Three with her "Here, chick-chick-chick . . . ." In the morning calm she is joined by Mrs. Webb, apparently come out to string beans, and the atmosphere is laid for a pleasant gossip. This, Scene Three, soon prepares us for the choir practice later in the act (because of that tickling feeling, Mrs. Webb had told her husband she "didn't know as I'd go to choir rehearsal to-night") and fills in a considerable amount of background about their own wishes and hopes and the interests of their husbands – men who are cornerstones of places like Grover's Corners. The chit-chat, then, is the main purpose, filled in with that secondary occupation of stringing beans.

The end of this scene provides a good example of an exit which should be rounded by proper acknowledgment of the characters. It finishes as the Stage Manager says, "Thank you very much, ladies" and then remarks to the audience, "Now we'll skip a few hours." By saying "Thank you" to the ladies he has acknowledged them, but since they take the hint and make their exit – with beans – his presence should be acknowledged in return so that the women leave the stage in character. Having accepted this intrusion, although perhaps thinking it a little strange, they then nod to each other before going about their later morning chores. The Stage Manager watches that their exit is complete before beginning the next scene, Four. If, however, he merely cut into their dialogue and they scuttled off-stage with no apparent thought to him or to each other, the effect would be jerky and untidy. Watch for this clear indication in a script of an ending of one part of the action and the beginning of the next (allowing the noise of the children to fade off to school, and then having Mrs. Webb start on the chickens). An audience likes to be presented with one thing at a time, in sequence; your appreciation of'this, and the collaboration of the cast towards ensuring a neat dovetailing of events, is an essential part of your work; and if done well, it carries no sign of your hand. Accomplished too slowly, and the action drags; too quickly, and it is hard to follow. Encourage the cast to sense these greater or lesser transitions by what you and they feel the author intended; this is collaboration not just in theory, but in practice.

With Scene Four we have a complete contrast on the lines of an Institute or Club Lecture, providing us first with all manner of geological, historical, and not quite meteorological facts, supplemented in phrase (b) by Mr. Webb and his information on local government and religion, inset by enquiries about attitudes to drinking, social justice, and culture.

Mr. Webb is tactfully dismissed, and leaves. Scene Five starts as the Stage Manager says, "Now we'll go back to the town," tells us about the afternoon calm, condensing the impression into mention of horses dozin', the buzzin' from the school buildings, Doc Gibbs tappin' people – and Mr. Webb comes out again, cutting his own lawn, watching his daughter as she returns from school, and then making a logical exit with his mower. The (b) phrase begins with George's entrance and provides an early recognition of the two young people for each other, and of George's hope from life: to own and work a farm. Then comes the (c) phrase – still part of the afternoon action – of Emily in conversation with her mother (beans again), which establishes the betwixt-between attitudes of the teenager and her growing awareness of herself.

Scene Five is followed by an interlude with the Stage Manager, giving more information on new developments in Grover's Corners set against the background of history. This allows time for the slow oncoming of night while the light, if possible, fades; and when the choir starts singing "Blessed Be The Tie That Binds," we are ready for Scene Six, starting with the line "Now we'll get back to Grover's Corners. It's evening." It seems logical for Emily and George to mount the ladders and do their homework, since we've had his mention in the previous scene of, "Gee, it's funny, Emily."

From my window up there I can just see your head nights when you're doing your homework over in your room."

Since the Emily-George phrases (and their ladder location) are the most important in this long scene, for from their courtship stems the theme and plot of the play, let us label them with an (a). Then you will find a series of subsidiary phrases weaving in and out of this main action of Scene Six through to the end of the act. So we have a (b) phrase immediately after the Stage Manager makes his exit following "The day is runnin' down like a tired clock." (His reappearance for the final lines of the act should be equally unobtrusive, when his purpose is merely to announce the interval.) We soon know what Simon Stimson thinks of the standard of the choir and of the Methodists; and then attention fades from them back to phrase (a) with George and Emily working away at their homework in the moonlight. This is followed by another touch of (b) with Stimson's "That's better; but it ain't no miracle," when we have a lead-in to phrase (c) as George's father (who has entered for a quiet bit of reading while his wife is away at that choir practice) calls George downstairs. There is a further inset of (b) as Stimson gives what amounts to a sound effects direction for the coming phrase. Meanwhile the author has again pre-set the coming action, for back in Scene Two, while preparing breakfast, Mrs. Gibbs mentions, "I declare, you've got to speak to George. Seems like somethin's come over him lately. He's no help to me at all. I can't even get him to cut me some wood." Phrase (c), then, is a father-son conversation showing some development in George's character, and a resolved change over the matter of the wood. On his exit Doc Gibbs remains reading, though the actor's sense of projection should fade until he again carries the action with the return of Mrs. Gibbs.

Phrase (b) is picked up again with the end of the choir practice, showing us more about the Town Drunk and the Town Gossip – and the public attitude of Mrs. Webb and Mrs. Gibbs to these two problems. This is followed by phrase (d) between Doc and Mrs. Gibbs, which establishes their private attitude towards Simon Stimson, with a transition in mood about a possible holiday, based on that so-called "legacy" she mentions to Mrs. Webb in Scene Three, and the fact that the wood problem is now under control. As the couple go up to bed there is a change back to phrase (a), this time between Rebecca and George on the one ladder. Then comes an (e) phrase between Mr. Webb and Constable Warren and Simon Stimson, which shows the latter's condition has deteriorated and, like Doc Gibbs, serves to bring the editor home. There is a final return to the (a) location as Mr Webb says good-night to Emily, still on her ladder, and in the last section between Rebecca and her brother. The picture is retained of George and Emily inevitably bound for Act Two, called by the author, "Love and Marriage."

DETAIL OF SCENES

Each phrase now has a purpose within the act, just as each act has a function within the play. Sometimes an author will plan these sections methodically, in advance: Henrik Ibsen, for example, made copious notes before he began writing his dialogue; but occasionally a play will seem to write itself, and the author is hardly aware of the phrases he has provided. But, whether they are conscious on his part or otherwise, they should be recognized by the director so that he may guide the cast, and eventually the audience, through the larger and smaller turns of the action which are a part of the form of the play.

Such a breakdown is an invaluable aid to coming rehearsals, for it will give purpose to the actors, help them to see the different sides of their characters, and avoid what can develop into the tedium of a director merely holding run-throughs of the play. It is far better to use the limited time available in this way, followed by a "run" so that each sequence may be appropriately joined, than to spend each rehearsal by starting at the beginning and going through to the end and back again until time has run out. An awareness of the phrases also gives a convenient reminder about the rehearsal schedule; if you list those of the cast in each scene, it will often be found that many scenes can be rehearsed by calling only certain members, thus saving the time of others – Emily and George, for example, have scenes together in both Acts One and Two. Then future run-throughs will give everyone a sense of progression through the various aspects of their character.

It will also be found that there is a literal shape (or beginning, middle, and end) to each scene. The purpose of Scene Three in Act One, for example, is, as we have already discussed, to provide further background for the older characters in the play. The beginning sets the location – outside; the middle section is based on the small inner conflict between Mrs. Gibbs and her conscience over accepting $350 for an old highboy, and this section reveals more about the characters of these wives and their husbands.

Though Doc Gibbs has not yet fallen in with the idea of visiting Paris, France, by the end of the scene, there is a sense that, with Mrs. Gibbs continuing to beat about the bush – and dropping hints from time to time – she will continue to hope for her ambition. Similarly Scene Six (c) begins when Doc Gibbs calls his son downstairs (at a time when Mrs. Gibbs is out at choir practice) and establishes George's present age, his ambition to become a farmer, and the fact that he has been letting his mother chop all the firewood. Doc Gibbs places a conflict in his son's mind by describing her working day; so conscience is at it again and from George's reaction we know the situation will change. By the end of the scene there is the good news that both George and Rebecca are to have a raise in their spending money; it is then rounded by the gentle embarrassment of both at George's need of a handkerchief, and this is relieved by Doc Gibbs' humor about his wife's singing voice.

When actors know what they are jointly trying to share with an audience and what is required of a scene, they have a good chance of playing well together. If, however, they were to play only according to their own concept of character – rather than to the joint concept of a scene – they could pull the play apart, giving solo performances which might have a virtuoso quality, but which would not necessarily be helpful to the total design of the play. But if they are loyal to the author they are likely to give better performances because they will be trying to work with, rather than against, the grain of the author's intention.

Such preparation will help give variety to the production. Certain scenes will be found to be more important than others and this will be of value when it comes to considering the blocking of the play. If each scene were to be performed within the same, as it were, key, there would be little subtlety of light and shade in performance; and, however sincere the approach, the audience would be likely to become bored and restless. As discussed in Chapter 1, every event has in some sense to be edited before it can be re-created so as to become a living experience for others. So variety is necessary, not for its own sake but as part of the clear communication of the play. While it can be invoked by various means, it should never be consciously utilized and merely placed upon scenes without rhyme or reason – as signified by the trap of such directions in acting editions as a "slowly," "quickly," or "quietly." The means used will include these key words, but it is best to think of them as progressive, so that the action builds towards, or away from, these suggestions. And, equally important, they should be used in comparison to what has gone before and to what is to come after. There can be no variety without the balance of comparison; comparison provides contrast (as, for example, light and shade to the painter), and contrast is an essential part of communication.

Similar means are used when progressing to a climax. Here, before considering that moment of reversal (and sometimes of recognition), look to see where it starts. You will find it usually coincides with the beginning of a scene, or at least a subsection of it, and as a reminder it is helpful to arrow the sequence – stemming from first growth till you reach the tip at a certain line, or a moment in the action. As the intensity of the conflict develops, the action will grow quicker, and with the build in pace there will be a similar rise in the pitch of voices (which can be controlled by ensuring that they do not start from too high a level) – just as in music the tempo increases and the melody rises before descending to the anti-climax (another contrast) which often rounds the sequence.

Thus a climax needs an awareness from the start; in the sub-section between George and his mother before the wedding in Act Two of *Our Town*, we have a build from his entrance through seven lines of dialogue until Mrs. Gibbs quiets him with "Why, I'm ashamed of you." Yet within this rise the entire sequence will need to be taken comparatively quietly (notice that she remarks, "If anyone should hear you") since the wedding group is already in position. There is an interesting contrast as she admits, "George, you gave me such a turn" and he then reassures his mother. They virtually pass the next section on to Emily and Mr. Webb; George is called to join them, and out of these episodes the wedding begins.

If you follow this breakdown of scenes through each act, you may find it will help you lay clear the structure, the characters, and the events of a play. Such an approach will guide your direction of each act and scene in relation to the whole, and will help you to a vision of the total result of the production. You will then be ready to finalize decisions with the designer, and to meet the cast at first rehearsals.

Rehearsals

READINGS

Some directors like to regard part of the casting sessions almost as readings of the play, and may start blocking (giving the actors their moves to memorize) at the first rehearsal. If there is time, however, best results will be gained through at least two readings of the play with all the cast present. They provide opportunity for character and situation to develop within the actors' imaginations without distraction or apparent pressure. This means that, when the blocking does begin, everyone, having listened with complete attention to all other characters, will sense the total impression and will have found part of the rhythm and inner change of tempo of the dialogue.

Before the Readings Show that punctuality is expected. Point out that theatre is a joint responsibility and that, whether concerned with the preparation of set, characters, or costumes, everyone is interdependent. This means attendance at all times as requested, though you may be able to divide later rehearsals and list *who* is expected *when*. Some delays will be inevitable, as the cast are held up at work and by late baby-sitters, so ask that anyone who is delayed calls through a message either to you or to the stage manager, and then you can at least change the order of rehearsal.

Ask the stage manager to be responsible for any discipline among the cast, since he will be responsible for it at performance. Without being too rigid, a notice on the call-board will give everyone a reminder of what is expected – and most will co-operate – so that consideration becomes a habit. Being alert for cues for entrances and noises off should also be ingrained within the actor; though at first he may be nudged by a friendly stage manager, he will soon learn that all parts of his performance are his own responsibility.

Should it become clear that some do not understand these points and you have to step in over the stage manager's authority, be firm and be soon. Prevention is always better than cure. It may be necessary to show that you neither expect nor take personal umbrage, for people work the better for knowing what is happening and for observing that the few rules are to be used. So avoid the development of sores and grievances in the background, and if you do have to "say your piece," switch key and, if possible, work everyone hard and with a new enthusiasm.

Remember that, as the stage manager is responsible for discipline within the cast, so you should be aware of any difficulty among the heads of the technical departments. Watch that results are produced by the time required. A designer who is asked to prepare a model and ground plan of the set with a week to spare – so that you may use them in preparation for the blocking rehearsals – and

Our Town: The Wedding Scene

Virginia Museum Theatre, 1958

appears with them only just before rehearsals are due to begin, may continue this pattern through the production. There is little you can do at the time except point out the problems and, if necessary, use a different designer in subsequent productions.

You will also expect reliability from the stage manager, for he is your chief assistant – and to have an assistant who is not dependable makes life worse than being without an assistant. He in turn will ask the same of his assistant stage managers, just as the actors rely on one another for attendance at rehearsal and for the learning of lines. Through this sense of interdependence a good production unit is built.

During the Readings   At the first rehearsal, or reading, most directors will enlarge on the résumé of the play already given at the casting sessions, and the designer will explain the model of the set so that there is a clear picture of how the stage is to be used. It may be that, with so little formal setting for *Our Town*, you have collaborated to provide different acting areas to clarify the locale of each episode for the audience, and that you have numbered these for use by the actors. Perhaps the theatre has an orchestra pit which is to be included in part of the action, such as the choir practice in Act One and the arrival and departure of the funeral party in Act Three (which would help give the impression of a graveyard on a hill). Steps would be required for the actors to reach the main stage from here, and extra lights and possibly platforms needed to make the area visible to the audience.

Now we come to the point where directors vary considerably in the whole process of rehearsing a play. Some spend time on a detailed examination of each character as they see it, which gives the actor a clear and ready-made intent but makes little allowance for his own invention; others barely mention interpretation. Some stress the visual aspect of the production, and a few may concentrate entirely on the atmosphere. Much depends on the play and the ability and experience of those involved.

While it is important that everyone has a clear sense of what is required of the production as a whole, it is a good rule neither to give, nor to expect, too much of the cast – and others – too soon. Ideally the interpretation of a role comes from the individual actor, for that is his job; yours is to help him, as necessary, express the ideas you sense forming and to guide his work within your concept of the theme and outline of the play. Trust in him and confidence in yourself will help you to encourage what is suitable and to stimulate his imagination via the author's words, so that he seems to do the greater part of building his character for himself. This requires invention and control on your part. It is so much easier to take his place and virtually say, "Do it like this." But he should perform on his own feet, not trying to be a carbon copy of what he thinks you want, but rather with both of you, in partnership, aiming for what you feel the author wants.

Outline each character; show his purpose within the play; as rehearsals progress, see if the actor can supply the details. Some will need little help; others a great deal. Rely on your judgment as to *who* needs *what*, and *when*. Often the most gifted require the least; but say when you are pleased with results. It can become a habit to take good work for granted and, within reason, every actor should know how you feel about the development of his role.

Try to let the reading run without too many interruptions. If you sense an actor having difficulty or veering off-course too soon, find the apt suggestion. A word here or there about the shaping of a scene, the eventual tempo required, and the climax of the play will gradually feed him material to take home and digest. Remember that he cannot take in, and give out, an interpretation simultaneously. He has some exploring to do; and the better the play, the more there is to find.

Keep your eyes and ears well open in case you have made a mistake in casting. If a change is essential, have a substitute in mind, try to be diplomatic, and make the switch as soon as possible. You can allow for this if you state clearly in advance that casting is provisional until the end of the first two or three readings or rehearsals.

If a second reading is possible, wait to give any cuts, changes, or scene divisions and phrases until then. The cast will appreciate the full continuity of the play and will begin to sense the development of their own roles.

After the Readings By the end of the second reading the actors should have a frame within which to conceive the theme and plot of the play, the physical setting, and the function of their characters within the total purpose (Simon Stimson, for example, and his problem provide one form of contrast, and Mrs. Soames and her gossip another). You have encouraged the cast to find the playwright's intention and to work in a sense with him through the basic medium of the theatre: the language of the play. Some core of a new being may have already begun to take shape within an actor, though it is unlikely that he is yet able to describe it in any way, let alone show it. To perceive is one thing; to reproduce in depth and with projection takes longer. But that is what rehearsals are for.

Remember to clarify rehearsal arrangements during these first sessions.

1. Check that everyone is available for regular rehearsals. If some of the cast have developed indispensable activities on Mondays, change the schedule to Tuesday, Wednesday, and Friday, or according to convenience – but make sure it is arranged on a regular basis. When the days and times are agreed upon, ask the stage manager to put this information up on the callboard so that everyone has a double check. Of all time-wasters, misunderstandings about schedule and lack of communication can be the worst.

2. Be sure everyone knows the date, time, and place of the next rehearsal.

3. Give a clear indication as to how long you expect the actors to take to learn their lines. If, for example, rehearsals cover a six-week period and the performance is in the seventh week, ask for Act One to be learnt by the end of the second week, Act Two by the end of the third, and Act Three by the end of the fourth (see Average Production Schedule). If eyebrows are raised, remind everyone that it is not until lines are reliable that any finish can be given the production; that most of this will be done in Week Five since Week Six concerns final run, costume parade, and the technical and dress rehearsals at which all elements – not just the work of the actors – must finally be co-ordinated. Encourage everyone to make a start on lines right from these early readings; ideally they should grow with the character, but four weeks is a reasonable time – and the sooner they're learnt, the better.

BLOCKING REHEARSALS

Now comes the third part of your main preparation of the play, which is to decide on the location of each sequence of action and to plan the blocking, or moves, of each actor within this frame. You will probably have discussed these locations in some detail with the designer, and so you will already have a scheme half in mind, but the mechanics should be clear for the actors. They are to perform the play to the audience and will need these tools with dispatch. An experienced director with a proficient cast might be able to play the process by ear, and suggest moves as the spirit wills without much previous thought; but at a different level this approach would be unlikely to produce results of a consistently high standard. The key to good work again lies in careful preparation, but the details will vary with each director, depending on his knowledge and experience, and his treatment of the play.

Preparation for Blocking Think of the plan you now prepare as a backbone for future rehearsals; it need not remain rigid and will not be perfect, often needing the practical help of the actors in working out certain moments; but it should serve as a clear reference, or point of departure, from which to begin.

Remember that the blocking is important in the successful communication of the play and should make good use of the designer's plan, the color of the costumes, the position of walls, doors, and furniture (imaginary or otherwise) and of different levels and screens, so that all contribute to the total effect of providing a final spectacle for the audience.

If you are new to directing, you may find it difficult to visualize the flow of moves, especially when a large number of people are on stage at once. Deciding on a logical pattern and then noting it in your script so that you can communicate it easily is a fascinating process, but it does take time and practice. The slow, sure method requires that you use cut-outs of scale figures on the model provided by the designer or, if more convenient, make a replica of the ground plan, using anything from chessmen to buttons to represent the size of the actor in relation to the space. If, after some experience, this process becomes unnecessary, discard it; your memory will improve, it will be easier to plan the moves, and you may be able to rely on miniature diagrams with initials, arrows, and hieroglyphics inserted directly into the script. The mechanics do not matter; the point is that you have clear reference when needed.

Imagine that the set is complete, the curtain up, and that the play is being performed to an audience. The obvious approach is then to begin at the beginning and block away until you come to the end. Even here some thinking ahead can be a help.

1. The staging of the climax of the play is the most important element in your scheme, because, as previously discussed, the

action should lead towards it, and it provides the focal point to which all else is related. Usually this staging is created by the designer (in collaboration with the writer) and in *Our Town* this "gift" on the part of Thornton Wilder is the emphasis of the vacant space among the graves Emily leaves, and to which we know she will inevitably return. He has also provided a natural locale for the Dead on the opposite side of the stage to that used for Mrs. Webb's kitchen in Act One, so that the reappearance of Emily's spirit in her familiar place makes the irony more clear and poignant. When she finally moves back to her station among the Dead, it will be visually significant if the cross is a long one, so it would be wise to block her on the far side of the stage in advance. Then she will be ready to take the move after the line, "I'm ready to go back."

2. Consider the end of the play, which usually comes soon after the climax; it will bring the action to some form of conclusion, and in certain plays will leave the audience with a memorable impression. The final lines spoken by the Stage Manager give a great sense of the continuity of life, and you would probably block him in the same place as at the beginning of the play (stories that begin and end the same way can be very satisfying). His near-casual "Tomorrow's going to be another day" could even let the audience feel that, if they remained in their seats a while, they would see the ghosts of further episodes among the descendants of the people who lived in Grover's Corners.

3. Look at the beginning of the play. The atmosphere set by the Stage Manager is important, and he will probably move from his base near the front of the stage to indicate the lay-out of the town. Synchronize the entrance of each character with his introduction, perhaps quickening the tempo from the early morning awakening to the bustle over breakfast, and allowing for a gradual change of gear into the routine of mid-morning (linking the blocking preparation with the preparation of scenes).

4. Relate these points to other acts, for each will have its own atmosphere, shape, and final impression. So we have a build from Act One with Rebecca rounding off the scene between Emily and George at the end of a typical day; the second act (with a change in the weather) picks up the thread with a coming and going of Time through their courtship and marriage, ending on a note of hope and happiness, with barely a sense of the tragedy that is to develop in Act Three. Such dovetailing is essential to the continuity of the play.

5. Remember that the emphasis of action will shift in the eyes of the audience according to locale. Consider the areas of the stage which will be most suited to the main scenes (the Webb and Gibbs kitchens up-stage and opposite each other, the graveyard probably in front of what was the Gibbs area), and then relate them to the minor scenes (the Howie Newsome episodes, and the Joe Stoddard and Sam Craig interlude which introduces the funeral).

Action placed directly centre will carry more point than scenes acted to one side; up-stage centre carries the greatest authority because all eyes (and the eyes of the other actors will direct the eyes of the audience) can be channelled towards the leading figure who, with the others down-stage of him, can address everyone and remain almost full-face to the audience. Traditionally scenes played down-stage and to one side carry a small point well and can be clearly heard, but may lack a proportionate visual impact.

When you know the locale of each scene, you know roughly where an actor comes to, and goes from, with each entrance and exit. Then, as you block the intermediary moves, you can plan them in connection with the shape of the whole play. Allow for the crowd-work within this pattern; if you sketch it in now, you can add the detail at the crowd rehearsal, when most of the other blocking is finalized.

As this form of visual chess takes shape in your mind and in your script, watch that you consider the relationship of the characters. The influence of one upon another may be shown by their proximity and grouping. Remember that, if there are any rules of blocking, the aim is to "show" the action of the characters to help the meaning for the audience. "Masking," for example, should be avoided; let the more important character stand up-stage and to the centre of the less important character, so that no one stands in a direct line between the audience and others on-stage. The same applies to groups, which should be arranged on a curve and "open"; if you are in any doubt, let the tallest stand up-stage of the shortest. These rules are constantly adapted, and you may break the famous one about *not speaking with the back to the audience*. If warranted, this is effective occasionally, and could be used by Emily during a part of her return in Act Three. It sets the imagination of the audience working and, through this involvement, could point up some moments better than showing her full-face. Be sure, however, that she is still audible; rules have reasons, and any adaptation needs an adaptable technique.

During Blocking Rehearsals   There are two main approaches to blocking a play with the cast:

1. A systematic plan for blocking through so many acts or scenes at so many subsequent rehearsals. Usually run to a certain schedule, this is a sure approach when, as almost always, a group is working against time.

2. A continuation of the development of the play and the characters as begun in the readings, the blocking being suggested as each move and change of scene and phrase arises, so that it is given concurrently within a broad progress. Likely to take longer, this does mean that the actor can continue to concentrate on his role without thinking of the moves as separate and then later having to blend them with the natural content of his lines.

Again the approach is not all-important and most directors will use either, according to need. The purpose is to help the actor in the time available so that he can note and later memorize *where* and *when* he sits, stands, and walks – and, if necessary, *why*. A good actor usually knows (unless mystified by a bad director). At the same time, the stage manager should insert the moves, numbered and described for future reference, into the prompt copy.

During the early blocking rehearsals, resist the temptation to feel there is not enough action going on, for the pace will be unavoidably plodding. It will quicken, however, when the moves are learnt, and can then be brought up to the natural tempo of the scene. It is better to use economy, and add ideas at later rehearsals, than burden the actor with fuss at the start.

Try to allow time for a run-through of the moves that have been noted at the end of each blocking rehearsal; then you can watch, the cast can try, and the stage manager can check what has been done. Here is your first opportunity to test your preparation of this section of your work. Will the moves help the play visually? As the cast becomes more certain of them, are they logical and unnoticeable – except when they need to be noticed? Since drama is said to be "character in action," do the moves reflect the characters? Do they make balanced and pictorial use of the stage?

Observe how the cast feels happy about most moves but uncertain in some, and collaborate over any difficulties; the actor often thinks of a good alternative and, since he is the one who does the doing, his experience and instinct may suggest what is suitable – later, if not sooner. You will need to find the dividing line, however, between discussion that is useful and argument that wastes time. The final decision rests with you.

After Blocking Rehearsals   Once the play is blocked, it is helpful to have a complete run-through, possibly running Act One without books, and it is useful to have the technical staff observe this rehearsal. Then, in their own preparation and at production meetings, their work is balanced by some practical knowledge as to the actual shaping and coming effect of the production. Discussion of any music, for example, is more satisfactory if whoever is to tape it knows the sequence to which you refer; the same would apply to those responsible for costumes, lighting equipment, and publicity. Cast and staff, however, should realize that the purpose is to provide everyone with a knowledge of the play, and that this run-through is not in any sense a performance.

OBSERVERS

One question which often arises during the coming weeks concerns people watching rehearsals. This should be discouraged on the part of the general public, for except under special circumstances (above) the cast should not meet an audience – even of two or three outsiders – until ready. Everything that is created must be created in private, and should not be brought to public light until the time of presentation. A writer rarely tells the details of a story he is preparing, nor does a painter describe a half-finished picture; this would be to give away a secret that has not yet quite formed. Members of the organization – probably paying dues – should, however, always feel welcome; they are not the general public, and this is one way of encouraging their continued interest in theatre.

PROGRESSIVE REHEARSALS

You are now on the way to becoming part-author of the production. The main author is, of course, the playwright; but there are others, who include the designer (your chief collaborator) and all the cast. You may want to discuss certain developments with various actors, just as the set and costumes were planned with the designer; but it is useful to remember Oscar Wilde's comment about division of labor but not of mind.

Rehearsals are now likely to become something of a struggle, with the cast trying to remember lines and moves and the director being able to do little about it. Much of the listening and inter-action evident at the readings disappears as everyone works hard enough to remember their own words and moves, let alone react to anyone else; and the blocking will probably look ragged. Suggest that the cast pair off and somehow meet, or at least call each other, between rehearsals so that lines and cues are heard in advance. For most people the first times without the book are rarely accurate, and are a means of finding out what they don't know rather than what they do know.

On a practical level, try to keep to the rehearsal schedule you have planned (see Average Production Schedule), which should divide the time allowed for each section of the play and for the final co-ordination of all departments. Out of the possible six weeks' rehearsal period, you will probably allot: the readings and some blocking to Week One (at the rate of three rehearsals a week); completed blocking of Act One and run of it without books by the end of Week Two; completed blocking and run of Act Two without books by the end of Week Three; and completed blocking and run – with possibly that run-through of the whole play, all without books – by the end of Week Four. Week Five will give some chance to polish; Week Six will allow for special crowd work and its integration with main rehearsals, followed by the technical rehearsal and finally the dress rehearsals. With such a routine in the weeks available, which never ever allows enough time for the finish everyone would like, try to see that the time is as evenly spread as possible. If the final scenes with Emily and her parents, for example, were barely rehearsed because there had been so much concentration on previous acts, the balance of the performance would probably be distorted, and the climax and the point of the play be lost.

Guiding the Actor   Theatre is by people, for people, and about people. It makes no difference whether the author has clothed his ideas and conceived his characters in terms that are animal, allegorical, or just us; the play still concerns people. Every actor represents a human being, and should blend his imagination with the author's to create one in which he, you, and the audience believe. He is the first judge of his creation; you are the second, and should be prepared to guide it – which means that, while giving him an apparently free hand, you also develop a clear sense of what you want him to contribute to the production. See that your actors become people, different people rather than variations of their own selves. These people will naturally be expressed through the actors' own personalities – and in that lies the value of their interpretation; but they should be more than mouth-pieces, figures in make-up and costume who sometimes appear and disappear on the stage, arousing little interest and no care. They are living, breathing, loving, hating, wishful, despairing people; little, or all, of this may show, but somewhere it is there. They are that essential ingredient which brings an audience to every level of theatre, for which not all the lights, the sound, the comfortable seating, and the magnificent décor can ever be substitute. These people evoke in us the human element, the seeing of ourselves as others see us, the sharing of laughter, sorrow, anger, and pride, and occasionally that sense of extra understanding which we may carry for the rest of our lives. Theatre is by people, for people, and about people.

Encourage results when you can and exercise patience when you can't; some actors are slow learners, and their hours of work may take time to show results. If you feel, however, that any are taking too little trouble, call extra line rehearsals for their benefit. Should this not help, give suitable warning, find a substitute, and (if at all possible) after a stated deadline make a change. Then stand by your decision. The feelings of anyone who has had a chance and missed it are not as important as the hurt he can do to others in the cast, to the play, and to the production as a whole. A *warning* and a change in time may be as opportune as a stitch in the same place.

The experienced actor will know how to present his role, but the beginner may need help; though if he is good his ability will include imagination and some natural technique. Observe the times when he may feel awkward for lack of knowing which way to turn or to commence a move. Point out that all physical movement should depend on the motivation and purpose behind it, and is often preceded by the reaction of one of the senses (sight, touch, taste, smell, hearing). In Act One Mrs. Webb feels it's time to change the subject, since she has listened to Emily's anxiety about her looks long enough, so she moves off with her beans, starting probably with the up-stage foot and, if with a turn, inwards – towards the audience and the centre of the stage; this means she remains open to the audience and they can see what is going on. Let everyone apply the same principle to the use of the up-stage (that furthest from the audience) hand or arm. If it would help, demonstrate the difference. But aim to be economical about demonstrating in the sense of giving a line and expecting parrot-like repetition from an actor. You are nearly always working against time and so may often have to use this apparent short cut, but try to reserve it as a last resort when all your other powers of suggestion, simile, metaphor, and cajolery are exhausted. Hook or by crook, to be consistent with the role, the line should come from, and belong to, the actor.

Some may find it hard to build on a sequence, and the light approach needed for the drug-store scene is lost while Emily and George try hard to find their words. Stimulate their imagination by asking them questions: How come their reaction to each other? What do they think of their parents and Miss Corcoran? Who are Louise? Ernestine? Helen? Cicero? Why does George suggest the wagon nearly ran over Emily? What's so special about sodas compared to phosphates? As this gives them something to bite on which, with experience, they should begin to supply for themselves, encourage their own "could we try this?" attitude, or suggest some adaptation of the original blockings so that invention becomes part of the rehearsal. Again judgment will be needed, for change for the sake of change will distort the thread of the play; so try to find a balance within the needs of the cast.

There will be hesitation in some scenes and it is part of your work to be aware of it, and to trace the difficulty. Perhaps the transition never quite resolves in the few lines between the end of the George and Doc Gibbs scene (Act One, Scene Six), and that of the town gossip, Mrs. Soames, discussing Simon Stimson with Mrs. Webb and Mrs. Gibbs. Mere repetition may look like hard work, but, and unless it is based on an understanding of what is required, it may land the actors in a pattern without meaning. The results may be untidy because Mrs. Webb can never remember the exact line, "I'll tell Mr. Webb; I know he'll want to put it in the paper," and she often fluffs, or stumbles, over the words. Perhaps she has not yet found an association in her mind of what the item is and what the gossip is about, and so has no imaginative context for her line. Find the cause and rebuild the scene, watching it flow in contrast to the previous sequence. In the same way you will hear a pianist take a run of difficult notes, practise them in slow motion after a change of fingering or tempo, and replace them within the context of the work.

When working with an experienced cast the director may now appear to do little; he allows the actor's instinct to explore the interpretation of his role. He may need to remind him of points which refer to his purpose and development: Mrs. Webb again might strengthen the beginning of her pre-wedding speech in Act

Two ("I don't know why on earth I should be crying") because she starts a new scene, and unconsciously the audience should be presented with a new rung in the ladder of the story. Discuss, or ask to see, further aspects of a character, so that with each rehearsal everyone takes a step forward in the study of his role. Encourage those in smaller roles, such as Professor Willard with his apparently absent-minded contribution of a few scientific facts, to see their purpose within a scene and their balance in the total play.

As the cast become free of their books and the lines and moves seem to arise logically – but intermittently – out of the dialogue, you will be able to see them reach for a form through which to express these new people. It should be a time of discovery, linked with trial and error, and puzzle and excitement, as they gradually find the underlying flow of thoughts and feelings which are crystallized on the surface by the language of the play.

Guiding the Speech   Now it is your work to see that this language – in the form of the actor's speech – should be heard, felt, and understood by the audience. A small theatre need present few problems in audibility, although slurred, untidy speech will always prevent communication; but there are monstrous auditoriums which set even the most experienced actor a challenge. This must be faced. One method is to ask someone who is a member of the group – but preferably a stranger to the play – to listen to a rehearsal. To you, the cast, the prompter, and the assistant stage manager, the lines and voices are already familiar; but the audience will come with a fresh ear, and an occasional test on a representative can be a guide. A voice calling, "Can't hear you" to an actor is usually an effective remedy.

Ideally the actor can only enlarge in terms of speech and projection what is clear in his mind and in his heart; yet, rehearsals being preparation for performance, you must soon insist that he "speak up." Again, however, to expect too much, too soon, can force decisions of interpretation for which he is not yet ready. The habitual mumbler might need reminders right from the beginning of Week One; the reliables may require a nudge around Weeks Five and Six. More matter for your judgment.

Another method directors instinctively use is to sit on the stage during reading and blocking rehearsals and, if conditions permit, move further and further away until at some time during final rehearsals they are roaming all over the auditorium trying the effect of speech and vision from every angle.

Unfortunately, rehearsal rooms are often too small for the fair development of speech and projection, and allow for little more than the taping of the ground plan of the set on the floor. Remind the cast that it will be essential to adapt not only to the different size of the theatre, but also to the acoustics. The rehearsal room may be bare, without drapes or upholstered furniture, offering only hard surfaces of plaster, wood, and glass which do not absorb but merely reflect the vibrations of the speaking voice. This means it is likely to be over-resonant, enlarging the voice out of proportion to the size of the room and requiring clarity without volume. If the cast realize this, they will be more prepared for the "feel" of the stage, where they may be surrounded by absorbent materials of canvas flats or heavy curtains, faced by an auditorium which seems like a hollow cave stretching into the dark. Only practice – and some prodding – under these difficult conditions can make for good results. It can be an excellent idea to have a vocal warm up – like an orchestra – for ten minutes before rehearsals begin, provided it is realized that good use of the voice and speech on-stage are an enlargement, and adaptation, of good normal speech. The put-on, the pedantic, or the plummy will sound false. Practice of the pear-shaped tones and clear articulation and good use of imagery (plenty of Tennyson, Gilbert and Sullivan, *The Rime of The Ancient Mariner*, and Shakespeare's sonnets) will sound and feel strange, but so does the first work on any technique, which in performance should always be forgotten. Any residue that is any good should gradually become incorporated, and then concentration depends not on the *how*, but on the *what*. If you are in any doubt as to what to practise, sing. It will get everyone breathing, relaxing, opening up, and using some vocal projection.

Guiding the Play　Guiding the actor should be balanced by guiding the play. Keep a watchful eye on the development of character and on the blocking. Actors will need to experiment, but naturally there must be some control within the original framework, for continual change of blocking and timing of moves or delivery of lines would have the same effect as an orchestra playing in different keys. That choir practice at the end of Act One, for example, needs less emphasis than the other phrases in the same scene, but be sure that, once the members have caught the spirit, they keep it. It can happen that the proportion is lost during the weeks of rehearsal, and that the choir over-plays or under-plays the phrase;

so ask them again to be aware of their purpose, the context, who they are, why they are there, and the required contrast. Expect concentration at all times.

Soon there will be considerable improvement at the end of each rehearsal, sometimes followed by a thud at the beginning of the next. It seems as if the scenes that were taking life might never have been rehearsed, and everyone is concerned. Just before the wedding, for example, Emily and her father, or George and his mother, were perhaps so within the action – and for the first time it took such a run that they are unaware how it happened; and now they find it hard to repeat. Since that rehearsal, their concentration has been broken and their attention has naturally strayed elsewhere – to the day-to-day distractions of earning a living or to keeping a home as a going concern; so now it may take a while before they can change gear for the creative approach necessary, and can summon the imaginative background. As they come to know these new people in their surroundings and reaction to each other, they will – with patience and a reminder that there is no chance for a second try at performance – retain the mood of one rehearsal and be able to re-establish it at the next.

Guiding the Production The best-laid plans can go awry, so via production meetings keep a watchful eye on the progress of the various technical departments. Difficulties have a way of appearing simultaneously: the producer has to take an unexpected trip; the publicity girl leaves the copy for the program on a bus and must prepare it again within a twenty-four hour deadline for the printers; the Emily ties her puppy in the paint-shop during rehearsal, and he mistakes the carefully mixed brown paint for gravy; the actor playing the Stage Manager has the flu – and chaos approaches. Whatever happens, keep faith with the production; even under normal circumstances the designer may be worried about the set or costumes, the actors forget their lines, or the play become ragged. Remember that in the saner moments of long ago few of you would have embarked on the enterprise without feeling, as surely as anyone can in advance, that the play was possible to present within the limitations and advantages of the group.

Now let us assume you are approaching Week Five – the final week of normal rehearsals, which should include a start on the crowd-work, prior to the final week of possible run-throughs and technical and dress rehearsals. To many eyes you have been concerned entirely with the cast; but you have meanwhile been giving thought to costumes, publicity, photo calls, suitable music, and all other paraphernalia of your function as director and co-ordinator of the artistic side of the production.

Your first concern, however, has been, and always is, towards the playwright. Be loyal to him. Though he may often be a plagiarist, he is the essentially creative person in the theatre because he starts only with the germ of an idea and the blankest of pages. As part-author of this production, use all honesty. It is your guidepost in the continuing trials, excitement, challenges, and satisfaction of working hard at something you enjoy, and will stand by you in the comprehensive rehearsals to come. For the director's influence can work in many ways; it is a considerable responsibility.

CROWD REHEARSALS

It is unnecessary to have the crowd attend early rehearsals, though it could help to invite them with the technical staff to that first run-through (probably at the end of Week Four). Then it would be a good idea to start their rehearsals during Week Five, preferably at extra times so that you do not lose time with the cast. Some directors would leave this work until the final week, Six, when there will be a great deal to do that can only be done then; it is advisable to space the load.

In *Our Town* the main rehearsal might take about an hour since the crowd scene lasts for only two pages and requires little individual work. If, however, you were preparing the mob scenes for *Julius Caesar*, these could take three or four sessions to complete satisfactorily, and it would be useful to have the assistant stage manager and the prompter walk through the moves of the leading characters so that the crowd would have a sense of both position and relationship before coming to a main rehearsal.

Before Crowd Rehearsals Crowd rehearsals take similar preparation to regular rehearsals, so you would block in their grouping for reference, as suggested in the main blocking of the play. When working with a large crowd requiring much movement and many cues (for example, in *Julius Caesar*, *Teahouse of The August Moon*, or *The Italian Straw Hat*) it can be a help to number each member in your planning and then have everyone wear his number at rehearsal, if necessary heading various groups under letters.

Follow the same approach to the detailed blocking of a crowd as you would to other sections of the play; for example, take into account the purpose and impression of the group, its location, and its relationship to the main characters and situation.

During Crowd Rehearsals Again your ability to communicate is important, and the crowd will need the following information:

1. An understanding of the crowd's purpose and effect. In *Our Town* these mourners could number twenty-five people, and even one not in tune with the scene could disturb the atmosphere.

2. Summarize the set – such as it is – and main blocking, so that everyone knows *where* he is going, *who* he stands next to, and the order in which he makes his entrance and exit. You will need time for rearrangement for height and size, remembering that this crowd has a dual function: the dramatic purpose of providing atmosphere and background with their open umbrellas centred around the coffin; and the practical purpose of bringing Emily on-stage while deliberately masking her entrance, so that the audience is led to believe that her spirit actually rises from that coffin.

Check two points: (a) That the mechanics of handling the umbrellas (provided by the prop-girl) are well-managed; few stages will allow room for twenty-five people to wait with them raised in the wings; so there will need to be a careful and, if possible, soundless opening on each entrance (and the reverse on exit), watching that there is neither injury to each other or disturbance of curtains on the way. When working on a small stage it might be safer to ration the number of umbrellas to one between two or three of the crowd. (b) Be sure Emily is fully-masked – hidden, that is, by the crowd from the audience until her cue for appearance at the beginning of the hymn. The wardrobe department would supply the dark cloak necessary, but it would be best for her to hand it to someone not holding an umbrella.

3. Suggest some interpretation by the crowd. The lighting is likely to be dim and the crowd may not "show" much, but each person belongs to this group for a reason and an association, and should participate in this action. The audience should be aware of these people as complementary to the main thread of the play.

4. It is likely that some of the crowd are making their first appearance on-stage, so a brief explanation of grouping (on a curve, to avoid masking unless it is deliberate) will make their position more logical, and help them to remember *where* and *why* they are needed in relation to others.

5. With the stage manager's help, check that the members of the crowd know *where* and *when* to wait in the wings, that they are clear as to their entrance and exit cues, and appoint a leader to be responsible to carry through their directions. The back-stage area is often confined, and advance decisions regarding the flow of traffic now could prevent silent snarls (with umbrellas) during performance.

Focus Try to allow time for at least two or three run-throughs of the crowd before rehearsing them with the lead roles. Remain aware of their use in relation to the total effect. Remember that a moving object attracts more attention than a speaking object, so watch for the necessary stillness and repose. Make sure that no one fidgets when Emily appears from behind the crowd; an audience cannot watch two things at once and, were attention to be divided at this point, it would develop a form of astigmatism. A director working with a cast who understands what is wanted can focus all eyes, almost as a television or movie director uses his camera, to say, "Now see this." Similarly, as he asks the actors to modulate or change their voices (Mrs. Webb and that pre-wedding speech), he clarifies events by saying, "Now hear this."

In all arts there is a certain manipulation, or craft, in the hand-ling of material for the sake of clear communication, which may be warranted but should not be apparent. Practised by a director who pulls the strings according to his own purpose, the results may be that of a puppeteer; used by the director who respects the material he is helping to create, the results are more likely to be faithful to the author's intent. Every good play contains its own truth, so be guided by the author's set of values.

The Final Week

The following elements should now be blended within the main-stream of ordinary rehearsals (Week Five) and not left to happen at the dress rehearsals, since they are needed as part of the actor's work:

1. The crowd should be incorporated within the action of the play.
2. Effects should be in use. In *Our Town* this would apply to those *sound effects* the director decides are necessary, such as the clank of milk bottles, the chickens, and that train whistle

(almost the theme sound of the beginning and ending of the play). If these are not yet available – there is a special record – ask for them to be called out by the stage manager or the assistant who will be responsible in performance.

3. Dummy props, supplied by the prop-girl, should now be in continuous use, so that the newspapers, soda glasses, etc. used in the production are available.

4. Appropriate furniture should be ready for the Webb and Gibbs homes, stools for the drug store, the correct number of chairs for the wedding and graveyard scenes, and the ladders for the end of Act One. Check with the stage manager that he has arranged which of his assistants is to be ready for setting (placing) and striking (removing) these objects.

5. A sense of the period (1901 to 1913) should now be established among the cast. Encourage them to think of the background, and ask the wardrobe department for a supply of practice skirts (or see if the girls can make their own) and a few jackets and suitable hats for the men. Once the women are enclosed in the high necklines and longer skirts of the period (watch their walks) and the men are trying the stiff collars, suits buttoned at the top (tight around the shoulders), and tight pants, a flavor will develop that is all part of the atmosphere of the play.

The actor needs a chance to assimilate these elements within his performance, and then he is more ready for the different conditions of the coming dress rehearsals, when he is still concentrating on the final development of his character.

With the last run-through in the rehearsal room, or under usual rehearsal conditions, you will now have a chance of seeing the play forming as a whole. Ideally the detailed work should be over and you can stand aside, noting any scenes or sequences that still need finish. Assess the light and shade of emphasis, for in a sense every scene is comparative and can only be judged in relation to every other scene. Try to estimate in your mind's ear and eye the balance of character and situation as enlarged for the theatre. Suggestions now can save alteration at the dress rehearsals when, if possible, the cast should not be asked to make major changes; but still be ready to nourish the actor's imagination so that he presents a full performance. There is always more to be discovered about a personality.

Now that the acts will be reasonably set and blocked, ask the stage manager to take note of the running time; it is bound to vary at coming rehearsals, and this record can be a useful check.

You are now watching the bare bones of the play for the last time. If it has a potential now, without all the effects of illusion which help create the medium of theatre – the proper lighting, full costume and make-up, the perspective and proportions of the stage – and if it begins to stand clear on a mere "four boards and a passion," then you begin to have a fair chance of sharing the lives and the story of these people with the audience.

TECHNICAL REHEARSAL

The technical rehearsal should be held before the dress rehearsals. If it has to be held during a normal rehearsal time, it is a good idea to arrange a line-rehearsal for the cast, taken by the prompter.

All heads of technical departments and their staffs, except for the wardrobe department, are required at this rehearsal, but should be able to leave once their supplies are checked. (You would not necessarily need the producer, for example, while you were doing sound effects.)

This rehearsal represents the deadline for: the designer and his set; the electrician and his lights; the stage manager and his supervision of furniture, properties, and sound and music effects. Their deadline is not Opening Night. It is essential that this is appreciated, for their work is a part of a whole, and the whole cannot be brought together and fused unless the individual parts are ready. And "ready" means in complete working order: lights up and connected, sound equipment on to play, and curtain operable. Much of this preparedness depends on the routine checking at those production meetings, but there will always be last-minute delays as bulbs blow, lights fuse, and someone cuts a finger.

Before the Technical Rehearsal Often it is not possible to rent the theatre much in advance, and instead of in a few days, which would be reasonable, all the equipment has to be assembled and the prefabricated set built in the few hours before this rehearsal can begin. This is known as the *setting-up* period and should cover the following points:

1. The set should be firmly in place and ready to be "dressed," which would mean with drapes, cushions, pictures, and ornaments available. In *Our Town* this would mean that the "sky" was up, and that the ladders and levels were painted. It is important that the designer realizes this finish is necessary, for when you come to the lighting any later addition or change of color would

make for a different reflection and absorption of light, requiring changes in the final lighting plot.

2. The same point about painting applies to the furniture and properties; and it is the responsibility of the stage manager, with the help of his assistants, to see that they are brought to the theatre and are ready on-stage or in the wings.

3. The lighting plot should be ready for completion. If you have a lighting designer, he will have prepared it after watching and studying the play and after some discussion with you. Often you will arrange the lighting yourself, and since this is a technical subject we will discuss it in greater detail within Chapter 4, on Design, with an account of a special lighting rehearsal. Remember that if someone is brought in to do it, however expert all the experts, the result must blend towards the total effect; so be tactfully but firmly prepared not only to use enthusiasm but also, if necessary, to curb it. If, in providing marvellous effects of design, light, and sound, the results attract attention to themselves, they are bad; but if they lead attention to the play, then, as far as the theatre is concerned, they are good.

As with your preparation of the blocking of the play, this plot should provide a scheme through which the lighting can be planned. Indicate the type of light, the source, and the required atmosphere, with a note of any special effects (the amount of time for the dawn to come up in Act One, and in other plays perhaps a realistic approach to car headlights, a fire, or a storm). A cue sheet should be worked out with the stage manager, which he can incorporate or copy into his prompt copy, showing the WARNING and GO signs of each change, including a brief note as to the type of change: DIM, as at the end of each act, or SLOW FADE INTO SILHOUETTE from Emily's "I'm ready to go back," completed over two pages to her "They don't – understand – do they?" and Mrs. Gibbs' reply, "No, dear. They don't understand." Give a second copy of this cue sheet to the electrician who will work these changes, and keep a third for yourself so that you will all be rehearsing with the same reference to hand.

4. The sound plot should be prepared in the same way as the lighting plot, and is the responsibility of the stage manager. Unless another expert is required, he will have the equipment ready and one of his assistants standing by to operate it.

5. If necessary, there will be a separate music plot, which will probably be prepared by you, and, with the help of the stage manager, the music will be on special tape or records so that

the exact number of bars and required fade or clear end is pre-controlled. The operation of these cues should be handled by an assistant stage manager, or a specialist, who has a certain musical sense, as mis-timing can distort an entire production.

6. If used, indicate the timing of the curtain to the stage manager, whether it is fast, slow, or co-ordinated with light, sound, or music cues – or with a line or move from the cast. Even with an assistant (traditionally, the carpenter) handling this effect, the stage manager is still responsible for the timing of every cue in the play.

It is useful to have two people as spare assistants at the technical rehearsal, as the assistant stage managers and the prop-girl are busy with their own work. One will be needed to help the electrician move tall ladders, focus lights, and re-label the switch board; the other will be needed as messenger between you in the auditorium and the stage manager backstage. In some larger theatres you may find there is instant communication via an intercom system; usually it is a more confusing process of "Shout!" "Can't hear you!" followed by a period of both speaking at once, and a start all over again.

Remember that the purpose of all this planning is to make the way clear for the actor when he comes to the dress rehearsals, and for the eventual success of performance, which depends on the co-ordination of all involved. The actor should be able to concentrate on the development of his character to help make the play a living experience for the audience, and should feel confident that light and sound changes will come at the expected time. A funeral of a curtain, for example, where a quick one is expected would spoil even the best of performances.

Use of these technical effects in the theatre may be judged *true* or *false* within the idiom of the play, for elaborate sets, fanciful lighting, or over-rated sound effects would ruin the simple convention of *Our Town*. Practice of the effects, however, makes for tangible results of timing and degree that are *right* or *wrong*. Once the arrangements are clear, they should be noted by the assistant concerned and practised until they are right. The early part of the technical rehearsal can at best make slow, steady progress; if it is to be done thoroughly, it cannot be done quickly.

Prepare for a siege.

During the Technical Rehearsal   You are ready to begin when setting-up is complete.

Directors vary in their method of running a technical rehearsal, and you are likely to slip into a routine that is best suited to the play. If it makes heavy demands on a particular department, it is best to work through those cues first. Lighting, for example, can add enormously to the spectacle of *Our Town*. (Although you would find that, if you had no resources and if it was well acted, it could, like all good plays, stand within the imagination of the audience without the need of complicated changes.)

Take each cue for a change of effect. Set the degree of light, the length and volume of sound or music, and the timing of each change – whether it is to be on, after, or before a line, move, or particular word.

Let's consider that Boston train whistle in the Stage Manager's first speech, which would come under sound effects. (Cue 1, SOUND, marked in green in the prompt copy.) The assistant operating this department would have the special record ready on the turntable or tape recorder, with the beginning of the sound marked on the grooves or play-bar, or indicated by the footage meter. The whistle should be heard after the word "Boston" at the end of the sentence "And in the depot, Shorty Hawkins is gettin' ready to flag the 5.45 for Boston." If it came in the middle of the sentence, Shorty would not be about to flag the train but would have done so a while back. Yet if there were too long a pause after that word, both the Stage Manager and the audience would have an uncomfortable and illogical wait before he can say, "Aya – there she is." Then the volume and length of the the whistle should be set, for if it were too loud with a jerk at the end, it would cause a jump that would intrude into the thread of the play; too soft with a weak fade, and it would sound like the mistake that it would then be. In each case your guide is what you consider appropriate to the mood and purpose of the scene.

Check the number of the change on the sound plot so that any reference needed is correct. Run the effect by having the stage manager read the speech (a quick, almost blah-blah-blah is enough) right from the WARNING to the GO signal. (For further details, see Chapter 3, on Stage Management.)

Now take each subsequent effect and work the change. Then take a break. You have broken the back of the work when each cue has been rehearsed: from the lowering of the houselights at the beginning of the play, to each further light change, to all music cues and intermissions, to the final raising of the houselights at the end of the play. A technical rehearsal can be very concentrated, and, if there is time for a run-through of all the effects, it will be the better for a fresh start.

Meanwhile, check with the stage manager in case he wants to redistribute any of the load backstage, to rearrange the stacking of scenery or furniture in the wings, or to try a more satisfactory school bell. He knows the conditions under which his staff are working at first-hand, and it is his job to take over the production from you and see that it can be run easily, which also means that it is run well. If each person knows what he does, then this run-through should not be a long process and will help establish confidence in the sequence of the play.

After the Technical Rehearsals You are now ready to co-ordinate the work of the actors and the technical staff, and are about to see the total result of many weeks' work at the coming dress rehearsal.

DRESS REHEARSALS

It is an exciting moment to see cast, costumes, set, make-up, lights, props, and furniture all together for the first time, and it usually provides fresh impetus for everyone's work. Try to start these, of all rehearsals, punctually, and if the technical rehearsal has gone well you should, with luck, now see the total production fit together like pieces of a jigsaw puzzle. Remember that with the final dress rehearsal your contribution to the production ceases; but the cast must re-create the play at every performance, and their efforts continue until the final curtain on closing night. You may find you are like a racehorse trainer, and – judgment again – will assess how far you can stretch the cast and still feel they have that extra reserve to carry them through until the end of a run.

First Dress Rehearsal This is always a long session, and it is a good idea to let people know how it will run. The order would be on the following lines: Costume Parade, Photo Call, Curtain Call, and Run-through. When there are two dress rehearsals, the first is often a stop-start process during the run-through to iron out any difficulties along the way (sometimes the co-ordinating of sound and light cues with the movement of the actors), and the director may give notes during the intermission when events which can be confusing are comparatively fresh in everybody's mind.

(a) *Costume Parade.* A costume parade should, like a technical rehearsal, be held in advance of the first dress rehearsal. If the play has a large cast and makes special demands on the wardrobe department (a production of Shakespeare or a big musical, *Hamlet* or *My Fair Lady*, for example), it is best to hold the parade as a special call at a separate time. For *Our Town*, with comparatively simple costumes, it would be usual to hold it an hour before the beginning of the first dress rehearsal, with the costume designer, wardrobe mistress, and any dressers present; for this, not Opening Night, is their deadline.

Ask the stage manager to have everyone ready in the wings; have the auditorium darkened and the stage lights brought up to their maximum for the play; and ask each character to appear separately. Check with the designer and wardrobe mistress for fit, general finish (pressing), and wear of costume. Some actors have a natural sense of period, and can use the angle of a hat, tie, or brooch to comment on a character; but watch for a wig, bow, or untidy waistline which can throw the balance of the total design. Check that wedding and engagement rings are worn as required. Real glasses should not be used, because of their catching the reflection of the lights; but, if glasses are regarded as part of the costume, the lenses should be removed, leaving the frame. Catch the wearing of modern wrist watches in a period play. Check make-up for color, neatness, avoidance of a mask or hard line around neck or forehead, and final effect of character. Watch hair styles, so that they are neither a caricature of a period nor so faithful that they distort a face.

Then call everyone on-stage together and ask them to stand in groups similar to those they will use in relation to family, neighbors, and crowd. You may need to discuss the color combination and contrast with the designer; for no matter how much thought, time, and care have gone into their preparation, it is not until you see the costumes under the lights, within the set and among the other characters, that you can assess their total effect. Should you feel that a change is needed, and a dress or jacket which seemed right in the sketches and fittings is unsuitable, now is the time to mention it. If the wardrobe department is relatively clear and has kept to its deadline, the change might even be effected by the second dress rehearsal. Make it clear that there is now no alteration of costume except from any notes just made, and that even this should be checked with you and the designer when complete.

(*b*) *Photo Call*. Because of publicity deadlines, certain photographs will be required well in advance, but the main ones are usually taken at the beginning or end of the first dress rehearsal. They provide the one tangible record of any theatre group and are of interest if they include details of the action of the play, the atmosphere of the set, and some of the characters and make-up. If possible, have them taken now; later everyone is weary, thinking of baby-sitters and of getting up in the morning, and their make-up has faded. Have ideas about certain shots, but rely on the photographer's judgment as to angle, lighting, and grouping. So much the better if he can watch the play and catch some of the action during rehearsal.

(c) *Curtain Call.* The "call" taken by actors at the end of a play in answer to the applause – if any – is their way of saying "Thank you" to an audience. An untidy or embarrassed-looking curtain call can spoil the impression of an otherwise satisfying evening of theatre. Unless part of it is especially arranged to music or as a tableau, it is taken not by the characters but by the actors as their own selves, and should be planned and then incorporated into the dress rehearsals. Explain the order in which the cast comes on, usually starting with groups of minor characters and building to a cumulative effect with the leads; or have the cast discovered on a curved line as the lights and/or curtain go up again; in either case have the leading characters in the centre. If you think, then, of Emily first, and balance her with George on one side and the Stage Manager on the other (alternate man/woman arrangement is best), you have a basis from which to continue. George's mother and father would come next in order on his side, and Emily's parents to the other side of the Stage Manager – and so through all the rest. Choose one person as a leader to start each bow or curtsey half a second ahead of the others, and rehearse so that they synchronize with the timing of curtain or lights, for this is a joint action of thanks.

(d) *During the Rehearsal.* Have that spare assistant by you again, as in the technical rehearsal, ready to take notes or run messages; make sure he has a flashlight that can be shaded, as a will-o'-the-wisp jumping around the darkened auditorium will disturb the actors. Ask the stage manager to check the running-time of each act and to observe any difficulties backstage. Give your own notes quietly, and insist on equal quiet in the auditorium. Some of the cast may want to slip through and watch part of the play, but there should be no missing of entrances or distractions that will affect the work of those either on-stage or backstage.

Even during the first dress rehearsal try to avoid breaking into the action, since everyone needs a sense of the flow and the different timing of their work and you need a look at the total perspective; also, you have to judge how much the actors need to strengthen their projection and adapt their performance to the size of auditorium. There may, however, be times when Emily, George, and Rebecca have trouble climbing those ladders in their costumes at the end of Act One, and then a quick repetition on the spot would help the final continuity.

(*e*) *After the Rehearsal.* When you give notes, try now, of all times, to make them as encouraging as possible. Dress rehearsals can provide the first stumbling moment when the play almost seems to take life and become an actual world – the final test before it is ready for an audience (without which it can never be complete). They represent a big transition from previous conditions for the actors, and some will have trouble adapting: to themselves and others in costume and make-up, to the changing lights, and to that fourth wall removed, or hollow in the dark. Show confidence in the outcome, and as far as possible avoid too many last-minute changes; complete rearrangement of grouping or alterations in blocking now would be more likely to confuse a cast, especially the newcomers, than add finish to the production.

Have a last check with all heads of technical departments, and the producer and publicity girl, in case of final requirements.

Final Dress Rehearsal Ideally this should be regarded as a spare rehearsal on the part of the director and as a complete run-through for the cast and technical staff and the stage manager (who is about to take over the production from you) with no stops, starts, changes, or notes in the middle – in the case of some directors, with not even notes at the end. (There is one who has a way of saying, "O.K., kids. You're in business." Nice if it happens.) More often it is a case of easing out the wrinkles of the first dress rehearsal, entailing a final trimming of the action and a clipping of time, for the pace nearly always sags the first time the cast are in the theatre.

Since most people have been preoccupied with their own work and performance at the first dress rehearsal, it is a good idea to call cast and staff on-stage before this final practice begins. Give a simple re-cap (not over five minutes) of your first introduction to the play at the original reading some weeks ago; sometimes your approach and interpretation will have changed, though with a play of clear action such as *Our Town* it is likely to have remained the same at base. Both you and the cast will have made many discoveries since then, but this is your chance to remind them of that all-important thread of the play, and to hope that everyone is sure of his purpose within the production.

Whatever happens, try to finish this rehearsal on a note of encouragement, yet with a hint that everyone has an extra length to go. End with a lift that will carry over into all the hopes and excitement and the hard work that go to make for a successful production.

Your work is now officially complete.

Performance

In one sense you are redundant at performances; in another you still have work to do. There is neither time nor opportunity to add to the production but, with care, you can watch that a standard is maintained and perhaps improved upon.

Appear backstage at a suitable time to bring good wishes, then leave. Space is usually limited and an extra body wandering round with nothing specific to do may be more hindrance than help.

Take your place in the audience and do not miss the Opening Night performance, or, within reason, any performance when the run is inside that of a week. The next couple of hours may be gruelling, but they are likely to be the most instructive you can have, for they are the only way of assessing whether you have succeeded in your work – of communicating *Our Town*, through the cast and total production unit, to the audience.

Be aware of the reaction around you. Listen for comments, fidgets, surprises. A laugh may come at an unexpected moment. Is this too much tension built into a scene not made to carry it? nervousness on the part of the actors? or a situation which carries humour to this particular audience?

Observe the performances carefully. Some actors will rise to the occasion and give more to their roles than ever before, finding a freedom which is one of the marks of accomplishment. Some may play down, and disappoint even though you feel they will improve later in the run. Others could show a lack of true discipline and unwittingly change moves, add business (actions), or alter lines at the expense of the balance of the play. Watch for development in an actor which would be useful in future casting.

Perhaps, if you are fortunate, you will be aware of an inter-play between actors which rises almost beyond expectation, is sensed by the audience and reflected in their participation in the events of Grover's Corners until every soul in the theatre is involved. Yet this process that may have been greatly conceived and highly organized remains at base: play. Keep it always in proportion.

Whatever the reception, be loyal to the cast. The underlying responsibility is yours, and the main comments will be based on your original approach to the theme and treatment of the writer. Good criticism tries to assess what has been attempted, though it may imply what should have been done. Bouquets will be deserved by the cast; brickbats will be deserved by you. Hard if you are working with inexperienced players to whom – unlike your so-called counterpart the orchestra conductor – you often have to impart all the basic skills, for they may not be ready to express what you wish them to communicate. Results will vary; points over which you have spent hours of rehearsal will be made and lost on different nights. But if those hours have been well used, the total shape for which you have all been striving should eventually be achieved. Somewhere there is a magic which may descend on the whole performance and invest it with the quality of a living experience.

Now . . . Turn towards a completely different type of play. There is no one way to direct and no one interpretation, but some authors demand more and give more than others. Adapt to the needs of Williams, Inge, Shaw, Chekhov, Moliere, Shakespeare, and Aristophanes; the best know the most about human nature and have the language to express it. By the challenges you meet, the knowledge you find, the conditions which you face – so will you develop, and so will your work grow.

Reading List

Directors on Directing, edited by Cole and Chinoy (Bobbs-Merrill).
The Director in the Theatre, by Hugh Hunt (Routledge and Kegan Paul).
Old Vic Prefaces, by Hugh Hunt (Routledge and Kegan Paul).
The Play Produced, by John Fernald (Deane).
Stage Directions, by John Gielgud (Heinemann).

3. The Stage Manager

The stage manager has an immensely interesting and satisfying job. He works in close co-operation with the director of the play, and is an essential person within the total pattern of the theatre. As his name implies, he literally "manages" the stage. All back-stage facilities and staff come under his administration, including the actors once the dress rehearsal is over, when, in theory, the director's work is finished. So that he may eventually take this full charge, the stage manager attends all rehearsals and necessary meetings.

His purpose is two-fold. He is: (a) the right-hand man and first side-kick or Horatio-Hamlet to the director, and (b) ideally, the considerate being who makes the way clear and easy at all times for the actor. While the director is finally responsible for *what* happens on-stage and has complete artistic control of a production, the stage manager is responsible for *how* it happens and has complete working control of a production.

When the stage management is good, it does not appear to happen, and the audience remains unaware of the activity back-stage, from the operation of sound, light, and music cues, to the pulling of the curtain. A critic may only give the department notice if it is bad, and even an adjudicator will take it largely for granted, unless it is exceptionally smooth in what he knows to be a difficult production. He will rarely give marks for it, but he may take marks off because of it. There is no hope-for-the-moment inspiration about stage management. Either the director is supplied with the pre-arranged lighting, or the actor given the correct property, or he is not. The results are direct, tangible, and right or wrong.

The stage manager is a practical person, and a first-class but unobtrusive organizer who enjoys working with people, from the director, whose work he helps transmit into performance, and the actor, whose needs he will foresee, to the newest and most assist-ant assistant-stage-manager, whose work he will supervise and encourage. He needs an instinct for preventing trouble before it happens and a good rhythmic sense to time the many cues in conjunction with the movements of the actor and the mood of the scene.

For an average production he will require on his staff: two assistant stage managers (known as a.s.m.s), a prompter, someone in charge of properties (often a prop-girl), and someone to "call" the actors (often a call-boy). It is possible, but not always advisable, to divide these three jobs among the two a.s.m.s. He will need a good stage carpenter (not always the same as a good ordinary carpenter, since he must continually adapt to less time and perhaps lesser materials), a reliable electrician (who has a proper understanding of wiring, etc.), a wardrobe mistress, and, possibly, a dresser.

For a heavy production which has many changes of scenery he will, in addition, require a crew to do the changing. The work of the stage-crew (or scene-shifters) should not in this case be done by his staff, who will have their own jobs to do in relation to the props and alterations to the dressing (finish) of the set. The stage-crew need not attend ordinary rehearsals but should be available from the time of the technical rehearsal.

To show the work of the stage management of a production we will divide it into four main sections: Preparation, Rehearsals, Performance, and Closing the Production, with an additional section on the work of a prompter, a prop-girl, and an assistant stage manager. So that the facts shall be as practical as possible, we will refer to a well-known play with which many of you will be familiar: *The Glass Menagerie*, by Tennessee Williams.

Preparation

The essence of good work in any field lies in careful preparation, and advance planning before early rehearsals will result in a smooth schedule later. Every play presents some difficulties, but the aim is to foresee and clear as many technical problems as possible, so that the cast will not be delayed in rehearsal while time is spent with the attention of the director and stage manager elsewhere. A good instance of foresight being better than hindsight.

As soon as you are asked to become stage manager of a production, read the play. You can become familiar with the plot and sequence of events, the characters, and the period, if any, and with details of background in relation to choice of furniture and

The Glass Menagerie: Amanda, played by Denise Ferguson at the Red Barn Theatre, August, 1962, directed by Marigold Charlesworth, designed by John Scott.   *Photo:* Lutz Dille

properties. Final decisions will rest with the designer and director, but you may be asked to collect suitable pieces, so advance knowledge will be a help.

In a detailed production of *The Glass Menagerie*, for example, there would be a need for all kinds of period knick-knacks dating from the late 'teens and early 'twenties of this century, such as kewpie dolls and ballerina shoes. Three items which would certainly have to be "managed" by you would be the enlarged photograph of Amanda's husband, the phonograph, and an elderly typewriter. Points to consider would be: how the photo is to be hung (from what kind of support, and therefore how heavy the frame can be), whether it is to be specially lit, and, if so, whether it will require special wiring. You would need to know if the director wanted a phonograph that was *practical* and would play of it's own accord when operated by Laura, or a dummy that would require its own music cue.

If you are often a stage manager in your community, it is a good idea to quietly docket the belongings in various homes. When there is goodwill towards the theatre, it helps to know where you can put your hands on a particular type of rocking chair, a pair of candlesticks, or the right kind of hassock and the day-bed for *The Glass Menagerie*. There is the story of a group who arrived in a city to compete in the finals of the Dominion Drama Festival, to find that their furniture had travelled in an unexpected direction. So they were without such necessities as a spinning wheel, a Dutch dresser, and an elephant's foot. But so well were local homes filed in the mind of a member of the host theatre that all these needs were supplied in time for their performance. Remember that, finally, the important part of the arrangement is that what is borrowed is returned on time, and in good order.

PRODUCTION MEETINGS

You will soon meet with the director, or preferably be called to a production meeting attended by the heads of other departments such as the designer, wardrobe mistress, etc., to hear of the director's approach to the production. The designer may already have a scale model, or at least a ground plan of the stage. Take note of this plan, for then you will be able to think of much of your work in a tangible sense, and details of doorways, platforms, and general proportion will all be useful as part of your working knowledge of the play.

You will now know if the stage is to be cluttered with furniture, props, and realism, or to contain only the barest necessities, such as the dining-table and chairs, day-bed, typewriter, phonograph – and the glass menagerie. Find out what the director requires of that photograph, if he is going to use the memory, or mood, music suggested in the acting edition of the play, and whether he prefers the phonograph to be practical. In that case, does anyone know a good source of old seventy-eight r.p.m. (preferably cracked) records? But if the actual machine is to be a dummy, you could put the effect on tape.

This will be a good time for preliminary discussion on any changes of set. The one change in *The Glass Menagerie* is the difference in the condition of the room between the news of Jim O'Connor's visit in the first act and his arrival in the second. Here you are helped by the author, who has allowed time for the changes during an intermission. The designer will suggest what happens; you will be responsible for carrying his ideas into effect. Note, for example, any extra cushions, chair covers, and light fixtures required.

Inquire whether a carpenter is needed, and if you are to find one. An obvious note, but occasionally it's the points we take for granted that cause the biggest slip. If there is a producer, he will be responsible for this; but no matter how large or small the production unit, the job still has to be done. Note any division of work between those who construct the set and those who make or provide any special properties. The carpenter might be asked to make the frame for the photograph, for example, if it is to have a light installed within it, while the property department would probably be asked to supply the dated table lamps and fixtures.

Ask how the budget affects your department, and what, if any, is the allowance. Know what items are to come under the listed headings so that you can mark any accounts that come to you accordingly. This will save considerable time for whoever keeps the books.

The stage manager is usually responsible for borrowing or hiring the furniture, so ask for guidance as to the exact type required, with particular reference to size. This should be in proportion to the set, as the set is to your stage. If the acting area is very small it would be a help, spacewise, to look for a drop-leaf dining table which could be folded when not required for the action of the play. Conversely, if the stage is large, an old-fashioned heirloom of a table would be effective provided that, like all furniture and props, it does not attract attention to itself; for of all the items in this play the only two which require emphasis are the husband's photograph and the glass menagerie.

Check whether an electrician is needed or has been found. Another obvious point; but it would be too bad if an ingenious lighting plot were planned and at the last minute no one was available to make the connections and work the switches. Again, where there is a producer, such arrangements will be foreseen; but in case it is your responsibility to find an electrician, it is best to have time to look for one. He is one of the key technical staff in an essentially practical way; for no matter how careful the planning, the lighting must be carried out by a competent person. Look for him in your community, and once you are sure he knows the technical side of lights and wiring, stimulate his interest in theatre. He will be guided by the director or lighting expert as to results, and it is possible he will soon become an addict for life. Like much of the work backstage, the electrician's job is satisfying because it is tangible, and challenging because each play presents difficulties which must be overcome. In *The Glass Menagerie* the director may want the lights so arranged that they pick out some areas of the stage, leaving others in shadow; while in the next production, say of *Teahouse of the August Moon*, a much brighter, lighter effect will be needed, and the electrician will have to change the color and control of nearly all the lamps. Because, like everyone, he often has to work on an economical budget, demands usually outweigh the supply of his equipment, and he has a puzzling time trying to gain every ounce of light without either overloading the board or underpowering the actors.

Inquire about a wardrobe mistress. She will take charge of the costumes and their condition once they are completed by the designer and his staff, and she may help in the making herself. In a four-hander such as *The Glass Menagerie* this position would not be essential, though if the play were to run for more than a week, cleaning, pressing, or mending could become important.

Unless pre-arranged by the director for some reason, you will appoint your own assistants, known as a.s.m.s. You should find that two are enough. It is better to have a few reliable people kept busy and happy backstage than to have many occupying the limited space with time on their hands. Too many cooks can spoil a theatrical as well as any other kind of broth. Look for people who are easy to work with and will co-operate well with the needs of the director and the cast. It is a help if they have had previous experience, but if not, be prepared to explain the reasons for *what* is done – *when*. Then you are training your own assistants, and their clear understanding now will make for a good technical staff in the future. If you are involved in a production with more than approximately twelve in the cast, you may find a third assistant useful. In this case it is customary to re-name the work, and you become stage director (the executive of the stage management world), and your chief assistant becomes stage manager, with the less experienced remaining a.s.m.s. By having one person more senior to the other two, so you can divide and scale the responsibility.

It may be your job to order copies of the play. Remember to inquire in good time whether they are available locally. If they have to be ordered from out of town, delivery could take from one to three weeks; if from overseas, six weeks. In this case see if the budget can take an air-mail parcel, since delay over scripts must be avoided. Find out the exact number required: you, the director, and designer will already have copies, but some will be needed by the technical staff as well as by the cast. In a large-cast play, some of the actors could share.

There will be more production meetings between now and the performance of the play. Often the early ones seem the busiest, but they can become very informal. Preparation is like the shape of a pyramid; have all the basic questions ready at the start and gradually they will be crossed off each list, until ideally only the routine of performance remains. Hold-ups, however, will occur, and probably everyone, including you, will forget or lose something on the way, so try to see that careful checking safeguards the production.

List the following points, and fill in details at subsequent meetings:

1. Date, time, and place of regular rehearsals, pencilling in extra sessions and week-ends near production time.
2. Arrangements for rehearsal space: the hiring, if necessary; the whereabouts of the key; and the time the building is closed each night.
3. Deadlines for set, costumes, and lighting requirements.
4. Date, time, and place of photo call.
5. Date, time, and place of technical rehearsal, dress rehearsals, and performance.
6. Reminder on insurance coverage regarding borrowed, hired, or company-owned sets, furniture, costumes, etc.
7. Time of the next production meeting.

PLOT SHEETS

Now is a good time to become familiar with the mechanics of the the play by preparing certain lists, known as plot sheets. You can "pull" much information out of the script with reference to the characters, furniture, props, basic lighting, sound effects, and music. You may be unable to complete some of these sheets in detail until near the time of the technical rehearsal, but by setting them out early and filling them in gradually you will avoid unnecessary pressure at the last minute. Reserve that for inevitable accidents, and meanwhile the sheets will give you a clear picture of what to allocate to each of your assistants.

The character plot should list in columns the characters in order of appearance, with space for the correctly-spelt names of the actors – these you can only fill in when the play is cast. (Later the list will provide the publicity department with a useful reference for press releases and program material.) Show the act and scenes in which each person appears, with a note on costume and any changes necessary. (Amanda, for example, will need street clothes, or at least hat, gloves, and purse, for the opening of Scene Two.)

The furniture plot should also be ready to list the items required in each act and scene. The best way to visualize this is to mark each piece on your ground-plan of the set; then, before rehearsal or performance, your eagle instinct will tell you if anything is missing.

List the properties on their own separate sheet, indicating the act and scene if it is a complex production, with columns ready to show their origin (for example, *wing, right, bookcase,* or *down-stage*) and any changes of position. Laura uses her glass menagerie in the second scene, but it must be in a suitable position by the end of the third scene so that when Tom hurls his coat across the stage it will inadvertently knock the figures to the floor. (In the case of breakage, have replacements ready for the following performance.) You can supply the details of the actual place on-stage as the director blocks the play, also noting on which side of the stage hand-props (those carried on by the actors) are laid out. Tom will need the key for the front door ready on the appropriate side of the stage, or he could have a hard time opening the fourth scene.

Work out a simple lighting plot which will be a useful reminder as to the time of day, for a change to evening will probably mean some change in the set: lights turned on, practical curtains drawn, etc. Note particular needs: *blackout* at the end of Scene Two, and, if available, a special effect for the photograph. In the first scene, as the family moves from the dining room to the living area of the room, the actress playing Amanda may need to plan her move to allow for the turning on of an extra light and the switching off of others. A mention of this to the director, if he has not checked it during the blocking, can help Amanda incorporate these actions from early rehearsals, rather than discovering them as extras to remember at the time of the dress rehearsal.

Make a similar plot for *sound effects* and, if necessary, for all music cues. The former will include any weather or crowd noises. Thunder, for example, may be suggested at the beginning of Act Two to aid the atmosphere of expectancy and Laura's near-sickness through excitement. Note the source of the sound (door-bell, for example, by the door), how it will be made (buzzer), and which of the a.s.m.s will operate it.

You now have a good working knowledge of the play, and are familiar with some of the problems that are likely to arise. This information will be useful in your purpose of being a reliable assistant to the director, and a guide to the actors with regard to the technical side of the production.

PROMPT COPY

The next important step is the preparation of the prompt copy of the play. As you will realize, it is essential that this is done before the director gives the blocking, or moves, to the cast.

The prompt copy is the veritable bible of the production. In it you will record every move, every WARNING and GO sign of every cue: entrances, lighting, sound, music, and curtain, etc. From this working copy of the play the show will be "run" by you at each performance; and whether you are giving one, one hundred, or one thousand performances, it is a must. Nothing that is in it can ever be left to chance.

Because so much information will be inserted, special treatment will be needed, or it would be hard to read the print for all the details pencilled around it. So there must be room for each note, and for the changes which will inevitably be made in subsequent rehearsals.

Take a clean copy and separate the pages. At first this will seem a terrible thing to do to a book, even a paperback acting edition, but you will soon become hardened to this very necessary process. Place the pages between the leaves of a large, hard-bound exercise book. If using only one copy of the play, make a strong fold along the inner margin of each page, and stick the fold to the leaf of the exercise book; this means you still have both sides of the play page available simply by turning over the fold. If you can afford two copies, however, stick each page firmly down, and you will have a firmer result, for a whole page of the play is less likely to come unstuck or be torn out in a moment of theatrical crisis. Instead of a regular exercise book use a good loose-leaf if you prefer it (especially handy if you have to insert detailed notes of crowd-work later). But be sure the ring-perforations do not get torn, for a loose-leaf that lost its leaves would certainly be unpopular when vital cues were missing.

You can begin to pencil in some obvious cues (DOORBELL, for example), though you will be unable to complete the details of the light cues until the time of the technical rehearsal. Each cue is composed of two signs: a WARNING, usually half-a-page ahead of time, and a GO sign. Usually a different color is used to denote each type of effect: green for each part of the sound cues, blue for lights, red for the curtain cues, or what you will. So a glance will tell you what is required at a certain moment, and in Scene Seven, for example, WARN DOORBELL would be written in green at the top of the page, with a line joining it to an arrow-mark half-way down the page and indicating GO DOORBELL as written in the script. Similarly, if the lights cues are to be in blue, there will be a blue WARN BLACKOUT sign half a page before the end of Scene Two, and GO BLACKOUT in blue on or after the final line of dialogue, as directed. All such light cues will be numbered at the technical rehearsal, so that even when set there is a term of reference if alterations are required and a clear order of operation.

Remember that the prompt copy must be both accurate and clear. As you complete it, bear in mind that if for some reason you were prevented from stage managing a performance, someone with knowledge of the work (probably, but not necessarily, an a.s.m.) would have to be able to "run" the show. This doesn't mean you are dispensable, for it would be as much a strain for everyone as working with an understudy on-stage, but anything can be done in emergencies. There will be times, however, when you may have to turn over part of a rehearsal to an a.s.m. while you arrange any special effects, hunt for furniture, or see about a thunder sheet. Then it is important that moves which the director may need to check, or cuts which the actors are not sure about, are all clearly marked.

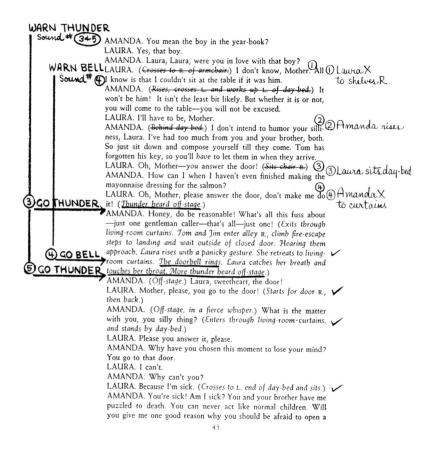

WARN THUNDER
Sound # ③+⑤   AMANDA. You mean the boy in the year-book?
LAURA. Yes, that boy.
AMANDA. Laura, Laura, were you in love with that boy?
WARN BELL   LAURA. (*Crosses to R. of armchair.*) I don't know, Mother. All ① ① Laura X
Sound # ④   I know is that I couldn't sit at the table if it was him.   to shelves, R.
AMANDA. (*Rises, crosses L. and works up L. of day-bed.*) It
won't be him! It isn't the least bit likely. But whether it is or not,
you will come to the table—you will not be excused.
LAURA. I'll have to be, Mother.
AMANDA. (*Behind day-bed.*) I don't intend to humor your silli- ② ② Amanda rises
ness, Laura. I've had too much from you and your brother, both.
So just sit down and compose yourself till they come. Tom has
forgotten his key, so you'll *have* to let them in when they arrive.
LAURA. Oh, Mother—you answer the door! (*Sits chair R.*) ③ ③ Laura sits day-bed
AMANDA. How can I when I haven't even finished making the
mayonnaise dressing for the salmon?   ④ ④ Amanda X
LAURA. Oh, Mother, please answer the door, don't make me do   to curtains
③ GO THUNDER   it! (*Thunder heard off-stage.*)
AMANDA. Honey, do be reasonable! What's all this fuss about
—just one gentleman caller—that's all—just one! (*Exits through
living-room curtains. Tom and Jim enter alley R., climb fire-escape
steps to landing and wait outside of closed door. Hearing them
④ GO BELL   approach, Laura rises with a panicky gesture. She retreats to living-   ✓
room curtains. The doorbell rings. Laura catches her breath and
⑤ GO THUNDER   touches her throat. More thunder heard off-stage.*)
AMANDA. (*Off-stage.*) Laura, sweetheart, the door!
LAURA. Mother, please, you go to the door! (*Starts for door R.,   ✓
then back.*)
AMANDA. (*Off-stage, in a fierce whisper.*) What is the matter
with you, you silly thing? (*Enters through living-room-curtains,   ✓
and stands by day-bed.*)
LAURA. Please you answer it, please.
AMANDA. Why have you chosen this moment to lose your mind?
You go to that door.
LAURA. I can't.
AMANDA. Why can't you?
LAURA. Because I'm sick. (*Crosses to L. end of day-bed and sits.*)   ✓
AMANDA. You're sick! Am I sick? You and your brother have me
puzzled to death. You can never act like normal children. Will
you give me one good reason why you should be afraid to open a

45

A Prompt Copy: specimen pages from a production of *The Glass Menagerie*

JIM. (*Rises.*) Well, Mrs. Wingfield, let me give you a toast. ✔
Here's to the old South.

AMANDA. The old South. (*Blackout in both rooms.*)

JIM. Hey, Mr. Light Bulb!

AMANDA. Where was Moses when the lights went out? Do you know the answer to that one, Mr. O'Connor?

JIM. No, ma'am, what's the answer to that one?

AMANDA. Well, I heard one answer, but it wasn't very nice. I thought you might know another one.

JIM. No, ma'am.

AMANDA. It's lucky I put those candles on the table. I just put them on for ornamentation, but it's nice when they prove useful, too.

JIM. Yes, ma'am.

AMANDA. Now, if one of you gentlemen can provide me with a match we can have some illumination.

JIM. (*Lighting candles. Dim in glow for candles.*) I can, ma'am.

AMANDA. Thank you.

JIM. (*Crosses back to R. of dining-room table.*) Not at all, ma'am.

AMANDA. I guess it must be a burnt-out fuse. Mr. O'Connor, do you know anything about a burnt-out fuse?

JIM, I know a little about them, ma'am, but where's the fuse box?

AMANDA. Must you know that, too? Well, it's in the kitchen. (*Jim exits R. into kitchen.*) Be careful. It's dark. Don't stumble over anything. (*Sound of crash off-stage.*) Oh, my goodness, wouldn't it be awful if we lost him! Are you all right, Mr. O'Connor?

JIM. (*Off-stage.*) Yes, ma'am, I'm all right.

AMANDA. You know, electricity is a very mysterious thing. The whole universe is mysterious to me. Wasn't it Benjamin Franklin who tied a key to a kite? I'd like to have seen that—he might have looked mighty silly. Some people say that science clears up all the mysteries for us. In my opinion they just keep on adding more. Haven't you found it yet?

JIM. (*Re-enters R.*) Yes, ma'am. I found it all right, but them fuses look okay to me. (*Sits as before.*) ✔

AMANDA. Tom.

TOM. Yes, Mother?

AMANDA. That light bill I gave you several days ago. The one I got the notice about?

52

These two pages reproduced from *The Glass Menagerie*, by Tennessee Williams. Copyright 1945 by Tennessee Williams and Edwina D. Williams. Reprinted by permission of *New Directions*.

REHEARSAL ROOM

Since it is unlikely that rehearsals will be held on the stage of the theatre which is to be used, it may be your job to check the facilities of the rehearsal room. Some details will be available via a production meeting, but you should have a key, or know that the room will always be open when required. Find out whether smoking is allowed, for such rules are strict in some buildings, and, if so, whether there are ash trays – large ones. Enquire about the use of any phone, pay or otherwise, since everyone is likely to need one at some time, and whether messages may be left. Try and find a clock if none is in the room, and if the building lacks a janitor you may need to check the supply of soap, paper towels, and toilet paper in the washrooms. If need be, some of this checking can be allocated to your a.s.m.s, but it is a good way of preventing those time-consuming moments when a director and cast can only stand and fume. It helps punctuality, and makes for a good impression on the cast – in whom confidence in a reliable stage management must be built.

Rehearsals

Make it a rule to be first in. Always bring the prompt copy, a clip-board, spare paper, and a supply of pencils.

BEFORE REHEARSALS

Prior to the routine of normal rehearsals, the director will hold casting sessions to decide who is to play the various roles. He may ask you to attend, to help notify those interested, and to see that the dates, times, and places are publicized.

Arrive with a sufficient number of copies of the play, or see that they are available. You will avoid missing a few if, until casting is complete, you see that they are returned.

Help the director by keeping a record of the names, addresses, and home and business phone numbers of those who attend, with a note as to height, physique, coloring, and a brief mention of any previous experience. He will see many people during the next few hours, and such notes can help focus his memory.

When casting is complete, make a list of the names, the roles they are playing, their addresses and phone numbers, and add your own and the director's (and producer's if you have one) to the bottom of the list. Give one copy to the director, put another in the prompt copy, and keep a third ready for the bulletin board. If the director asks you to notify those who are cast, try to do so as quickly as possible; then everyone hears directly and not by rumor or second-hand.

It is a help to have a bulletin board ready in the rehearsal room. If you ask the cast and your staff to watch it, you have a double check for all notices which will be called out and then pinned up. There are always arrangements to be made about rehearsal times, costume fittings, dates of special work on songs, and individual study; the cast may have enquiries to make about borrowing certain items for costumes; and the a.s.m.s may need a special appeal if they have difficulty in supplying the prop-list.

Check with the director (or producer) whether copies of the play are to be given out free of charge or not, and if they are to be returned at the end of the production. When the cast first meets, keep a list of those who receive copies from you, and then you have a check for the record.

After the director has cast the play and perhaps held some readings for everyone to sense their roles, you have one important job to do before he blocks the play: to prepare the rehearsal room so that the ground-plan of the set is clearly indicated. Although a surround of chairs with suitable gaps for entrances will do, it is not very satisfactory since they are so easily moved out of place. If possible use masking tape, with different colors clearly outlined on the floor for any change of set. This ensures that the arrangement and proportion of the acting area remain the same for the cast, even when they transfer from this untheatrical room to the working stage of the theatre.

Since you will not be rehearsing with the real furniture (there is no need to do so, and it could get badly damaged), place substitutes in readiness. Three upright chairs together will suggest the day-bed, a stool the hassock, and a hat-stand the floor lamp. If the rehearsal room is used for a different purpose at other times, it may be good diplomacy to clear everything to one side at the end of each rehearsal. Always show the a.s.m.s, however, that you expect a tidy working area, and ask them to keep everything, including dummy props or special items of costume, in good order.

See the prop-girl and explain the requirements of the production. Ask her to make out a prop-sheet, and then check through it with her. If she is inexperienced, explain that tables, known as prop-tables, are placed on either side of the wings, and it is from these that the actors will pick up any hand-props, and to these that she should eventually return them; she must also know the position of all props to be set on-stage. She will collect the various props by a certain deadline (she may need her own assistant, or one of your a.s.m.s if it is a specially heavy or difficult list to find – she might, for example, take a while to locate a goat for *Teahouse of the August Moon*); but meanwhile she should find some "stand-in," or dummy, props for the cast to use as soon as they are struggling through the play without books. Early practice with any small ornaments to represent the glass menagerie, with old mugs or cups and saucers to represent Amanda's coffee and dinner set, will help the actors rehearse with their lines and moves as much as with their props, until they all become an integral part of their performance. Once you have allocated such work, show that you expect it to be completed as a matter of individual responsibility, and encourage results as they appear. It is a matter of dividing your labor, helping where necessary, and double-checking everything as a matter of routine.

The stage manager should be the first to arrive at any rehearsal in order to prepare the way for the director and the actors. In a play requiring many scene changes you will know in advance which scene is to be done first, and have the appropriate furniture and props in position ready for the rehearsal to begin. Then note, for example, that any platform or steps used either in the rehearsal room or on-stage, are safe, free of wobbles, and easy to step on or off. This will help eliminate clumsy exits and entrances, and may avoid broken limbs. Allocate the job to an a.s.m., but try the steps yourself before the beginning of rehearsal.

The director is likely to ask you to maintain any discipline among the cast in relation to punctuality, and to quiet at rehearsals. Within reason, expect both these qualities. If necessary, it is you who will have to *keep the peace* at performance, so it is best if the authority comes from you at rehearsal. These qualities are part of the self-discipline of the theatre; once they are a habit, they become invisible – but ingrained. Most people will co-operate once they understand that theatre is a co-operative effort, and that noise or lateness on their part doesn't matter but keeping others waiting, or disturbing them at work, does. A few requests early on will establish the habit, as everyone appreciates they have a joint responsibility – in regard to each other, the director, and the play.

DURING REHEARSALS

The stage manager attends each rehearsal, becoming familiar with the needs of the director and the actors and with the order of events, gradually adding all important information to the prompt copy. This will include cuts, possible changes in the order of scenes, and the marking of pauses in the action. If there is room, have a table ready near the director so that you do not have to work with the large prompt copy balanced on your knees.

When the director blocks the play, you have a routine task which can provide a constant reference for many later rehearsals. Note in the prompt copy every move that is given, in correct order, to every actor. Put a circled number by the appropriate line of dialogue or italic print in the play; put the corresponding number neatly in the margin of the actual book, where you have room to write a simple description of the move. Start the numbering afresh at the top of each page, or you could run into the thousands by the end of a complex play. Be sure that the acting area is clearly defined; for example, "② Amanda enters from door U/L (*up-stage left*) and crosses to table, R (*right*)" or "③ Laura moves slowly to phonograph D/L (*down-stage left*)." When working in a production with a large cast where many moves are concurrent, have an a.s.m. near you to keep double watch that this record is correct. Then, as rehearsals proceed, you can act as a prompter for the blocking. Actors do not always memorize their moves quite as carefully as their lines, and should you see them wandering hopefully out of place, a quiet word to the director before a tangle becomes too involved is a good instance of prevention being better than cure.

See that an early trust is built between the cast and the prompter, who should always sit, traditionally on a stool (to prevent him from falling asleep?), in a corner at the side of the stage. There, undisturbed, he can see and hear the actors. Resist the temptation to "throw" a prompt yourself, and do not let it come from anyone other than the prompter. Once again it is a case of rehearsal being practice for performance, and it is important for the cast to become acquainted with the voice which, if necessary, will come to their help in time of trouble. A prompt from a familiar voice is easier to catch than one from a stranger. Make it a rule that no one speaks to the prompter while rehearsal is in progress, or asks to borrow his copy. Momentary distraction, or even temporary loss of that script, could occur at a moment of need.

As the blocking is completed, check the dummy props for rehearsal with your a.s.m.s or the prop-girl, and note that the collection of real props for performance is progressing. Make arrangements for their storage in a special box or cupboard, for which a lock or *keep out* notice is advisable to prevent someone unwittingly disturbing the precious pile.

Occasionally the director may be detained, sick, or unable to attend a rehearsal. If he has not left special instructions, take a run-through of acts or scenes in which the lines or moves are shaky. Or you could hold a word-rehearsal, which helps ensure that the cast know their lines so well that they come as the natural and almost automatic expression of their characters. Or suggest they each take a mutter-through of every line, incorporating it with each move they make, so that the cast appear to be moving around the rehearsal space in a disorganized, mumbling maze. Either method helps their eventual concentration on the reaction and development of character, without having to think consciously of what they say, or do, next. Remember, however, that whatever kind of rehearsal you do take, it is your business always to endorse the director's work, and never to change it. He is sure to listen at any time if you have suggestions, but make them to him rather than directly to the cast.

There is an etiquette of working in the theatre as there is in any activity – business, art, or sport – where a group of people pool their talents towards a common aim. Naturally leadership, backed by division of labor, is required, and it is as well for every one to recognize that there is a line between their own and other departments. So individual ideas which are often a help to the final results should be mentioned to the head of a department, and then it is his prerogative to pass them on to the people who will carry them out, and, if he is a reasonable person, he will give you credit for the change. But if everyone threw in their own ideas all the time – and you and the a.s.m.s, for example, began telling the actress playing Laura how to interpret the role – the result would be chaotic. When all concerned in the production were asked to participate, they had a choice of saying "Yes" or "No," so the affirmative is taken as meaning they realize there must be a last word in each matter, and that the decision of the director – like that of an editor – is final.

Maintain a routine check on points to raise at coming production meetings. Have you got the necessary deadlines for costumes, lighting needs, photo call? If the dining recess in *The Glass Menagerie* is placed by the designer on a slightly higher level than the rest of the set, can the carpenter have this ready a week in advance, so that the cast can practice the feel of it even in the rehearsal room? A truck will be needed to collect the furniture from various homes and locations, and to return it when the run of the show is over; does anyone know of a friendly truck and driver, or is there allowance in the budget for hire of these services? Find out if the director has decided on the colors for the lighting of the play, and check with the electrician whether new transparencies, or mediums, have to be ordered. Cheaper ones tend to fade and tear, so it is as well to go through your stock rather than take its condition for granted. All such items will be needed in time for the technical rehearsal, and it is your job as foreman-of-the-works to see that everything is ordered and ready. Contact your nearest theatrical supply house for a catalogue and details of lighting needs, and add a request for information as to their range of theatrical make-up.

Keep the prompt copy neat and up-to-date. What has to be scribbled in at rehearsal should be made neat at home. Mark the WARNING and GO signs for cues as they become finalized, and if in any doubt, check them through with the director before the technical rehearsal. Just prior to this rehearsal he will probably give you a special lighting plot, which will give you further details to mark into the copy; but number them during that rehearsal, since changes are likely to be made.

At the end of each rehearsal make it a routine to call out, and post on the board, the time of the next. Notify anyone who left early of any changes in the schedule. Check with the director to see if anything further is required, and with the a.s.m.s as to their particular work. See that the room is left tidy.

Be last out.

TECHNICAL REHEARSAL

Now you have come to the end of the regular rehearsal period, and the play is about to take its full shape. There should be opportunity for at least three rehearsals on-stage, the first of which should be purely technical so that all tangible sides of the production can be co-ordinated. The cast is not needed at the technical rehearsal; it is better to let them rest, or have a word-rehearsal, than keep them waiting during the time-consuming adjustment of lights, the trial and error of sound and music cues, and even the timing of the curtain.

Naturally, if a play is being given the simplest possible production and there are no changes of effect or music, a technical rehearsal will be unnecessary. However, even in a one-act play having a few cues it is a good idea to take thirty minutes or so at the beginning of a dress rehearsal and run the cues through (while the cast is dressing and making-up) than have a slow, uneven rehearsal which can be both muddling and trying for everyone concerned. Time, like labor, is often best divided.

The routine of the technical rehearsal has been discussed in the chapter on the director, and once it starts you follow his lead, acting as a messenger between him and the electrician and whoever is operating other effects. But meanwhile you have some work to do with the a.s.m.s, and should be available to help wherever needed.

Before the Technical Rehearsal   Be first in.

If the set is a complex one, arrangements should be made for the designer and carpenter to be in the theatre some time in advance. However careful or fortunate the planning, delays often seem inevitable, and you may arrive to find the stage littered with wire and cable, while sawing and hammering resounds through the theatre and you wonder how long it will take to create order out of this chaos. Help where you can be of use, but whatever the state of the theatrical nation, be sure to go through your check-list.

Check the tape-recorder or record player and set the volume for the speakers, remembering that when the theatre – hopefully – is full, the bodies will soak up the sound, so it can afford to be a bit louder than you would otherwise expect. See that recordings are ready – from the anthem, to introductory music, to interval material. (These special requirements should be supplied by the director or music expert in advance.)

Three notes will be useful on a notice board (placed in a central position near the stage-door, or outside the dressing-room area):

1. Ask all backstage staff to wear rubber-soled shoes. They may need to move quickly, and will certainly have to move quietly.

2. List the number of each dressing-room and those who will share it, and have an a.s.m. post the names on the appropriate doors. If you cannot do this now, be sure it is done before the first dress rehearsal, so that the cast know where to go on arrival.

3. Ask the cast to keep clear of the prompt corner, the lighting-board, the tape-recorder, etc., and to remain quietly in the wings (or dressing-rooms if space is very limited) until near the time of each entrance.

Avoid taking for granted that everybody knows about such points; there are newcomers in every production who would rather learn from a written reminder than be barked at for getting in the way.

If you find unauthorized people coming backstage, be polite and firm about the rule of *sorry, no admittance.* They may have heard a rumor that you are doing a play, and appear with the best will in the world all ready to help. Remember that they may be interested in future work, but unless there really is something useful they can do, explain that the production staff were chosen some weeks ago, and suggest that perhaps next time they would like to inquire well in advance. Anyone wandering around who has little idea of the fact that every object backstage has a use and a place may out of curiosity pick up a prop or record, and inadvertently put it down in a dressing-room or leave it in the auditorium. This could upset everyone's careful preparation, and should never be allowed to happen.

Check that a small working-light is available in the wings – both sides if necessary, but particularly by a lighting-board and your own shelf or desk. See that such lights are well masked and do not "leak" on to the stage, otherwise a blackout could produce a first-class crisis.

Since you are now working in a public place, and after the next rehearsals will have not only the cast but, with luck, a large audience in the theatre, check that you have a list of emergency numbers ready and on display by the phone. These should include a doctor, the fire hall, and the nearest hospital. Think of any accident on-stage or backstage as being your responsibility with regard to summoning help, while any mishap in the front-of-house area would be the responsibility of the house manager. Though if there is an intercom to the front office, you can co-ordinate your efforts immediately.

Aim to see that the preparations of the designer, carpenter, and electrician are ready for the director to begin the technical rehearsal on schedule. Hard – but try. If there have been delays in the construction of the set, for example, nothing can hurry the process, and it must be structurally sound. The framework of flats, if used, must stand upright, so that walls show no join and support is invisible but sure; doors and windows must open and close as required; and platforms must be safe. Provided everyone is working with a will, time and patience will see the job done.

Check that all props have been brought over to the theatre, and are ready to be placed in position as soon as the set is completed.

When the stage is clear of all equipment, have it swept, and help lay the stage cloth, or carpet, for that part which is an interior scene. Check with the designer about the placing of the furniture, and when he is satisfied have the corner-marks chalked on the floor, so that if anything is moved during the action or changed as part of the scenery, its correct position is there for future performances. The designer will also arrange the drapes and cushions; take careful note of this arrangement, for it will be up to you to repeat the total effect at each performance. Set out the necessary props or ornaments and check any food with an a.s.m. – the breakfast in Scene Five may need the cereal plus the hot coffee for a realistic production. Fortunately Tennessee Williams has so arranged the main meal of the dinner during Jim O'Connor's visit that it is eaten during the lapse of half an hour between Scenes Seven and Eight.

Remember that glass should be taken out of picture frames, and mirrors be lightly soaped. This will avoid their reflection picking up the stage lights and destroying the illusion of reality for the audience. If cigarettes are lit on-stage, as perhaps by Jim in Scene Eight, check that the lighter is in good order or that there are reliable matches; should these be used from a book or box set on-stage see that a few are half-pulled ready for use. This will help a small action flow without unnecessary fumbling.

By now the lights should be mounted, connected to the circuits, and ready to be focussed, waiting for the director and/or lighting expert to rehearse the cues for each change. Very soon the set will come alive, and all of you present will observe one of those exciting moments in theatre, when the model which you first saw weeks ago, and the ground-plan you have used during rehearsal, cease to be mere unidentified measure and dimension, and assume sudden reality through the use of line, color, form, and light.

During the Technical Rehearsal You will find you need to act as liaison between the director and designer sitting in the audience and those working the various changes of cue backstage, because they will be mostly out of sight and probably – with the curtains and the distance – half out of hearing. Give the WARNING and GO signal for each cue, and when the correct volume of thunder, degree of music or light, or speed of curtain has been established, take a minute to mark the timing and level, as necessary, in the prompt copy. When each cue has been set, the director may, if time permits, take a slow run-through followed by a quick one. These will show any difficulties that have yet to be eased, and will develop everyone's ability to think ahead towards the next cue.

If this were a full-scale production of a play involving many changes of scenery, you would be likely to take extra rehearsals on your own with the stage crew only, arranging exactly *who* does *what* and *when*, *where* each piece of scenery and furniture is to be stacked, and the best order for future use. Full changes during an intermission rarely present the worst problems, because reasonable time and good light are available, but those between scenes require the utmost care. Be prepared to practise a change again and again, finally using a stop watch if you wish; for a long wait is bad for the audience, the actors, and the play.

After the Technical Rehearsal Before leaving at the end of the technical rehearsal, see that everything is in good order for the first dress rehearsal to begin. When possible (some theatres are locked at certain times and there's no changing the arrangement), see that props are re-set, that any utensils used for a meal are washed, and that records or tapes are stacked in place, and note if anything which has been broken or damaged requires repair or replacement. Finally, check adjustments to the set – unfinished paintwork, change of drapes, different cushions, another floor lamp – and try to have these alterations made before, rather than after, the dress rehearsal.

Remember that the purpose of the technical rehearsal is to ensure smooth running of all technical requirements for the director, and to have everything in readiness for the actor. The fewer changes that then have to be made, the better chance the cast have of concentrating on, and finally achieving, a better standard of performance. Some changes are unavoidable, but with careful preparation these are more likely to be practical ones linked with the work of the cast than a complete and time-consuming re-arrangement of light or curtain cues. The actress playing Laura, for example, may find the small table by the day-bed too high for her to use easily, and will ask for a lower one; or Amanda may discover that the saucers for the coffee cups are so rounded that she finds it hard to carry a cup and saucer without the sound of a wobble. Actors have to make a big adjustment at the time of the first dress rehearsal: suddenly they are faced with the real set, furniture, props, and costumes and make-up on each other, glaring lights, strange acoustics, and a variety of sensations which eventually help, but can at first break, their concentration.

Reliable stage management can be a wonderfully certain rock in the suddenly different world that now confronts the actor.

Be last out.

DRESS REHEARSALS

A costume parade will be necessary before the first dress rehearsal can begin. Unless the cast is a large one, the parade will probably be held at the beginning of this rehearsal, so be sure everyone realizes this means ready, dressed, and made-up on time. Suggest that the cast will be expected in an hour prior to this, though most, if they are wise, will allow longer.

While the actors are preparing, double-check your own lists, even though some points were re-set after the technical rehearsal; for bulbs can still blow, the tape-recorder can refuse to work, or the "traveller" curtain can reveal a tendency to jam. Go over each point with the a.s.m. concerned, checking furniture, practical doors and windows, platforms, props.

Be sure that all the actors have arrived; it's better to start making phone calls and tracing someone thirty minutes before than three minutes before the curtain is due to go up. There is rarely a real emergency – more often it's, "Sorry, took-a-rest-and-fell-asleep" or "Had-to-eat, and-dinner-wasn't-ready"; but a prod at dress rehearsal may save the same thing happening before performance.

Operate the *call* system – by intercom, a.s.m., or call-boy with a knock on the dressing-room doors – with the "half" as "Half-an-hour, please," the "quarter" as "Fifteen minutes, please," and similarly at the "ten" and "five" marks; finally, "Three minutes, please," and then "Beginners, please." These reminders are more than mere formality, for they help the actor judge how much time he has for the various stages of preparation. See that everyone concerned appears without delay on the last call, and because the curtain should never be delayed by a late actor, advance each call by three minutes.

During this last half hour check the dressing of the set – the drapes, angles of cushions, steps, etc. A chair in an unexpected position, or a change in the angle of the day-bed can "throw" an actor, and as far as possible everything should be as intended by the director and designer, and so as arranged in rehearsals.

Ask the director for a reminder to the cast that once the costume parade is over decisions as to costume are final. There can be no use of a different suit or dress, or even alteration in the color of gloves, stockings, or stoles. This is another obvious point, but it can come as a surprise to find an actress wearing something different on Opening Night simply because she thought it would be nice.

Inform the cast how the rehearsal is expected to run, for people work the better for knowing what is to be expected. With the costume parade first this is likely to be a long session, so find out from the director whether he will give notes between each act, and which of these intervals would make a good coffee-break. Warn everyone to be ready to come on-stage at these times.

While the costume parade is being held, you have the chance of a final check within your own department, for unless the group is very understaffed this parade would rarely be your responsibility. When all else is ready take a moment to glance through the prompt copy, so that you know the order of the opening routine right from the time of the WARNING signal to the seating of the audience and the lowering of the houselights. Then clear the stage, and be sure everyone is ready in position.

While the rehearsal is running, note any mishaps which may be a little rough on the action of the play. The director, in the audience, will catch obvious mistiming of lights, but there may be other hitches: perhaps an a.s.m. has forgotten to warm up the tape-recorder after it was mistakenly turned off, rather than down, and a music cue was late; or the other a.s.m. may have buzzed the front door bell early – he was on the opposite side of the wings to you and because of the movement of the cast on-stage had difficulty in seeing your WARNING sign, was afraid he'd miss the GO sign, and buzzed away. Aim to work out and re-run such points after the rehearsal.

While the director is giving notes, ask him to mention that no one should leave the theatre without a quick check with you. Sometimes there are individual points about costume, make-up, the timing of a move with a light change that has to be altered, and if possible such points are best seen to immediately, not left to the next rehearsal, or just prior to performance.

When all is over, re-set everything just as you did after the technical rehearsal. Tidy the wing-space, and at all times remember a "Thank you" to your staff.

Be last out.

The second dress rehearsal should, like all others, start on time, and it should represent a final run-through without stopping, exactly as in performance, with the director giving notes as necessary at the end.

His job is now over, and the production is your responsibility. He has nothing left to do and can be of little help backstage, since by reason of his own job he has been unable to practise and prepare for any other duties. If the production has built steadily, however, he should feel confidence in your control, and be ready to take his place in the audience during performance. Then he can assess the one sure test of all creative effort – communication.

Performance

BEFORE A PERFORMANCE

Be first in.

Check your plot sheets with the a.s.m.s and check the lighting, music equipment, and so on exactly as in the routine of the dress rehearsals. Check the set, furniture, props, and the arrival of the actors, and operate the call-system.

Expect silence in the wings and quiet in the dressing-rooms, and ask the actors to double-check the props they will use (the glass menagerie, key, cups, paper by typewriter). See that they keep away from the front curtain; it may be fun to discover a peep-hole and count brothers, sisters, husbands, wives, but the odd bulges caused will make an interesting impression on the audience.

Have a time-sheet ready, or be prepared to note the running time of each act and the total for the performance. This can provide a useful check for the director if he feels some parts were quicker or slower than in rehearsal, and wants to know which.

Either tie the prompt copy to your desk, or have it with you everywhere you go. Decide where to keep it between performances, for it should never be lost or mislaid.

Reflect confidence, even though you may not feel it. Should anything serious happen, don't panic, for this affects others, including the actors. Deal with the trouble, if possible quietly, and if you are careful few others need realize there is anything amiss. If, for example, you forget to bring a tape with a certain sound effect, send an a.s.m. home for it while you take over his work; if it doesn't arrive, improvise – you may find unexpected talent for making car noises or sounding like a zoo. If this is impossible, warn the actor concerned and explain what has happened so that if necessary he may adjust the line of dialogue. If you notice the cast or any of your staff getting over-excited, give them something extra to do or double-check (more powder on the make-up won't do any harm) so that the right kind of excitement, which is good, can be used towards concentration on the matter in hand – of presenting a particular play to an audience that is now arriving.

As the final calls are being made, run over in your mind the opening routine, according to your cues used in the technical and dress rehearsals. Usually with "Three minutes, please" there is a WARNING signal to the house manager and auditorium (sometimes a bell, or flicking of the lights). The electrician pre-sets the stage lights for the opening of the play, and then after "Beginners, please" the actors take their places, often followed by the anthem. (Listen for the thumping while the audience is reseated before starting further cues.) There may be introductory music while the houselights are lowered to half, dimming to a blackout. There will be the fade or end of music, a signal for the curtain – it rises, and the play has begun.

DURING A PERFORMANCE

Maintain the habit of thinking ahead. It will make for smooth running, and allow time to avert trouble should it appear. Rely on your instinct here; if you sense someone is liable to miss an entrance, or suddenly guess that the actress playing Amanda has left the street clothes necessary for the opening of Scene Two in her dressing-room when she should have them ready in the wings, send an available a.s.m. or the call-boy at once to check. The intuitive feel for what may go wrong, almost before it occurs, is one of the marks of a good stage manager.

Be ready for any scene changes. Supervise, and help where needed. You will do better to double-check the work of others than to rely on a do-it-yourself campaign.

Remember that the fall of the curtain does not mean the end of that series of cues. During a scene break there is likely to be music to cover the brief interval while an actor changes or props are replaced. During an intermission there will be houselights to raise and lower; never leave an audience forgotten and in the dark.

Be sure the cast is ready for the curtain call. It will have been arranged by the director at the dress rehearsal, but because it has not had regular practice, some actors can forget how soon they will be needed. When the curtain call is taken, signal for the closing before the curtain is fully up, or open, for then it is possible to give it a continuous movement with a good sweep. And when it is finally closed, remember your final cue: HOUSELIGHTS.

AFTER A PERFORMANCE

After each performance *strike* (or clear) the last set and if necessary re-set the first. In *The Glass Menagerie* this would mean replacing new light fixtures for old, taking covers off the chairs and changing some of the props so that once again the atmosphere is ready for the contrast which is created for the arrival of the Gentleman Caller. As after recent rehearsals, see that any table and glassware are washed, and breakages replaced.

If the run of the play extends for more than a few days, arrange for a quick laundry, cleaning, or pressing service for any costumes that become heavily soiled. In a large production this would be the charge of the wardrobe mistress, but even then their return in time would still be your concern, as you are finally responsible for all items used on-stage, or backstage.

If you need another slogan, try: "Never leave anything to chance."

Once again, see that all is tidy, close windows, and turn lights off in the dressing-rooms, and unless there is a janitor lock the stage door. The house manager would do the same in the front-of-house area.

Be last out.

Closing the Production

This process takes more time than the few hours after the closing of the curtain on the final night. So, as with all previous work, request help from the a.s.m.s in advance or you can unwittingly be left holding much to do single-handedly.

Supervise the striking of the set, which will be done by the carpenter and his assistants, and the a.s.m.s if required. As soon as possible have the a.s.m.s collect all hired or borrowed furniture, drapes, rugs, props, costumes, equipment (such as lights, dimmer-board), and music, and arrange for their return. Check any need for the repair or cleaning of these, inform their owners, and let them know when they will be back. If necessary, ask the cast to return their scripts.

Add any new belongings to an inventory for the group – perhaps the girlish frock of a certain period, worn by Amanda, has been donated to the wardrobe. The same might apply to the picture frame of the famous photograph, and someone else might donate the phonograph. See that they are carefully stored, and it won't be many seasons before your group has a useful core of adaptable belongings that may be re-cut or re-painted for use in future productions.

Complete the prompt copy with photos of the set, the cast, and any particular details of costume or make-up; add a program; and return it to the officers of the group. It cannot be used again, for a different director, cast, and designer all working in a different theatre would create the need for an entirely different prompt copy.

It may serve a purpose as a record.

One day it might be of interest in a theatrical museum.

Staff

THE PROMPTER

Like all those concerned with the stage management of a play, the prompter needs one special quality – reliability. There is an art in prompting – similar to that extra sense of the stage manager – of providing a form of mute accompaniment to the dialogue. The function of the prompter is to assist the cast in finding, and maintaining, the dialogue of the writer, and if they have confidence in your ability to sense their needs, confidence in their own work will grow.

Try to attend the first read-throughs of the play to catch the flavor of the production.

Then with pencils handy (never use a pen on a script; there are likely to be many changes) be at the first rehearsals, and take careful record of the cuts as given by the director. Check these, and any changes in the order of scene or of dialogue, with the stage manager. It is important that you both have the same version of the play on record.

Watch for breaks in the dialogue filled by movement, and listen for and mark in any pauses, taking note of their varying length. Remember that your signs should have meaning for others: unless the director has arranged for an understudy, you should remain the prompter for all rehearsals and performances; but if you were sick or detained, someone else should be able to read your hieroglyphics.

The hardest time for the actors is when they put their books down for the first time, and struggle through their lines from memory. You will soon find the kind of help each wants from you: the actor playing Tom might ask for immediate prompts; the actress as Laura may wish more time to find the line for herself. Always point out paraphrasing, for apart from upsetting the proper arrangement of the writer's dialogue, it is hard on the rest of the cast, who rely on the rhythm as well as the sense of the lines to provide their own cues. As rehearsals develop, you will develop a second ear for the sound of the actors' voices, and know almost before it happens when a prompt is likely to be needed.

At first, throw the prompt loud and clear, for until the lines are really familar the actors may need a good, solid nudge. But you will soon be able to form an invisible partnership, whereby you prompt in such a way that the sound is barely audible to the audience and yet an actor can hear it easily and will not come out of character when receiving it.

It is a good habit to keep a pencil in hand and run it a couple of lines ahead of the current dialogue. Then you can keep an occasional eye on the action of the play, and yet if necessary refer to the line for an immediate prompt.

As run-throughs are held, do not interrupt, unless the actors are so far off the script that they are unable to help themselves back on. But keep note of paraphrasing or of difficult passages, and afterwards mention them quietly to the actors in question. The director will usually sense continual mistakes, but if he doesn't, point out the worst passages to him.

Never lose concentration during performance. By then half a syllable from you will probably be enough to help the actor; but should something serious happen and someone start bringing in lines from Act Two when everybody else is still in Act One, be as skilful as you can in following them, and try to throw one firm line which will set the action in the right direction again.

Never lose your script.

A good prompter can contribute a great deal to a production and, with careful preparation during rehearsals, much of the credit for a trouble-free performance is due to the person who occupies a stool on the side of the stage, and who supports the cast through thick and thin.

THE PROP-GIRL

Properties are usually handled by a person labelled "props," and often by a prop "girl" (as opposed to the calling of the actors, which is always handled by a call "boy").

The work of the prop-girl can be done by an a.s.m. for a simple production, and consists of collecting, and being responsible for, all properties used during the action of the play.

Start by reading the play, and attending an early read-through so that you know something of the characters concerned and the sparkling-new or old-and-dowdy qualities needed in the items they are going to handle. Then make a preliminary list, and check it with the stage manager's plot sheet. Do not rely on the list at the back of an acting edition of the play, for this applied only to a particular production and may be used as a guide rather than as a final count.

Watch the blocking rehearsals so that you can record the on-stage and off-stage position and origin of each prop, and then as soon as possible assemble a collection of dummy props for the actors to use in subsequent rehearsals.

Check with the stage manager as to whether it is your responsibility to find all, or only some, of the props. In a historic play many will be made in a special department and designed as part of the production, but in a modern play you may be asked to beg or borrow all of them. It may take you a while to find possible sources of supply, but this is where an inquiry on the notice-board may help. You will soon have a fascinating time unearthing dated telephones from basements, old fringed lamp-shades from attics, and an ancient typewriter from some past playroom. Remember that, as far as the owner is concerned, the most important part of borrowing is the return, so make clear such arrangements in advance.

Know what is required of food on-stage. You may be asked to supply the actual tea and coffee and edible objects, while the a.s.m. arranges and prepares them for each performance. The traditional boar's head, sucking pig, and enormous turkey for a zany banquet would probably be supplied and made of papier-mâché by the design department; but a realistic set of bacon and eggs could be required for a realistic production of a modern play.

Set out the prop-tables on either side of the rehearsal-room stage, so the cast can become accustomed to using the dummy props from the correct source, and check that they are replaced after use – for everyone should think ahead to the next rehearsal, or performance. Then have similar tables ready in the theatre.

Go through hand-props with the wardrobe department, if any. These would include props used as part of costumes, such as gloves, hats, lorgnettes, and spy-glasses.

Keep your plot sheet tidy and up-to-date. Someone else might have to help or take over from you. Keep track of any alterations made during rehearsals, for the director may cut lines or even a whole scene, and this could obviate the necessity for some props, or you may be asked to supply different ones.

Keep a duplicate copy of your plot sheet, and never lose either. You will find satisfaction in the job you are doing as each prop is used at the right time and place, and miraculously returns to you – rather like a boomerang – ready for future checking.

THE ASSISTANT STAGE MANAGER

The assistant stage manager is an indispensable link in the chain of stage management; the job requires someone who can be reliable and punctual, and who enjoys working with others.

Read the play, and find out *what* the stage manager wishes you to do, and *when.* Make out your plot sheets carefully, knowing what furniture you may be asked to help look for, or be responsible for when it arrives.

Always follow through on what is required. Otherwise someone else has to do it, probably at the last minute because it was assumed you would be responsible for it, and this makes what was arranged as an equal load into an unequally heavy one for others.

During rehearsal, think ahead to what will happen in performance, and you will be the better prepared. If it is your assignment to have hot tea or coffee ready for the stage – for Tom, for example, in Scene Five – or china and glassware to be used in a meal, realize the need to wash them afterwards, and perhaps even have them ready in time for a subsequent scene. So have detergent, a towel, and a bowl ready as necessary.

Keep your own supply of pencils, notebooks, and safety pins around you when you move into the theatre. You will be surprised how useful paper clips, thumbtacks, scotch tape, and a staple gun may prove; the stage manager can run out of these essential supplies, and your own cache may be needed in emergencies.

Be prepared for all the theatrical winds that blow. Being an a.s.m. is an excellent way of finding out all that goes into the making of a production. There is much to be learnt from watching and listening to rehearsals and seeing different directors and actors at work. And the more experience you eventually gain about the various departments of theatre, the more you have to contribute to an understanding of the approach and problems of other people's work. Meanwhile you may find yourself doing anything from sweeping the stage, operating the curtain (traditionally done by the carpenter, if there is one), standing by as an emergency dresser for a quick-change in the wings, encouraging nervous actors (keep aspirin handy), handling coffee orders for the entire company – anything from these to taking notes for the director. You will soon find you are involved in essential work among a group of people who are together helping to make of a printed play a living experience for the future audience.

Thus the art of stage management – and it is an art if accomplished unobtrusively and well – is the art of careful, complex organization, in which the work of one person neatly dovetails into that of the next.

To the newcomer to the theatre it may appear to be a routine of constant rechecking, and it is. For nothing is created for public consumption without such exacting work, whether it is a car – which will require a designer, precise blueprints of every part, the making and assembling of each into top condition for its new owner – or the setting up of an organization to create a new magazine – needing decisions as to the choice of articles, layout, printing, and advertising. You may think these cases do not quite parallel the theatre, for while everyone concerned will be hoping to make a good living out of them, your interest in theatre may be as a hobby, so that you are not concerned with the same attitudes. Yet whether you are earning a living at it or doing it as a part-time interest – either hoping it will lead to a career in theatre or for the enjoyment of the contacts you make and the shared excitement of putting on a play – the approach is the same.

There are no short cuts. Whatever the level of production, the jobs still have to be done. No performance of a three-act play which is going to attain any worth-while standard, and therefore be worth doing, can be properly mounted without a director, actors, stage manager, prompter, and a.s.m.s all carrying out their appropriate jobs, any more than an orchestra at any level can play without the conductor and a full complement of instruments. How various groups approach each job is often an individual matter, largely dependent on experience. The stage manager who has a dozen or so shows to his credit may find he can do without his plot sheets, and run it all by memory; and it's fine to bend the rules to your purpose when you know they exist. But since the theatre is a very public art, every show presented should be the expression of the best you can achieve. Then the public, without which we cannot perform, will grow. So use time well, be glad to do good plays, and take all care.

Reading List

Stage Manager's Handbook, by Bert Gruver (Harper).

4. Design

The designer of a play is the architect of an entire world. He provides a setting for the action and a background for the actors which is practical, logical, and evocative. When the curtain rises there is a sense of expectancy, provoking immediate participation from the audience as eyes, thoughts, and feelings fly to the stage, picking out significant points, making sense of them, relating all into an impression; surprise may follow, but readiness awaits.

Ideally our architect also designs the costumes, and has some say in the make-up and total appearance of those who are to people his world, in the lighting which will make it visible, and in the introduction to the public via posters and program cover. The visual elements are then closely related, and the audience will view the production through one vision. In practice, however, it is rare to find someone with the talents and necessary time available, although it is a help if one person can plan both set and costumes. Usually this person has some training or knowledge as an artist, and if someone else should design the costumes, he still contributes his knowledge of dressmaking or tailoring. The first two sections of this chapter are intended as a guide in applying this experience to the needs of the theatre.

Many may be involved in the total process of design, which we will consider under the headings of set, costume, lighting, and make-up, but final decisions should rest in the hands of one person – preferably the set designer, who measures the words and creates the world, then provides the surround in which the characters live. The director in turn has the responsibility of editing the work of all these departments so that he may co-ordinate each effort towards his approach to the play. As mentioned elsewhere, "There may be division of labor, but there must be no division of mind."

Set

The final result of any design depends on the strength and suitability of the original concept, and the ability to plan what is practical according to available material, labor, and conditions. When, for example, Ellen Terry's son, Gordon Craig, prepared the design for *Hamlet* at the Moscow Art Theatre in 1912, he required a series of massive screens for which he tried stone, timber, metal, and cork; because of the shapes, none appeared feasible. Finally the director, Stanislavsky, had to use unpainted canvas on plain wooden frames; unfortunately they were difficult to move, giving the stage-hands much trouble. After the last rehearsal they were re-set in position, ready for opening night, when one swayed and fell, upsetting all the others like a pack of cards. Somehow the damage was mended while the audience was coming in; but the curtain had to be lowered for each scene change, destroying the continuity of action which had been the main purpose of the design.

The result of any planning cannot be fully assessed until the set is actually built, painted, and "dressed," or finished, given its main source of life, which is provided by the lighting, and then viewed from a distance. All of this is hard to estimate from sketches, so they should be followed by a scale model as a first discussion point; for no matter how many ground plans, elevations, and careful sketches are presented, the proof of this theatrical pudding is going to rest in dimensional reality. A model will make it easy for the actor to visualize future conditions, will avoid possible misunderstandings with the director, will be a first step in communication to the many hands who are to help a-building, and will enable everyone to retain the spirit of the original concept.

All the coming research, knowledge of the play, and conditions of the theatre will require a synthesis – a pruning and then arrangement – of the essential. The essence is the important quality – catch that, and let the details follow. Sometimes it will come from the total atmosphere, sometimes from the emphasis of a focal point. Selection is the means, through choice not of what to put in but more often of what to leave out. The aim is to suggest, or reveal the situation, rather than cross the t's and dot the i's with explanation; always leave something for the audience to do.

This world will possess no life of its own. It is an effective use of space whose function is to be ready for the ensuing action. Like music written specially for a ballet, it's chief merit will be as a form of accompaniment, often decorative but saying little if separated from its partner. Sometimes, for example, people hang costume designs which are attractive in themselves instead of other pictures on their walls; unless for a personal association, they rarely hang sketches for a set design, for this is complete only when seen in relation to the play. Unlike a usual picture it must be suitable for a change of action, probably both in time and in place, and be adaptable to the two hours' – and more – traffic of the stage; yet this background must at all times satisfy the eye, and possess a symmetry of line, form, and color. If, allowing for an initial gasp, it continues to attract attention, it is either because the production fails to hold, or because the set dominates, retaining the eye rather than leading it to the action.

The design has to incorporate a dual purpose: to suggest the spirit of the play and, without appearing to do so, to effectively mask the immediate wing and backstage area, and any border and side lights. The whole space could deliberately be left open in a non-set play such as *Our Town*, but it would be important to check that the wings were as much in shadow as possible, and even then those off-stage would need to move only when necessary, since a half-seen actor or prop-girl could detract from the action on-stage. Lights should be carefully focussed so that there would be no spill into the eyes of the audience.

The designer is a mixture of architect, interior decorator, sculptor, painter, master-planner, and collaborator – the last quality being the equal of any other combination of talents. His preparatory work on the play can be divided into four parts: Reading, Discussion, Research, and Result.

PREPARATION

Careful preparation on the part of the designer is of the utmost importance; in collaboration with the director he is about to pre-set the whole tone of the production. Both, however, will adapt; the director, in particular, may vary his views since he will be working with the less predictable and more human material of actors; but once the designer has made his choice of material, he is likely to spend a considerable proportion of the budget, and there will be little to spare – of either time or money – to make allowance for change. It is vital that his decisions are made with as full a knowledge as possible of the needs of the director, the actors, the play, and the theatre.

Reading Read the play as all others should read it, first trying to gain a total impression as a taking-in, rather than any form of a giving-out, process. Read it many times; let it settle and then seep before ideas can be expected to percolate. Sense the theme, plot, atmosphere of the locations, changes in time, the imprint of the people on the places and of the places on the people, and all the action – inner, outer, emotional, physical, and maybe intellectual – which is to be enacted within this future world.

Discussion   Meet the director and hear his approach to the play. Some designers might have tangible ideas at this early time; but, however exciting or good they may be, they will have little value unless geared to the director's requirements. Pin down his concept of the production to date; he may as yet have a general rather than a detailed approach in mind, though in some cases he will indicate exact needs and supply the designer with a required shape for the set. It is often hard to say who contributes most to the final result; and it does not matter, as ideally both pool their resources in this important collaboration. The total design of the production will be an inherent part of the spectacle, and each will help to form and shape the other, until the influence of the two collaborators is completely interwoven. The result of their suggestions and decisions should be so joined that no one is aware that this spectacle has been contrived.

When an acting edition of a play is used, just as the director should avoid repetition of suggested blocking and past interpretation, so the designer should be prepared to plan his own set. All arrangements were probably among the best that could be achieved, as suited to those conditions, and as conceived by that director. Repetition would make void the designer's function, turning him into possibly a good stage carpenter but contributing little that is creative to the production.

Until a director and designer know each other's work, there are bound to be a number of preliminary discussions, probably in the nature of a search and as a preparation for discovery about the play; after which, both will have considerable research to complete before ideas can be considered in concrete terms.

Research   The designer will now need to collect certain facts at many levels, so that, knowing the line which the director hopes to follow and having perhaps his own glint of an idea, he may ensure that the result will be practical, even if some modifications are necessary to make it suitable.

(*a*) *Background.*   Consider the particular history or geography in relation to the play. The house in *The Cherry Orchard*, by Anton

Chekhov, for example, is not just any country house at the turn of the century, but it is a Russian house, indicating a certain type of society and reflecting present, as well as past, owners.

This research could entail some interesting hours in an art gallery, museum, or public library, looking for illustrations, paintings, and photographs of interiors, exteriors, and the countryside. It may be possible to talk to someone who emigrated from Russia at the time, or whose parents might have memories of that kind of house. The eventual design will not necessarily be realistic or reproduce all this in detail, but will be a compound, or synthesis, of what is relevant, reduced perhaps to the simplest possible terms. As suggested for the director in Chapter 2, become immersed in the period, and try to compile a scrapbook of any loose references, for some of these facts would be useful for other plays by the same author, or for others of the same period and setting.

(*b*) *The Play in Detail.* Readings of the play should continue, but now with definite objectives in mind. Related to conditions, what type of setting is likely to be best? How is the director planning to stage the climax, and what shape will be most suited to the action at this moment? How many entrances are needed, which is the more important, and where will it be placed? If there is to be a change of set, how can this be achieved quickly and easily? But if a permanent set is used, are different locations to be indicated? Is the director likely to require certain angles, steps, or elevations?

These practical considerations are of equal importance to any artistic approach to the design. If the play means placing a large cast on a small stage, somehow the area must look large even if it is not. If it means placing a small cast on a large stage, in what is meant to be a confined space, it must look confined even if it is not. If the men are to be seen wearing stovepipe hats, the height of doors and archways should be checked for clearance; if the women's costumes are to include farthingales (Elizabethan) or crinolines (Victorian), then doors must be wide enough for them to pass.

Gradually ideas for the total layout will begin to materialize, sometimes emanating from one focal point which will also crystallize the spirit of the play. In *The Glass Menagerie*, for example, this might stem from emphasis on the large photograph of the father. Consideration of suitable furniture and properties will follow, linked with a total color scheme; and all should be expressed within a certain idiom so that a total unity will always be preserved.

(*c*) *Idiom.* The idiom, or language, of the design should be consistent. If a certain historical period is chosen it should be adhered to, or anachronisms will result; furnishings will often reflect character and circumstance, and the *dressing* of the stage will be carefully chosen, indicating the atmosphere through ornaments, cushions, books, pictures, and all the paraphernalia of living. The stage manager is usually responsible for assembling these items, and so they should be discussed with him in advance.

(*d*) *Type of Setting.* A set has many requirements: it should be light and look solid, or occasionally be solid and look light; it should be easy to move, and look permanent; it should be simple to make, and look intricate; it should be reasonable, and look expensive. All this without any appearance of the thought, time, and effort in either the preparation, construction, or painting. The result should seem inevitable; in a new play, appearing to be a logical outcome of needs; in a well-known classic, expressed in such a way that the audience thinks – "Of course!"

There is the elaborately realistic box-set of painted canvas flats, lashed together and braced to the floor (or, for the quickest changes, sometimes flown wholesale from the flies); it may have a ceiling to match, and it will contain all the trappings of a real room: the dressing, as mentioned above, curtains that draw, and doors and windows that open and close.

The permanent set is more economical: an enormous staircase could be a functional background to *Macbeth*, placed against drapes of a neutral color; cheaper still, it is possible, especially when aided by good lighting, to place a minimum of objects (sometimes cutouts) against this same background and convey a complete world. Place an impressive coat of arms over a high-backed chair, seat an elderly gentleman in black robes and a wig, and you have a court of law. Put a garden bench, real shrubs in tubs – or faked and cut-out ones – on-stage, add some elevation with the suggestion of a terrace, balustrade, and steps down, and Olivia's garden could be ready for many of the scenes in *Twelfth Night*.

Another economical and effective design is the skeletal set, or mere framework of a room, which can be suggested by a wooden outline, or even by wooden supports with ropes in between. The surround is inset within the usual drapes of the stage so that the wings and backstage area are still masked. It is best if these drapes are dark, preferably black, and better still if they are of velvet; then when the lights are focussed into the inset area any spill is absorbed rather than reflected. The result creates a limbo against which the characters, their costumes, and the furniture are picked out with a stereoscopic clarity, the effect presenting a spectacle which can give simple, but added, attraction to the play. Practical doors and windows can be incorporated within this frame, and real or cut-out furniture placed within it. Total illusion is completed by the imagination of the audience.

Such a design requires care in the support, which must be neither flimsy nor visible. The whole construction may be hinged, standing like empty screens; but any additional bracing or wires would have to be hidden. Whatever type of scenery is used, however, must stand firm. Doors that wobble on opening and won't stay shut on closing will attract attention; a window that won't open when it should could alter the whole course of the action; and a picture that is not hanging straight could cause more comment than anything else in the play.

Whatever the world to be created, much can be suggested with almost nothing, provided that the "almost nothing" is significant. If the choice has meaning through an immediate association and conveys the *where*, the *when* and the *what*, then even the minimum of setting can fulfil a proper function.

(*e*) *Conditions: Theatre and Budget.* An essential part of the designer's concern will be with the conditions of performance, and he should know the following facts before he can safely finalize any ideas that are developing about the eventual form of the set:

1. Dimensions of the stage, including acting area, wing space, and width and height of the proscenium opening.

2. Details of building and paint facilities, and general workshop equipment.

3. Labor, experienced or otherwise.

4. Previous material which may be used again.

A major problem will be a careful check of sight-lines, with particular reference to the extreme side and centre seats of the front row, and, where relevant, to the front and back of the balcony. The set should be so angled, and the wings and lights so masked, that the audience can see all that it is intended to see on-stage, and none of what it is not intended to see off-stage. This is known as major masking; minor masking consists of suitable backing for doorways, windows, and fireplaces so that when doors open or curtains are drawn the audience is faced with a continuation of the set, rather than bare wings, walls, and half-lit figures of staff and actors in the background. Where elevation is used, either as platforms on-stage or as risers for the seating of the audience, such height may need accurate measurement, or the tops of heads or of scenery may be cut off.

Watch for any immovable hazards in this particular theatre. They can include radiators on the back wall of the stage; overhead

Set Design: 1. Preliminary Sketch

Note how some features of this original idea were later modified in both the model and the finished set (page 137).

This set was designed by Brian Jackson for Act 11 of *The Pirates of Penzance*, directed by Tyrone Guthrie for the Stratford Festival of Canada, 1961.

and floor pipes in difficult places; or steps cut through the apron down to the orchestral or audience level. Sometimes the floor of the stage is raked, or sloped from back to front, so that the set must be angled at base to compensate, or it will stand crooked, look crooked, and put perspective out of joint. There may be generous wing space on one side, not on the other; and there may, or may not, be a cross-over, or way behind the acting area.

Then the budget, plus all these conditions, will do much to determine results – though, given a strong concept, the initial flavor which the director and designer require will be maintained. The budget will be discussed in collaboration with the producer, and it may cover the total design department, with the allowance divided according to the needs of each section. Sometimes the designer is notified, like everyone else in the production, that the total budget will have to be managed on a shoestring, of which he will only be able to spend just so much. Sometimes an organization can be lavish and the producer will ask each department for an estimate of potential needs; always price this at a little over rather than under the margin; people who stay within the budget are regarded as reliable, and will establish their credit for later productions. There is usually, however, a perpetual challenge in the theatre of adapting to limited circumstances, and producing the required impression takes ingenuity and imagination. The eventual answer to most problems lies in simplicity, which requires clarity of design.

An average estimate for the total design budget is twenty per cent of production costs; and it is a good policy to splash when necessary, and economize when possible.

Result   Now, with luck, some kind of imaginative yeast will begin to rise; and, allowing for alternative ideas, alterations, trial and error, instinct, plus all the above considerations, will tell the designer that a certain result begins to look right and to feel right. After the barest of glances at the program, the audience should find immediate meaning in the result, so that the *where*, the *when*, and the *what* they are seeing can immediately be assimilated, and then left to cultivate the coming action. It may even seem like an activating agent so that all, or part, of the set becomes as important as the protagonists, assuming the proportions of another character. In *The Cherry Orchard* the house – and the orchard – becomes the symbol of a life which a seriously-laughable family wishes to preserve. In *The Glass Menagerie* the set could represent the genteel poverty which is part of the villain of the piece.

CONSTRUCTION

The first results of the designer's ideas will probably be in the form of color sketches for preliminary discussion with the director. These will be followed by a ground plan (or bird's-eye-view of the stage), by elevation, and then by a model which should be to scale, usually a half-inch to the foot. The model should include representative figures of the characters – also to scale – for the design must be suited to the size of the stage, to the proscenium opening which is to frame it, and to the number of people it is to house.

Scale Should this question of scale be overlooked, it could lead to major, and expensive, last-minute changes: each item will appear to be well constructed in the carpenter's shop, and painting will go according to plan; but with all set up on the actual stage, the proportions will be wrong and the reason hard to find. Then there is almost no alternative to starting over again with a different design – since the present one is unlikely ever to look right on that stage – resulting in a crisis which could have been avoided, and which may deprive the actors of enough rehearsals in the proper setting for their characters. Experience can be a tough school.

Modification When the designer takes the scale model to the director, there will almost inevitably be modifications. These can include suggestions as to slight changes of color and layout, and perhaps for a different angle or position for a doorway if more room is needed to clear a group who will often be downstage of this focal point. For meanwhile the director has been working out a preliminary blocking from the ground plan so that he can begin to plan for rehearsals and check that the design will work.

These collaborators then reach agreement so that both can start building: one, the world; the other, the people. The designer now makes working drawings so that the carpenter, his assistants, and the painters may soon go to work.

So the designer begins a further process of collaboration. Sometimes he is a carpenter himself, but if not he would be wise to help where he can, and supervise, rather than intrude, where he can't. He should be able to rely on a carpenter who can construct a full-scale set from his drawings. Assistants, however, are always needed, and it is advisable to spread the work and plan a schedule, thus avoiding too heavy a load falling on to too few willing hands. It is a good idea, if necessary under the carpenter's guidance, to allocate

Set Design: 2. Scale Model   *Photo:* Peter Smith

Set Design: 3. Finished Set   *Photo:* Peter Smith

certain parts of the set to each assistant: some being responsible for the flats; others for the door and window frames; some for special treatment of furniture, perhaps adding top shelves to a cupboard to turn it into a dresser; still more for the construction of special properties. Then, as available, they can turn to painting, finishing, and finally to helping set up on stage prior to the technical rehearsal.

Building   The main unit of scenery is known as a flat, or flat-piece – cotton or canvas, stretched, tacked, and then glued to a wooden frame. The width is usually a stock size of five feet, nine inches, depending on the material, which is sold in bales either thirty-six or seventy-two inches wide (so there is allowance for shrinkage). They are rarely constructed less than twelve inches wide. Height will vary according to the requirements of the theatre and the needs of the designer: in mammoth auditoriums they have been known to reach thirty-six feet; most range from ten to eighteen feet.

The wooden frame is cut preferably from Northern or White Pine, using strips of one-by-two's and one-by-three's. Care must be taken, in assembling, to see that all angles are square. The material is laid on the completed frame, and then treated with glue so that it will shrink, presenting a firm surface for paint. The flats can be joined at the back by hinges or by cleating, and can be further supported by braces angled to the floor, or by jacks and weights.

This flat-piece is immensely adaptable, and within the wooden frame a variety of doors, windows, and archways can be constructed. Carefully handled it is easy to store, and the initial small investment can provide some years of use; the canvas may wear and tear, but a good frame, which must be properly constructed, will wear forever.

It is a help if any part of the scenery which will be most used by the actors can be constructed first, and painted and finished later. Sometimes doorways, platforms, and stairs may be available from past stock, but rehearsal with the near-real things will be as important as rehearsal with practice costumes and dummy properties.

Painting   The flat will require two primers of paint; whiting is a cheap medium, or any mixture of leftovers may be applied. Whatever the coat, however, it will go on the better for being warm. Always mix enough for present needs, with a proportion of special glue which contains size; the paints are powder paints, and, like the size (sometimes called carpenter's glue), can be bought at most hardware stores. The size must be soaked in water, and then cooked, preferably in a form of double boiler. Take every possible precaution that it does not burn; it has a strange smell at the best of times, but should it ever catch, an invasion of skunks would be like perfume in comparison. The final proportion of size to paint varies, and, like the eventual color, should be tested and allowed to dry; add a quarter-teaspoonful of Lysol when the mixture is right, to prevent the paint from going rancid. Too little size and the paint will crumble to powder; too much and it will flake and crack; without any it will never even stay on the flat. Old flats can be re-used by scrubbing them down with water, and then treating them again exactly as above.

FINAL RESULT

Then comes the exciting moment when the designer supervises the setting-up on-stage, from the laying of the stage-cloth (carpet) to final touch-up and painting. If the design has been well conceived, the result will be as the director, the stage manager, and the actors hoped, and the new world will create its own form of expectancy. It is unique, and there will never be another world quite like it, for each designer will interpret the same play in a slightly different way. There it stands, awaiting the light, the costumes, the people who are to use it, the audience who are to view it, and the particular production for which it alone has meaning.

The designer will check all construction for firmness, probably followed by a double-check by the stage manager, and try the sight-lines from extreme seats in the auditorium. He will then arrange the furniture and dressing of the stage, aiming to have everything as ready as possible for the technical rehearsal – which is the deadline for the set department.

The designer will probably want to see, if not participate in, the lighting rehearsal, so that best results are obtained for the play, the actors, and the set, and to watch the costume parade to ensure that the people are consistent with this world, and the world with the people.

The stage manager should now know the exact position of the set, and the position of all objects on-stage. After the dress rehearsal he takes over the responsibility of seeing that the same conditions are repeated at each performance. A carpenter, or someone who can do running repairs, should be on hand during the run since the designer's work, like the director's, is virtually finished before the performance begins.

Then, when the production is over and the set is finally cleared, the stage will return to its own natural void: waiting, then, to contain other worlds suited to all kinds and conditions of society, from kind hearts and coronets to cabbages and kings.

Costume

First appearances count for much; normally it takes time to come to know people, but in the theatre we have at the most two or three hours. In accordance with the role, appearance, therefore, needs an immediate impact, suggesting more about the life, the conditions, and the personality of each character than in chapters of description or weeks of acquaintance. The main problem of the designer is to make the first glance effective and then consistent to all needs of the play. There is no time for puzzlement, or for too much attraction, yet even in the case of a Richard Crookback the result should be pleasing to the eye, or the audience might concentrate on the good characters and tend to ignore the bad.

Costume in the theatre, or in varying proportion in any of the lively arts, is an enlargement, a comment, and a focus on the use of costume in real life. While it is a revelation of personality and may, like hand-writing, disclose other traits sometimes unknown or unheeded by the wearer, it has a further use which distinguishes it from real life. Instead of being an extension of ourselves, it becomes, in the arts, an extension of others – a means of interpretation of the life of a complete, but imaginary, individual. Careful choice, even of one essential part, can tell as much as the selection of one item on the set tells of the history of the room. That wondrous scarf of Alec Guiness in the movie *The Ladykillers*, or the sight of a Malvolio, glorious in cross-gartering, remains with us. The effect of the visual is immediate, and will be retained where much else fades.

Some form of dressing-up is a primitive and integral part of all ceremony, religious and civil, ancient and modern. Shriners wear hats and priests wear vestments, mayors wear chains and judges wear robes, each garment having a special significance, an eternal idea expressed by a symbol, which may have been used through the ages as a torch or link with mankind. These symbols make it permissible for the wearer to perform a ritual for which he might otherwise be thought unhinged, making him free to carry out his office. So it is with the actor, who dons the clothing and assumes the form or symbol of others, also making it permissible, and acceptable, for him to perform – or to act.

The preliminary work of the costume designer is similar to that of the set designer, so we will consider it under the same headings of Reading, Discussion, Research, and Result. The costumes should be regarded as an outcome of the set, and as both are an outcome of the language of the play, they can be regarded as branches of the same tree.

PREPARATION

Reading   Read the play; first, as suggested for others, for a general impression, and then re-read it many times, until it has been digested. Creative ideas can only surface when they are based on factual knowledge of the theatre, on research, and on an instinctive grasp of what the author is about in his expression of theme and his use of character. Sketches will eventually be prepared which will be a first indication of the author's people, so take every chance to become well acquainted; with discussion, and with care, the sketches will bridge the ideas of the director and the actors. When working with a familiar cast the results are often an interesting blend of the actor's own looks and of the character he is to become.

Discussion   As already mentioned in the previous section, the work of a designer is based on collaboration, but in relation to costume a further element is required. Whereas the set designer provides a link between playwright, director, actor, and audience, the costume designer provides a link between the set and the actors, ensuring that the people become the world – so that the audience may see the play through a vision that is consistent.

The costume designer, then, should have discussions with both the director and the set designer, perhaps hearing the general approach and sensing any first indications regarding the set, so that all talent is combined towards the play. Again results, no matter how decorative, would be of little value if they had small reference to the production in hand.

Once the shape of the set is established, the next important decision will be in relation to color, depending on the type, the time, and the place of the setting of the play. Choice of period would help pinpoint impressions when research begins, though it would be important to consider whether the fashions are to be highly of the mode and contemporary with the date, or, as with the majority of people, slipped back a few years, since few can afford the latest that are available. Choice of place could also affect the color since this is influenced by light. *Romeo and Juliet*, for example, could be produced in a Renaissance world; if set in Italy the heat and the colors of the climate would lie ready for use; if the setting were less literal, relating more to a time than to a place, then the scheme might be more sombre and suggestive of tragedy. (But not too much so, as this is a tragedy of youth, and not, like *King Lear*, a tragedy of age.)

An early discussion of the lighting would also be useful as this should preserve and balance the total color; amber mediums, for example, will do much for yellows in the set and in costumes, whereas the same tones would look brownish if lit by blues. There might, however, be a need for those blues if there was to be any fading to a gathering storm or much moonlight, in which case the designers might reconsider their scheme to preserve the intent of the lighting.

All decisions, of course, eventually pivot around the director's approach to the play; if he views *Twelfth Night* with melancholy, then color-scheme and lighting are bound to reflect this flavor; if he sees it for the most part (Shakespeare is too varied to be tied) as a witty and early comedy of manners, the result will be more positive. Comedy, if it is to be gay, must be light, vibrant, seen; tragedy is not always dark but is likely to be heavy in comparison. Visual unity then places the audience in tune with the action.

Research   The costume designer is now faced with detailed and often interesting research of all facts pertaining to the play and to the production, of which finance will be a first consideration.

(*a*) *Budget.*   As already discussed, the budget for costumes is usually divided among the total needs of the design department. Where it may be necessary to make over a number of past costumes, it would be as well to check what is suitable, so that as needs are clarified it will be possible to estimate expenses.

(*b*) *Staff and Equipment.*   Although it is marvellous how an expert dressmaker can be found in the shape of the friend of a friend, and people can appear when needed, it is a help to know something in advance of future cutters, sewers, and finishers. It is safer to think in terms of simple designs which can be used by willing but not always experienced hands, and created with reasonable speed, than to prepare intricate sketches which might be magnificent in detail, but could prove almost out of reach of the labor available.

The staff of the costume department is headed by the designer, who, even if he is unable to tailor and sew, should be able to supervise and be responsible for the schedule and organization, usually aided by a wardrobe mistress who acts as a forewoman of the whole process. Rather as the stage manager helps the director, she will help in the ordering and matching of materials, supervising the handling of the work and checking that what is taken home to be finished is returned on time, so dovetailing this form of assembly line.

Equipment varies enormously, often according to the vintage of the group. A start can be made with a sewing-machine, large table, iron and board, and sinks for washing and dyeing, usually located in somebody's basement. As a wardrobe grows, so it needs housing, preferably in the theatre or near the rehearsal room, with adjoining space for a workroom.

Lists will play an important part in work which is liable to pass through many hands, and there will be no time for misunderstandings. They will be required whether costumes are rented, made, or supplied by the cast. It is always a better investment to make than to rent, though it can be safer to compromise at first by making for the women and renting for the men. When there is a supply to be adapted, there will be more time to think about tailoring; initially it could be difficult to mount a whole production from scratch.

(c) *Background*. Read and research the total surround of the play. Costume is a reflection of a time and a place and should never be regarded as an isolated subject living between the covers of well-illustrated books. It catches the line and complements the color of architecture, furniture, pictures, and hangings. Look at the bulbous legs of Jacobean furniture, then the ornate spindles and high backs of Restoration; note the parallel legs and long waists of the men. Look at the drapery, fuss, and lace round Victorian windows; then note the frills, the bustles, and the whole line of the women – made all the more possible by an invention of a Mr. Singer, marketed in the 1860's.

Go to all possible sources of background – wherever available to the art gallery, museum, libraries (lending and reference, historical and fine arts). Try the public archives, art schools, and technical colleges, and for special details find historians, teachers, and travellers. If the play is set in a cottage in Ireland, find out about the life before thinking about the costumes; if in the southern states, find colored slides, pictures, and articles in the *National Geographic Magazine*. Then facts on costume are ready to be absorbed and, if based on this sense of place or period, can be absorbed accurately.

Note the silhouette of the costume; the outline of the apparently square, squat bodies of the Tudors, the heart-shapes of the Elizabethans, and the elegant droop of the My-Fair-Lady Edwardians. Consider the texture of the fabrics: the opulence of silks, the luxury of satins and velvets, and the no-nonsense broadcloths which became so popular during the Age of Reason. See how color, linked with fabric, turns in and out of fashion catching the mood of a period, of conditions, and of place. Look at the pastels of dimity and cotton, apparently delicate but faded, because dyes could not withstand much washing or sun; and note the difference between the penny-plain and tuppence-colored fashions which usually distinguish rich from poor.

Like the research of the set designer, little of all this may show, but the facts will be there for later if not for present needs, so begin a scrapbook of every possible reference. The result will be a compound, or synthesis, relevant to the characters and the play, ensuring unity of approach and control of effect.

Then comes the need for ingenuity, for few groups can afford to buy suitable materials in exactly the right color. So the costume designer is often faced with a challenge; for example, how to give the impression of power and prestige, without even a nest-egg of past costumes as a base from which to start. Poverty presents fewer problems, but may still reflect the characters' past, or the incongruity of other people's hand-me-downs which may imply a special comment of their own.

The answer lies in the ability to adapt, with the knowledge and imagination which can take the cheapest materials, line them, visualize shading and trim at a distance – and under lights – and bravely plan ahead.

(*d*) *Details of the Play*. Read the play again, and read it many times, until ideally the characters become so familar that meals could be ordered and households arranged. Previous research will fall into place as a pattern gradually emerges, of colors and line according to the set, of the flavor of the play and the taste of the people. Before results can be useful, however, there may be certain requirements to check: the number of scenes and any changes of costume – with special note of a quick-change; obvious needs, indicated in the text – Tschubukov in *The Marriage Proposal* remarks on Lomov's dress clothes and white gloves; some costumes should allow plenty of room for padding – Sir John Falstaff; and others require pockets for containing letters and change. Accessories should be noted – hats, purses, parasols; and then all this information put to the creative part of the designer's work – the interpretation and suggestion of character.

When coming to a play, an audience may hope to see a spectacle, but the real magnet of the theatre is people in action; good costumes can help to create both. Clothes cannot, however, any more than make-up, create a performance, though a good actor always gives life to a costume, instilling the outward form with the spirit of the person.

Result To be effective in the theatre, the result, as we have mentioned, may be based on reality, but is an enlargement and interpretation of reality, rather than use of the real thing itself. Consider those family heirlooms often stored in the attic: Great-aunt's wedding-dress, Granny's ball-gown, Grandpa's morning suit, or the strange taste of Mother's first formal. Apart from their condition, which may be faded and in some cases worn, and the fact that they were bought or made for someone who would hardly be identical with the character in a play, put them on a stage and they will probably lack life. Similarly the display of authentic costumes in a museum rarely seems vital and has little projection, for these clothes were an extension of a real person rather than an interpretation of an imaginary person who, living in an imaginary world, needs to be imaginatively created. Costume in the theatre is not merely to be worn for what it is, but deliberately to be seen for what it shows.

EXECUTION

Costume in the theatre is liable to an amount of movement to which it would rarely be exposed in three hours' traffic of ordinary life. Ophelia's dress may appear to be gossamer, but needs strength to withstand all the twistings and turnings of her madness; the suitor, Lomov, and Natalia, his intended, in *The Marriage Proposal* are bound to be active in their space of thirty minutes; and while Amanda's dresses may look a trifle tight – smaller sizes make you feel younger – for one who is such a fussy mover, they should be doubly secure at the seams.

JOSEPHINE 5'4½"

ACT II

LACE EDGE

CUT SLEEVES

CREAM

YELLOW

TO DANCE

Costume Design: 1. Preliminary Sketch

This costume was designed by Brian Jackson for Josephine (played by Marion Studholme) in *H.M.S. Pinafore*, directed by Tyrone Guthrie for the Stratford Festival of Canada, 1960.

In addition to being practical for the play and wearable for the actor, stage costumes should also be pleasing to the audience, both in action and repose. The material soon to be chosen should light well, look well, and move well – and hang, drape, float, or fly. Emily's wedding dress will be more effective if it looks ethereal to the audience, and feels ethereal to her; Hermione in *The Winter's Tale* will need the appearance of a statue, yet the line must fall well when she moves.

Sketches   The original sketches of the designer's ideas are unlikely to finalize results; there may be many rough outlines and different color-schemes, until, with juggling, the puzzle begins to fit. Dresses will be switched and changed here, hats there; lines emphasized or reduced; colors made to clash or harmonize; until all proportion seems right for the production. Within the main scheme, contrast will be invaluable, just as it is part of the director's work to establish contrast in casting; and in helping the actors to avoid catching another's tone of voice, so their costumes will be designed to ensure that where they sound different, they also look different. This is even more important in plays without sets; though the first scenery lies in the language ("How sweet the moonlight sleeps upon this bank," and that part of Grover's Corners which is described as "on a hill-top – a windy hill-top – lots of sky, lots of cloud – often lots of sun and moon and stars"), the second lies in the costume, supplemented by light. The audience need not be in doubt as to location; a glance should be sufficient to tell which army is preparing for battle there, or in whose parlor these people are sipping tea here.

Trial, error, and experiment will follow, with perhaps many drafts of some costumes, until the result feels right and fits into the whole. Once a basis is conceived, this time of gradual polish can be among the most interesting of the designer's work; it is similar to the process of the actor after he has learnt his lines, and of the director when blocking rehearsals are over: something is at last down, and there is an existence, capable of change but ready to be moulded, adapted, and modified.

Modification   The plans of a costume designer may seem to be like Malvolio's mention of a "very true sonnet – Please one and please all," and some modification of sketches will usually be needed. They should be fully discussed with the director, the set designer, and, because of his eye on expense, the producer, if he is interested;

and they should be checked in relation to the model of the set, grouping of characters, and interpretation of the director's approach.

Alterations should then be settled, agreement reached, and, if possible, the results shown to the actors, of whom some will be more interested than others. Whatever the comments, the designs must now stand, the actors be measured, and the materials ordered. Should there be need for further change, it should again be discussed and checked, for the director's decision must carry the final word.

Taking Stock   Needs should be finally balanced against what is in stock, and it is a better policy to think of building any garment from a ready foundation rather than to start each from scratch. A man's shirt, for example, with long sleeves, frills at neck and cuffs, and a heavily embroidered front, can be built from an ordinary one in good condition. Heavy coats may be made from old ones, with the addition of deep (perhaps fur) trim, more length, and a good lining. Hats will again be simplest if a previous one is used, or at least if a shape is bought from a local dressmakers' supply.

Measuring   It can save time to ask the cast to complete forms for their measurements at home, though to be certain it may be better for the costume designer and/or wardrobe mistress and assistants to do this in person, catching people before or after rehearsal. These details can be filed away as they could be useful in future productions. Ask the girls to wear similar foundation garments to those they will use when in the play; check hair length for the period so that no one has a drastic cut just when the length is needed; and enquire if anyone plans to change their color, as a switch from redhead to blonde might mean changes in the total scheme.

Buying   Buying, based on the size of the budget, will depend on a list made from the costume sketches, with what is on hand subtracted. Sometimes, because of certain discounts, large stores are the most reasonable. If possible, it may be best to contact people in the textile business who are interested in helping the organization. Actual arrangements for ordering should be cleared in advance with the producer or business manager; occasionally hundreds of dollars may be involved, but the responsibility should always be settled, and a system established which simplifies the handling of accounts.

Costume Design:
2. Final Design

Costume Design:
3. Finished Costume
Photo: Peter Smith

So that all garments can be cut with a liberal fullness, it is a good policy to buy plenty and buy cheap, rather than to skimp on expensive materials. Often a mention that this order is for a theatre and for a particular play brings extra interest from the sales staff, and can result in all kinds of windfalls: broken lines, or slightly damaged material at reduced prices. Search for material that will light well and look well at a distance – often not the same as material that looks good close to. Sometimes the dreariest of silks can look lush and opulent when distance and light lend enchantment.

There is one key to success in costuming a play, and that lies deeper than the outward show; for the secret lies in the lining. Costumes that are unlined will look flimsy, be flimsy, and lack any body of their own in action or repose; but a lining will support the cheapest of materials. So be sure to buy an almost equal amount of cotton or bleached or unbleached muslin (depending on whether it is to be washed or dry cleaned) as of the other fabrics, and the result will complement and not detract from the production.

It is often hard to find exactly the right color, price, and texture to cover all the planning intended, and some ideas may have to be changed to fit in with what can be bought. If possible, ask for samples of any doubtful choices so that they can be discussed with the director and set designer.

Watch patterned materials carefully; usually too small a print will look fussy or indeterminate on-stage; it is better to present clear batches of color than to distract with detail.

When the buying is complete, pin swatches of each fabric to the appropriate sketch; this will help in remembering *what* goes *where*, and in arranging *who* deals with it, *when*.

Making The routine of the costume department now depends on the hands available; a few reliables are sometimes better than the many who are said to make work light, since dividing work takes time in itself; it is best to try and create a team which will work well together. Plan a schedule which will spread the load, perhaps on an assembly-line basis, so that the more experienced see to cutting, fitting, and finishing, and the less experienced to the hemming and binding. Arrange deadlines for fittings of costumes from leads to crowd, so that the final deadline of the costume parade will at least come with an expected rush rather than a sudden, last-minute panic. Sometimes the designer or wardrobe mistress prefers to start with the most difficult costume first; it may take more time than others but, once finished, is a hurdle completed, and it will then be easier to see how the schedule can develop.

The test of each garment lies in the cut, and patterns will often have to be made from trial and experiment; those in the fancy dress section of pattern books are not always suitable (though it may be possible to adapt from some), for the line is unlikely to be historically accurate. Experiment, then baste a trial garment from old material, or lining, until the right silhouette is found. When possible, remind the cutter to leave a reasonable amount of material for seams, for these clothes are an investment to be used many times, and will spend their lives being altered to suit different figures, characters, and periods.

Fittings will be a vital part of the schedule, and the first should be held as soon as shoulder and underarm seams are ready; then the waist can be adjusted and, if the right shoes are worn, the hem length decided and the line marked; remind the girls about their foundation garments, as they can make a considerable difference to fit and to length.

The lining should be cut and basted to each piece of material so that seams include both sections, making for a firm result which will also aid later alterations. Fastenings should be large, of the hook-and-eye or snap variety, which can be bought in strips by the yard and machined directly into place; they avoid time with buttons, and particularly buttonholes, on the part of the maker, and fumbling on the part of the wearer. Zip fasteners are more expensive, but may be best for a very quick change; otherwise they can be a hazard; should they catch material or skin, they will cause a moment of decided crisis. Any padding required should be used from the very first fit, and allowance should be made for it in the cutting; always secure it round the back of the neck, over the shoulders, or into the upper garments somewhere, for any parting of the ways might be disastrous. Tights can be ordered from a theatrical supply house, and it is safest to buy white and then use a dye; men should always wear a dance belt underneath.

As fittings progress, remember to check results from a distance; if possible, stand fifteen feet away and ask to have a couple of lights available with the basic colors to be used in the lighting. The designs will be planned with this sense of projection, and their success will depend on this essential effect.

Trimming The trimming of a costume tells the story of the wearer, and should complement the line and any sense of period. Creatively used, it can make a simple costume; it does not have to be lavish and, carefully chosen, it can do much to suggest a tarnished, or aged effect. Aging should first be provided in the deliberate shading of the costume, for which scene paint with size (which won't wash) or a spray-paint (which will) may be used; this process can also give a sense of added texture to cheaper, but lined, materials. Remember that aging would also apply to accessories, and as much in modern as in period dress; some hats, shoes, and gloves are likely to be soiled; appearance may be linked with occupation, and grooming will not be immaculate all the time – not every housewife always wears a clean apron.

Let all that should attract be noticeable; a bold line of braid or one large bow is better than fussy detail; and let all that glitters – glitter; precious stones the size of cough drops may look bewildering elsewhere, but on the stage will tell their story at a glance. Trimming brings the costume to that interesting time when whatever is added, or subtracted, has something definite to say about the character within.

COSTUME PARADE AND DRESS REHEARSALS

The deadline for the costume department is the costume parade, which should be held prior to the first dress rehearsal. The wardrobe mistress and any dressers should be ready with all the emergency equipment of needles, pins, and thread; ideally, if the fittings have gone according to schedule, each actor will know *what* he is wearing *when*, and how to put it on. Costumes should be pressed and ready, and make-up applied before actors dress. In practice, a last rush is nearly always unavoidable; but somehow all costumes must be produced at the parade, or it would be like holding a lighting rehearsal with half the equipment missing.

The wardrobe mistress will take over backstage, while the designer, with the director, checks all costumes from the auditorium as the cast assembles on-stage; the total effect of groups and individuals against the set will be noted. If colors seem different, a change in the lighting might bring back the intended effect; if possible, the costumes should be seen through a quick run of the range of any light changes; one process is a filtering, the other a reflecting, of light, and each is best used when it complements the other.

Note the actors' use of costume during dress rehearsals: their whole posture, sitting and standing, and their walk; all should fit, like the skin inside a glove. The director will have suggested the modes and manners during ordinary rehearsals; but watch that girls, for example, do not cross their legs when sitting in long skirts: (a) it was not done, and (b) it spoils the line of the costume. Watch that the taking on and off of hats is well-managed, and, if necessary, ask for plenty of practice – the same with gloves, and the use of canes and parasols. However good the design and cut of the costume, it is not complete until use becomes second nature.

Check that the wardrobe mistress has arrangements for any laundering, cleaning, and pressing ready for the run. Once the play is on, she will be responsible for maintaining the standard of the costumes; like the stage manager who takes over from the director and set designer, she takes over from the costume designer, who, once the last dress rehearsal is over, virtually retires from the scene. Be ready to help, however, with tidying and storage at the end of the run, and see that any inventory is kept up-to-date.

Attend opening night and, if possible, watch further performances to see the costumes in the wear and tear of character in action. Assess the blend and contrast of color, the use or suggestion of texture, and the total movement against the background of the set. Be alert for comments or for criticism, from actors or from audience; digest, and then put all experience to use for the next time, when there will be a different challenge, requiring further ingenuity, of preparing designs for an entirely different group of characters.

Lighting

The primary purpose of lighting in the theatre is to light the actor. The secondary purpose is to complement the background and atmosphere of the set. The actor performs on a platform so that he may be seen, and the auditorium is darkened so that the audience may sit in shadow, therefore seeing him with a greater brilliance than we see people in ordinary life. Without being obvious, the lighting attempts to reproduce all the effects of natural light – of sun, moon, or even stars – and of the artificial light of candles, oil, gas, or electricity. Occasionally it may be required to supply the fireworks of a thunderstorm, the effect of rippling water, or the appearance of a perfectly ordinary ghost.

Once the actor has been considered, the next requirement is for the audience to sense the atmosphere, which is closely linked with time, place, season, and weather. Day or night, summer or winter, and rain or shine will, in turn, influence the place that the stage is to become, whether it be a blasted heath, a castle at Elsinore, or a country house in spring with a cherry orchard in bloom. As a stage lighted without variation would be stale, flat, and unprofitable to look at, emphasis can be added through the contrast of highlight and shadow. Then eyes are directed, hints taken, and the audience can assimilate both action and atmosphere without being consciously aware of the design. In this sense, stage lighting could be regarded as a form of subliminal advertising; like other departments of theatre, if it is really good it will appear so logical and suitable as to pass unnoticed, except to the discerning. Stage lighting exists, then, not for the sake of the light but always for the sake of the play, and follows the famous saying that "the height of art is to conceal art."

DEVELOPMENT

The approach to lighting has suffered more than one sea-change in the long career of the theatre, for although a comparatively late arrival on the scene, the equipment has already undergone a couple of revolutions, and currently seems in the middle of a third.

There was no need for artificial lighting until theatres were enclosed in the early seventeenth century; with few exceptions, all public performances from the time of the Greeks to just after Shakespeare were given in broad daylight, and indications of evening or night were given by the carrying of lanterns, candles, or torches. Then, for nearly two hundred years, lighting was provided by candles and occasionally, as in the case of the footlights, by oil; both sources gave trouble to the eyes and noses of the audience, and allowed no possibility of dimming either on stage or in the house. The actors could see the audience, and the audience could see each other. (See the illustration on page 22.) By the middle of the eighteenth century, chiefly owing to Garrick, naked candelabra were masked so that the light did not glare direct, and there were attempts both to conceal side lights and to provide greater intensity by the use of reflectors.

While the need for more power was long recognized, it could not be supplied until, with the innovation of gas in the early nineteenth century, the first revolution in stage lighting occurred. As with the next revolution sixty years later, gas was originally used outside theatres, in foyers, and on staircases – finally, as equipment developed, reaching the stage. Gas lighting was first used for a performance in 1817 at the Lyceum Theatre in London (later to become the home of Henry Irving), beating a neighbor, Drury Lane, by a month. Like other contemporary theatres, the Old Vic. (née the Royal Coburg), which was built in 1818, was lit by oil, but gas was installed in all parts of the theatre in 1836.

The power of this new brilliance was exploited to the full and exposed every nook and cranny of the stage. The glare-direct became the glare-reflect; and the audience could barely see the actors among the blaze. The object became light for the sake of light, and mere shadows were left to be supplied by the scene-painter. Soon, however, the pressure could be controlled and came under the care of the prompter, who in one theatre in Paris managed a board of eighty-eight stop-cocks, or valves, which controlled nine hundred and sixty jets requiring twenty-eight miles of gas-piping; by such means intensity could be varied, and even a complete blackout achieved. But progress, as usual, brought its own hazards, and safety measures were lax; fire, always a constant danger, destroyed three hundred and eighty-five theatres within the first seventy-six years of the nineteenth century.

The second revolution was created by the new source of power known as electricity. Again, like gas, it was tried first in the front-of-house sections of the theatre, and soon gave instant light on the stage with far less danger and far greater intensity. Belasco records that it was first used in performance at the Californian Theatre in San Francisco in 1879, and in 1881 it was installed at the new Savoy Theatre in London (which was specially built by D'Oyle Carte for the Gilbert and Sullivan operas). Irving at the Lyceum, however, continued to use gas, and was one of the few to experiment with what Ellen Terry described as its "thick softness." It was found that color could be added to the light by filtering it through cotton or muslin blinds, and some managers undoubtedly created tremendous effects for their Gothic castles, moonlit grottos, and scenes labelled "Boudoir of The Fairy Baneful." But much of this magic was created for its own sake and, except among the better managements, little was done to co-ordinate final results. Meanwhile Irving was creating a minor but important revolution, being the first to establish the custom of dimming the lights in the auditorium while a play was in progress.

Crude as the approach to lighting may seem, however, we should remember that it was only during the end of the last century that first attempts were made to create an ensemble in the theatre. A Swiss designer, Adolphe Appia (1862-1928), saw lighting as a unifying element between actor and set, and was among the few to regard it as an integral part of design.

With electricity providing a safer, more intense and variable source of power, new theories could be put into effect. Parallel with the incandescent lamp, a new form of dimmer control was developed, and the first type to be widely manufactured was the variable rheostat, or wire-resistance dimmer, which still remains in use all over the world. Operation now passed from the hands of the prompter into those of the stage manager, who, until fifty years ago, was also responsible for much of the direction of all that occurred on stage. Even today his responsibilities include running the total performance, and so he may continue to give the cues for each change of light.

The assistant who sets up, connects, and works the equipment should be an electrician with a good knowledge of circuits and supply. To entrust what is often the most expensive and technical of all equipment in a theatre to someone who knows little about maintenance would be unwise; but once a good person has been persuaded to do his first show, he is likely to be fascinated for life. There is a constant challenge to produce different effects with often limited resources, and there is also more than a tinge of satisfaction in sensing the value of timing in the theatre. This occurs in partnership with actor or stage manager, as when completing a cross-fade or mastering a blackout dead on cue, and is usually an inherent part of the "ham" that lies buried deep even in this most technical of all stage technicians.

PERSONNEL

All the lighting equipment in the world is only of value when properly operated by two essential people: the technician, or electrician, and whoever is responsible for the lighting design. His function is to create suitable conditions of light to illuminate the actor and to suggest a proper surround for the world of the play. Sometimes this person is the set designer; sometimes it is an expert brought in to do this one particular job, who will then be known as the lighting designer; sometimes it is the director himself. In opera, ballet, and lavish spectaculars it is customary to call in a lighting designer. There are set designers, however, who consider that lighting is an essential part of their work. In either case, some of the load of the visual side of the production can be lifted from the director's shoulders, and he can concentrate on his work of directing the action of the play. Again it becomes a question of collaboration, but one in which the director must have the final say; so he should be able to suggest what is wanted, discuss results with tact, and know when alterations might be needed. The more experts and assistants involved, the clearer must be the director's concept, and the more able he must be in maintaining communication at every level. He would be wise to know something himself of the apparent mystery of lighting.

EQUIPMENT

The purpose of stage lighting equipment is to control the direction, intensity, and color of light so that the actor may be clearly seen and the background noted under every possible condition of natural and artificial light. At this point, however, it is important to establish that, while the principles of lighting remain the same no matter what type of theatre or arena, installation and equipment vary according to the type of stage available. The following discussion is generally applicable to the conventions of proscenium-arch and end-stage productions. A helpful, detailed account of necessary adaptations to the needs of open, arena, or thrust stages may be found in the last four chapters of the booklet, *Stage Planning 1971*, published by Rank Strand Electric (for addresses, see listing at foot of page 252).

Lights may be divided into two main types, and each should be used in its proper function and in an appropriate position. They are known as *spotlights*, which will pick out, or spot, the actor, and *floodlights*, which will provide general areas of light.

Spotlights The distinguishing feature of a spotlight is that the diameter of the beam can be controlled as to size and, in some cases, as to shape and brightness. One of the main groups of the spotlight family is the ellipsoidal-reflector spotlight, for which various makers have their own terms, such as profile spotlight, or mirror spotlight, or leko (derived from the names of the designers, Levy and Kook). We will refer to this type of spotlight under the generic term of *pattern spotlight*. It has a plano-convex lens and shutters near the lamp, or bulb, which can give a clear-cut rectangle, a triangle, or a circle of light; it can also, by means of mirror-reflectors, project a clear beam with a throw of from twenty to over seventy feet (or one hundred and fifty feet with some types), depending on size and adjustments. The shutters are particularly useful in avoiding spill in an unwanted area such as the top or side of the proscenium arch.

1. Fresnel Spotlight. 1,000w.
2. Bifocal Spotlight. 1,000w.
3. Fresnel Spotlight. 500w.
4. Profile Spotlight. 500w.
5. Junior Spotlight. 250/500w.
6. Floodlight. 200w.
7. Batten (Border Lights).

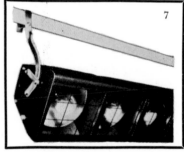

Photos: Strand Century Limited,
a company within the
Rank Organization

The pattern spotlight may also be used for projecting shadows for special effects, such as church windows, crosses, candles, or trees, and the diameter of the beam may be varied by means of an *iris* (adjustable shutter).

The main problem in lighting the actor is to provide him with sufficient intensity in every possible part of the stage, and the hardest place in which to do this is near the front of the stage; lighting from over the proscenium arch will cast the strangest shadows, and footlights – particularly for anyone coming within six feet of them – will cause an opposite distortion. The need, therefore, is for lights which can direct a beam onto this area from the distance of a front-of-house position, and pattern spotlights are made to supply this demand.

Ideally they should be hung at an angle of from thirty-five to forty-five degrees from the horizontal, for which a first balcony is often too low but a second is likely to be better. When these are unavailable, special perches, or pipes, may be fitted and either slung from the ceiling or used as towers from the sides of the auditorium. Although it may seem illogical to hang them from such height, and instinct may suggest it would be preferable to direct them from eye level onto the actor, it would then be found that the beam would spill right to the back and possibly to the sides of the stage, causing strange shadows of actors and furniture. The source of most light in our everyday environment comes from above, for even artificial light is used to reflect downwards, imitating the accustomed direction of sunlight.

There is a further point to apply to the direction of light: it should come from the diagonal, so that both sides of an object – and particularly of an actor's face – are visible; furthermore, shadows can then more easily be eradicated by providing a reverse source of light. Frontal lighting would fade the set and actors back into the one-dimensional glare of the early use of gas and electricity, and would mean that every time someone turned his head or moved to one side, a proportion of him would be lost in his own shadow. We live in an environment, however, in which the sources of light are rarely equal, and so an expert would suggest that pattern spotlights should be directed diagonally, be hung if possible from slightly different heights, and finally be set at different intensities so that there is a careful balance of shadows.

So much for the down, or forestage, acting area. Now we come to a group of spotlights with the advantage of a stepped-lens, which provides a soft edge to the beam while still controlling a certain area of light. These are known everywhere as *fresnels* (after the inventor, Augustin Fresnel, 1788-1827, whose experiments led to the development of lenses still used today in lighthouses). Their beam may be varied by moving the lamp towards, or away from, the lens. In some fresnels the beam angle can be as narrow as seven degrees and as wide as seventy degrees. Because of the soft edge, however, the result will spill and reflect over a wider area than the same opening in a pattern spotlight, unless special masking devices are used.

Fresnels are hung from horizontal pipes (battens) or gas barrels, and from vertical booms (boomerangs) or towers, over and to one side of the stage; they are usually directed diagonally from a first pipe, just behind the top of the proscenium arch, down towards a centre-stage area, and sometimes from a second pipe towards the up-stage area. The second pipe can be valuable since the up-stage area can otherwise be somewhat of a dead spot as far as the actor is concerned, though another form of light, which we shall discuss next, is used to illuminate the set.

Floodlights   The purpose of floodlights is indicated by their name. They are made in varying forms and are used as a secondary form of light to add interest to the set and as an aid to atmosphere. The most familiar are portable *floods*, which can be mounted on a floor stand or clamped to a pipe for additional top light.

Floodlights are now used mostly in strips as *border lights* (battens) and are wired in two, three, or four circuits – several lamps to a circuit, which, as we shall discuss later, may be controlled by a dimmer to allow for flexible shading and for mixing of color. One form of border lights installed in most auditoriums is hung from the last pipe for the specific purpose of flooding the back-drop (back-cloth) or cyclorama, otherwise known as the sky cloth. These have been named *X-rays* (sun-rays, or rear batten) and are an essential part of any lighting equipment, for without light on the cloth there can be no sense of distance necessary for outdoors or sky. To give an even spread, they should be hung four to eight feet away from the cloth and, where light can also be used from ground level, should cover the cloth in the proportions of two thirds flooded by the X-rays and one third flooded by the lower, or *groundrow*, strip-lights.

The next general source of lighting provided by floodlights is perhaps dear to the theatre because it is unique and rarely used in any other medium. Footlights are now also known as strips, but

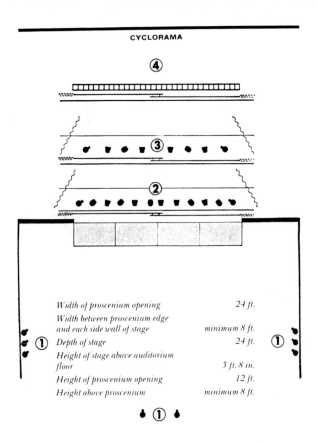

CYCLORAMA

④

③

②

Width of proscenium opening	24 ft.
Width between proscenium edge and each side wall of stage	minimum 8 ft.
Depth of stage	24 ft.
Height of stage above auditorium floor	3 ft. 8 in.
Height of proscenium opening	12 ft.
Height above proscenium	minimum 8 ft.

1. Front-of-house Spotlights
2. No. 1 Lighting Barrel
3. No. 2 Lighting Barrel
4. Cyclorama Lighting Barrel

Profile Spotlight
Fresnel Spotlight
200-watt Floodlight
Batten (Border Lights)

Courtesy: Strand Century Limited

A basic lighting scheme for a proscenium stage

may still be referred to as *floats*, the one term of stage lighting that has been in continuous use since the beginning. These lights were known in Italy by the sixteenth century, and in England by the time of the Restoration, imported by way of France. Originally made of wick threaded through cork which floated in troughs of oil, by the time of Moliere they had evolved into unconcealed candles, later to be hidden behind metal reflectors. They have recently been almost banished from the theatre, since it is reckoned that pattern spotlights are more than adequate to light that down-stage area which was always the concern of the floats. There may be theatres, however, where it is hard to counteract excessive angles of those top-lights, and then the floats, carefully used, can compensate. But they should only be used for this purpose, will rarely need to be brought up to the fullest intensity – or they could create shadows on walls and ceiling – and should be watched that they do not leak too much distracting light onto the proscenium arch.

Floodlights can provide a further source of light for any backing which masks doorways, windows, and arches. This will require an even spread, usually of one or two single floods, which should be used to reflect light bounced, as it were, off another near surface. When such entrances are used by actors, the confined space would provide bad shadows and a strange effect if these floods were directed straight on to the actors.

New Developments The third revolution in stage lighting is currently taking place and is related not to a new source of supply, as in the case of gas and electricity, but to new sources of power and control. These relate to a new type of lamp, and also to electronic developments providing simplification of even the most complex control systems.

Interestingly enough, both these developments have been made feasible largely through new demands of lighting for television. The recent proliferation of studios of various sizes, coupled with the special requirements of color television, have made money available for research and have created a market for new products.

A new type of lamp, for example, is much smaller than the conventional one and is known as the tungsten halogen or, as it was originally called, Q.I. (quartz iodine) lamp. The tungsten halogen lamp can provide higher efficiency and a longer life of up to ten times that of its conventional equivalent, and will provide over eighty per cent full lumen output throughout its life. This benefit is derived from a self-consuming chemical process that regenerates the tungsten which, in the traditional filament, gradually blackens the envelope, or bulb. Some retrofit-type tungsten halogen lamps may be used in present equipment, but they should, because of their expense and certain parameters of operation, be installed only in consultation with a supplier. They fall, for example, into two categories: one of high efficiency and color temperature of 3,200 degrees Kelvin upwards, short life; another of lower efficiency and color temperature of 3,000 degrees Kelvin down, longer life. The former would be used in supplying the higher color temperatures required in television, while the latter is technically and economically more suited to the needs of the theatre. Where there are special needs, however, such as projection and follow-spot apparatus, the former lamp would be used to give every possible lumen in overcoming surrounding light levels.

Control Whatever the lamps used, however, the equipment is brought under control when the electrician connects it to the *control board* (switchboard) in circuits – groups of so many lights not exceeding a certain total current, each group having its own switch. Each circuit also has a safety device, which is usually a resettable circuit-breaker although fuses can still be used. Occasionally, with certain types of electronic equipment, it is necessary to use both circuit-breakers and fuses to provide complete protection against short-circuit and overload. Then each circuit (but not necessarily each light) is linked with one of the most important items in the entire theatre, the dimming equipment – dimmers being used to control the intensity of all lamps by regulating either voltage or current.

The second feature of the current revolution in stage lighting concerns the transition of this equipment from the cumbersome and antique to the ease and mobility afforded by solid-state miniaturization. Among the devices which have given reliable and world-wide use in recent years, for example, is the variable rheostat, or wire-resistance dimmer. This is now giving way to the silicon-controlled rectifier, or Thyristor, in which dimming is achieved by chopping the wave cycle. The result gives greater technical efficiency and allows dimming of the lamp without loss of energy through resistance.

The components of such a board are modular and may be connected in pre-wired sets. If servicing should be required, a manual will help diagnose faults, and immediate repair or replacement of the offending section is guaranteed. A pre-fabricated system can be built into a control desk, which may range from a twenty to an eighty-and-up circuit format. Thus, whether a dimmer module is to suit the needs of a basic school system or the most complex and computerized needs of a large opera house, the actual components remain the same. It is of interest that, where a computer hook-up is available to provide instant recall of any lighting plan once recorded within the system, valuable use could also be made of it within the business section of the theatre. When linked with the box-office, for example, ticket reservations could be processed as quickly and simply as airline reservations.

The remote-control dimmer represents the first advance of the technological age into the theatre. It has come about because of the growing use of directional lighting, in which, for best effect, each light should be controlled by an individual dimmer. Although this aim cannot always be achieved, it has led to a considerable increase in the number of dimmers. But a much smaller board can now control a larger number of lights and can be installed in a convenient position for seeing the stage, which ideally means in a booth at the back of the theatre. The operator can then synchronize all changes with the action much better from his unrestricted viewpoint, and can establish a greater sense of the actual "play" of light. Smaller desks can also be mobile, mounted on wheels and attached to the dimmer board by a special cable resembling those of the life-support systems used by astronauts. A further advantage with the more elaborate boards is a pre-set control; this allows for a "ghost" preparation of a subsequent change of light, while the present settings are held; then one master control operates the change, and the new setting, in turn, is held while the next is pre-selected. By means of electronic grouping facilities, this process can be arranged on some boards to pre-select twenty light changes. A computer or other memory-storage system could provide for hundreds of pre-selected changes.

The majority of theatre groups are unlikely to need or to use some of the more complex pre-set boards, but these controls are being installed in some of the newer high schools and in the large multi-purpose auditoriums which are built for the needs of an entire community. They are, of course, expensive, varying according to need from as much as ten thousand dollars in some high schools to one hundred and fifty thousand dollars in civic auditoriums.

Maintenance The final requirements we need to consider in connection with lighting equipment include:
1. Power supply, especially in the case of new buildings, should always be adequate to fulfil future needs rather than being geared

Control Boards: 1. 20-channel, 2-preset control panel for use with Thyristor dimmers. 2. 40-channel, 3-preset control wing. 3. 240-channel Thyristor installation with automatic memory system at the London Palladium (England).

Photos: Strand Century Limited

to present requirements. To bring in additional heavy cable at a later date would be an expensive business and would add considerably to the cost of new equipment.

2. All facilities should be kept in good condition if efficiency is to be maintained. Inevitably lights generate a certain heat which will collect dust, and all reflectors should be cleaned and checked each season; similarly *pigtails* (cord) and receptacles and hangers should be inspected regularly for wear and tear.

3. It is important to check the *lamps* (bulbs) since all are designed for a different purpose; it is useful to remember that the efficiency of a lamp can drop off by as much as eighty per cent by the end of its rated life. This, however, as stated above, does not apply to the new tungsten halogen lamp, which will maintain at least eighty per cent efficiency to the end of its rated life.

4. Color mediums should also be cleaned, checked, and reordered as needed.

Color　Because the great intensity of the lamps and their reflectors have a bleaching effect on all objects which they strike, color mediums are used in special frames in front of most stage lights; though the real expert could still achieve highlight and shadow and dimension by the most subtle use of dimmers. As will be found in the following section of this chapter, on make-up, the prime object of these color mediums is to replace what the increasing power of all this equipment takes out. The wider the variety of color needed, the more lamps will be required, for it would be hard, if not impossible, to keep changing the color in any one frame during the course of the play.

There is, however, sometimes confusion as to the most suitable colors to use, because most of us think of color in terms of three primaries: red, yellow, and blue. But these are primaries only in relation to pigment. In stage lighting we are concerned not with the subtractive processes of color mixing, but with the additive process, in which the primaries are red, blue, and green. The mediums act as filters so that, if light of each primary color is shone from three different sources onto one area, the resultant color is white. Because the color can be proportioned, this is a more complete white than that produced by a plain, unfiltered lamp.

As stage light is filtered it also loses intensity, for the strong mediums of those red, blue, and green primaries hold back the light waves of other colors; a green medium, for example, allows only green to pass. Allowance can be made for this reduction in intensity by using paler mediums, or pastels, such as pinks, golds, and mid-blues. By this means, a suggestion of "warm" and "cold" spots – or high-light and shadow – can lend to the stage variety and dimension, which can ideally be so acceptable as to pass unnoticed. The colors should be carefully placed in the pattern spotlights and fresnels so that, while providing interest, they are also blended from their different sources to avoid patches of color. These are sometimes called color shadows and can cause an actor's complexion to pass through interesting phases of pink and yellow as he walks across the stage.

The practice of using the primaries in floodlights, especially in the strip-lights of X-rays and floats, is often continued, for they can balance the background where fullest intensity would detract from the needs of the actor. In addition, all three primaries may be mixed to provide other colors by varying the intensity on the appropriate dimmer circuits. So where the fullest range of sky effect is required from night to day, the primaries could be so blended and varied; but if the sky were to remain the same throughout the action, and to suggest broad daylight, the careful mixing of different blues, with perhaps a touch of green among the color mediums, would give the required result – possibly on two circuits, thus releasing a dimmer for another light or set of lights.

Color mediums are sold in sheets of approximately sixty different shades, and are available through stage lighting firms and many theatrical supply houses. They can be ordered by shade number and are made of a durable medium known as Cinemoid, which is a self-extinguishing acetate.

EFFECTS

Lighting effects are specially prepared for a specific illusion and will require more planning than a simple dimming to suggest a sunset, or the highlight and shadow of moonlight. They often need co-ordination with sound effects such as the hiss and roar that can accompany the flames of a major (off-stage) conflagration. Storms on land or sea may not only require clouds and plenteous lightning, but thunder (of metal sheet) and howl of wind (supplied by a wind machine made of stretched canvas wound over a wooden drum.)

Two lighting effects which can be achieved simply and usually without additional equipment are the silhouette and the special magic of soft distance achieved by use of a scrim. The silhouette is created by the use of light behind the form or body to be outlined, and is especially effective for clarity and a sense of distance when used in conjunction with a good sky-cloth.

A scrim is a gauze cloth weighted at the bottom which, when lit from the front only, looks solid and may be painted as part of the set. But when the front lights are dimmed and the stage behind it is illuminated, the effect leads the eye into a pastel of color which can give the other-worldliness of an old diorama.

THE LIGHTING REHEARSAL

The approach to a lighting rehearsal will depend on who is to light the play and at what point he joins the production unit. If it is to be done by a lighting designer, he should be invited to early production and design meetings so that there might be clarification of needs and facilities regarding budget, total color scheme, and director's intentions. Ideally the lighting designer would then, like others, acquire a thorough knowledge of the play, attend some rehearsals to be sure of the growing mood and atmosphere, and become familiar with the major part of the blocking so that he is able to unify setting and action. When the director does the lighting, the preparation will grow as part of the total rehearsal period in collaboration with the stage manager, who will signal each lighting cue, and with the electrician, who will operate each change.

Preparation   Prior to the lighting rehearsal, which can be held as part of the technical rehearsal, a lighting plot should be prepared, indicating trial ideas such as which pattern spotlight, fresnel, and flood would be hung and would shine where, what color mediums might be needed and the approximate intensity required by each source. Since lighting is such a practical matter, an experienced person can save time simply because he knows how to attain results without too much experiment. But, once the main principles are understood, no amount of careful plots and paper plans can actually do the work itself. Neither can they take into account all the comparative influences of reflected light (from set, costumes, and floor cloth) and the vagaries and advantages of equipment. Once requirements are known, there is no better approach than actual practice in a darkened theatre with an assistant available, a good electrician on the board, and a set ready for action.

Arrive armed with certain facts, and see that the electrician, sometimes through the stage manager, has advance notice of particular colors or special needs, such as firelight or shafts of sun or moonlight. Keep in mind the weather, season, and time of day for each scene, and maintain a clear concept of the total atmosphere.

Equally important as plans for a basic scheme are the decisions as to changes of light, which should only be made in relation to logical needs. Sometimes the more equipment there is available, the more tempting it becomes to supplement the action by changing colors and thus modifying the emotional effects which are intended to convey the mood of the characters. But always be guided by what would be appropriate to the needs of the actor and the purpose of the scene. If in doubt, eliminate, or know the answer to "Is that light-change really necessary?" Main indications will lie in the script, and will include definite changes of time, place, and condition as well as direct changes, such as turning a switch on or off, opening or closing curtains, or lighting candles, oil, or gas.

These changes should be discussed with the stage manager, who will automatically mark most of them, with the appropriate WARNING cue, in the prompt copy of the play (see sample WARN and GO for light cue on page 105). Then a cue-sheet will be prepared, every cue for a light-change being numbered, so that to some extent the lighting rehearsal can be planned in relation to the direction, probable color, and total changes of light to be made throughout the play.

Setting of Light The hanging of lights and preparation of the set should be complete before the lighting rehearsal begins, and all concerned should have a copy of the cue-sheet from which they will eventually work.

The first need is to follow the basic purpose of lighting the actor, and each spotlight – pattern or fresnel – should be focussed on the main acting areas and checked on an a.s.m. for visibility, and on the set and background for spill. To avoid eye-strain on the part of the assistant, they should be set at a low intensity until it is time to check for color and final settings; remembering the different heights of the cast, ask the a.s.m. to stand, sit, and walk. It is important to realize that what an audience cannot see it usually finds difficult to hear, and a beam of light must catch a face rather than a costume, for even lip-reading – and certainly facial expression – play a part in the double purpose of making the actor both visible and audible. Allow time for adjustment of beams, changing shutters, or altering an iris.

When focussing is complete, add the color mediums; then, beginning from a blackout, bring up the lights area by area; first the spots and fresnels, then the borders and special floods, to the required intensity. If necessary, add a touch from the footlights, but only to counteract the shadows from any excessive top-light, and remember to test their low intensity on the a.s.m. Develop a memory for color and a sense of the required contrast of light and shade, asking the assistant to move everywhere so that there is a constant check on the acting areas in order of their use and in relation to any changes of light.

Now the basic settings of the dimmers can be noted, providing a mean from which to start all changes. If, as in *Our Town*, a considerable range is needed, from night to day and back to night, it will be well to set the maximum darkness and lightness so that there are extremes within which to work. There may also be certain limits to establish so that, in a tragedy, scenes of comic relief do not provide too marked a contrast or, in a comedy, any serious scenes do not become too dark. Such planning will vary according to different designers and directors and to the needs of the play. It may, for example, be helpful to ask the a.s.m. to bring some of the costumes on stage to make sure that the lighting will complement the total color-scheme, as hoped; for, by their reflection or absorption of light, the costumes can influence the final results. It would save time to experiment with different color-mediums on them now, rather than wait for the dress rehearsals when there will be much else to be done.

Finally the cues for each change should be rehearsed and checked on the cue-sheets. When each setting of the control board has brought the lights to the right intensity, the electrician will need time to note them on his copy of the cue-sheet. In the case where highly sophisticated controls are available, as in some large arts centres and theatre complexes, the cues are recorded in the control equipment's memory system. The human process can still be accurate but will take time, being similar to the working of sound cues as discussed in the technical-rehearsal section of the chapter on the director. An average three-act play could have well over fifty changes to be rehearsed, and these, after focussing, could take three or four hours to set.

Now we return to the real test of a good electrician, for although he usually takes his cues at a signal from the stage manager, he should develop a feeling for the exact moment of the change, whether coming on a word, line, or curtain (and this is always easier when he is able to see the action on stage). The final proof of successful lighting lies not only in making the actor visible and in affecting logical changes, but in the timing of each change so that, for example, twilight darkens the stage ready for mention of it in the action, or a shaft of sunlight from a fresnel comes up as a curtain is drawn, or a pattern spotlight comes up as a switch is turned on. In the latter case, be sure that the "practical" lamp is low-powered, or too much of a contrast will make it difficult to see the actor because of the glare.

When all the cues have been set, allow time for a run-through. At the beginning of the dress rehearsal check special timing – especially the sequence to be used for introductory music, the lowering of houselights, and the opening curtain; or, for the lighting of a lamp, establish the understanding needed between the actor concerned and the electrician – for however carefully worked an effect may be from a technical standpoint, everyone has a slightly different sense of timing.

Always remember that the secondary purpose of lighting in the theatre is to complement the background and atmosphere of the set. The primary purpose is to light the actor.

Make-Up

The custom of going to the theatre is an age-old ceremony. Ceremony is the clothing of an idea, and setting and costume are a literal part of that clothing. Make-up, as an extension of costume, is another part, and together they are an expression of personality.

When a character make-up is used, it still serves the purpose of the original function of disguise (a straight make-up should complement, or embellish), and, by enlarging them, heightens the features to be emphasized. The degree of enlargement originally depended on the size of the theatre and the importance of the character, for the very first form of make-up was the mask. The larger the mask, the stronger the expression and the more dominant the character appeared to the audience. Gradually this was superseded by the painting of the actual face – or natural mask – of the actor through varying the shape of the eyebrows, adding a grisly scar, using friction on the cheeks, or affixing a wig or a beard. With the coming of enclosed theatres, the use of artificial light began to impose the need for the disguise both to look natural and to compensate for a featureless effect. The brighter the lights, the more they rob the face of its own form and color, taking away what they are there to supplement.

The compensation for the power of artificial light, plus the function of clarifying the features, is the purpose of all make-up in the theatre. The principles of painting the face are thus linked with the principles of lighting; they are aids to vision, adding dimension through highlight and shadow, or "warm" spots and "cold" spots. As lighting is a part of setting and costume, so make-up has a natural place in our chapter on design.

There is no mystery about the practice of make-up, and it should be as much a part of the actor's craft as his ability to learn lines for each role. The face being a natural reflection of his total preparation it should be painted by him – how can anyone else know quite what he wishes to convey? In the movies and television, however, the process is usually done by an expert since a more technical knowledge is required. The audience, or camera, is closer, the lights are more intense and come from more unnatural angles, and the make-up must be carefully toned and acquire a neatness and finish that will never show the join of a wig or the retracing of an eyebrow, even under the closest of close-ups. The make-up artist then works in close collaboration with the actor, sensing individual needs and the director's approach to the play.

But it is poor practice always to allow make-up for the stage to be applied by an expert. The rules, such as they are, may be learnt, but cannot be applied, overnight. Guidance is usually available from someone, though what cannot be learnt in person does exist for the most part in books. But the essential part lies in the practice. Even when you are experienced and it all seems easy, it is a good idea to spend a couple of evenings each season on a practice period, either on your own, or if possible with others in your theatre group. This is an excellent way for the beginner to begin, and by passing on your own experience you may have an interesting time finding out just *what* you do, *when*, and *why*.

We will discuss stage make-up under the following headings: conditions, materials, and canvas of the face; and then you will be able to make a preliminary start for yourself.

CONDITIONS

A large theatre will require one scale of performance, projection, and make-up; a small theatre, another; so it is important to be adaptable, and to take the intensity of lighting into account. This comes from artificial sources, and instead of natural top (or sun) light it will flood and spot the actor from front and sides, from directly overhead, and occasionally from the feet. Not only must color and features be replaced in an otherwise bleached mask, but allowance should be made for natural shadows to counterbalance this unnatural effect. These shadows will provide an added depth to what is already a curved surface: each hollow curve of the face having a natural shadow, and each prominence attracting more light, or what is known as highlight.

The color of the light will have some bearing on the materials to be used: an amber light makes the skin look sallow and sick, and would need the compensation of more rouge without orange to restore a healthy effect; a light shade, known as Surprise Pink, is popular for the opposite reason, for this retains the healthy glow without emphasizing the natural yellow in our complexion. Blue, in a moonlight scene, would make heavy rouge and lipstick over a dark foundation eerie and blackish – for red will not reflect blue. In most productions, color in the lights will be carefully mixed, carrying a suggestion of change through the lighter mediums now available, which in turn add their own depth and dimension to the actors and the set. Ask the director or lighting designer if there is to be any predominant shade or intensity, which will also be linked with the color of the set and costumes, since allowance may be needed within each individual's make-up.

So much for the actual conditions on stage. They should be balanced by conditions in the dressing-room, which should always be painted in a light color to reflect light and never be equipped with fluorescent lighting, which has no resemblance to the equipment used on-stage. Naturally the full range of color and light cannot be duplicated, but there are some essentials, which include:

1. A wall-mirror and lights round it, over a table or bench.
2. Two lights just above and on either side of the head so that the working area can be seen and a symmetry established.
3. A firm chair or stool.
4. Washbasin and waste paper basket available.
5. Somewhere, the use of a long mirror at a distance which, coupled with strong lights, will help the actor assess the final result and the blend of make-up with costume and hand props.

MATERIALS

Until approximately a hundred years ago most theatrical make-up was of the powder variety. The colors were blended from pigments which were sometimes poisonous, owing, for example, to the use of a lead base. Although the skin might be cleaned and prepared with a grease such as pomatum, the powders were mixed with water (or plain lick) and some gum, and in spite of final powdering this gum tended to leave a shiny surface. This meant that the surface could crack if applied too heavily, or if overworked under emotional stress, or might simply melt and run under lights that were already hot, if not powerful.

Then sticks of grease paint, made from a special formula of pure fats and with colors free from lead, were introduced. These were far more satisfactory because they were safer, looked and blended with the skin better, and, because of their grease foundation, largely counteracted the trials of perspiration. The original grease-paints to be manufactured on a commercial level were invented by a Wagnerian opera singer, Ludwig Leichner, and have been marketed on a world-wide basis since 1873.

The first grease paints were sold in tubes and tins, but make-up is now available in other forms. They include a pre-mixed liquid make-up which is applied with a sponge, and even a return to a greaseless, solid variety that is mixed with water.

We will discuss the use of the Leichner sticks since, while there are many other good makes, these remain the best-known, are certain in quality, adaptable, and those most commonly used.

The basic equipment is inexpensive and any initial outlay depends on how elaborate you wish to be. As with any new activity, it is best to start with the essentials and then, like a golfer graduating to different irons, acquire more as your needs develop. A good beginning could be made with the following:

Standard Size Stick, Form C – #2 (Pinkish) or #2½; #5 (Ivory-yellow) and #9 (Brown-red).

Form G, liners – #22 (White), #25 (Lake), #28 (Brown), #42 (Black), #326 (Dark blue).

Form G, Carmine – #1, #2, #3.

One light, one dark tin of blending powder (or many people prefer Johnson's Baby Powder, which allows the full variation of shade and color to come through).

"Spot-lite" eyebrow pencils – one black, one brown.

For women, one bottle of black Liquid Cream Mascara.

For men, one foot of crepe hair in a suitable color and a bottle of spirit gum or a tube of latex.

With an investment of approximately \$15-\$20, you will still have allowance for cold cream and for further colors which you will eventually need; most of this supply will last well over a couple of seasons, and it will never need replenishing all at once.

Other requirements include: a good mirror and lights, as previously mentioned; some cotton batting and facial tissues; towel, soap and water, orange sticks, wooden matches, or paint brushes for lines and finish; hair brush and comb; and some newspaper on which to lay out the paints and powder. Now you are ready to begin working on your canvas.

CANVAS OF THE FACE

Straight Make-up 1. Always start by greasing the face with cold cream – not too thickly, enough for a light smear, and then a good wipe. Do not leave any residue for this is only a preparation and not a foundation.

2. Now apply the foundation, Standard Stick #5 for both men and women – three or four liberal strokes each on forehead, both cheeks, nose, and chin, and a touch on the neck. Smooth this well in, and smooth it evenly – into your hairline (women often wear a band to keep the hair clean), and taper it into your neck and round to the ears. Be sure it is evenly distributed around eyes and nose; there should be no "mask" or dead ending anywhere, but rather a natural blend into the rest of the skin. The result will be a strange yellow, but now the canvas is ready for the first indication of the role: a blending of a basic color, or complexion.

3. Men now use #9 or, for a particularly healthy character, #15; women, #1½ for the delicate, or up to #3 and a touch of #9 for the ruddy. The result will be startling at first, but if you remember that you are putting back what the lights take out there will be some judgment of the final effect. There can be no exact definition of what to use since everyone starts with a different complexion, and will adapt slightly different means to attain the same result. Smooth well in as before – eyes, nose, etc. – and then stand back to judge at a distance, and to compare or contrast with others in the cast.

4. When satisfied with the color and blend, work down through the features, to avoid later smudging, starting at the eyes and on through the cheeks and lips. For a straight make-up the eyebrows will follow their natural color, but should be strengthened if they are somewhat light, using a brown or black pencil as suitable.

MIDDLE-AGED WOMAN

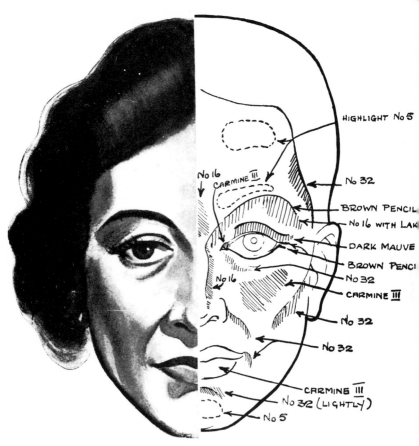

HIGHLIGHT No 5

No 16

CARMINE III

No 32

BROWN PENCIL

No 16 WITH LAK

DARK MAUVE

BROWN PENCI

No 32

CARMINE III

No 32

No 32

No 16

CARMINE III

No 32 (LIGHTLY)

No 5

You are dealing with a mature face, still essentially young. Ageing should not be overdone, the complexion remains warm and alive.

FOUNDATION Use Greasepaint Standard Stick or Spot-Lite Klear make-up in tubes. Select shade from list on page 4.

SHADING Use No. 32 Dark Grey as indicated, also No. 16 and No. 16 mixed with No. 25 Lake, creating subtle pools of shading accentuated by highlights.

HIGHLIGHTS Use No. 1½ or No. 5.

EYES Define clearly with sharp lines along lashes. Eyeshadow should harmonise with colour of eyes and extend slightly upwards and outwards. A touch of Lake will give a tired effect. Apply Mascara to your lashes. Use Heating Cosmetic for glamour.

LIPS Use Carmine according to type, outline sharply following natural line.

POWDER with Blending Powder firmly over make-up, using Rose or Neutral shade. Brush off surplus and then apply a slightly warmer tone of Finishing Powder (Apricot-Peach or Brownish).

Apply Liquid Make-up to neck, arms, and hands.

Courtesy: Leichner of London

LEICHNER MAKE-UP CHART No. 5

ELDERLY LADY

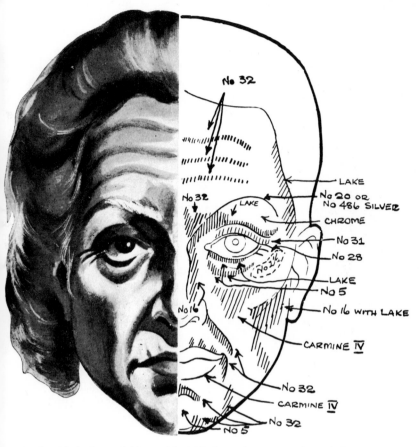

No 32

No 32

LAKE

No 32

LAKE

No 20 OR
No 486 SILVER

CHROME

No 31

No 28

LAKE
No 5

No 16

No 16 WITH LAKE

CARMINE IV

No 32

CARMINE IV

No 32

No 5

In the elderly face wrinkles and facial hollows deepen, muscles and tissues sag, and the skin looks sallow, frequently very delicate.

FOUNDATION Use Greasepaint Standard Stick or Spot-Lite Klear make-up in tubes. Select sallow or pastel shades according to type.

SHADING to be soft pools smoothed out, and accentuated by a sharp line of Lake or Dark Grey at deepest part of shadow. Use mostly No. 25 Lake and No. 32 Dark Grey.

HIGHLIGHTS can be accentuated. using No. 1½ or No. 5.

EYES define clearly with sharp lines along lashes using No. 25 Lake or No. 32 Dark Grey. For eyeshadows use Mauve, Purple or Lake, or No. 31 Light Grey. For eyebrows No. 486 Silver or No. 22 White Liner.

LIPS Use Carmine IV lightly.

POWDER with Rose Blending Powder firmly over make-up brush off surplus.

HAIR Grey or White Hair Powder. Also No. 486 Silver Cosmetic for silver streak.

Don't forget neck, arms, and hands.

Courtesy: Leichner of London

Rather than following the natural horizontal line, a better effect can be gained by gently tracing in with light strokes the actual growth of the hairs, so reinforcing the brows. Now practice begins to count, for the brows must be symmetrical and neat, and a sense of control will gradually develop. Having brought back the eyebrows, as it were, into focus, the next step is to enlarge the eyes. This can be done by adding a careful band of white (Liner #22) with brush or orange stick underneath, and a triangle of white at the outer corners, literally increasing the whites of the eyes; gently underscore with a thin shadow of lake, so using a small highlight and natural shadow which many people have just under the eyes, and outline the corners with an arrow of lake. Add some shadow to the lid (#326 Dark Blue liner if it suits), a touch if you like, of Carmine #1 to the inner corner of the eye (it is said to add sparkle, or accent, to that little pink blob), and a start has been made.

The nose will look after itself unless you wish to narrow a broad one. In that case, shade off the wide base on either side with a touch of lake (the color that resembles the deepest, or shadiest, shade of our otherwise pinkish skins) and then highlight the resultant higher point, or central ridge, with a brush of pinkish white #1½, or #5 in an intimate theatre where the lights are not very powerful.

Add a suitable amount of rouge to the cheeks, being sure it has the symmetry of an equal amount on each side. Men will need the barest touch, boys a little more. It is a good idea always to blend this from a central spot, out; some say from a central triangle, out.

The color and shape of the lips will depend on the type and age of the character: the younger you are, the lighter the Carmine; the older, the more blue is added, so then use Carmine #3. Some people like to use a brush to gain a clear, controlled line, others can do it directly from the stick. Again, symmetry and neatness are all-important. If you have used the foundation and basic color on the lips, they help provide a smooth base on which to edge the required outline. The color should match the rouge – some people use identical Carmine for lips and cheeks. Men, of couse, will not need lipstick – just a firm application of #9 with a clear outline. On a basic make-up there is nothing further to add before powdering, which will give a finished, mat appearance and help soak up any perspiration. Always re-check whether more powder is needed by intermission: some people stay "mat" right through a performance; others appear to drink it up and need an extra dusting.

5. Any whiskering, such as beards, moustaches, and sideburns should be added after powdering. But before powdering tone in some dark brown (or dark blue if likely to be a very stubbly individual) towards the area; this will avoid a sudden, unnatural line, which looks especially hard on a young face. Apply cold cream and gently wipe away some of the color and grease already on, to give a firm foundation and clear surface for the spirit gum to grip. Cut the strip of crepe hair (mohair is better, though more expensive, if you can get it) and straighten its natural frizz by damping it carefully with a sponge. Thin it, leaving a fair allowance for trimming when on, and shape it, remembering that it builds from under the chin and is not a hard line of frizz. Then, with the whiskers laid aside, apply spirit gum or latex to the surface of the face. Place the hair carefully on it, and as you begin to mould it into the fashion required, apply the firmest possible pressure with a clean hand, preferably armed with a damp cloth or sponge, and maintain this for a good sixty seconds. Check that it feels firm, and then trim or thin as need be, adding a final shape with the scissors.

6. Some women touch up the eyelashes with mascara after powdering, and this is sufficient for a small theatre. False lashes are best for anything large. They are more expensive but very luxuriant, come with their own adhesive, and can be used again and again.

7. Remember that hair-style plays a part in the framing and final finish of the make-up. Everyday aids such as sprays, perms, and rinses now give such control that wigs are less worn than previously; toupés often give a necessary touch for men, and women use a false "switch" for added length and padding. It's as well to consider any need for a longer or shorter style during the rehearsal period.

8. Make-up can be removed by plain soap and water, by cold cream, or liquid mineral oil; the process demands plenty of facial tissue or towelling, and should be followed by a good wipe and wash. Men will find it helpful to treat areas covered by whisker with an application of rubbing alcohol to ease the spirit gum; then grasp the hair firmly and, as in taking adhesive tape from the skin, give one firm pull.

Character Make-up The subject of character make-up, or an adaptation of your own appearance to reflect, for example, a different

LEICHNER MAKE-UP CHART No. 4

MIDDLE-AGED MAN

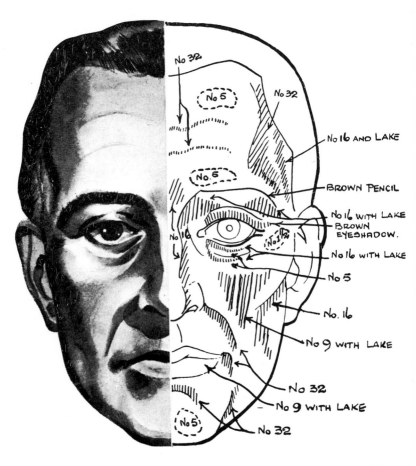

You are dealing with a more mature face, firm, and essentially young with a normally healthy complexion.

FOUNDATION Use Greasepaint Standard Stick or Spot-Lite Klear make-up in tubes (select shade from list on page 3).

SHADING Use No. 16, or No. 16 mixed with No. 25 Lake, and No. 32 as indicated, creating pools of shading, not hard lines.

HIGHLIGHTS Using No. 1½ or No. 5.

EYES Define clearly with sharp lines along lashes. For eyelids use Brown, the addition of No. 25 Lake or No. 32 Dark Grey creates tired effect.

LIPS Use No. 9 with No. 25 Lake, or Carmine III. Don't overdo.

POWDER with Rose Blending Powder firmly over make-up, brush off surplus.

HAIR No. 486 Silver Cosmetic on hair at temples adds a subtle touch of ageing.

Courtesy: Leichner of London

LEICHNER MAKE-UP CHART No. 6

ELDERLY MAN

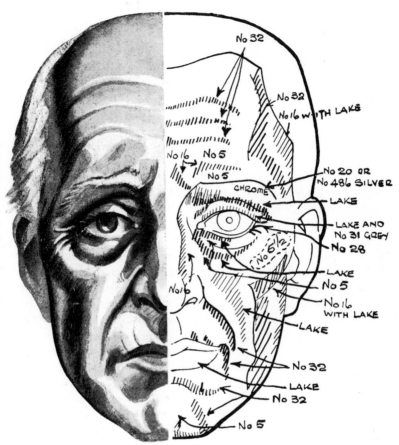

In the elderly face wrinkles and facial hollows deepen, muscles and tissues sag, and the skin looks sallow, frequently very delicate.

FOUNDATION Use Greasepaint Standard Stick or Spot-Lite Klear make-up in tubes. Select sallow or pastel shades according to type.

SHADING This should be sharp with a thin line drawn at the deepest part of the shadows. Use mostly Nos. 25 and 32.

HIGHLIGHTS To be pronounced, using No. 5.

EYES Define clearly with sharp lines along the lashes using No. 25 or No. 32. For eyeshadow use No. 25 with No. 16 or No. 32. White, Dark Grey, or No. 486 Silver Cosmetic should be applied to eyelashes.

LIPS Very careful use of No. 9 with No. 25.

POWDER Apply Rose Blending Powder firmly over make-up, brush off surplus

HAIR White or Grey hair powder, or No. 486 Silver Cosmetic.
Remember to make-up hands and neck.

Courtesy: Leichner of London

personality, or the process of ageing, would take a chapter in itself to discuss in any detail. But basic principles are a guide to first practice.

Character is told in the face by the habitual pull of muscles on the bone structure; if this is to be usefully adapted, then an important rule becomes: Know thyself. Look at, touch, and sense the concave and convex surfaces beneath the skin, until you almost have a feel of the bare bones; just as an artist studies the anatomy of the whole body, so should an actor know the anatomy of the face. Then try and experiment with a further rule, that every natural shadow (deepened with lake) has its own highlight (using #20 as a contrast). Learn to visualize the grotesque near-to effect with the finish of powder and then lights, and results will come with practice and control of the medium.

The eyes can be changed in setting, width, and size. Bring in the brows, shade near the bridge of the nose, and you have a narrow effect; take out the brows (using a firm amount of that original #5 and base color), then reshape to a surprised, half-moon curve, with little shadow in the surrounding hollows or setting, and a different personality emerges. Assess the lines on the forehead; the intense and worried person may have deeply etched "tramlines"; find any of your own, apply a gentle line of lake with orange stick or sharpened match, smooth in with a finger without smearing, add the resultant highlight of the now more prominent fold above, smooth again, and the forehead tells its story. For better control, think of lines as the shadows they are, and use a camel-hair paint brush with a good body thinned down to a fine point, applying the lake with this from the liner, and then smoothing out with a dry brush rather than the finger. Similarly, find any trace of five o'clock shadows, or bulges under the eyes, or the rise and fall of a few double chins, and deepen the shadows and strengthen the highlights. Always use the fingers, or brushes, to apply the colors rather than taking the greasepaint, or liner, straight to the skin as this can make for a clumsy result.

Then round out or hollow the cheeks as necessary, and apply the same principles to the nose: foreshortening, for example, by shading the top of the bridge, then adding a snub effect with a highlight on the tip. The mouth can become wider, fuller, straighter, or smaller, and the chin prominent (highlight the jawline, shade just above) or receding; but consider every feature in relation to the whole. The surface of the canvas must be as consistent as the interpretation of a role.

Naturally, aging depends on your own present age, but wonders can be done either way. To become older a lighter base will be needed, and the process must again be consistent, with the careful suggestion of the shrinking of skin upon bone, carried right through to the neck and the hands. Use less rouge and lipstick, avoid eye shadow and let the eyes stand "in" rather than "out" – the setting will change more than the eyes themselves. There is no one way to become old or young since it varies with each character as it does with each person, and age is largely a reflection of attitude.

Remember that make-up is a complement to acting – an aid and not an end in itself. Ideally every role portrays a different person, each growing from within and to some degree inhabiting the actor's face. Make-up should reflect and suggest the inward attitudes and outward behavior, rather than sketch an imprint on bare canvas. It should not assume a fixed expression, or the face would become immobile and distorted, but should be a mirror of the manner in which this person uses his muscles, and therefore of his way of expressing himself. Aim for a neat finish, in keeping with the character, and use economy of means. Clear suggestion is better than caricature, and will be noted and filled in by the audience.

Make-up was originally a mask to show the features. Painting the face now combines this purpose with compensation for powerful lighting; like costume, it is an extension of personality. Costume within a proper setting is an integral part of ceremony. Ceremony is the clothing of an idea. The clothing of an idea is theatre. And theatre is about people.

Reading List

SET

Scenery for the Theatre, by Harold Burris-Meyer and Edward C. Cole (Little, Brown).
Stage Scenery – Its Construction and Rigging, by A. S. Gillette (Harper).
Proscenium and Sight-lines, by Richard Southern (Faber & Faber).
Stagecraft and Scene Design, by Herbert Philippi (Houghton, Mifflin).
Designing for the Stage, by Doris Zinkeisen (Studio).
Designing and Painting Scenery for the Theatre, by Harald Melvill (Rockliff).
Complete Guide to Amateur Dramatics, by Harald Melvill (Rockliff).
Amateur Theatrecraft, by Percy Corry (Pitman).

COSTUME

Costuming for the Theatre, by Josephine Pasterak (Crown).
Making Stage Costumes for Amateurs, by A. V. White (Routledge & Kegan Paul).

Historic Costumes for the Stage, by Lucy Barton (A. & C. Black).

The following would be among the many useful as reference books:
Drama, the Costume and Decor, by James Laver (Studio).
Five Centuries of American Costume, by R. Turner Wilcox (Scribner).
Handbook of English Medieval Costumes,
Handbook of English Costume in the Sixteenth Century,
Handbook of English Costume in the Seventeenth Century, all three by C. Willett and Phyllis Cunnington (Faber).
English Women's Clothing in the Nineteenth Century and
English Women's Clothing in the Present Century, by C. W. Cunnington (Faber).
Masterpieces of Women's Costumes of the 18th and 19th Centuries, by Aline Bernstein (Crown).
Costumes of the Western World, edited by James Laver (6 vol.) (Harper).
Costume and Fashion, by Herbert Norris (6 vol.) (Dent).
Accessories of Dress, by Katherine Lester and Bess Oerk (Manual Arts).
Mode in Hats and Headdresses, by R. Turner Wilcox (Scribner).
Corsets and Crinolines, by Nora Waugh (Batsford).
A History of Everyday Things in Ancient Greece,
A History of Everyday Life in Roman and Anglo-Saxon Times,
A History of Everyday Things in England (Vols. I – IV, 1066-1914), all three by Marjorie & C. H. B. Quennell (Batsford).

MAKE-UP

Practical Make-up for the Stage, by T. W. Bamford (Pitman).
Stage Make-up, by Richard Corson (Appleton-Century-Crofts).
Magic of Make-up, by Harald Melvill (Rockliff).

LIGHTING

Stage Lighting, by Frederick Bentham (Pitman).
Lighting the Stage, by Percy Corry (Pitman).
Stage Lighting, by Geoffrey Ost (Herbert Jenkins).

Theatrical Make-up, by Richard Blore, a one-hour tape with accompanying diagrams, is available on loan from Malabar, Toronto, in Canada and agents of Leichner, London, elsewhere.

5. Production

The Producer

The producer is to a play what a publisher is to a book; they bring into being, manage, and then make known their offering to the public. In the theatre, as the director is the artistic partner, so the producer is the business partner in the building of a production.

Any outline of his work should be related to the organization and experience of each theatre group since it will vary according to needs and capability, and according to different productions of the same play. Ideally an established group works on oiled wheels and the producer is a clear-desk executive who makes the early decisions, sometimes in collaboration with others, regarding budget, deadlines, equipment, and personnel; who allocates the work, appears occasionally to check that it is completed, and, from material supplied, makes out a business report at the closing of a production.

In practice, however, and especially where concerned with a new group, the producer is an able businessman, a marvellous watchdog, an ideal chairman (who knows *what* needs to be done, *when*, and *by whom* before a meeting starts), and a diplomat with whom people enjoy working – so that they will even return for more. While the director is creating a team of actors, the producer is building a parallel team of people in wardrobe, carpenter's shop, publicity, and box office, each under its own head. Co-ordination and supply for all this activity is the basis of the producer's work; his function is to take such management off the director's shoulders so that he may concentrate entirely on the artistic approach to the production.

SELECTION OF STAFF

It is possible for a director to be, as it were, an itinerant fly-by-night of a casual laborer; since actors, while individually special, are basically the same everywhere, a director can move to groups and communities with more or less hazard according to his talents. But a producer is less likely to be transient, for he has to be an expert in local conditions, and these can vary enormously. It is best if

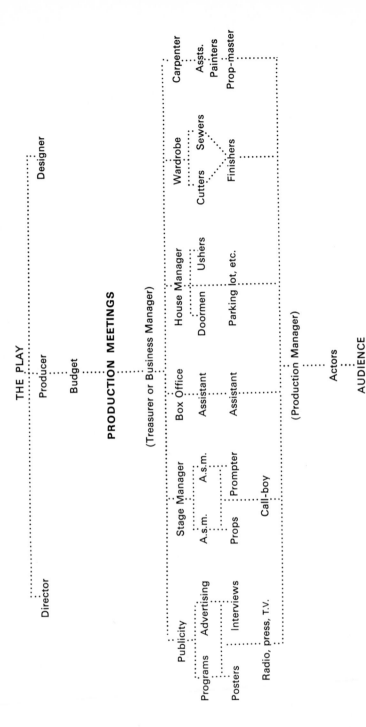

THE PLAY

Director

Producer

Designer

Budget

PRODUCTION MEETINGS

(Treasurer or Business Manager)

Publicity

Stage Manager

Box Office

House Manager

Wardrobe

Carpenter

Programs

Advertising

A.s.m.

A.s.m.

Assistant

Doormen

Ushers

Cutters

Sewers

Assts.
Painters

Posters

Interviews

Props

Prompter

Assistant

Parking lot, etc.

Finishers

Prop-master

Radio, press, T.V.

Call-boy

(Production Manager)

Actors

AUDIENCE

the partnership between producer and director continues through most of a season, and it may even continue for many years, for it takes more than a few productions to meld a composite team. Both are usually selected by officers, or a committee, of the theatre group, though who is chosen or comes first is like sorting the order of the chicken and the egg, and does not matter so long as their ability to collaborate, based on agreement of approach, is established. Then the producer helps, if necessary, suggest the names of available designers and generally places the director in the picture of the group.

The diagram opposite will list and help clarify the personnel soon to be required, at least in a large organization and for a heavy production – that is, one for a theatre seating approximately 600 or over and a play with a cast of more than a dozen, involving changes of costume and having elaborate sets; in smaller organizations and for lighter productions, the personnel will be scaled according to need and availability. In all cases, however, the producer should be prepared to nominate the head of each department, and to suggest suitable assistants.

The main work of the heads of the departments is covered in other chapters. The title of the treasurer or business manager has been bracketed not because it is unimportant, but because, where an organization is young, the accounts should in any case be personally checked by the producer. When creating a system where so many others are involved, it can save time to do a known part for yourself. But, as the number of productions increases each season, so the treasurer becomes a Very Important Person.

Similarly the production manager has been bracketed; this work is sometimes labelled *producer's assistant* or occasionally *production secretary*. The title is unimportant, but the position arises as the work grows and the organization becomes more complex. The producer must continually think ahead, and it becomes essential to find someone to follow up routine matters – preferably a person who keeps up to date with the progress of all, and who can be contacted at any time with such desperate enquiries as: Is there a phone backstage in the theatre? Has the price of Theatre Night seats been decided yet? and Where is the tape-recorder usually rented?

It is advisable at first to keep the number of staff to a known nucleus of reliables, who will know something of what is wanted, rather than retain an army of high-sounding titles (*dramatic adviser, costume co-ordinator*) whose existence suggests more sound than action and whose work should already be covered by someone else.

RIGHTS AND ROYALTIES

Before the choice of play can be made final, and before too much time is spent and expense contemplated on a particular play, there is an immediate *must* in every producer's diary. When a play has been published for less than fifty years, inquiry should be made of either the publisher or the author's agent as noted in the printed edition about two points: (a) availability of performing rights, and (b) the price of royalties for the first and subsequent performances – sometimes an inclusive fee for the run, or sometimes arranged on a sliding scale which diminishes after the first one or two performances.

It is essential to establish that rights are available before a production begins. They are a form of licence which must be held before a performance of the play can legally be given, and are occasionally withdrawn in a certain area because, for example, a touring company is due, and two productions at the same time would be detrimental to business either way. There have been cases where groups have omitted to clear this important question, resulting in the last-minute cancellation of their production and a sad waste of time and money.

The royalty fee should be cleared at the same time. It can vary by thirty dollars or more per performance (approximately from twenty to fifty dollars for a three-act play), and so presents a solid item which will be important in estimating the budget.

When applying for these rights, be sure to state whether they are for amateur or professional performance since the fees vary. There was a recent omission by one group about this; an account for royalties was submitted and paid immediately (with the best intentions) without anyone checking with the producer, who then discovered the professional scale had been charged. A refund appeared unlikely, and, even if it did come through, would not be cleared in time for the production. All this happened, unfortunately, when the producer had been guarding every cent to allow for a badly needed intercom between distant dressing rooms and the stage manager's desk. No one can catch every item of business at once, but this example is another reason why it is best for the producer to have everything, especially accounts, directly under his eye at the first. Once a system is established, these duties can later be delegated to others.

THE BUDGET

The producer has charge of preparing the budget for each play, but on certain points will need close collaboration with the director and designer. A balance must be struck between needs and what the group can afford, often requiring practical imagination and plenty of ingenuity over the repainting and use of available equipment. During the depression, for example, one designer was told that the allowance for the set would be forty cents; he stripped and re-made previous flats, found a series of pipes to create special lighting shadows, bought only some additional paint and a much-needed brush, and kept within his budget. However, every group wants to improve on, and add to, equipment, and the producer will have the responsibility of deciding between the time to lie fallow and the time to spend.

Expenses will vary enormously with each group and the conditions under which it works, but the following are among the main items to be considered:

1. Royalty.
2. Scripts.
3. Rent, including rehearsal room where necessary, and use of any office and box-office space, plus the cost of the theatre.
4. The production: material for set, costumes, props.
5. Additional equipment: renting of lights, tape recorder, etc.
6. Publicity, including printing of tickets, posters, flyers, programs, any letterheads, envelopes and postage, and display advertising in the press.
7. Personnel: for example, director's fee.
8. Transport: of furniture, sets, to and from theatre.
9. Parking lot: rent and/or attendant.
10. Miscellaneous: upkeep of equipment (light bulbs, rewiring, etc.), extra cleaning needs, janitor's services, dry cleaning.

Against these will be balanced the one major source of income: ticket sales. These should never be estimated on one-hundred-per-cent capacity houses; it is wiser and safer to build the budget on an estimated break-even at approximately fifty per cent, that is, a half-full house at each performance. Attendance usually works out to less than this at the beginning of the run, but far more at the end. All of which can have some bearing on the price of tickets, and on the choice of play.

Minor sources of income should include program advertising; when this is well managed, most groups estimate the money derived from this source to cover at least all publicity expenses, as in (6) above. When available, refreshment facilities should again cover costs, or in a large operation can be rented out in the form of a concession.

Whereas most production costs, such as rent and printing, are fixed or unavoidably set, there can be choice in some respects. Royalties can be avoided when the classics are produced, but, unless performed in modern dress or by a group with an ample wardrobe, they can be expensive to mount as far as set and costumes are concerned. Similarly the majority of groups do not pay a director's fee, and will wait to mount varied and complicated sets until they have an abundance of carpenters and material.

Probably the most constant variable lies in the cost of the set. Costumes and lights are a must, but the greatest economy can be exercised by the designer. The producer should discuss needs carefully with him and with the director, so that whatever funds are available are put to the best use for the production.

Some groups plan their budget on a percentage basis, making a proportionate allowance for each expense. In this case it is good to allow for any unexpected margin by allotting a good twenty per cent to that mysterious column labelled *miscellaneous*. Whatever – and however – the decisions reached, it is important that the producer impresses on all concerned that individual allowances cannot be exceeded; one department winging off on a financial spree – and the planning of the whole is valueless. In estimating a budget, most people try to list their expenses at slightly over, and not under, their needs; this makes the results look more reliable when the final report is handed in to the organization, thus paving the way for future plans.

Then, before the budget goes into operation, it is best to arrange and discuss a system for the accounts. Ideally all payments should be made by one person, and it is sometimes arranged by signed voucher and/or the establishment of a special account with local stores, through which someone from each department (stage management, wardrobe, etc.) may be able to order and buy materials. They should sign and give the receipt to whoever keeps the books. If the entries are kept up to date, the producer has a reasonable chance of maintaining a firm eye – and hold – on the budget. And the financial position can indicate that everyone is keeping to schedule.

SCHEDULE

The essence of a producer's work lies in control of progress; and he should know how all departments are faring, and whether any need extra help, or have been delayed through late delivery of materials. Deal with smaller problems as soon as possible; if shelved, they can accumulate. There should always be a weather eye open for the first-class crisis which most productions have a way of creating – when the director's firm decides to move him, the leading lady is hospitalized, or the threat of demolition hanging over the rehearsal-room comes into immediate effect and all costumes, properties, furniture, and cast need a new home within a few hours.

The best way of maintaining this control is to work out a production schedule, discussing details with department heads, and placing copies in certain hands and on bulletin boards. Then, as with the budget, impress on everyone that it is important they keep to the schedule since all the work is inter-dependent. A lighting rehearsal cannot be completed until a set is painted, or the color of the costumes assessed until the lighting is right, or the set used by the cast until the paint is dry. The process is similar to building the house that Jack built, but in a large production there may be a hundred-and-one Jacks.

The producer has his own routine within the schedule which will vary with each organization, but the following are among his first responsibilities:

1. As soon as the necessary rights have been cleared, through the publisher or agent, arrange the booking for the theatre. There is usually a form to be completed and a deposit to be made; if not, the arrangement should be put in writing, stating dates of performance and the rent, including so many rehearsals in the theatre (usually enough to cover one technical and one or two dress rehearsals) and the hours of each. Sometimes groups are surprised to find a ruling that the building must be closed by midnight or eleven p.m., which can shorten their expected rehearsal time.

Once these dates are finalized, the publicity department can send out a first press release announcing the production.

2. Make arrangements for a suitable rehearsal room covering times to be used, any rent, and when and where a key is available, etc. The space will probably be used by other groups and for other purposes, and it is best to avoid confusion.

3. Some groups may also require space and equipment for building and painting scenery. The workshop should have easy access and a large door, or the situation could become like that of the boat which a man builds in his basement and then can't move out of the house.

4. The wardrobe department will require a place in which to work; preferably one where, as the organization grows, it will be possible to keep and store costumes.

5. Office or desk space will be needed by the producer. It is a help if this can be near or off the rehearsal room since it makes for a good central meeting place.

6. As soon as possible a production list should be completed of everyone's home and business phone numbers, and circulated to all heads of departments; the director may have a sudden idea about a doorway to suggest to the designer who will pass it on to the carpenter, and quick communication is important.

7. The producer should keep files of all business transacted for each production. They can provide useful reference for the future, and should make it reasonably possible for someone else to take over if one of those crises were to develop round the producer himself.

8. He should become aware of any provincial and local regulations concerning fire precautions, which can require the flameproofing of drapes, etc., and of those governing exemption from Hospitals Tax for a non-profit organization. Application for this exemption would be made in Ontario, for example, to: The Comptroller of Revenue, Hospitals Tax Branch, Parliament Buildings, Toronto 2.

9. Insurance is a further point to be considered, and it would be well to make enquiries of the various companies about coverage, including any damage by fire or theft, etc. to costumes, properties, equipment, and furniture.

PRODUCTION MEETINGS

Production meetings play a very important part in the successful planning and co-ordination of the actual management of mounting a production. They are called and chaired by the producer, and it can be a good idea to hold them on a regular weekly basis, with all staff attending and submitting a quick report as to progress and any particular needs. These meetings will become informal, but at the same time will help to keep everyone informed and maintain a sense of participation within the whole. Emergency meetings may still become necessary for a few staff at a time; but then they will be able to concentrate on the extraordinary business, knowing that routine matters will still be checked.

It is worth remembering, however, that while discussion is useful and a pooling of ideas sometimes may open avenues for the publicity department, or suggest sources for the borrowing of furniture, they can be time-consuming unless put into action. Once decisions have been made, it is the producer's job to allocate the work and then check that it is done by the time required. This can sometimes be difficult when people who are experienced in their own lines, but inexperienced in theatre, and who are giving voluntarily of their own time, do not appreciate at first that delay or lateness can affect many others. The designer, for example, may take the posters to a printer who will do an excellent job for no charge; or a good photographer may be interested in helping by coming to take publicity shots; then in both cases the pressure of everyday work catches up, and after much inquiry they deliver wonderful results, but a week or ten days behind schedule – and all the while the producer must exercise tact. So when paid work is allocated (ticket printing, advertising, etc.), state the deadline; with voluntary work, explain the position, and a clear understanding may just tip the balance.

It is advisable to keep some check of attendance at production meetings, because people are unavoidably late, have to leave early, are out-of-town, or just plain sick. This can be just the time when decisions affecting their department are discussed and made, and it is so easy to assume they are then known, which creates a ripe situation for misunderstandings to develop.

REHEARSAL PERIOD

As the cast go into rehearsal, the producer sets the production staff in motion. If necessary, he will put through orders for material for the set and costumes, or, if this is done by the departments, he will keep an eye on their budget. With reference to our Average Production Schedule at the beginning of the *Handbook* (six weeks' rehearsal, one week run), he will want to know by the end of the second week, for example, that the order for tickets has already been discussed and sent by the box office manager to the printers, that the artist has started the design for the posters, and that the director, designer, and/or stage manager have decided which properties may be found by the prop-girl and which should be made by the carpenter or special property man. By the end of Week Four he may help with putting the posters out, settle arrangements with the box office manager for advance sales to begin the following week, and know that costume fittings have started, that the publicity department is going ahead with press releases and planning for radio, television, and press interviews, and that, if the director and cast are ready, all staff will be invited to that first run-through of the play without books. While not a performance, this represents a first deadline for the cast and is a good way of ensuring that staff have first-hand knowledge of the production.

During Week Five front-of-house staff will be selected and checked with the house manager, the program will be at the printers, and the box office should be able to report some advance sales. When inquiries come in for Theatre Night parties, try to arrange for them early in the run, for if the critics give favorable notices and the word-of-mouth publicity is good, business is more than likely to be bursting at the end of the week.

Week Six will be the busiest time. The producer is usually involved in checking that there is transport and labor for taking scenery, furniture, props, and costumes over to the theatre; that any costumes and equipment being rented have arrived; that the theatre, including dressing-rooms, is clean; that deadlines for the technical rehearsal are being met; and that complimentary tickets are going to the right people.

When the theatre is rented – often at a fee which takes quite a proportion of the budget – it can be a good idea to impress on both staff and cast that the equipment provided within this fee is expensive and should be treated with respect. Within reason, make clear that it is advisable for everyone to keep to his own department, so that only the electrician handles the lighting board, those in stage management the sound equipment and properties, and the stage crew the scenery, just as in performance.

PERFORMANCE AND AFTER

Once the play is on, the producer, like the director, has officially little left to do except provide a check-point to maintain the standard of the production. If any rented equipment, such as lights, goes wrong, he contacts the firm and arranges for substitutes. And he would do well to bring all accounts up-to-date, check the nightly "take" from the box office, and so have an immediate picture of the income which is expected to balance the budget.

At the close of the production the officers of the group may ask him to make out a simple report on the budget. Meanwhile he is likely to be thinking ahead, making resolutions about the next play in relation to personnel, contact with various firms, dates, and deadlines. Good planners never cease.

There is, however, one tangible thing which the producer can do for the future: make a file or compile notes, perhaps in loose-leaf form, of all possible facts and information which would provide a useful reference for anyone else coming into his job in that particular organization. This could include:

1. A copy of the membership list, and of any committees and officers, which is always kept up-to-date and contains home and business phone numbers.

2. A similar list of those who have served recently as cast and staff.

3. Notes on the theatre(s) used by the group: dimensions of stage; their equipment – lighting (and power), sound, drapes (and colors); dressing-rooms; scene-dock; paint-shop; seating arrangement and capacity; foyer, box office, and office facilities; phones.

4. Usual rehearsal room arrangements: location, space, rent, phone, etc.

5. Usual wardrobe and general design arrangements: location, storage, rental firms.

6. Usual stores with whom accounts are opened – printing firm, dry cleaners, source of mimeographing.

7. Kindly lenders who are often a source of furniture and properties.

8. Copies of recent production schedules.

9. Transport firm.

10. Names and addresses of play publishing firms.

The Publicity Girl

A play is incomplete until it is performed to an audience. It is one of the few products which has to be sold before the public actually sees what it is getting – buying a ticket is very different from buying something as tangible as a car, a book, or a radio.

It is the work of the publicity department to announce the coming production as widely as possible, to promote interest and to arouse curiosity so that an audience will be attracted to the performance and be prepared to pay for their seats some weeks, days, or certainly minutes in advance. Through this work the department completes the circuit of playwright-director-designer-actors-staff-to-audience. We will refer to the head of this department as the publicity girl since, although the work is often done by a man, in most groups there is usually a need for all spare men to do the heavier work on the set and lighting, which will rarely be done by women.

The publicity girl may do all the following work single-handed, or she may have many assistants, one perhaps heading each section. The more divided the work, however, the more carefully it must be co-ordinated; so in addition to being a good organizer she must also be a good supervisor. The essence of her work lies in timing; publicity that is put out too late will reach the press too late to be read by the public too late and, however valuable the material, could result in no audience. Publicity that goes out too early will create an interest that will sag. Always follow up material, and any possible leads. If you can, make it convenient to deliver some publicity in person; the contact is invaluable. Then a number of short, carefully geared announcements will feed fuel to the interest. Like every other aspect of producing a play it needs preparation and planning and, where others are concerned, a follow-through to check that assignments are completed – and completed on time.

The publicity girl works closely with other members of the production staff so that her own work is co-ordinated to the needs of the play. She will discuss budget for the department and suitable allowance with the producer – although as you will find, many hope to cover their expenses with income from advertising in the program. She will listen to the plans and ideas of the director and designer so that her material will have a suitable approach. She will know prices of tickets, and, where there is no business manager, discuss possible arrangements and ideas for block bookings and Theatre Nights with the box office manager.

It is very important that all information which goes out is truthful, correct, and concise. It should never be misleading – announcing a cast list, for example, before agreement has actually been reached. It should contain correct spelling and the right phone numbers, etc., and be completely reliable. Written material should be short. This is circulated by what is known as a press release to all public channels in the area – radio and television stations and all papers; it should be neatly typed in double-spacing, headed *For Immediate Release*, and be no longer than one side of the paper. Three hundred words, or less, is enough at a time. After the first, or general, release, which announces the play, the place, director, well-knowns in the cast, the dates, and the producing organization, each subsequent release should be channelled to a different aspect of the production: playwright, actress, theatre, director, or pet dog. See that there is an address and phone number on each release so that further inquiries can easily be made.

Main coverage of this material will deal with:

1. The play, and any particular interest: its own history, what previous critics have said, first stars, etc.; some hint of the plot (never the whole story); leading characters; special location.

2. The cast: previous fame, experience, local notoriety.

3. The author: international or local, celebration of a birthday, centennial, etc.

4. The director – previous experience, local productions, other organizations.

5. The producer, or producing organization.

Similarly it is best to gear any "spot" announcements for radio and television to one aspect of one of these topics, with the essential details as to play, place, and dates. If possible, channel all interviews in definite directions so that, while the "plug" is maintained, there is a certain control over a wide coverage.

The following diagram will help explain the work of the publicity girl and show how the department may be divided:

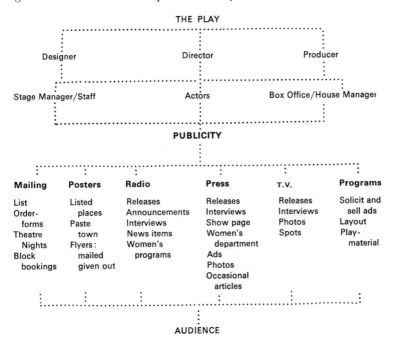

THE PLAY

Designer   Director   Producer

Stage Manager/Staff   Actors   Box Office/House Manager

PUBLICITY

Mailing	Posters	Radio	Press	T.V.	Programs
List	Listed	Releases	Releases	Releases	Solicit and
Order-	places	Announcements	Interviews	Interviews	sell ads
forms	Paste	Interviews	Show page	Photos	Layout
Theatre	town	News items	Women's	Spots	Play-
Nights	Flyers:	Women's	department		material
Block	mailed	programs	Ads		
bookings	given out		Photos		
			Occasional		
			articles		

AUDIENCE

The arrangement of the above work will vary with different organizations – programs, posters, and mailing list, for example, might automatically be done by separate people; but somewhere there should still be co-ordination under the heading of publicity. Suppose that through the order forms, or direct contact with the box office, or even through the producer (it makes no matter who – the point is, you should still get the news) an organization buys the house for a complete Theatre Night before advance booking even opens – this is news; circulation of it might encourage other groups to do the same thing, and, even if they don't do it now, they might for a subsequent production, for publicity operates on a long-term as well as on a short-term basis. A report that a certain night is already sold out will look good when you place the display advertisements in the papers, and it would be as well to warn the cast to have their friends book well ahead for other nights. But . . . be sure the arrangement is complete, that there is some form of agreement, and that you have the right name of the organization. Facts must be accurate.

With reference to our Average Production Schedule of two weeks' main preparation, six weeks' rehearsal, and one week for performance – let's see how the work of the publicity department will best be co-ordinated with that of the entire production unit.

PREPARATION

Read the play.

Find out as much as you can about the various stages of the director's and designer's approach, so that without giving too much away you can form an extension of their work. The closer your collaboration, the better you can present the necessary information to the public.

Discuss the budget for your department at early production meetings. Your main expenditures will be: printing of tickets, posters, programs, and flyers (small handbills); stationery and mail-order material; display ads in the newspapers. Try and assess the amount of each item – through previous program costs, or estimates from firms. It would be too bad if all your allowance were spent and you suddenly realized it was time to place the ads for the papers – with no money left for them. Your main income should be from program advertising. This will require planning regarding prices that are reasonable and provide a fair chance of covering all the above expenses.

As soon as the play is cast, send out a first brief press release. Number this, and all future releases, and file a copy with a list of those to whom it was sent. Then you will have control of *what* has gone *where* – and *when*; do not miss any papers or radio stations; ideally coverage should be universal within the area, and it should be synchronized.

WEEKS ONE AND TWO

Attend early readings of the play to sense more of the director's work and to become familiar with the cast. List their names – correct spelling – and phone numbers, and gradually collect a brief biography from each person; this could tie in with later interviews, photographs, and ideas for Hobby Corners or Teen-age Columns.

Discuss the design of posters with the artist so that if possible they can link with the design of the whole production (occasionally they might be done by the designer himself), with some flavor of the set, costumes, or theme of the play, and see if this can be carried through into the program cover and even to the flyers. Remember that a poster should be geared to the needs of the theatre, and that, no matter how pretty or artistic the appearance, it has a dual purpose: to attract suitable attention to the play, and to provide information. This information should include the following: name and location of the theatre, box office, phone, name of play, director, stars, writer, and producing organization, and dates and time of performances. These are vital statistics, and should be noticeable. Check that the result is approved by the director and producer before the expensive process of printing is to begin.

Arrange for the addressing of mailing-list envelopes in advance, so that they will only need stuffing when the details and possible order forms have been printed or mimeographed.

Decide on prices for the program ads, and send out a letter to previous advertisers. Contact new possibles, with details of size and price range.

WEEK THREE

Solicit program ads personally or with the help of your assistant – thus following up your letter, being sure to check back on previous advertisers.

Find out the policy about complimentary tickets from the producer, and then start what you might call your courtesy list, so that with each production some go out to those stores who habitually display posters, to the radio stations where they give interviews and help with spot announcements, and above all to the critics. The length of the list will depend on the size of the theatre, for a group must always aim to break even on total production costs, and this can only be done through the sale of tickets. In a large theatre when there is not too much evidence of advance sales for the first few nights of a run, it is a good idea to "paper" the house – that is, send out many complimentary tickets, judiciously, to people who are known in the community and have a definite interest in theatre; for although in some part the critics will influence the later sales, there is nothing like word-of-mouth recommendation for bringing people to the play. So, particularly in later weeks, keep in close touch with your box office manager, but prepare now in case you need to put such a plan into action.

Send out a second press release, feeding interest with information, this time geared perhaps to the play. In larger cities most of your material should present facts which editors will place among many similar announcements. In smaller centres short articles on some aspect of the production are often welcome; similarly, radio stations may prefer an item which is ready to be read aloud. Both approaches are useful, and it would be worth inquiring about any preference among the press, radio, and TV people in your area.

Then follow up with ideas about possible interviews for the cast, director, and writer, if available.

Make arrangements for a photo call for the following week; this is often done through the papers, or you may find there is a local camera club who would be interested in helping here. Check with the stage manager and/or director as to suitable day, time, and place for certain members of the cast, seeing if any costumes could be supplied by the wardrobe department, and if make-up can be used.

Check that the posters are back from the printers.

WEEK FOUR

Distribute the posters, listing special spots: certain restaurants, coffee houses, or bulletin boards. For this you will need assistants, who should help to literally paste the town. A good poster continually attracts the eye wherever people go and is a constant reminder of the coming production. Aim to see that nobody can miss it.

Attend the photo call, and try to see that the results will tell something of the action of the play. Give the photographer the correct spelling and order of names of the cast and their characters.

Let the next press release follow up the photos with some facts about the cast.

Finalize decisions about the program cover with artist and/or director and producer.

Contact those who may be holding a display or small exhibition in the foyer, and plan with the house manager for a suitable time when this may be brought in and arranged. These often include exhibitions of pictures, photographs (theatrical or otherwise), past costumes, the design of present ones, old posters, and/or properties and how they are made. Any of these would require its own press release and publicity, whether as an added attraction or as related to the coming production.

WEEK FIVE

Finalize layout and all production details for the program; send to the printers; and, when ready, check proofs.

Aim to start interviews with the director, author (if local and/or available), and cast. Spread the press release to news stories on the cast, via other interests in the Women's Column and news on a career or past travels in other sections.

Keep in close touch with the box office manager when the advance sales open, for this department can provide proof of the publicity pudding, and can in some measure reflect how your own work is progressing.

WEEK SIX

This will be the busiest week for everyone concerned, but all their work will be wasted unless it continues to be made known to the public. It may be difficult to filch an actress out of rehearsal, so perhaps you can arrange for a taped interview in a coffee break; you might have a photographer get a shot of the wardrobe department at work on final touches; or see if you can interest a reporter in watching part of the lighting rehearsal.

Plan the layout and insert the display ads in the papers. These are likely to be among the most expensive items in your budget, and insertion should be carefully timed. Keep them as simple as possible, but aim to attract the eye; if you take the copy in personally, the assistants will help you select suitable print and any border.

Check progress of advance sales, and any special guest list and seating plan.

Arrange and attend the main photo call at the first dress rehearsal.

Send out a press release, if possible with some comment on these ticket sales, with a form of reminder that the play is next week; include any news of Theatre Nights.

Programs should be back from printers.

In addition to an exhibition, and depending on facilities, it may be possible to arrange for the sale of copies of the play in the foyer, and to include other works by the same author, and any recordings. Contacts with book and record stores could produce a good response, but make sure that the person who is to handle the sales knows the price of each item.

PERFORMANCE

Now that we have come to the week of performance, there is little new to be done except follow up previous contacts. Be present before opening night when an exhibition or display is being arranged. Try to have photographers take pictures of some of those who attend the opening; encourage interest via the social columns, and be aware of the various comments.

Be present to meet groups who come for Theatre Nights, and have an ear open for quotable reactions to the play.

Send out a press release on progress: figures on attendance, if they are good, may be helpful. If necessary, nudge the public with a follow-up and interviews.

Keep copies of all clippings relevant to the show; some of the publicity you send out may get little response and never appear in print, but just keep plugging. As the group creates a standard and attracts attention to results, the activity will grow more newsworthy.

Similarly keep all criticisms and ask for any transcripts of radio and television comments. One copy will make interesting reading for the cast on a bulletin board, another should go into a scrapbook along with photographs of the production.

Balance the books, keep track of unpaid accounts, and forward all details to the producer's department. Assess results so that conclusions can be put to work for the next production.

The Box Office Manager

TICKETS

Tickets are the lifeblood of the theatre; they are the equivalent of dollar bills, and should be treated with the same respect. Without these printed slips the theatre could not exist, for every production takes money to mount: whether on the scale of a Collegiate Festival or a Broadway *Camelot*. Expenses can only be met by box office returns, and it is to achieve at least a balance, or preferably a profit, that the budget and financial pattern of a production are planned.

Printing After the producer has agreed to the price of tickets, they become the sole responsibility of the box office manager, no matter how many assistants are available to help him. His first job is then to arrange for their printing, for with their prices, range, and the seating plan before him, he can assess needs accurately. Once the number is known, tickets will contain the following information:

1. The name and location of the theatre.
2. Name of the play and the producing organization.
3. Date and curtain time.
4. Price of ticket.

Where seats are numbered, the following points are duplicated with a tear-off section, one part for the doorman, one to be retained by the holder:

5. Area – if necessary, indicating balcony, main floor, and any special entrance.
6. Row.
7. Seat number.

Large organizations may even have items (3), (4), (5), (6), and (7) above in triplicate, the third part being the audit stub from which the other parts are torn, and which is retained by the box office at the time of sale. Audit stubs can then be balanced by the equivalent cash in the cash box. This is a good way of accounting for every ticket, sold or unsold, though it will be a little more expensive in the printing. The other apparent way – checking the doormens' stubs with cash-to-date – is unlikely to be accurate, for sometimes people buy tickets and then do not attend.

When all tickets are the same price, it is helpful to have them printed in different colors for the different nights, keeping to the same colors for subsequent productions. Then everyone concerned with the selling or handling of them will know immediately that they are for the right night.

Another use of color is to denote any variation of price, which is usually connected with different sections of the theatre, and this is particularly helpful for ushers and doormen.

Tickets will take about ten days to print, and should be ordered to be back in time for advance sales to begin. These sometimes open two weeks – more often one – before the week of Opening Night. But proofs, if any, should be carefully checked. The real responsibility begins when the tickets themselves are delivered. They should be checked again, like a pack of cards, to ensure that the correct number is available for each night and, if necessary, that the number at each price is right. From now on they are the equivalent of so many hundreds – or thousands – of dollars as far as this production is concerned, and the box office manager should plan a clear system of distribution, sales, and returns.

Distribution   In a small organization it is sometimes customary to give out so many tickets to each member of the cast and production unit, on the assumption that if everyone sells a dozen or so the house is half-sold for the run, and therefore less effort, time, and money need be spent on publicity. In this case the tickets are usually numbered, by hand, so that whoever gives them out knows *who* has *what;* the remainder are then handed to someone delegated to advance sales who should be – but is not always – the box office manager. Occasionally this arrangement works happily, and a few people may even over-sell their allowance and come running for twenty or thirty more. This creates a difficulty however; although everyone is meant to turn back unsold tickets by a certain date, they don't always, and the supply is depleted. Complications develop when the public calls in and no one has any tangible means of knowing exactly how many tickets are still available for each night, which could be serious when dealing with inquiries for Theatre Nights and might result in a loss of business.

The cast can just as easily canvass friends, find out how many seats are wanted, and call in the result; some may feel a ticket-in-the-hand acts as a better "sell," but this slight advantage to the few is nothing to the overall advantage of all tickets being handled by one person – and assistants – from one place and one phone number, which will facilitate the ease and accuracy of all bookings. So it is advisable to keep them under the eye of the box office manager,

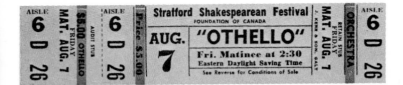

STABLES THEATRE
146 Crescent Rd. - 924-9318

APRIL
26

FRIDAY EVENING at 8:30
THE IMPORTANCE OF BEING EARNEST

Admission $1.50

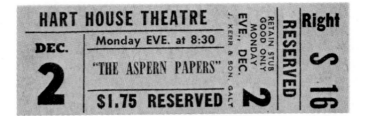

Tickets: Some Examples

and not distribute any unless in return for money. If tickets are booked by telephone, envelopes should be available, the tickets slipped in, and kept in appropriate sections for different nights, with the number, price, and name of the eventual owner clearly marked on the outside.

Complimentary Tickets   The box office manager should inquire about the policy regarding complimentary tickets, sometimes called house seats, which would be determined by the producer; from him, the director, and the publicity girl, the box office manager would extract any special lists so that these tickets are held before others go on sale. More requests are bound to come in, so it would be wise to put aside the total allowance for each night. Keep in touch with the publicity department on the results of advance sales when they start; for if they do not promise much, extra pressure may be required; while if they are selling well, that alone is news.

KNOWLEDGE OF THE PLAY

Everyone working in the box office should read the play, have some idea of the director's approach, and, if possible, attend a rehearsal – particularly that first run-through, to which all technical and production staff may be invited. The public is going to ask many questions, and, as with a car salesman, there's nothing like knowing your product: When is it? How do we get there? What time does it start? Who's in it? What's it about? Where does it take place? How many intermissions? What time is the final curtain?

SEAT PLAN AND RACKING

When seats are reserved and numbered, the box office manager will find it a help to prepare and have mimeographed a seating-plan of the audience, numbering each row and seat, so that with every sale the appropriate number is marked off. This makes it easy to check at a glance the seats still available and, if necessary, to show their exact location; but it will require a separate plan for each performance. Sometimes, however, the public is referred to a permanent plan which is encased within the box office window, while the manager uses his racks as reference.

Ticket racks are an important part of box-office equipment. They are boxes of slots, holes, pigeon-holes, or what-you-will to hold the tickets in order of the seating-plan for each performance. Since advance sales and the actual box office are rarely in the same place, it is a help if they are portable; useful older ones can sometimes be found at a reasonable price with a sliding or fold-down door and a lock. *Racking* the tickets accurately is another means of ensuring that the public is sold the right ticket; but it is always best to double-check and look again at the date, seat, row, and price before completing any sale.

TYPES OF SALE

Box office personnel are often, as a result of publicity, the first contact between the public and the play, and whether as a voice on the phone or as a face at a window or behind a desk, the aim should be: to please. Those concerned with every level of theatre do well to remember Samuel Johnson's advice, "For we that live to please, must please to live." In the case of the box office this means that the customer is always right. No matter what the public asks, or how long their inquiries take, each request should be handled with the same care and consideration.

Sales are made through some, or all, of the following methods, depending on the size, policy, and growth of the organization:

1. Subscription is often used by large, established groups, and is an excellent way of ensuring a percentage of future attendance and income by offering seats for so many plays at a certain reduction in price. Such a program is planned well in advance to offer variety and balance, and often in March or April of a previous season plays are already under discussion for the next season.

2. Mailing lists are an effective form of publicity and a good way of promoting sales to people who, having a definite interest in theatre, have requested advance notice of each play. The simple filling-in of a form and enclosure of a cheque and stamped, self-addressed envelope becomes, like a subscription, a painless way of buying tickets. These notices usually go out two weeks in advance of the opening of sales to the general public, so that these people have the next chance after subscribers of reserving the seats they want. Many organizations keep a book, or forms, ready in the foyer at each performance, or print details in the program, to acquire continual additions to these lists.

3. Advance sales are then advertised as open to the general public, when it is also a good policy to accept reservations by phone, taking the seats reserved out of their rack and putting them aside in their appropriate, named envelopes – but asking people to pick

them up at least twenty minutes prior to curtain time. If there is a run on sales they cannot expect the box office to hold them after this time when they have not been paid for, though naturally most managers will oblige for as long as possible.

4. Direct sales are the immediate cash or cheque transactions on the night of performance. If the theatre is in a central location, it is best to be optimistic and open the box office well in advance of each performance – if possible by four-thirty or five p.m., as people may find it convenient to drop in for tickets on their way home from work.

When selling, try to fill the house from the front of each price range in blocks to the back, using the centre sections first, so that the audience will become corporate and the actors have a body of people to play to; nothing is harder than performing to a scattered audience. Similarly, do not leave more single seats than are necessary, or it will be difficult to group couples and parties together as the house fills. Avoid selling seats across an aisle. Should a group have to be broken, explain the situation and use any advantage in a change; perhaps people have to be seated behind each other, and will prefer this to being dotted over the house when everything is nearly sold. If they have to be on the side, explain they will be nearer to the stage; or, if further back, that they will see better because these seats are raised.

Be polite but firm when that wonderful thing happens and House Full notices are posted. If some people do not understand and clamber and badger for non-existent tickets, try to persuade them to buy early next time. (Sell some now if humanly possible, or persuade them to go on the mailing list.) Always aim to encourage customers for the future. Both they and the box office are losing out when people have to be turned away, but the theatre must continue to woo the public if ever it is to be the other way around. Do not sell more standing-room tickets than are allowed, or have extra people stand or sit in the aisles. This would prevent the enjoyment of people who bought tickets in time and would infringe fire and safety regulations, so doing the theatre – and the organization – no good.

BALANCING THE BOOKS

It is advisable to make up the books on the night of each performance, keeping all records, checking, and banking up to date. List how many tickets were sold, at each price, by subtracting those gone from the racks from the total number available, remembering to list complimentary tickets apart since they produce no direct financial return. Balance the total price of those sold (if necessary, previous lists will note how many of each house were used for subscription, mailing, and advance sales) with cash or cheques received, and the amounts should be equal. Deposit the cash in a safe, or bank it, according to custom, and at the end of the run all records are then complete and easily available. So the wheel has turned full circle; theatre money, or tickets, is back in the bank again in the form of ordinary dollars and cents.

The House Manager

Actors are the servants of the public. During each performance the house manager represents them, and the producing organization, as host to the public. Like any good host he sees that all is prepared for their arrival. His care extends from the moment they enter the parking lot (where one is available) to their entrance into the foyer, covers easy access to the box office, checkroom arrangements, washroom facilities, attendance by doormen and ushers, refreshments at intermission, disposal of cartons and cigarette butts, and a ready ear for comments and complaints.

His concern is always for the convenience and safety of the public. He is responsible for all activity in the front-of-house, and has final authority over this public section just as, during performance, the stage manager has over the backstage or private section of the theatre. Where the house manager is resident, he represents ownership – whether of a private individual, university, or public corporation – and has charge of all facilities and usually of all rental arrangements.

He enjoys meeting people, is a good supervisor, and has many assistants; but as one manager explains it, "Something goes wrong in the ladies' john – you fix it."

PREPARATION AND STAFF

The member of a theatre group who acts as house manager should read the play and know the production, for he is bound to be involved in conversation and be asked questions about it. He would be wise to attend at least one run-through and, if possible, a dress rehearsal. After checking first with the producer, he should begin selecting his staff. When operating within an established organization he usually has a fair line of experienced people to draw upon, but if helping to start a new group he may, like others, need to check certain points which will be new to them.

His staff will include:

1. Parking-lot attendants.
2. Doormen.
3. Ushers.
4. Check-room attendants.
5. Refreshment staff.

1. Parking lot attendants should be available to help the public, and if possible to post signs at the theatre indicating the location of the lot, and to see that the approach is clearly marked; they will need flashlights, masked to avoid glare. The route from the lot to the theatre should have a good outside lighting. One group welcomes its guests with a line of candles in glass chimneys along the path.

A good policy is to arrange for police supervision of the parking lot. This can be done by calling the local police office; when available, they will usually permit off-duty officers to take this charge and any payment involved would be between the officers concerned and the organization.

2. Doormen will check politely that everyone has a ticket, and will tear off and deposit stubs, as required. Their number depends on the size of the theatre; sometimes their work can be handled by one or two at a central barrier, but with a large auditorium it will be quicker to have doormen, if not at every section entrance, at least dividing the streams of main floor and balcony traffic. They should remember to check that each ticket is for the right performance, and then indicate the location of the seats.

3. Ushers should know the arrangements of the house, or if seats are not numbered should help place people together without leaving too many gaps, memorizing spaces as curtain time draws near. They will need an adequate supply of programs and, possibly, of flashlights – some theatres are dimly lit even with the house-lights full-on, and steps can be a hazard to the elderly.

It is best to arrange that, within reason, the ushers have a uniform style of dress, for it would be strange to see some girls in formal wear and others in blouses and skirts. Boys look neat in white shirts, quiet ties, and grey pants. Whichever style is chosen, it is best to remember that the ushers are part, as it were, of a "welcome" committee, and not a part of the show.

The house manager would be wise to check that the ushers know where to wait during performance; whether in or outside the auditorium, they will realize that quiet is a necessity. Sometimes they leave after everyone is seated, but they may be needed at intermissions to stand at the bottom of the aisles checking that people do not wander up on the stage where they could be in the way. Anyone who wishes to go backstage should be directed round to the stage door at the end of the performance.

4. Check-room attendants perform another useful service, and like others should be both fast and efficient. Suggest that they attend to one person or couple at a time. If they take in a number of coats, hats, and scarves together, they are likely to confuse the accurate giving out of each check to the right person, and everyone will want to avoid delays after the performance.

5. Where there are refreshment facilities, staff will be needed at each intermission. One person will be responsible for their work, but the house manager should check that their preparations are quiet, especially where they operate near the auditorium doors. Better to have everything ready in advance and suspend activities during each act than disturb the audience.

It would be advisable to make the contacts for staff at least two weeks in advance, for it often takes a while to track down people who have enough free evenings. It may be necessary to fit in some for some nights and some for others, and to check that all understand equally *what* is required, *when*.

The house manager should be on hand if any exhibits or displays are being arranged in the foyer, and collaborate with the publicity girl over the reception of any special guests. He would help to see that any disabled persons are conveniently seated; in some auditoriums space may be made in certain rows for wheelchairs.

Cleaning and janitor arrangements, and the locking and unlocking of the theatre, all come under the house manager's supervision, so that all care is taken to see that the house is ready for its guests.

PERFORMANCE

Staff should arrive about forty-five minutes before curtain time, the house manager an hour before. The public can arrive early, and usually begins to be seated half-an-hour in advance.

Final arrangements should be checked with the stage manager. Ideally his calls backstage of "Three minutes!" and then "Beginners, please!" are synchronized with signals in the foyer by bells, lights flicking, or recorded announcement. Then the doormen tactfully begin to close the doors so that all are seated just before curtain time. If it is clearly stated when the public buy or reserve their tickets that latecomers will not be seated until the first intermission, people do in time respect this policy. It avoids that poor five or ten-minute wait which creates a lag in expectancy, and which is bad for the actors, the play, and the performance. Those who have come early should not be disturbed, so that concentration is lost and there is a lack of contact with the actors, whose many weeks of preparation should in turn be met with the courtesy of quiet.

In practice, however, there should be some link with the stage manager before he gives the CURTAIN UP signal. A great rush at the box office, or particularly bad weather, can delay people, and the final clearing of the foyer should be managed with diplomacy.

Occasionally there may be difficulty over tickets, and staff will look to the house manager for assistance. Usually it is a case of people sitting in the wrong row. Sometimes it is the rare nightmare of finding that there are apparently two sets of tickets for the same seats; a knowledge of how carefully the box-office staff check their sales almost certainly results in the discovery of "right tickets, wrong night" (though "wrong theatre" has been known), which was caught by neither doormen nor ushers. Preference is always given to those who hold the right tickets; but if the wrong nighters wish to stay, and if there is room, it is customary to exchange their tickets.

Once the curtain is up, the house manager sees that there is complete quiet in the foyer; he is then available during intermissions to meet the public as a good listener and to assess reactions to the play. He should keep his eye on the rule that refreshments are not taken into the auditorium, because of later litter and noise, and, because of fire regulations, should watch smoking; and he should supervise the call signals.

The house manager finally sees the audience out, investigates any lost property, checks the supply of programs, sees that refreshments are cleared and all is ready for the next performance, makes sure the box office is closed, and, except for the janitor who locks up, should, like the stage manager backstage, be last out.

Reading List

Producing the Play, by John Gassner (Dryden).
The Business of Show Business, by Gail Plummer (Harper).

6. The Actor

When an actor prepares for an opening night, he is about to participate in a ceremony that is a special form of ritual. The rites of the theatre ask that actors and audience be ready by a certain time in different parts of the same building, without seeing each other first. The audience then sits in darkness and the actors pretend no one is there, while using words that are not their own and behaving as if they were people other than themselves. Everyone knows none of the action is really happening, but through the magic of the theatre – sometimes called the willing suspension of disbelief – they do believe in it at the time, and are sometimes haunted by it for a long time afterwards.

Actors and audience accept the conventions involved, and both, in a good performance, contribute their own roles. It is as if going to the theatre involves a game of mutual schizophrenia, for the actor says "I am" and knows he is not; and the audience agrees "you are" and is aware that he is not. It is all a question of timing: the actor performs so only on-stage, the audience only in the darkened auditorium; at other times the action seen might be judged lunatic or deranged. This participation provides the advantage which the theatre has over the more mechanical mediums of the other lively arts of movies, radio, and television, resulting in that tremendous here-and-now, in flesh-and-blood sense, officially known as immediacy, that is unobtainable where an audience is removed from the performance and therefore has no influence. In the theatre there is interplay, not merely between actor and actor, but between actor and audience. This adds an ephemeral quality to each performance because it is fashioned at that particular moment for that particular audience; and as an audience becomes corporate, so it assumes a personality. It is this sharing of the same play with different personalities that makes acting so fascinating, and perhaps the liveliest of all arts; a happening, by people, about people, and for people. When the audience's disbelief is completely suspended, they are involved in the age-old pleasure of being told a story, with the extra delight of seeing it in action. And as the curtain falls at the end of a production, perhaps everyone who has played his part has reached a little greater awareness of the triumphs and the tragedies of other human beings, and therefore of themselves.

Acting is a deeply individual affair. Apart from a viewpoint of a role, there is a variety in the means by which it may be expressed, and in the personal equipment which the actor has at his command. So much depends on where we start, and with what. Like make-up, everyone begins with a different complexion, as it were, of personality; and while all may have Hamlet in mind, the question is, which Hamlet? or Emily? or George? or Laura? or Amanda? If we start from the surmise that, just as each director is part-author of a production, so each actor becomes part-author of his own role, we will agree that each version will of necessity be based on the work of the original author. Given good material, then, every hint for each move or inflection can be found somewhere within the lines, and often the less authorship added by the actor the better, for it would become superfluous (though, as we shall see later, that is not the end of the affair). Given poor material, the actor may have to do far more to build from far less; and in this sense, by using much of his own authorship, some actors can make their reputations. A most famous example of this would be Irving in *The Bells*.

Either way, it is a question of interpretation, and it is important that an actor recognize this point. Unlike a novelist, sculptor, painter, poet, or composer, he is not creating from life at first-hand but at second-hand, being largely dependent on another's creation. He is similar to a musician, or a dancer, or a singer, who look for their material to the composer and/or choreographer. It is a dependence, however, that works both ways, for from Shakespeare to Molière and from Williams to Wilder, authors will always require actors, good actors, to complete their work. Without the physical presence of each character – and the director's control, designer's concept, and often as many concerned backstage as there are ground crew to an aircraft – a play cannot rise off the printed page and assume its particular reality.

The actor is the one person among all these who faces the public. His art is individual because it is personal, for he has no medium other than his own self; and his total physique, his mind, heart, and personality are the parts of his one instrument. Where a singer, for example, whether in *Traviata* or *South Pacific*, or a dancer, whether in *Sylphides* or *Pal Joey*, is continually guided by the music and by a visible conductor, the actor is guided by nothing more than the benefits of rehearsal, the collaboration of other actors, and his instinctive sense of each audience for whom he times and shapes his performance. He does this not in the way of becoming self-conscious, but in diverting his consciousness so that he may share the role and the play with others. Perhaps a good actor can be likened to a good salesman: the patter is the same; the product is the same; but they both have a further point in common: they adapt to their customers.

Within our outline of the actor's work we will concentrate on the development of his approach to a play from the time he first hears of the coming production, through casting sessions, early readings, to blocking and subsequent rehearsals, dress rehearsals, and performance. Within this pattern we will insert time for the different kinds of preparation, for since acting is partly an interpretative as well as a creative art, there is need to give careful consideration to many points concerning the play, which can be common to almost any role. We will refer to those plays we have already discussed, *The Glass Menagerie* and *Our Town*, rather than confine attention to the development of a single role; but to widen our scope and show that all is applicable to a whole range of authors, we will also refer to two contrasting plays by Anton Chekhov, *The Marriage Proposal* and *The Cherry Orchard*.

Reading the Play

As soon as you hear that a group is about to produce a particular play, make it your business to find a copy and read it. Then there will be some chance of knowing if you like it, and of finding if you believe in the characters. Plays with a straightforward theme and story will not present much difficulty; but if, for example, a classic such as *The Cherry Orchard* does not mean much at first, give it time; we rarely like what we cannot comprehend at some level; but if we continue to look into it, then, as with a more complex picture or symphony, an instinctive understanding may develop.

Read the play many times; already one or two characters will appeal, and at this point almost anyone is likely to reckon the size of a role, even to pages and number of lines. It is as well, however, to remember the famous saying about there being, "no small roles, only small actors." When you have discovered theme and plot, which we have discussed elsewhere, try reading some of the scenes out loud; this can help the characters and situations come alive, and provide useful practice for the casting session.

Occasionally people find the mechanics of reading aloud difficult, and since, especially for a newcomer to a group, casting can largely depend on it, time should be made for some practice. Remember that the aim is to lift the printed words off the page so that no one is aware that they are being read; the lines should sound as they are intended to become – speech, spoken as the logical outcome of character. We are dealing now with dramatic dialogue, which is a carefully selected form of speaking-writing, rather than the descriptive or narrative prose of reading-writing. Punctuation, for example, should be seen and noted by the reader, but not heard by the listener; in speech it becomes an integral part of the flow and change of thought and feeling, which is dependent on the two factors of the sense-grouping of words and the amount of breath they require. The combination of these breath-sense groups results in what is known as phrasing. There is a wonderful example of mistaken phrasing in the Prologue at the beginning of the play of Pyramus and Thisbe in Act V of Shakespeare's *A Midsummer Night's Dream*:

If we offend, it is with our good will.
    That you should think, we come not to offend,
But with good will. To show our simple skill,
    That is the true beginning of our end.
Consider then we come but in despite.
    We do not come as minding to content you,
Our true intent is. All for your delight
    We are not here. That you should here repent you,
The actors are at hand and by their show
You shall know all that you are like to know.

Read this passage aloud, as punctuated; then change the punctuation and therefore the breathing according to the sense, and you will see what was really intended.

Note punctuation, and always use it in a practical sense. Apart from the actual choice of words, it is the only other guide the author can provide as to interpretation, and in this way it is similar to the time signature and phrase marks which the composer uses in music. Commas will indicate continuity (and so usually a rising voice); semicolons and colons call for slightly more of a break within the frame of the sentence; periods usually represent the end of an idea (but ideas can come tumbling out, and many are often spoken on one breath); and paragraphs indicate the end of a section.

If the speech were to be broken by a breath at every punctuation mark, or even at every period, the result would become overcareful and unnatural, sounding more like a pedantic piece of reading than flowing, thought-and-feeling-propelled speech. To gain a good continuity of reading by phrase and meaning, rather than by punctuation mark, and to have time to digest the further meaning and changes between each phrase, it is essential that the eye travels ahead: half a line is a must: one to one-and-a-half lines will give a greater sense of freedom.

Practice of sight reading for the actor should be as systematic and careful for words as for the musician who needs the same accuracy in relation to notes. There a teacher will often mask a bar after the player has glanced at it, forcing the eye to look ahead, and training the memory to retain what is to come while present notes are being played. Similarly, if there is difficulty with ordinary reading, find an object that will mask a line (an envelope will do); look at the line, then cover, or mask, it, speaking from memory as the eye travels to the next line, before that one, in turn, is memorized and then masked. At first this will be difficult, halting, and probably inaccurate, and cannot be expected to sound natural; but even after ten or fifteen minutes a day, with a week of perseverance there will be improvement, and, given a month, the mechanics of reading can be mastered.

Once this freedom is gained, all the imaginative process can be brought back. The characters, situations, imagery, thought, and emotions can be spoken unhampered by hesitation. The eye can look ahead, sort out puzzles and difficulties in advance, and the reading, when good, will sound not like reading, but like speech. Then, by the time of casting sessions, there will be some sense of control; it should be possible to listen to, and give, what the director requires, to listen to others, and to adapt to further suggestions.

Casting

Listen to any resumé the director might give; his approach to the play will be the key to the production. In *Our Town* and *The Glass Menagerie* this is not likely to differ very much from the clear outlines of character provided by the author. When we allude later to *The Cherry Orchard*, however, which is open to a wider interpretation, we shall see how much this initial approach can influence all preparation, and we shall discuss a scene which could be conceived in various terms.

Casting, as mentioned in the chapter on the director, falls into two main categories: *to type* and *against type*. Similarly, it is possible to define roles under the categories *character* and *straight;* that is, either distant or close to an actor's own age, physique, nationality, and personality. A suggestion of these main types is important in certain roles: Sir Toby Belch and Sir John Falstaff, for example, are unlikely to be played by tall, thin actors, or Sir Andrew Aguecheek by a short, fat actor. It is best, however, to conceive every role as a character role, in that each will differ to a greater or lesser degree from the actor's own self. As no two sets of fingerprints are alike, so no two people are identical, and an actor will create a far wider variety of experience by seeing each role as different than by thinking, emoting, and reducing each solely according to his own approach to life. While his own self is the essential beginning, he needs to expand and explore out from this base, putting himself in the place of Tom, or the Gentleman Caller, or Emily, or Varya, and creating, with imagination, from the character's viewpoint. The process of rehearsal and private study will help the actor discover what this view is, and then a new and unique person can gradually emerge.

Be ready to try a variety of roles; particularly if you are a newcomer, it is a good policy to aim for as wide a range as possible. Be willing to start as a Second Dead Woman rather than think, "Emily, or bust." Ability may exist, but usually has to be proved; if chances do not always come at first, try, try again. In the theatre perseverance and being around can often do as much for the future as for the present. If you still have no luck, and yet there is a genuine interest, try other departments. There are far more things to be done than is ever dreamt of in the outlook of many actors, each department making different demands and in turn offering a different sense of accomplishment. Somewhere there is a place for everyone who is prepared to make a place; and if it isn't at first exactly what you want, it could lead to other developments later.

Casting is usually a competitive affair. In large organizations, eighty or ninety people can appear for the chance of a dozen or so roles; in small groups six people may turn up where twelve are needed. Keep both ears open for the director's suggestions to others, and try to be adaptable when it comes to your own turn. If possible, look up from the script when reading and establish a link, or rapport, with anyone reading with you by listening to their lines, so building a chain of action and reaction. All other aspects being equal, awareness of others and the development of a scene as a whole are points which could bring a role in your direction.

Before the end of the casting session be sure to ask, if it is not announced, about dates of performance and probable times of rehearsal. Then anyone who is likely to be away, or who knows other commitments are due, would be wise to mention the fact – now. Casting can be an intricate matter requiring much juggling; no director is pleased to spend time and thought on it only to find that someone is then unavailable. So explain the position before, not after, casting is settled. There are always likely to be further productions, and a good reading now need not be wasted, and may always be remembered later. When decisions are final, however, and the dates cleared, note the time and place of first rehearsals.

Now that you have been offered a role, read the play again, both silently and aloud. Lay the ground for learning the lines, but do not consciously work at them until after the first rehearsals; a role takes time to grow, and if the thoughts and feelings are forced into a mould too soon, the result might run off at a tangent before the director has had time to indicate a more detailed approach than in the resumé at casting.

Remember that, when the writing is good, the lines are characteristic of each role. Because they are pertinent to that one person in that particular situation, Emily's lines could not be switched to Laura, or Amanda's to Mrs. Gibbs, or George's to Tom. They also have a rhythm suited to that personality, and are orchestrated so that the sound complements the sense. There are many approaches to a role; some actors, for example, start large and gradually whittle their performance down to the degree for which they are seeking; others start small and then build. If the lines are first read with the greatest simplicity and if there is any sensitivity in these matters, the actor cannot help but find some grain of the author's intention. To this can be added that special quality of a personal concept of the role which will give, as it were, an individual salt, pepper, and relish to the lines. As they are fashioned and then used, they will come alive; and provided they are spoken as the outcome of the character, they can ideally be enlarged and projected to any size of theatre, and still retain their original intent.

Reading Rehearsals

Make it a habit to be punctual at all rehearsals. The stage manager and cast should be ready a few minutes before each call, so that everyone is ready to begin when the director arrives. If he is held up, the stage manager often starts the rehearsal so that time is not wasted. If you know you are going to be late, or may even have to miss a rehearsal, realize that this always affects others. One late arrival can delay the work of the entire cast. So call the director or stage manager in advance, and if it is not possible to contact anyone directly, leave a message. Once you have been given a copy of the play, usually called a script, never lose it. It is going to contain many signs and hieroglyphics that only you can decipher, and that would be of little value to anyone else. At the back of your copy, take note of the rehearsal schedule and any changes, of any special calls for costume fittings or photographs; and list the phone numbers that are likely to be useful: of the director, stage manager, and those in the cast with whom you need special rehearsals.

Many actors then underline their cues or the last couple of lines, or sentence, before their own speeches; many also underline their own lines, sometimes in a different color. When it comes to what is often the hard jog of learning, those with a pictorial memory may retain this shape of the page as an extra reminder of their lines; both can help in avoiding troublesome pauses and "I'm sorry's" in finding the place during early rehearsals.

This underlining will also be a reminder about one essential point in speaking, or reading aloud, the words of a play; unless a pause or break in the dialogue is clearly indicated, cues must be picked up with a dovetailing continuity. This means the development of a special sense of timing which soon becomes habitual, must always be linked with special care in listening, and is as important to the actor as learning the use of the pedal is to the pianist. Take a breath through the mouth for speech (through the nose is too long and too noisy) as the previous actor comes to within half a line of the end of his speech. Then the subsequent dialogue follows with no lapse and this continuity provides the basis for the pace of the whole production, which will vary but must be capable of a good flow. Nothing is more deadly to the action of a play than a lie-down-and-die break at the end of every speech while someone heaves in a breath. Dialogue is written to be spoken; the flow of ordinary conversation should be repeated on the stage.

Concentrate on any further introduction which the director now gives, and take a careful look at the model of the set which should be produced by the designer. Sketch your own copy of the ground plan in the back of the script, making allowance for two or three plans where there is any change of set; memorize the position of entrances and placing of furniture. The sooner a sense of each location is developed, the less time is likely to be lost in rehearsal.

The town of *Our Town* would be carefully planned even though it is imaginative, while the Wingfield apartment in St. Louis would be comparatively easy to visualize. Each act of *The Cherry Orchard*, however, would be different. The set of the nursery in Acts One and Four would be similar in outline but not in detail, for by the last act only a small amount of furniture would be left and there would be trunks and packing-cases about the room ready for departure. Act Two takes place in a field near a ruined chapel, with perhaps the orchard in the background, and distant telegraph poles winding towards the suggestion of a small town; the third act would be of a sitting-room separated by an arch from the drawing-room, where a dance is taking place. The location of all these points, both on and off-stage, is going to provide one outline of the world in which a future character is to live.

We will assume that the director spends the first two rehearsals after casting in readings of the play. With other business, such as the resumé and discussion of the model, it may only be possible to read it once in this way, though twice is preferable. Listen to any suggestions, mark the script accordingly (with a pencil in case of alterations), and remember to incorporate them later, if not now. Above all, use these readings as a time to listen: to the play itself, to the interplay of character, and especially to other characters in your own scenes. Action in a play is similar to that in life, being a continuous process of the interaction and reaction of persons and events, the one influencing the other. Nothing just is: there are always underlying reasons and causes. In life the result is often untidy, disarranged, and apparently without meaning, until we can perhaps understand from a perspective of time or of distance; but the continuity is present, and unending. In a play the result has an immediate meaning because it is arranged by the dramatist, and if you watch and listen carefully, each unifying point will arise out of his dialogue, and you will become aware of the situations in relation to the whole. Most directors will guide the cast in this respect, but every actor should be prepared to do some investigating for himself.

These readings can be interesting because there is a sense of spontaneity among the cast; as yet there has been little repetition and the lines have a genuine first-time-thought-felt-spoken ring about them. Try to retain a memory of this; the interpretation is now mostly instinctive, and can seem easy and feel right (although sometimes a role is a puzzle until almost opening night). The instinctive approach can be one of the truest gauges an actor has;

held in the imagination, it can give focus to all the coming work on the role.

The next main group of rehearsals will be concerned with blocking the play; for a full-length production this can take six rehearsals, including re-capping of previous acts, as indicated in the Average Production Schedule. Once the first readings are over and blocking rehearsals start, begin to learn the lines, so that this double process can grow together. Allow approximately an act a week. This would seem like hardship to some, placing unwanted pressure on the memory and forcing the role too soon. It is essential, however, that there is an understanding of the difference between what is desirable and ideal in theory, and what is necessary in practice; and in practical terms there is usually a very limited time in which to prepare a play for performance.

Many directors suggest that everyone has his lines heard as they are learnt, a form of rehearsal for rehearsal; some actors forget, lose the continuity, or make slips the first time they try without the book. If this first time is left in every case to an actual rehearsal, the result is bound to be stumbling, and will be more an exercise for the prompter than early practice of the inner and outer action of the play for the cast. Make a point of finding someone who will cue you before first rehearsals of a new section to be memorized. Certain lines or speeches are often more difficult than others, and this is a good way of finding out what you really know, and then working on what you don't.

As much collaboration and confidence is required by actors in each other as by every other department in theatre. An independence and freedom of the mechanics of the words and moves is needed which can only be based on sure and thorough practice; in a sense, only then can detailed rehearsals begin. Memory, however, plays only one part in this process of learning the lines; there is much else to be considered before they can be expected to become the logical outcome of character in the actor's mind, as perhaps they once were in the mind and heart of the playwright.

It is useful to regard early rehearsals as an introduction to the play, and to your role. Then you are ready to begin the major part of preparation with an approach in mind, rather than jumping to conclusions too soon. Preparation, however, being a process that never really ceases, will continue through all the weeks of rehearsal, and may still leave something to be learnt, even during the run of the play.

Preparation

The dialogue of a play is like the tip of an iceberg: ninety per cent can lie underneath. It is this underlying thinking-feeling-intuitive process of the thoughts and ideas of an imaginary human being that the actor now begins to sense and to discover. Then the dialogue will grow out of the personality, seeming to develop as a matter of association rather than as a dull matter of learning by rote. This working through to the core of a role can take time, thought, and study, and may be labelled under different terms; some refer to it as the *spine* of the person; others consider it as the sub-text, or parallel imaginative base of the dialogue, linking the underlying action and re-action.

Finding a way through to the heart of a character will vary with each actor and with each role. While no amount of preparation and research can actually make a performance, any more than costume or make-up can provide a finish without the person within, it can spread horizons, widen the approach, and help the actor place the role within the context of the play. Then there is a perspective, and the greater the knowledge and resources, the more the imagination has to draw on, and the more rounded the eventual belief in the character.

ASSESSING THE PLAY

The director's resumé, and your private and public reading of the play, will give the main indications of theme, plot, and action. Then it can be helpful to consider three questions: What is the purpose of the play? What is the function of the character within this purpose? What has the character to learn – what, for example, is the tragic flaw which undermines his own interests? The answers help provide the solution as to how the role may be performed. The main conflict can be the result of the difference between the purpose of two characters, or between one character and the total situation, or between one character and his inner self. The action of *The Glass Menagerie*, for example, is based on Amanda's purpose of seeing Laura married; this is opposed by Jim's understanding with Betty, which is outside Amanda's control; it is also opposed by her own eagerness to better their lives, and by her daughter's shyness, aggravated by that slight physical defect. In *Our Town* there is a comfortable sense of the same hope of Mrs. Webb for Emily, but it creates no conflict because it is fulfilled.

The above examples are comparatively straightforward, but when we come to a more complex play like *The Cherry Orchard*, opinions are bound to vary. Some will say the main theme is of an old order changing; others that the play is the tragic reversal in Madame Ranevsky's life; still others will see it, as termed by Chekhov, as a comedy – of the serious absurdities of life. While it contains all these elements, a director would stress one to make his point, rather than give an equal importance to each. Beginning even with Stanislavsky, however, directors of this play have misinterpreted Chekhov's terms for it, and he was dismayed by first results. This is an interesting example of yet another conflict: between the creative artist, who is said to be not always conscious and fully aware of all he creates, and the interpreter, who takes and fashions a work sometimes more on his own account than with respect for the original intent. The actor's work, however, is always guided by the director's approach.

If the people in *The Cherry Orchard* are regarded as tragic figures, then Varya, the adopted daughter of Madame Ranevsky, can be played as sensitive and keenly aware of the possible reversal in her life when, near the end of the play, she apparently comes to do some final packing in the old nursery. Lopahin, who has bought the property, has been told she is in love with him, though he may doubt that this is true; but he does know that he is expected to propose to her:

VARYA: It's very odd, I can't find it anywhere.
LOPAHIN: What are you looking for?
VARYA: I packed it myself, and I can't remember.
LOPAHIN: Where are you going now, Varvara Mikhailovna?
VARYA: Me? I'm going to the Ragulins'. They've engaged me to keep house for them – to be housekeeper, or something like that.
LOPAHIN: Oh, at Yashnevo? That's about fifty miles from here. Well, so life in this house is over now.
VARYA: Wherever can it be? Perhaps I put it in the trunk. Yes, life here is over – there will be no more of it.
LOPAHIN: And I'm off to Kharkov now – by the same train. A lot of business to do. I'm leaving Yepihodov to look after the place. I've taken him on.
VARYA: Have you?
LOPAHIN: This time last year we had snow already, if you remember; but now it's fine and sunny. Still, it's cold for all that. Three degrees below.

VARYA: Were there? I didn't look. And then the thermometer is broken.

A VOICE: Yermolia Alexeyevich!

LOPAHIN: Coming!

Guided by the director, both performers would know the purpose behind the scene. Lopahin, feeling that he cannot move out of his social sphere (his father was a serf on the estate which he has now bought), assumes that Varya, though poor, would not accept him, and at some point selects a moment of excuse. Varya, using the luggage as her excuse for being in the nursery, and hoping for what does not come, would also select the moment when she knows Lopahin will not propose. If, however, she was played as a passionate creature, both in love with him and wanting to avoid the life to come at the Ragulins', her reaction would be strong. If she is "the perfect fool, but very good-natured," "a nun, a foolish creature" and "a weeper by nature, so that her tears ought not to depress the spectators," as Chekhov wrote in his letters and telegrams, her reaction would probably dissolve into another of those weeps.

Once the line of purpose becomes clear within a play and within a scene, it becomes easier to establish the development of the character, with particular reference to three points: (a) the order of events as they occur on-stage, (b) the life of the person before the curtain rises, and (c) unless he dies, his life after it comes down. What was Lopahin like before, and what will he now become as a result of owning the property? In *The Glass Menagerie*, what was Tom's upbringing like, how does he break away from home, and what eventually happens to him after the episode of the Gentleman Caller? In *Pygmalion* (*My Fair Lady*), what of the difference between Eliza as a flower girl and the Eliza who owns a flower shop, as developed within the action of the play? The total purpose, therefore, and the before, on-stage, off-stage, and after life is all part of the consistency of the character.

Now it would be useful to do some research both within and without the play, so that there is a continual delving from the general aspects of any background – history or geography – to the selection of these facts in relation to one particular role.

Anton Chekhov (1860-1904)

BACKGROUND

Where does the action of the play take place, and what other circumstances may influence the character? The setting is not merely a question of the suggestions of the writer and designer, but an awareness on the part of the actor. The design for *The Glass Menagerie* could be a simple skeletal set; but the cast would find it helpful to consider the total atmosphere – provided by the color of the wall-paper, the drapes and when and where they were bought, the thousands of similar meals eaten off the dining table – and the unseen areas of the apartment: the kitchen and its worn linoleum on the floor, the bleak outlook from the window into a brick wall, the entrance via the alley and the fire-escape landing.

The research for *Our Town* would be wider, because it is set in a period other than our own; even though the whole conception is imaginary, the research must be just as painstaking. In *The Cherry Orchard*, consider the flatness of the countryside, the architecture, furniture, costumes, music and favorite instruments, painting and sculpture, and the total life of the people. Think of the house, outside and in, the colors, the views from the nursery, the river where Madame Ranevsky's son was drowned, and the driveway by which everyone enters and leaves the house. Become immersed in this past until it becomes the present of the character; then there are images, associations, memories to be used, all helping towards creating a composite person.

Since acting is a question of interpreting as well as creating a role, find out something of the author, the development of his own life, and any particular influence he may have had on the theatre. Chekhov, for example, was a doctor, and grandson of a serf who managed to buy his family's freedom at five hundred rubles a head, twenty years before serfdom was abolished. By the time he wrote his last play, *The Cherry Orchard*, in 1903, he was already well-known as a journalist and writer of short stories. His first plays, including the one-act comedy *The Marriage Proposal* (1889), were of direct action, telling a story as it happened; his four later plays were of indirect action, more concerned with the reaction of characters to major events which took place off-stage, having their climax, such as the selling of the property in *The Cherry Orchard*, in the third rather than the fourth, or last, act. In 1904 this doctor of souls as well of bodies died of consumption, as he knew he would, at the age of forty-three. His plays did for Stanislavsky and the Moscow Art Theatre what, perhaps in lesser degree, Synge and Yeats did for the Abbey Theatre in Ireland, and O'Neill for the Provincetown Players in the next decade. A prolific writer (he had already published over four hundred stories and articles when he qualified as a doctor at the age of twenty four), he was a great traveller, and a doctor who cared deeply enough about the human condition that he undertook research at his own expense at a convict settlement in Siberia. He also possessed a quiet and joyous sense of humor. The characters in his great plays, therefore, are rarely superficial, and he establishes in a supremely organized fashion much of the disjointedness of life: the conversations at a tangent; the lack of communication; and whole families who never quite listen to what any one member really has to say.

Although there will be something of the author in every play he writes, it is usually in his early ones that his own life is more reflected, or in some way written out, than in others. In the case of O'Neill, for example, his personal tragedies are always evident in his longer plays; and there is much of Williams in *The Glass Menagerie*, with Amanda and Laura modelled to some extent on his own mother and sister. Thornton Wilder's sheer good nature, that of a bubbling Mr. Pickwick, shines through his plays, and he has a fascination for reducing time to tangible everyday occurrences – from the stage manager's commentary in *Our Town* to the dinosaurs on the lawn during the ice age of *Skin Of Our Teeth*. So become familiar with the writer as a singer would with his composer, a reader with his poet, or a photographer with his subject.

LANGUAGE

The language of a play is the medium of the writer's expression, and should be treated with respect, learnt as written, and not altered during rehearsal or performance, any more than musicians would change the notes of a symphony. In the case of a new and untried play there is likely to be change and experiment with the lines, but these, if possible, should be made in collaboration with the author.

Remember that words have a sound as well as a sense; most actors tend to make more of one than the other; ideally they find a marriage of both. This quality was termed by Elsie Fogerty, one of the greatest teachers in the English theatre and founder of the Central School of Speech and Drama, the "musical significance of sound," and every actor would do well to read her article on Speech in the *Oxford Companion To The Theatre*.

The meaning and purpose of words will subscribe to their sound. Sense the imagery, the idiom of verse, of prose, the contrasting expressions of character, the shaping towards the climax, and, above all, the rhythm. This can be the key to the inherent manner of expression (style) of the total production, of the playing of each scene, and the action and re-action of each character. Rhythm is there to be used by actors and director, suggesting the flow of a scene, including the pauses, which have a length and rhythm that are part of the whole, and the stress, or lilt, of the accent which the author has in mind.

A famous example of rhythm in speech is Professor Higgins' comment on and repetition of the "wood-notes wild" of Eliza's father, "I'm willing to tell you, I'm waiting to tell you, I'm wanting to tell you." This underlying quality of rhythm and pertinent use of phrase often imposes such a strong form on a character that every actor invariably catches the author's mould and will interpret the character in a similar way; but by lending his own personality to it, he also places his own seal upon the role. Such eternal figures grow larger than the confines of a theatre, and the Mrs. Malaprops (*The Rivals*), Lady Bracknells (*The Importance of Being Earnest*), Amandas (*The Glass Menagerie*), Sir Toby Belches (*Twelfth Night*), and Professor Higgins' (*Pygmalion*) are, and will be, familiar to many generations in all parts of the world.

The actor's sense of rhythm is important. What he senses from the writer he passes on to the audience as the base, though not the whole, of an integral part of his equipment: timing. This almost mathematical sense of how to pace a line or a move, wait for a laugh, point a word or look, or react to another character or situation, is a quality that cannot be taught, but with experience can best be learnt from good writers and audiences, and with guidance from a director.

It is important to realize that there is a close connection between the results of rhythm, sound, and meaning. A word or phrase altered, or that is stubborn in coming to the memory, can mean not so much poor expression on the part of the author, as the fact that the actor has not yet been able to assimilate it within the frame of the character. Then, again, such alteration can throw others in the cast since the elimination, even of a syllable, changes the rhythm; change in rhythm, to their ears, brings a change in the melody; and change in melody results in a change in meaning; and so the author's true intent is lost. Another actor, when one small difference throws his listening out of gear, can look at you, for example, as if he has never heard the cue before. While he should not fall into the trap of listening to a mere pattern rather than to the actual words, he has to rely to some extent on what is to come so that he may continue within the expected context of his own performance. So the medium of the writer is incomplete until given the final clothing of speech. Ideally an actor's voice becomes the mirror of his imagination, reflecting all the subtlety of feeling and thought experienced by the character; all use should be made of the sensations within each image, those of our five senses of touch, taste, sight, smell, and hearing. If Constable Warren in *Our Town* pictures Simon Stimson, "rollin' around a little," the audience will receive a similar picture. When Amanda describes her visit to that depressing business college, she will need to clothe the author's words with her own memory of the situation – the entrance and layout of the school, the color of the walls, the arrangement of the desks – and create, with belief, a concept of an off-stage character: the typing instructor. Similarly, Varya in *The Cherry Orchard* will want an image of the Ragulins if she is to know and to convey what she feels her life as their housekeeper may become: what of her relationship with them – friend of the family or lonely help? how many children do they have? and what, if anything, of her future? or will she remain there for life?

FOREGROUND

So far we have been concerned with a process of thinking around a character and situation, and now it is time to delve from the general to particular conditions. We have mentioned the total purpose within the play, within the character's life, and within a scene; so now particular influences and relationships with others should be included. Obviously those in *Our Town* seem happy and normal, but there are complications between mother and son and mother and daughter in *The Glass Menagerie*, based partly on a conflict of purpose and partly on the economic life of the family. The careful poverty aggravates the situation, becoming almost as important as another character. It would be interesting to imagine the same people under different conditions, and to consider what would have happened if the Wingfields belonged in a higher income bracket; the plot would be similar, but perhaps acted out among split-level housing and country-club surroundings.

The economic and social conditions of *The Cherry Orchard* are again part of the fabric of each character, but with the added contrast of the servants, soon to become the equals of their present employers, who are fated to be permanent exiles in Paris.

Next, consider the dialogue in detail with reference to the two most often made points about character – in a play, as in life: what they say of others, and what others say of them. Take into account not merely the surface value but the total regard and underlying needs which may color the relationship. Amanda, for example, is strangling her daughter with too much outward concern, and trying to live her own youth again in her. While genuinely fond of both her children, and still loyal to the charm of the husband who has left her, she pours all her affection and ambition towards them with the best of intent – but with what result! Part of the growing into the skin of a role is to sense the intaking and outgiving of these impressions of others, and then it becomes possible not only to act, but to re-act. Similarly, a gradual knowledge of what Laura and Tom really feel about their mother can help avoid those uncertain moments in coming rehearsals when a performance lives during the dialogue and dies when silent. It will create a consistency of that line, spine, or what-you-will, and provide a reason for much of the on and off-stage behavior.

Look carefully at the climax of the play, and see how this turning point influences, or is directly or indirectly influenced by, the character you are creating. Somewhere this will make a difference even to minor roles, and the shaping of the climax will be the eventual test of individual ability and of the whole production. The actual release of emotion will, like the intensity, vary considerably, depending on the language, the situation, the character, and the interpretation. Laura, for example, has four words of first reaction to Jim's excuse for not being free to contact her again, and after his "I've got strings on me, Laura" speech, all she does is mutely hand him the broken unicorn. He asks her three questions before she finds a two-word reply as reason for her gesture. Then her only other line is in agreement with her mother in wishing Jim good luck; but obviously much, though deadened on the surface, is happening within. This is an instance where the actress fills in what the author, through a minimum of dialogue, has suggested.

In *The Cherry Orchard* the climax comes, as previously mentioned, at the end of the third rather than the last act; and the reactions to Lopahin's news that he has bought the property vary from Varya's throwing down the keys and exit to the sudden release in words of the buyer, and the silent weeping of the past owner, Madame Ranevsky.

Within this total framework, it will become possible to see the shape of a role: the development of this human being as he or she influences, and is influenced by, events, and by others – all arising out of conflict. With study, the shape will sharpen into focus until an outline becomes familiar.

All of which is just as much applicable to comedy as to tragedy. Let's consider Lomov, the suitor, in Chekhov's *The Marriage Proposal*. The story is outlined within the title, and the purpose of all three characters is the same: to arrange a wedding between Lomov and Natalia, regarded as a piece of good fortune by her father, Tschubukov. Everything, then, should be plain sailing: the suitor is thirty-five, and a neighbor, and Natalia is – not young. He is, however, extremely nervous, and his appearing in dress clothes complete with white gloves, both perhaps to give himself courage and to honor the occasion, unfortunately creates more of his self-made conflict. By the time Tschubukov sends in his daughter, we know all about Lomov's weak heart, palpitations, trembling lips, pulsing temple, and sleepless nights from a soliloquy that has, like all good speeches, a continuity, shape, and climax of its own. One misfortune of his condition is piled upon another until, once he has got to sleep, all is succeeded by something worse: a terrible cramp in the side.

He is now in such a state of nerves that Natalia's entrance doubles his agony, and for half a page he is almost wordless. Then she comments on his clothes and it seems he is about to propose, when he mentions the subject of certain meadows as a part of his inheritance. The conflict over their rightful ownership begins casually until, with Tschubukov's entrance, it has mounted to a full-scale argument, and now becomes a conflict of two against one. Each remark, whether about embezzling uncles, dipsomaniac ancestors, or limping mothers, rises to a row that causes Lomov to retire, physically wilting but mentally fighting still. After Natalia has discovered the real reason for his visit, he returns, still almost punch-drunk from the fight, but weakly determined to stick to his principles. She cleverly changes the subject to hunting, and for half a page there is peace. But a second and more violent conflict begins with argument over the price and merits of two hunting dogs. In spite of the short lower jaw, Lomov defends his Ugadi most hotly; but his palpitations grow worse with every insult while, between gasps, his heart bursts, his shoulder seems torn from its usual place, and he again collapses. Father and daughter assume that he is dead, but he revives and she declares she is willing;

dazed, he accepts, and as Tschubukov fetches champagne, the conflict over the dogs begins all over again Curtain.

Purpose, action, conflict, reaction, momentary defeat, further conflict, apparent death, and a revival. Few plays contain half as much in so short a time, or provide more opportunity for actors both in character and in situation. What they say about themselves and each other is a marvellous reflection of their own selves: Lomov with his perpetual palpitation of the heart and hammering of the arteries; Natalia telling him, "You needn't scream so! If you want to scream and snort and rage you may do it at home, but here please keep yourself within the limits of common decency"; and Tschubukov's "You're an intriguer, that's what you are! Your whole family were always looking for quarrels. The whole lot!" Then Lomov calls him an intriguer in return, asks what makes Natalia scream, and declares her father is no hunter and only rides to flatter the count. Many of the charges and countercharges contain common truths that are part of the delight of the play, and are perhaps one reason why it is already a minor classic. They include Natalia's "I have always noticed that the hunters who do the most talking know the least about hunting," and Lomov's "It was only the principle of the thing – the property isn't worth much to me, but the principle is worth a great deal."

Rehearsals

Here, then, within the script, lies a whole fabric waiting to be fashioned by the actor. First, however, it must be given a form and pattern before it can be fitted, which brings us to the next stage in the sequence of preparing a character for performance: the rehearsals mainly concerned with the movements of the play and usually referred to as blocking rehearsals.

BLOCKING REHEARSALS

This type of rehearsal has already been discussed in some detail in the chapter on the director, and for a three-act play blocking is likely to take a minimum of six rehearsals. Including re-caps to ensure that Act One is not forgotten while Acts Two and Three are blocked, each act has the chance of approximately two blocking rehearsals. Concentrate on what is required, and note your moves directly into your script, in pencil for there may be changes. Try to be accurate, for although the stage manager will also keep a record, it can waste time to have to keep re-checking where and when you *do* move.

The progress of these rehearsals may seem slow and sometimes confusing to the less experienced. Laura, for example, might consider she is being left in one place for a long time with nothing apparent to do; and, after all, acting is doing. But remember that blocking rehearsals can only move in very slow motion, and that a couple of pages which might take five minutes for everyone to take down moves and walk through carefully may well take less than half that time to perform. Acting is also concerned with two kinds of action, inner and outer, and in varying degrees most roles provide a combination of both. Because Laura is sitting still, it does not mean there is no development of character. In some productions she might remain sitting on the edge of the day-bed for much of Scene Two, and in this case the more static she is the more a contrast can be achieved with her mother; but within, she is continually reacting to Amanda and to the entire context of the situation.

It is a good rule for the actor to realize he should take, follow, and try the blocking as given by the director. There are bound to be some difficulties, so at the end ask if there could be alternatives or, if the atmosphere is conducive, make suggestions that would feel more suitable. A good director will usually encourage actors to try their own "doing," for they are the ones who have to carry it out; but he must have the final decision. Remember that each performance will be seen by the audience in relation to other performances, and in relation to the whole play; the actor may imagine, but never literally sees, the final result, and it is the director's work to co-ordinate, with the co-operation of many, the total effect.

Ideally the link between actor and director is essentially one of collaboration: a partnership in which the actor is guided in his particular role so that it may fit and grow within the total concept of the production. If the partnership is to be creative, it needs, like any other, to be based on trust and respect, so that the collaboration is carried through in word and in action.

The approach to lead roles is usually discussed with the actors concerned, and is likely to be suggested for the main body of the cast during the time of the first readings. So by the blocking rehearsals there is a common ground of agreement as to what the director hopes to see and what the Amanda, Laura, or Lomov hopes to build over the next few weeks. Once this has been established, and both director and actor have accepted the responsibility of the production and the role, it is an unwritten law in the theatre that both honor their side of the arrangement. They will make changes and will need to experiment, for both are necessary if the play and the role are to be fully explored and discovered. Should a marked difference of opinion, however, become apparent, it is the actor who complies with the director, realizing that having accepted the role – which no one is ever forced to do – he then abides by his side of that unwritten law. Acting is essentially a group activity, and each member of the cast has this responsibility to the group, which should come before personal considerations. A good director will instil enthusiasm for the production so that all are prepared to sink differences towards a common end.

Be sure at this time to try and learn the number of lines indicated by the director for each rehearsal. One person, for example, having to read Act Two now, is likely to be stumbling later when the rest of the cast are beginning to sense a flow of action and response. This could cause further delay if he is still plunging into Act Three while the others are capable of a complete run-through without books.

Even when you seem to know the lines, keep working at them; many actors make it a habit to thrust the book into friendly hands at home, or at a coffee or lunch-break at work. It is also a good idea to make time to have extra rehearsals of certain scenes. Sometimes the Natalia and Lomov, or the Amanda and Tom, might make it a point to arrive at ordinary rehearsals half-an-hour early, for an essential part of a good performance is absolute confidence in teamwork with others in the cast.

FIRST RUN-THROUGH

There is now progress in two main areas: work at home in studying the role, linked with a gradual mastery of the mechanics with others during rehearsal. So the imagination begins to create a new and unique character. This brings us to a major point within the Average Production Schedule: the first run-through without books, which should be possible by the end of Week Four. Remember to be alert for all entrances and any *voices off* that might be your responsibility, for now the action will run at approximately the same pace as in performance, and these moments can appear much more quickly than in previous rehearsals. When on-stage, listen to others from the heart of your own character; when off-stage, listen to the development of the whole play, and sense the atmosphere of the production. If there has been a re-cap of each act during the blocking rehearsals, this run-through should go reasonably smoothly. If it is attended by production staff, as suggested in the chapter on the director, it should give everyone a tangible idea of first results, and can provide a sense of flow and clear sequence of events for the cast.

The run-through will also bring to light certain gaps in continuity, and scenes and speeches that need particular work. Note these, and resolve if possible to clear them before the next rehearsal of that section. Try to develop this awareness of an individual sense of constructive criticism, for while there will be experience with many other actors, directors, and audiences, this personal standard can be applied in the case of every production, and it remains within an actor to guide him in any role he ever plays.

PROGRESSIVE REHEARSALS

The first run-through without books is likely to provide a surprise which has so far been cushioned by intensive study of lines and concentration on blocking. There are now probably only two weeks left prior to opening night. Since Week Six will include technical and dress rehearsals, the coming week (Five) is often the period of most solid development of a character, though this cannot always be expected to coincide with results; it can take a while to learn to express what lies within.

Every actor, and every artist, experiences at some time the problem of knowing, hearing, seeing how he wants to do something; such intent is important in any communication; but, like sincerity, while a beginning, it is not always enough. It is as if the craft of a medium must be mastered before it can be used to any purpose; so the painter has to learn control of his brush, and the pianist of his touch; for sheer imagination and dogged emotionalism, for example, can suppress and tie in knots the very qualities that an actor is trying to convey. There is a need for the release of his intentions, and by understanding that his own self is his only instrument, the actor will soon realize that he needs a control of that instrument – as an athlete of his body, and a singer of his voice – and therefore of total co-ordination of all its members. Mention has already been made of the inner muscle of the imagination; continuing practice will improve the range and control of any muscular action: inner, of the mind and heart, as expressed in outer action of the body. When the actor can use these means as part of a well-tuned instrument, he has the beginnings of what is known as technique, and the purpose of technique is his ability to communicate with, and often to move, an audience.

The actor, for example, needs breath, breath, and still more breath to provide the motive power for his voice, so that he may adapt phrasing to character and meaning, pick up cues, project and place a channel of sound so that his speech may be heard, felt, and understood under all conditions. He should always remember that if speech is to flow, yet control and point the speaking-writing of the dialogue, he requires a precision of articulation, and an ear for the rhythm of the writing and the sound of the character. Like the muscles mentioned above, it is as if he needs two kinds of ear – again, inner and outer; one hearing what is wanted within, and in a sense pre-setting the instrument, and the other, an outward ear, assessing results. Both these ears will depend as much on the imagination, set off by the playwright, as by observation of how people sound in real life. In this sense the actor has a further storehouse through the eye, known as the kinesthetic sense, by which he may observe a movement, retain it through his muscular memory, and be able to repeat it months or years later as part of the imaginary character he is then creating. When a performer uses merely these retentive qualities of eye and ear, he is a mimic, an imitator of life; when he uses them to create, via the playwright's intention, he becomes an actor, an interpreter of life.

Gradually there comes an ability not only to attain, but to repeat; otherwise it is bewildering to find a scene feels right at one rehearsal, and has gone the next. This is a natural hazard in any learning process, which usually progresses through plateaus of learning so that higher levels are achieved for certain glimpses of time, and then elusively sink into valleys before rising again to show further results. This development can, however, be balanced by that awareness of memory (behind eye, ear, and feeling) of how a scene was played, or a move or turn made, in relation to the purpose behind it. This ability to develop and repeat with consistency is one of the marks of experience, and every minute of rehearsal should be used with concentration. Then the conscious *how* can be dropped, retained as unconscious habit, and the *what* will shine through. Changes in blocking, suggestions on the implication behind a line, alterations in the timing of a sit or a stand, however, all need to be incorporated at the first rather than the fourth or sixth try. Even with concentration, there will be occasions when a wise director will suggest that you work on such moments at home so that there is time for a new approach to percolate.

"*Work on that at home.*" How often actors are given this note by a director, and perhaps wonder what it means. How can you "work" on anything so ephemeral as the moments in time when you are trying to become another human being? Is it not possible to rely on the inspiration that must surely come, the "It'll be all right on the night" attitude?

Inspiration never arises out of nothing, cannot be relied on, and is usually the result of sheer, hard, and apparently non-productive work. Only then does the accumulation of thoughts, facts, and ideas, half-perceived, slip suddenly into place, and the process behind the lines of Amanda, or Madame Ranevsky, is understood.

To work in private, at home, means to delve, experiment, hear inwardly, and try outwardly until a line or move can be spoken or made as you feel the character intended. Do not be afraid to analyse, to find out *what* is hard, and, if possible, *why*; often preparation is a breaking down into small parts so that each facet of character and situation may be seen and felt, and then re-built again into a whole that will grow in rehearsal and last through the run of performance. All the feeling in the world cannot be conveyed on a voice that lacks breath, by speech lacking precision, or through lines or moves that are uncertain. If it helps, put breath-marks in your copy of the script, arrow the minor and the major climaxes in different ways, plot out the development of this person – realizing that by performance all is so assimilated that, while such detail exists, it is also unnoticed. An audience comes to see results, not the wheels within.

Remember that in a good play there are as many sides to a character as windows to a lighthouse; we see Amanda losing hope after the incident of the business college, and finding it with the advent of the Gentleman Caller. As in our own personalities some of these sides are more predominant than others, and shine in reaction to different people and to different circumstances. The hardest of hearts will be vulnerable, and the warmest of hearts will cool somewhere; but this may be shown, or seem to escape, only at one moment in contrast to the main trend. It is a trap to try and convey everything about a character all at the same time.

Few actors are going to know immediately (a) *what* they want to do with a role, and (b) *how* to do it; their work would probably lack depth if they did. So do not be afraid of making mistakes – that, in a sense, is what practice is for – but time will be saved in rehearsal if some of the experiments are made in private. The greater the role, the more there is going to be to discover, and finally to share, with an audience.

Further development Meanwhile co-ordination is required, not just of one actor and his instrument, but between all actors – in concert. One breath late, one line lost, a reaction out of proportion, a move timed too late or too soon, and all the efforts of a team have to be re-built, whether a small team as the trio in *The Marriage Proposal* or a larger team as in the third act and party in *The Cherry Orchard*.

The underlying rhythm or beat of a scene may have to take precedence over the actor's individual approach; if he is wise he will blend his ideas with the needs of the scene. Lomov and Natalia, for example, need to build to a minor crescendo (this is the first of a series of battles, and a grand fortissimo should be reserved for the last) with their, "The meadows belong to me!", "Us!", "Me!" for Tschubukov to return and say, "What's going on here? What's he yelling about?" Each of these monosyllables comes on a strong beat, the climax coming, as in music, with a rise in pitch and a corresponding increase in tempo. Even a short sequence such as this requires a timing which can be repeated so that Tschubukov can make his entrance. Depending on the size of the stage and the design of the set, he may have a way to come before he says his line, which will be wanted from the right place at a certain moment. Once achieved, these lines could require repetition, until they seem to arise automatically out of the situation, as seen by each character.

Remember that even in a small rehearsal room it will be a help to establish a sense of projecting speech, trying the character for size, as it were, for the much larger space which it must soon fill. It should not be necessary to have to rely on reminders from the director, and, if some projection is incorporated into regular rehearsals, it will be much easier to bridge the greater gap at the coming dress rehearsals.

Actors differ greatly in their approach to acting and to a role; there are no golden answers, or short cuts in the studying. There is a perpetual search for the way that seems true and faithful to what the author has written, as interpreted by the actor and guided by the director until gradually re-created with each rehearsal and so made ready for performance.

Bear in mind that what you may have rehearsed one-hundred-and-one times is always a first-time happening to the character and to the audience, and that this requires a discipline within the self and with others which differs from that of the painter, composer, playwright, and poet, who work in seclusion. You always rehearse and perform with others, and always at specified times. No one can act merely when the psyche moves him, or down tools and think of something else when he knows that a fallow period is upon him, one of those plateaus in the development of learning. There is a continual responsibility to many others, which is also part of the tremendous satisfaction of participating in a good production and of helping to create an entire world, from virtually nothing more than the printed words on a page.

As they become more familiar with a character, and to help them retain the associations and reasons for action and re-action, some actors join what is underneath and supporting the text by writing in a sub-text to their script. A few will do so in entirety, copying out their lines in triple-spacing with ample room for these invisible lines; others merely add the conjunctive, or joining, thoughts. Some star their copies with reference to previous thoughts, moments from which a crisis grows, or development from one transition to another. All such points should be regarded as aids; they can be the results of considerable study, but could not in themselves make a performance. Be prepared to use whatever seems to help a role at a particular time, and to vary the approach, for every author and every play will make slightly different demands.

Inner resources At some point it is essential to experience the situations as vividly and imaginatively as possible and, since we learn and develop by parallels of what we know, this can first be done by putting the actor's own self within a memory of a similar situation. Few actors will have experienced rows with their mother identical to that of Tom and Amanda in Act One, Scene Three of *The Glass Menagerie;* but, being human, most are bound to remember something of a few arguments on which to draw. Few people may have owned a house and land which has been in their family for centuries as in *The Cherry Orchard*, but on another level we may have lost something material that is just as important to us, leaving a similar gap in our lives. Then, sensing how the loss might feel, it becomes easier to put ourselves in the place of our character and realize the full implication of a particular scene.

There will, however, be situations which an actor is unlikely to have experienced: shutting up an old house (like Firs, the eighty year old servant in *The Cherry Orchard*, realizing perhaps for the first time the futility of his whole life); or being a girl who has a lame leg and an emotionally hurt mind; being dead in one sense in *Our Town* and in another in *The Marriage Proposal;* or in other plays becoming one who murders, steals, commits crimes of commission or omission, or who is rich where the actor is poor, or poor where he is rich. While actors should, ideally, be able to communicate any, or all, of these qualities to an audience through imagination and belief, any actor will find it easier to convey some than others. And although all audiences should react in the same way, some will be more capable of receiving these impressions than others. Then there will be a sense of recognition of the situations and of the flaws, the failures, and the solutions of the characters, leading to a feeling of identity, and so of participation in the action. All human beings are capable of far greater depth and resources of emotion and extremes of conduct than we ever encompass in reality, and somewhere the potential exists. It is these tremendously adaptable inner resources for which an actor has to search; then he can use them to build an approach to almost any role. The greatest need is likely to come at the climax, which brings about the reversal, or turning-point, of the character.

The climax of the play The climax will bring some form of release or reaction; it may be implied and delayed, with the actual moment taking place off-stage. When Laura realizes Jim is not free, she says very little, but probably reacts far more to herself later. A sense of this moment often helps the total understanding of the character, and it is this quality which can give value to a performance. A good Amanda can show she is ridiculous, brave, and gay, but will also share with an audience something of *why* she became like that, *what* she wants from life, and *how* she tries to get it. Since we all have a measure of these qualities, perhaps somewhere within there will be an added compassion, for "there, but for the grace . . ., and under those circumstances . . ." This understanding becomes a tool which gradually illuminates the character for the actor, who can then, via his one instrument of his own self, share his interpretation with each audience.

So much for the rehearsal and study of a role; the total rehearsal period is likely to be interspersed with costume fittings, photo calls, and perhaps publicity interviews for which, again, everyone should aim to be punctual.

DRESS REHEARSALS

Dress rehearsals represent the final co-ordination of all aspects of a production for performance, to which reference has already been made in previous chapters. There should, if possible, be two, of which the second may be regarded as a preview so that actors may have their final practice with an audience. The first is usually preceded by a costume parade and may be a stop-start affair, so that wrinkles may be ironed out as they appear – for example, the timing of lights with cues, or difficulty with the opening and closing of practical doors and windows. The second dress rehearsal should, in theory, be a complete run-through, with a minimum of notes to be checked at the end, so that, as nearly as possible, it represents the conditions of performance; in practice, however, this depends on the readiness of all departments, including the cast, and on the judgment of the director.

Arrive with plenty of time to spare to be ready in costume and make-up for the costume parade. It can also be helpful to take a look at the set first, as it will always come as a surprise after customary work in a bare rehearsal room. If it is reasonably ready, and you can do so without getting in anybody's way, try out the furniture, doorways, and properties, moving through certain lines, testing the feel of the set, and rehearsing a few lines aloud to sense the acoustics of the theatre.

Make up carefully, and in relation or contrast to others; the servants in *The Cherry Orchard*, for example, are likely to have more rugged complexions than the family which does no work. Think of the costume as being the final skin of the role, but at the same time be practical and check any hand-props or those that you carry on-stage with you as part of the costume, such as gloves, hat, stick, or purse.

Listen for the sound of the call of "Half an hour, please!" and the others which follow, so that you are aware of the time left before being needed. When the final call comes, go into the wings, or on-stage, as requested. After your costume has been checked, remember that there should be no alterations unless requested and then re-checked with the director; the same should apply to make-up. Few dress rehearsals can be run without some delay, so try to use extra time for concentration on the role, or for quietly going through a few scenes with others. Remember that silence in the wings will be essential. Clear what is often crowded space in the entrances as soon as you come off-stage; during any form of scene-change the cast should again clear the stage, leaving everything to do with the set in the hands of the stage manager and his staff; but it is always wise to note that any props you will use are ready and in position. Make it a firm rule always to replace any properties used; ideally they should boomerang back, as it were, to the appropriate table in the wings. Similarly, take care of your costume, and have any changes organized so that each garment is ready in proper order. Do not leave any garment lying around; hang, or fold it, and similarly leave make-up tidy and ready for further use.

Think of what are now the additional elements of costume and set in relation to your character; use them and incorporate them into the performance. If a chair is placed at an unaccustomed angle, change it as your character might; if someone leaves a door open which should be closed, close it as your character would; small emergencies will happen, and when a prompt, for example, is needed, again stay in character.

Belief in a role implies knowing what the character would do under every and any circumstance. Acting can be regarded as one of the best possible examples of positive thinking, and if the actor assumes, "I am," he will be, and the audience will agree. Within this assumption, however, rests a degree of vitality which could be termed will-power; it is one thing to act convincingly for the self, but another to inject the words of the playwright with such life that a total image is projected to hundreds, or possibly thousands, of people sitting at some distance from a stage. This will to project with clarity and with intent is part of the magic of acting; using his own self as his medium, it enables an actor to transmit an image of something that he is perhaps not, but in which he momentarily believes. Whether this power is termed magic or hypnotism, it catches, through a certain empathy, the imagination of the audience. Then together they see a beautiful woman transmitted by an actress who is plain; an old and ugly man by an actor who is handsome; age where there is youth, and even youth where there is age. All stemming from the actor's courage of belief.

Listen carefully to the director's notes; he is now able to assess for the first time the total result of the production in the theatre, and is bound to ask for minor changes. The main work of the actor is now often concerned, however, with managing the technical side of his performance, and with enlarging it so that he can project to all parts of the theatre, without losing or changing the essence of the role. At the first dress rehearsal one or the other of these sides is usually predominant; by the second, both should be combined, and so a new character is ready to be shared with an audience.

Performance

Now the ritual of performance is about to begin. Depending on the role and the play, it begins for many actors early in the day; many concentrate, consciously or otherwise, on the role they are to play for some hours prior to curtain time. When conditions permit, this can be a useful form of final preparation, a synthesis of all the previous weeks of study and rehearsal.

Unseen by the audience, the actors will arrive about an hour in advance; unseen by the actors, the audience begins to arrive half an hour in advance, and by a different entrance. The actor goes through the necessary and often reassuring routine of making-up and putting on his costume; the audience, too, will be dressed for their share in the ritual, probably in their Saturday, if not Sunday, best. Actors react differently to their routine; some grow quieter and quieter, retiring into their roles as they assume the outward form, using this hour as a time of growing concentration; others find it hard to keep their excitement within. Both can become infectious, and the trend may well depend on the type of play about to be performed.

Avoid any last-minute rush, and be ready for the call. Concentrate on the action to come, and use any nerves in a positive way – towards a greater sense of awareness, in being sure there is a good breath for the opening line, or in hearing it with that inner ear which will help provide control. Keep thinking ahead; an exit in one scene, and time off-stage, can be used in preparation for the next; keep well back in the wings until needed, and do not anticipate an entrance by being visible to the audience. Should anything happen and someone forget to make an entrance, improvise; if the lights fuse, keep going – they may soon be mended; if you need a prompt, accept it in character; retain the role at all costs, and the audience will retain the illusion.

Be alert for any laughs; not for their own sake, but because the action needs to be suspended during the sound or else the audience will miss the following lines. Start again just after the peak of sound has been reached: too soon, people's enjoyment will be cut and they will be bewildered; too late, and the bubble of action will die. It may be necessary to "cap" the sound even as it falls, for if the following speech begins too softly the opening words would also be missed. Judgment can only come with experience, and with instinct; avoid relying on these moments, for each audience, having a different personality, has a different funny-bone. A howl one night can produce silence the next, much depending on the way the line is said; while known to be funny to the actor, the line is rarely so to his character, and it is unwise to treat it obviously. This would become what is known as "playing for laughs," which might satisfy vanity a little, but which would also distort the character at the expense of the play.

Every performance requires an inner discipline, a summoning of resources, and the greatest possible concentration on the shaping of the role. Most actors will retain some awareness of results – that self-critic at work – but should aim for them through the character and for the scene as much as for the sake of personal development. It is not hard to discover little tricks to make an audience laugh; a tiny gimmick such as the raising of an eyebrow can be enough. Nor is it difficult to distract from the focus of attention by the smallest of moves, for a moving object is always good advertisement. It is easy enough to misplace a move, or find a sudden mental blackout so that it seems impossible to remember anything of what comes next (though if the weeks of preparation have been well-founded, a certain habit, similar to the reflex action of breathing or blinking, will break through and restore the broken pattern). But it requires an invisible and positive self-control to retain what is needed for the production, and to polish and replenish each moment in proportion, and to the best possible degree, for every single performance.

Be ready for the final curtain call, either as rehearsed at the end of the dress rehearsal, or as posted on the cast bulletin board. Take this as your own self, and not in character; it is your chance to say "Thank you" to an audience.

POST MORTEM

After the performance comes the criticism; occasionally invited, public, and spoken, as in different kinds of adjudication; often public and written, as in the press. In either case, and no matter what the result, it should be accepted with grace. Too easy a satisfaction with good results can cause a downfall later; resentment at what are judged poor results would leave little room for improvement, which can only be developed by fair criticism, well used. Most of us believe only in what we want to believe; the greater the indignation, for example, over what is considered unfair criticism, the more there may be a rejection of a germ of truth. If it were that unfair, no one would bother to believe, and so there would be nothing to reject.

Acting is a very public art; nobody has to do it, but through the mere fact of needing an audience, actors must become aware of public reaction. Nobody creates something only to bury it, unseen; or we would have a strange state of scientists undiscovered, painters unviewed, and writers wishing to remain unpublished. Nothing is, until it is communicated. If an actor links what he has tried to do with the impressions that his audience has received, then he has one way of assessing his very ephemeral art. This he may judge by formal criticism, as above, and by informal, but not necessarily uninformed, criticism of friends and family. It is all a question of opinion, and signs are sure when they all lead in the same direction; but they rarely do. Then again an actor needs to discover within his own self not just what he wants to believe – but what is worth believing.

So he fashions his own instrument to interpret, to create, and to share, each element complementing the other until, together with all concerned in a play, the actor discovers the meaning of the word "artist" as originally intended by the Greeks, and becomes simply – and perhaps greatly – a joiner.

Reading List

Mask or Face, by Michael Redgrave (Heinemann).
An Actors Ways and Means, by Michael Redgrave (Heinemann).
Method or Madness, by Robert Lewis (Samuel French).
An Actor Prepares, by Constantin Stanislavsky (Geoffrey Bles).
Building a Character, by Constantin Stanislavsky (Methuen).
Creating a Role, by Constantin Stanislavsky (Geoffrey Bles).
My Life in Art, by Constantin Stanislavsky (Geoffrey Bles).
Make Believe: The Art of Acting, by Edward Goodman (Scribner).
Voice and Speech in the Theatre, by Clifford Turner (Pitman).
Actors on Acting, edited by Toby Cole and Helen K. Chinoy (Crown).
The Players, by Lillian and Helen Ross (Simon & Schuster).
Actors Talk about Acting, by Lewis Funke and John E. Booth (Thames and Hudson).
The Actor and his Audience, by W. A. Darlington (Phoenix House).

P.S.

Every chapter in this book has emphasized the interdependence of one department of theatre upon another. Good theatre is built on the choice and acceptance of leadership, and on collaboration which is based on sound administration. Many talented and gifted people may come and go in any theatre group – in acting, design, publicity, or wardrobe; all the inspiration in the world, however, will crumble without the co-ordination of each department, and without the goodwill of everyone involved.

Two approaches can be useful in creating a favorable climate for such co-operation: (a) if arrangements are made public within a group, everyone knows what is happening at the appropriate time; (b) if responsibility is delegated, most people will work well, knowing what is happening and feeling they have a contribution to make towards the whole. But much as they would like to, few members can afford to give more than limited time to theatre; and sometimes because of inexperience the work takes longer, and so is subdivided more than would otherwise seem necessary. A do-it-yourself approach can seem easier to heads of departments and be tempting when newcomers may not realise that deadlines are just as important in theatre as, for example, they are in journalism. While there may be initial disappointments, in the long run the delegation of responsibility will build a strong production team, and this is important if standards are to rise and abilities to develop.

The sense of collaboration with others towards a common aim can be one of the most satisfying aspects of participating in a play. It is a quality that depends much on mutual respect, and can exist easily within an atmosphere in which it is possible to say, without being taken personally, "Let's change that" or "What about this?" or "I'm sorry, I was wrong. Let's try. . . ." Such an approach entails considering plans and results not for what they can do for an individual but rather in the light of what the individual can do for the production as a whole. Ultimately there is little room for those who see theatre only as a means of self-expression and enjoyment.

"The play's the thing," and it must take precedence over personal differences, for it is the unifying element between actors and audience, and between the different departments and individuals involved in the production. When the wish to create a unity is genuine, the atmosphere becomes very stimulating.

Theatre is an art, not a therapy. But, like music, painting, or any creative activity where there is delight in the medium, it will give back to those who contribute. The Stage Manager in *Our Town* says, "You've got to love life to have life, and you've got to have life to love life." Similarly, you have to lose the self to find the self, and you find the self by losing the self. Only by giving himself to the needs of a production, for the sake of the play and the total unity of effect, can the member of a group find in theatre the satisfaction and sense of personal identity that are among its chief rewards.

Participation in community theatre can lead to a lifelong interest which creates a fund of experience and a wealth of contacts among people. It is more demanding than many other community activities, carrying a responsibility to others and requiring often nine, or more, hours of rehearsal a week if any standard of performance is to be reached. But, when the infectious excitement of a good audience is felt by everyone in the production, all the hours of preparation fall into place and thoughts soon fly from achievements of the present production to the challenge of the next.

The building of a production – from scratch to opening night – becomes a fascinating undertaking. In a few weeks a group of people who may have barely met before blend their talents and their energy to form a whole new world – in some cases to transform their own selves into something surprisingly different. So a new potential is discovered, and new values are expressed. Such development is particularly noticeable in high-school and teen-age theatre groups (formal drama is rarely given to younger people on any scale). Moreover, when the play on which everyone is working is good, it becomes an adventure in the use of the most apt and concisely expressed language for an occasion. Besides being satisfying to hear and to speak, such language provides values which help insure against poverty of personal expression; these may take time to percolate, but they can have a lasting influence.

In schools the director carries a particularly heavy load, often supervising all departments single-handed. But sometimes there is good co-operation from other teachers: those in music help with any singing, those in woodwork with the set, and those in art with the total design and the costumes. Such communal preparation builds a sense of active participation among members of the eventual audience, who will see and test the final results of their own work.

Each year a theatre group becomes a new and interesting compound of personalities. The situation rarely remains static, and the complexion changes with the injection of personalities with greater and fewer skills, and with more and less talent. In time, and as standards rise, more people will be available for roles and for general participation. Within a few years growing numbers may lead to a split, friendly or otherwise, and a part of the group may re-form, so creating further theatre. The birth of a new group brings its own excitements, leading to a secondary period requiring a steadier approach. If this transition is weathered and the first few years show development, the group has a chance of becoming established in the community. Ultimately a theatre group is as good, as much fun, and as inventive and imaginative as the people who create the total organization.

Meanwhile, whether playing leads, becoming an apprentice, or designing the set, take every opportunity to see other theatre; and supplement all by reading. A variety of knowledge and experience is needed in the theatre, and the reading lists at the end of the chapters in this book will take you further in any subject of particular interest. Some writers will mean more to you than others, and many say the same thing in slightly different ways. It can be an advantage to re-read some writers every five or ten years; a knowledge of basic principles will provide a foundation which may be viewed from different angles, and if your outlook is to develop it is bound to change. But above all read widely, and read to develop the imagination. This quality, well used, is one of the richest of our inner resources and can fill the many corners of our lives. It is the essence of the theatre, and lies at the root of that understanding by which we give life to our beliefs. It gives form to ideas that are eternal, through characters that are occasionally immortal; and it enables us to identify with our heritage, resulting in that distillation of experience which we somewhere share with the ages.

Now the actors are finishing their make-up, and the house is coming in. The call-boy is doing his rounds, the electrician setting the lights, and the stage manager and his staff checking their equipment. The ushers are busy, and the box-office staff are selling the last tickets. The director has made his tour of good wishes. For a moment the stage is silent. Soon it will be peopled by a special world, to be re-created at each performance by actors and by audience, and by the many whose names are on the program. The final calls are being made; the actors are assembling:

"Beginners, please!"
"Quiet, everyone."
"Houselights."
"Curtain – going up!"

General Reading List

Here is a list of general interest covering books of theatrical history, biography, autobiography, criticism, etc., including a few works on ballet:

An Introduction to the Theatre, by Frank M. Whiting (Harper and Row).
The Passionate Playgoer: A Personal Scrapbook, edited by George Oppenheimer (Viking).
Art of the Theatre, by Edward Gordon Craig (Heinemann).
Curtains, by Kenneth Tynan (Atheneum).
Dramatis Personae, by John Mason Brown (Hamish Hamilton).
Theatre in Spite of Itself, by Walter Kerr (Simon & Schuster).
Reflections on the Theatre, by Jean-Louis Barrault (Rockliff).
The Rediscovery of Style, by Michel Saint-Denis (Heinemann).
Return Engagement, by Norris Houghton (Putnam).
Seesaw Log (including *Two for the Seesaw*), by William Gibson (Transworld).
Renown at Stratford, by Robertson Davies (Clarke, Irwin).
Twice the Brinded Cat Hath Mewed, by Robertson Davies (Clarke, Irwin).
Thrice have the Trumpets Sounded, by Robertson Davies (Clarke, Irwin).

The Fervent Years, by Harold Clurman (Dennis Dobson).

A Pictorial History of the American Theatre, 1860–1960, by Daniel Blum (Chilton).

A Picture History of the British Theatre, by Raymond Mander and Joe Mitchenson (Hulton).

See the Players, by Maud Gill (Hutchinson).

Curtain Time, by Ruth Harvey (Houghton, Mifflin).

Garrick, by Margaret Barton (Faber & Faber).

Richard Brinsley Sheridan, by Lewis Gibbs (Dent).

Kean, by Giles Playfair (Geoffrey Bles).

Prince of Players: Edwin Booth, by Eleanor Ruggles (Peter Davies).

A Pride of Terrys, by Margaret Steen (Longmans).

Ellen Terry's Memoirs, by Edith Craig and Christopher St. John (Gollancz).

Irving, by Laurence Irving (Faber & Faber).

Oscar Wilde, by Hesketh Pearson (Methuen).

George Bernard Shaw: Man of the Century, by Archibald Henderson (Appleton-Century-Crofts).

Chekhov, a Life, by David Magarshack (Faber & Faber).

Stanislavsky on the Art of the Stage, edited by David Magarshack (McGibbon & Kee).

Diaghileff, by Arnold Haskell (Gollancz).

Theatre Street, by Tamara Karsavina (Heinemann).

Come Dance with Me, by Ninette de Valois (Hamilton).

Dance to the Piper, by Agnes de Mille (Little, Brown).

The Book of the Dance, by Agnes de Mille (Paul Hamlyn).

And Promenade Home, by Agnes de Mille (Hamish Hamilton).

Dancers of Mercury – the Story of Ballet Rambert, by Mary Clarke (A. & C. Black).

A Life in the Theatre, by Tyrone Guthrie (McGraw Hill).

Act One, by Moss Hart (Secker & Warburg).

George, by Emlyn Williams (Hamish Hamilton).

Eugene O'Neill, by Arthur and Barbara Gelb (Harper).

Brecht, a Choice of Evils, by Martin Esslin (Eyre & Spottiswoode).

The Theatre of the Absurd, by Martin Esslin (Eyre & Spottiswoode).

Anger and After, by John Russell Taylor (Methuen).

Effective Theatre, by John Russell Brown (Heinemann).

Public Domain, by Richard Schechner (Bobbs-Merrill).

Improvisation For The Theatre, by Viola Spolin (Northwestern University Press).

Towards A Poor Theatre, Jerzy Grotowski (Odin Teatrets Forlag, Denmark). (Methuen.)

Brecht On Theatre, translated by John Willett (Methuen).
World Theatre, by Bamber Gascoigne (Michael Joseph).
Experimental Theatre, by James Roose-Evans (Studio Vista).
Tyrone Guthrie On Acting, by Tyrone Guthrie (Viking).
The Empty Space, by Peter Brook (MacGibbon and Kee).
Tynan Right And Left, by Kenneth Tynan (Longman).
The National Youth Theatre, by Simon Masters (Longman).
A Stage In Our Past, by Murray Edwards (University of Toronto Press).
The Actor At Work, by Robert Benedetti (Prentice-Hall).
Adolphe Appia, by Walther R. Volbach (Wesleyan University Press).
The Victorian Theatre – A Pictorial Survey, by Richard Southern (David and Charles).
Speech For The Stage, by Evangeline Machlin (Theatre Arts Books).
New Theatres In Britain, by Frederick Bentham (Rank Strand Electric).
Stage Lighting, by Richard Pilboro (Collier-Macmillan).
The Concise History of The Theatre, by Phyllis Hartnoll (Thames & Hudson).
For general reference:
Oxford Companion to the Theatre, by Phyllis Hartnoll (Oxford).

Magazines

Plays and Players (Hansom Books Limited, Artillery Mansions, 75 Victoria Street, London S.W.1.).
Performing Arts in Canada (49 Wellington Street E., Toronto).
Drama (British Drama League, 9 Fitzroy Square, London W.1.).
New Theatre Magazine (University of Bristol, Drama Department, 29 Park Row, Bristol 1, England).
Theatre Quarterly (Methuen Publications, 2330 Midland Avenue, Agincourt, Ontario).
Educational Theatre Journal (A.E.T.A., John F. Kennedy Centre, 726 Jackson Place N.W., Washington, D.C. 20566).
Theatre Crafts (33 East Minor Street, Emmaus, Pa. 18049).
The Drama Review (32 Washington Place, New York, N.Y. 10003).
Theatre Design And Technology (USITT, Queens College Theatre, Kissena Blvd., Flushing, N.Y. 11367).
Tabs (Rank Strand Electric, 29 King Street, London W.C.2, England; Strand Century Limited, 6334 Viscount Road, Malton, Ontario.

Glossary

apron a forestage projecting in front of the proscenium arch.

audit stub the third section of a printed ticket, retained by the box office at the time of sale for later auditing.

backcloth see *cloth.*

backing material which forms the literal back of the set, masking the wings by, for example, filling the space in or immediately behind the gap made by a fireplace. In a conventional box set backing is needed also behind window frames and behind doors that open or stand open.

backstage the total area of a theatre behind the proscenium arch or, where there is an open stage, behind the back wall of the stage.

blackout 1 the condition of there being no light on stage. The cue may be sudden (to point a line as at the end of a revue sketch) or slow (to suggest or maintain an atmosphere, as on a slow dim and fade to blackout). 2 a forgetting of lines or moves; a temporary loss of memory.

blocking the director's planning of the moves, or physical action, of the play and his giving of them in early rehearsals to the cast. These moves then become the choreography and, with the set and costumes, the visual explanation of the play.

the boards a term once synonymous with *stage*, which is a platform constructed from simple wooden boards. The area is the natural centre of attention in any theatre, and so "four boards and a passion" are among the first requirements for performance.

borders 1 masking material, usually drapes, hung above and across the stage to mask sources of scenery and light from the audience. 2 a row of lights hung behind such drapes, also called *border lights*. (Known in England as a *batten* or *pipe*.)

box office manager the person responsible for all activity connected with the ordering, printing, and selling of tickets. After a performance he must account for sold and unsold tickets against the money received.

call a request for actors to appear at a certain time for a definite purpose: *rehearsal call, photo call, curtain call* (which is, in effect, "called" by the audience), etc. "Beginners, please" is one call that every actor knows.

call-boy   the person responsible for calling the actors before each performance, traditionally known as a call-*boy* even when actually a girl. Now this job is often done by intercom., though this can be a disadvantage unless the system is two-way. Every call needs a response, so that there is a verbal check that each actor will be present when needed.

casting   the decision as to which actor should play which role. This decision is in the hands of the director; where actors are known to him, it may be made in part before a *casting session*, though it is more often made after this chance of a trial run. Where there is some choice, good casting is one of the most important elements in the creation of a sound production and, on a long-term basis, in the building of a group.

catwalk   a narrow bridge above and across the stage, or in the roof of an auditorium, giving access to lights and/or scenery.

clear the stage   leave the stage. "Clear the stage, please!" is a stage manager's request for a clear working area. The opposite request is usually, "On-stage please!"

cloth   1 a *backcloth*, a hanging cloth forming the back of a set, often painted in perspective to portray an exterior background, such as the view through a window, or as the main background to an exterior scene (for example, one set in a wood or in front of a building). The style may merely suggest a certain setting, or it may be completely realistic. 2 a *ceiling cloth*, a roof lowered onto a conventional box set. 3 a *stage cloth* or *floor cloth*, a covering for the bare boards of a stage. It may have a neutral color, or it may be treated as part of the set, for example painted green to represent grass or patterned as a large rug for an interior scene. 4 a *sky cloth*, a plain blue backcloth used to represent sky. See *cyclorama*.

complimentary ticket or **house seat**   a free ticket, by custom offered in pairs to critics and, where possible, those who have helped with the production; for instance, the designer should see the set and costumes in action, under lights, and from among an audience, and his assistants should be able to see the results of their work. In addition, they are often sent to those who help the theatre by displaying posters, lending furniture, etc.; in a large theatre some such tickets may be available for friends of the cast. But complimentary tickets should never be given out indiscriminately; tickets in the theatre represent money, and it is only by their sale that production costs can be covered.

control board   a panel for switching and for varying the intensity of individual lights and series of lights, also called a *switchboard*.

costume parade   a detailed check of the costume, make-up, and total appearance of each actor. It should be held prior to the first dress rehearsal.

cross   a move across a stage. It may be indicated by referring to the actor's left or right or, more often, by specifying "above" or "below" (behind or in front of) a piece of furniture, a part of the set, etc.

cross-over a clear passageway behind the set or backcloth by which actors and staff may go from one side of the stage to the other while a performance is in progress.

cue a signal for an effect (of light, sound, music, etc.) or for speech. In the stage manager's prompt copy a cue is always marked in two parts, WARNING and GO. An actor's cue is usually the last line or sentence of the preceding speech; he should underline this line or sentence and memorize it as if it were included in his own part.

curtain 1 a cloth hung or flown behind the proscenium arch to divide the stage from the auditorium. The timing of the raising and lowering, or opening and closing, of the curtain at the beginning or end of an act or scene is as important as the timing of any sound effect, light cue, etc. 2 the end of an act or performance. 3 a curtain call.

curtain call a raising and lowering, or opening and closing, of the curtain at the end of a performance, by which the cast acknowledges the audience's applause.

cut 1 to delete from the script, lighting plot, music plot, etc. 2 a passage deleted from the script. 3 a move or effect that is no longer required.

cyclorama a curved screen going right across the back of a stage and having a smooth surface on which light may be played, of particular use in giving the effect of distance to bring inside the theatre the most elusive of all natural elements — the sky. Developed in Germany, it was originally constructed of concrete and made to curve inward toward the top as well as toward the sides, so that it resembled an incomplete dome. The term is now applied to, in large theatres, a vast blue or near-white cloth hung on a curved track and, in small theatres, a simple blue backcloth; in either case, it must be completely free from seams or wrinkles. Also called *sky cloth*.

debut a first appearance, like the maiden voyage of a ship: "Mary S., who plays Emily, is making her debut in this production."

depth the distance from front to back on a stage. The depth of a stage is measured from the edge of the platform to the back wall. The depth of a set is usually less, for it must normally begin behind the line of the curtain and end in front of the back wall so as to leave room for a passageway, or cross-over. The depth of the acting area may be further limited by the impracticability of lighting the full area of the set.

dim to decrease the intensity of light; fade.

director the person responsible for the entire artistic approach to a production. He is the invisible conductor of the eventual performance, and is the accepted leader of the total production unit, working through producer, designer, lighting designer, stage manager, and, of course, actor. (In England often called the *producer*.)

double   to play two, or more, roles in one production. Doubling of small roles often makes it possible for a relatively small group to produce a large-cast play.

down-stage   1 the part of the stage nearest to the audience. 2 at, on, or toward this part of the stage. See *stage directions*.

dress   to trim and supply furnishings for a set. When a set is dressed, it is ready for use and decorated as required by the designer, who must approve the finishing touches. See *dressing*.

dresser   an assistant of the costume department who helps members of the cast put on and change their costumes, usually required only when there are many changes of costume, or several quick-changes, in a production. Sometimes a dresser assists a particular leading player, and is then responsible for the cleaning, pressing, and general care of her (sometimes his) costumes. Dressers are usually not needed until the first dress rehearsal.

dressing   trimmings, furnishings, etc. put on to complete a set after it is painted and after the furniture is in position. It includes drapes, cushions, candles, light brackets, pictures, ornaments, and other stage properties. Such finish is similar to the trimming of a costume, and it can be equally important in suggesting an atmosphere or establishing an appropriate sense of period.

dressing room   a room or cubicle backstage in which one or more actors dress, make up, and, unless there is a green room, wait for their entrances. Traditionally, the best dressing rooms are those nearest the stage, and these are allocated to the leading players on the basis of the size and significance of their roles. In small theatres, quiet is essential in the dressing rooms during every dress rehearsal and performance.

dry   1 to forget one's lines. 2 an actor's forgetting of his lines: "a terrible dry in the third act."

effect   an impression, produced by design and usually arranged mechanically or technically, which supports the illusion provided by the actors. Some examples are: a change of light, the operation of a wind machine or thunder machine, the sound of a car starting or a door closing. Effects are usually handled by the stage management, though actors often do their own "door bangs," etc. In fact, everything cued by the stage manager is an effect.

false proscenium   an inner proscenium arch which, by enlarging the frame of the stage, narrows the overall opening through which the audience sees the set. It is often used to make a large stage either appear smaller or accommodate a set originally built for a smaller stage.

floats footlights. *Floats* an old term, sometimes still used, derives from the original type of these lights, which consisted of pieces of cork threaded with wick and *floated* on a trough of oil.

fly to raise scenery out of sight of the audience. This can be done in large theatres by means of a system of ropes and pulleys; the scenery is lifted straight up into the space (*the flies*) above and behind the proscenium arch, a space which has to be at least as high again as the height of the arch. With careful planning and sufficient equipment, several sets can be flown at the same time, providing a speedy and efficient method of effecting scene changes.

flyer a small advance notice or handbill to advertise a production, usually printed but sometimes mimeographed, etc. Flyers are mailed or given to members and others to distribute when posters go up and publicity is in full swing.

fly-gallery a gallery from which to work the ropes used in flying scenery. It extends along the side wall of the wings, from behind the proscenium arch to the back of the stage.

fly-rail a wooden rail which runs along the fly-gallery and to which ropes and rigging are made fast.

focus 1 the setting of the size and angle of a beam of light. 2 in a production, the invisible pointing by the director, working through the cast, of moments of special significance.

F.O.H. Front of House, that area of the house, or theatre, which belongs to the audience; the auditorium, entrance foyer, etc. For example, lights hung in front of a balcony or from a pipe across the auditorium are referred to as F.O.H., or front-of-house lights.

footlights a strip of lights, set in a trough along the front of the stage. They can be an advantage under certain conditions, but they should be used with care. See the discussion of this point on page 162. See *floats*.

gelatins transparent mediums used for diffusing and giving color to stage lighting, now mostly replaced by a flameproof material known as Cinemoid.

green room a meeting-room for actors, in which they can relax, see friends, and, when ready for performances, await their entrances. It was originally known as the *scene room;* the present term was first used in the late seventeenth century, probably derived from the color of a particular room. Such rooms are now rarely built, and actors remain in their dressing rooms.

grid a framework which is built above the stage (at the top of the flies) and from which scenery may be hung.

house 1 a theatre, which may be called a house in a similar sense to that in which a church or a temple is so called. 2 informally, an audience: "A good house will be appreciated by box-office and actors alike." 3 the auditorium.

houselights the auditorium lights.

house manager   as representative of the theatre organization, the "host" to the audience in his "house." He is responsible for the front-of-house section of the theatre, as the stage manager is responsible for the backstage section.

house seat   a *complimentary ticket.*

iris   in a pattern spotlight, an adjustable shutter used to vary the sharpness of the beam.

kill   1 delete, a more emphatic term than "cut." To kill a certain beam of light is to eradicate it, deleting its source from the lighting plot. 2 to cut into or smother by interrupting. When an actor speaks too soon after the beginning of a laugh from the audience, he kills the laugh.

language   the total selection and arrangement of words and phrases used to express character and situation in the action of a play, as opposed to the spectacle, or visual aspect, of the production.

legs   tall, relatively narrow curtains used as part of a set for masking the wings. Legs are usually used in pairs, one on either side of the stage.

lighting booth   a small room in a theatre, usually at the back of the auditorium, from which to operate the control board. Now common in newly-built theatres, it must have a clear view of the stage; the electrician can then control the "play" of lights more effectively than if he had, as in the past, a constricted view from beside, and often above, the stage.

line of sight   a straight line, imaginary or drawn, indicating the direction of the eyes from any seat in the auditorium to the stage or to a particular point on the stage or set. Ideally, theatres should be built and sets designed so that all lines of sight are clear and uninterrupted.

mask   to interrupt the line of sight so as to prevent someone or something from being seen from all or part of the audience. Backing is used to mask the wings and other off-stage areas. Actors should not be placed so that they mask each other, unless such masking is done deliberately (for example, Emily has to be masked before her entrance in Act III of *Our Town*).

medium   a transparent plastic filter used to diffuse and give color to the light from a spotlight or floodlight. See *gelatin.*

mime   1 the use of gesture and movement alone to convey character and situation; acting without words, sometimes done to music. As an art form, mime has a language, or grammar, of its own, derived from the Commedia Dell' Arte. Whole performances are sometimes given in mime, but the art is always of value in the training of an actor. 2 an actor who performs in mime. 3 a play enacted in mime. (Also called *pantomime*, which originally meant "a person who mimed everything.")

O.P.   opposite prompt, used to denote the side of a stage, usually stage right, opposite to the prompt side (P.S.), which is traditionally stage left. Both abbreviations are useful in labelling flats or other pieces of scenery on tour or for an intricate set-up.

open stage   a stage open to the audience on three sides, having a permanent background and no proscenium or front curtain. The Elizabethan stage, as at the Globe Theatre, was the original type, and recent examples are to be found at Stratford, Ont., Chichester, Sussex, and Minneapolis, Minn.

orchestra   1 in the ancient Greek theatre, the "dancing place" used by the chorus. **2** in modern theatres, the place where the orchestra, if any, plays: (a) Where there is a proscenium arch, the musicians usually have an orchestra pit just below and in front of the stage. (b) Where there is an open stage, the musicians play from an orchestra gallery, which is usually behind and above the back of the stage. **3** the part of the auditorium that is or would be on the same level as the orchestra pit; the main floor of the auditorium. **4** in some theatres, the *orchestra stalls*, referring to the rows of main-floor seats nearest the stage.

pantomime   1 a Christmas play with words and music, primarily intended for children. **2** originally, an actor in mime. **3** mime: "The whole performance was done in pantomime."

plot sheet   a list prepared by the stage manager or by an a.s.m. on his behalf, itemizing the requirements for a production. Separate lists, or plot sheets, cover such aspects of the production as: characters, furniture, properties, music, and sound effects.

practical   working; able to work. A practical window is one that opens and closes. A practical table lamp is one which switches on or off when an actor operates the switch, as opposed to a light that is actually operated from the control board by the electrician, who must synchronize with the movements of the actor.

pre-set board   a control board on which the operator may set in advance many changes of light, each one being operated on cue by the action of one master control.

press release   an official announcement notifying the press, radio and television stations, and other publicity channels of future arrangements. It should be simple, double-spaced, and precise; and care should be taken that all information is supplied to all the proper people at the same time. For further information see pages 196 and 197.

producer   the person responsible for all the business and administrative aspects of the production. Since he makes the performance possible, supplying the material aspects of a production, he should work in close partnership with the director, who creates the artistic aspects. In England he is known as the manager, while the name *producer* is often given to the person usually known as the director.

prompt book   the copy of the play always used by the prompter and marked by him for pauses, places where actors seem expecially liable to "dry", etc. It must never be lost or borrowed. Compare *prompt copy.*

prompt copy   an interleaved copy of the play in which the stage manager records every move and every cue for each kind of effect. It is the "bible" of the production, and from it the stage manager runs each performance. See pages 102–105 for further information and sample pages.

prompt side   the side of the stage on which the prompter sits, usually stage left.

property or prop   1 any small article set on the stage (and so belonging to, or the property of, the stage), as opposed to larger articles of furniture. 2 a *hand-prop*, an article, such as a letter, which "belongs" to a character and is brought on-stage by him. 3 a *costume prop*, an article, such as a purse, sunglasses, or sword, which is a part of an actor's costume.

prop tables   tables set in the wings, accessible and yet out of the way, for properties to be taken on and brought off-stage during a performance by the actors. While, like everything else backstage, they come under the supervision of the stage manager, these tables are the direct responsibility of the prop-girl (or boy). She must be sure that, before a performance, all necessary properties are placed ready and in proper order on the prop tables; during a performance, she must ensure that the actors replace properties they bring off-stage; she must then re-check the tables against her plot sheet for the following performance.

proscenium   1 the part of the stage between the front curtain and the auditorium (the term is not used of theatres where there is an open stage). 2 the *proscenium arch*, the frame of a stage behind which the front curtain rises and falls (or opens and closes). It virtually divides the audience from the actors, creating what is known as "the picture-frame" stage.

proscenium doors   in Restoration theatres, two doors that opened onto the forestage, or remnant of the apron, on either side and in front of the proscenium arch. They were reduced to one door as the area of the forestage became smaller, and disappeared in the eighteenth and nineteenth centuries, when the entire performance retreated behind the proscenium arch. The space originally occupied by these doors was later given over to the audience in the form of boxes. See the pictures on pages 22, 24, and 25.

proscenium stage   a stage framed by a proscenium arch.

P.S.   prompt side. See *O.P.*

racking   in a box-office, the placing of tickets for each performance in a specially-made rack and in the order of the seating plan. It enables assistants to see any remaining seats at a glance, thus helping to give quick and efficient service.

rake a slope given to the stage of many older theatres, especially in England and Europe, giving a grade of as much as ½″ to the foot from front to back of the stage. It was intended to help those upstage or at the back to be more clearly seen from the auditorium, which was level; but it created many difficulties in the construction of scenery since the base of each flat or other piece had to allow for this slope. In modern theatres, the stage floor is normally level but the auditorium is raked.

repertoire a selection of plays which comprise a company's offering for a season and which can be alternated at each performance. Often called a *repertory* and so confused with the following entry.

repertory 1 Often called *rep*, a system of presenting a series of plays, each of which is performed only for a certain length of time and is discontinued when another production begins. Each production may be performed for one week, two weeks, three weeks, or even longer. Weekly and two-weekly rep. is continued in England on a year-round basis; in North America the systems appears usually only in summer and is known as *stock*. 2 a theatre or company presenting plays under this system.

revolve or **revolving stage,** a round platform set into or on the floor of a stage and able to be rotated, usually by means of a motor. It can be used for changing sets quickly (two sets, for instance, being built back to back) or for suggesting a change in location without interrupting the action or lowering the curtain.

rigging the system of ropes and their supports, etc. by which scenery may be flown. See *fly*. It should be kept in good condition and treated with the same respect as the rigging of a ship. Because so much work in older theatres required the handling of ropes, many of the stage hands, or stage crew, were sailors. They could be relied on to work the ropes, and they are still in demand as workers backstage.

road touring. *On the road* means on tour. A *road company* means a touring company of a production, as opposed to, for example, the Broadway company. (Short for *railroad*, the development of which made touring companies in the United States possible.)

run 1 the duration, or total number, of performances of a production: "We are going to do a well-known comedy and try a two week run." 2 a continuous rehearsal of a passage, scene, etc. without any interruption or break in the action. 3 to rehearse a scene, act, etc. in this way: "Let's have a ten minute break and then run Act II."

running time the duration of a scene, act, or play in performance. The stage manager should time each scene and act during final run-throughs and during dress rehearsals, and he should continue to keep such a log for each performance. If, then, an act is seen to be playing much faster or slower than usual, there is probably something wrong which needs attention. The house manager and the box office need to know running times as early as possible before the first performance.

run-through a continuous rehearsal of an act or whole play, without interruption by the director or any break in the action. It is usually held only after the act or acts concerned have been rehearsed in some detail. See Average Production Schedule for a suggested time for a complete run-through.

set 1 the scenery and all that it includes and contains; the whole physical setting as seen by the audience. 2 install or place on-stage in its proper position: "The stage manager should check that properties are correctly set before each performance." 3 to arrange and then retain as part of the permanent plan of production. The lights involved and their levels of intensity are set for each cue at the technical lighting rehearsal. The procedure for music cues must be set in the same way.

setting line the furthest point down-stage to which scenery and furniture may be set to allow for proper clearance of the curtain and good lighting.

set up 1 to build and finish a set on stage. 2 *set-up* or *setting-up*, the process of building and finishing a set on stage. This operation must be completed before the technical rehearsal. If there is a change of set in the play, there will have to be a set-up after each performance.

spectacle the entire visual aspect of a production, including the scenery, costumes, and grouping (the arrangement of actors on the stage); the entire setting and the use made of it. It may be delightfully simple, or it may be magnificent and impressive. Ideally it is an integral part of the director's interpretation of the play; no matter how elaborate or how bare, it should be used never for its own sake but always to support the intention of the production.

spill unwanted light spilling onto the set or elsewhere. A badly tightened or poorly adjusted spotlight may spill onto the proscenium arch. A stage manager's working light spilling onto the stage may destroy the effect of a blackout.

stage direction in the script of a play, an instruction to actors or director which is not part of the dialogue. In so far as they refer to actors' moves, they are given in terms of the actors' point of view, his left and right as he faces the audience. The stage is also thought of as being divided into areas labelled "up" and "down," terms derived from the slope on a raked stage. See *rake*.

stage director a chief, or executive, stage manager of a heavy production requiring a large staff and more than one stage manager.

stage door the backstage entrance of a theatre, which should always be used by the cast and production staff. The front-of-house entrances are used by the audience, but visitors backstage after performances should come round by the stage door rather than walk across the set or through the wings.

stage manager   the person responsible for the management of everyone and everything in the backstage area. He has final authority over all activity behind the proscenium arch. He is in charge of the running of every performance, and, after the dress rehearsal, he in effect takes control of the production from the director.

stock   in North America, the repertory system. It usually functions during the summer only and is often known as *summer stock*. The term derives from the old resident companies which were attached to one theatre or group of theatres, choosing from a permanent "stock," or repertory, of plays; these companies were contrasted with the touring, or road, companies which gradually became more numerous and more popular as the railroads were extended.

strike   to clear or remove. It is sometimes necessary to strike certain properties or articles of furniture between acts, for example to show the passage of time. If there is a complete change of scenery, it may be necessary to strike one set in order to set the next. In such cases a set should be cleared and stacked in the order in which the pieces will be needed for resetting.

tabs   the front curtain, sometimes still called "the blind." Most such curtains are now raised or lowered, but originally the tabs parted in the middle to portray a tableau, of which *tabs* is an abbreviated form; although this practice has died out, the name has remained.

technical rehearsal   a special rehearsal held by the director for technical staff only, especially for lighting and the setting of all effects cues. It should be held well before the dress rehearsal, on a separate day if the production has many effects and is technically complicated. It is valuable in helping to ensure reasonably smooth running of the technical side of the dress rehearsal.

tormentor   a masking flap or flat between the down-stage end of the set and the proscenium arch. It "torments" inquisitive eyes in the auditorium by preventing them from seeing into the wings.

trap   a door in the floor of a stage, allowing actors to ascend and descend, to appear and disappear. Traps used to be widely used in pantomime, melodrama, etc.; one kind was the *bristle trap*, which was composed of brushes the same colour as the stage floor and which, being almost invisible, made the disappearances and reappearances made through them all the more spectacular.

traveller   a running curtain which can be pulled across the stage behind, and at any distance back from, the tabs, or front curtain. It is often used to preserve continuity of action, allowing a set to be changed behind the traveller while the action continues in front of it; the traveller, or *traveller curtains*, can then be opened at the proper time to reveal the new set, again without interrupting the action.

underdress to wear one costume underneath another that is required first. When the time comes to change costumes, it is necessary only to remove the top one — a useful way of managing a quick change.

understudy an actor who learns the lines and blocking for a major role so that he is ready to take over in case of sickness or accident to the regular player. Because of the limitations of time, understudy rehearsals cannot usually take place until after Opening Night. Sometimes, however, a production is double-cast; this system involves virtually double the normal rehearsal time, but it does give experience to double the number of actors and allows, if the run is long enough, more people to play roles in front of an audience.

up-stage 1 the area of the stage furthest away from the audience. The director will often place an actor in an upstage position when it is important that all eyes are led towards him. See *stage directions*. 2 to put oneself in a position further up-stage than other actors. To do so without the blessing of the director is irresponsible.

walk-through not quite a slow run-through, but the slow rehearsal of a particular scene or passage, often done to sort out a technical difficulty such as an awkward move or the mistiming of dialogue with the handling of properties. The actor's sense of character and emotion is usually dropped during a walk-through so that he can concentrate on mechanics, or technique. Then, as with a pianist who has rearranged his fingering, the same section should be run two or three times to set the new pattern and to establish a smooth connection within the context.

wardrobe mistress the person who has charge of all costumes once they are completed by the designer. It is her responsibility to check arrangements with the dressers and to supervise the cleaning, storage, and/or return of costumes after use.

wings the side areas of the stage, unseen by the audience, which provide access to the stage, space for the changing and temporary storage of the scenery and furniture, and room for the prop tables, for floodlights on stands, etc. It is essential that the wings, under all circumstances, are kept as clear as possible. They are a working area for many people, often poorly lit as all light must be directed onto, not off, the stage, and it is obvious that stage entrances must be kept as clear as possible. A good stage manager will keep the wings as uncluttered as the deck of a ship.

DATE DUE	